MORVELVING

An Erviad Novel

The Mourning Sword
BOOK ONE

By C. J. Switzer

For anyone who loves adventure

A tale of the Ervos,

Abandoned by gods, who crossed the Rift,

To the fell hands of the Fates.

—*The Erviad*

TABLE OF CONTENTS

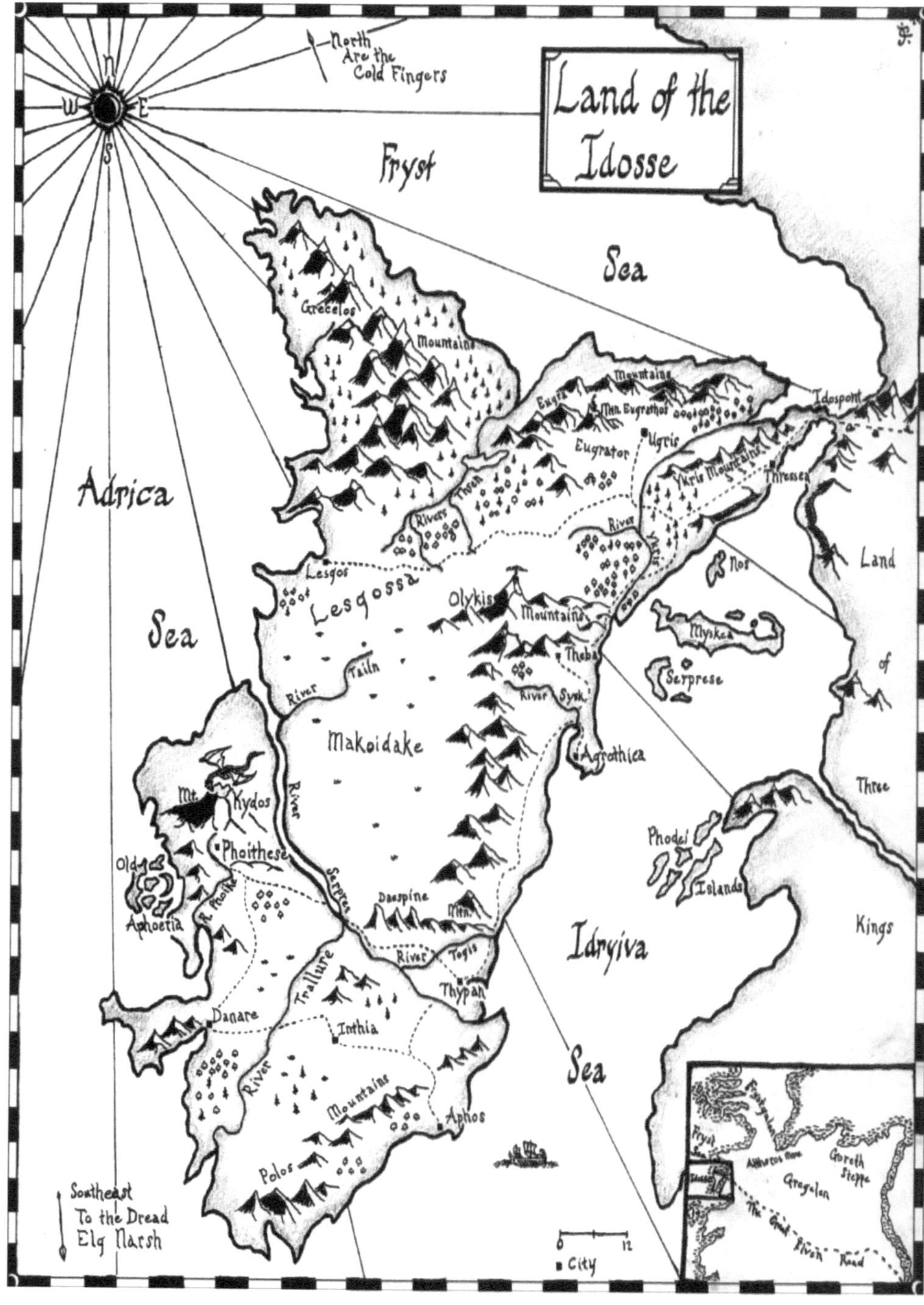

North
Are the
Cold Fingers
Land of the
Idosse
N
W E
S
Fryst
Sea
Grecelos
Mountains
Mountains
Eugra
Mtn. Eugrathos
Idospont
Eugrator
Ugris
Adrica
Ykris Mountains
Thressea
Thren
Rivers
River
Sea
Lesgos
Lesgossa
Olykis
Mountains
Land
Nos
Myskea
Theba
of
Serprese
River
Tailn
River
Sysk
River
Makoidake
Agrothica
Three
Mt. Kydos
River
Phodei
Phoithese
Old
Islands
Kings
R. Phoike
Aphoetia
Serprea
Idryiva
Daespine
Mtn.
Trallure
River
Togis
Danare
Thypan
Inthia
Sea
River
Mountains
Aphos
Polos
Southeast
To the Dread
Elg Narsh
6   12
City
Fryst
Althoros Rive
Goreth
Steppe
Gregolon
The Great Elvin Road

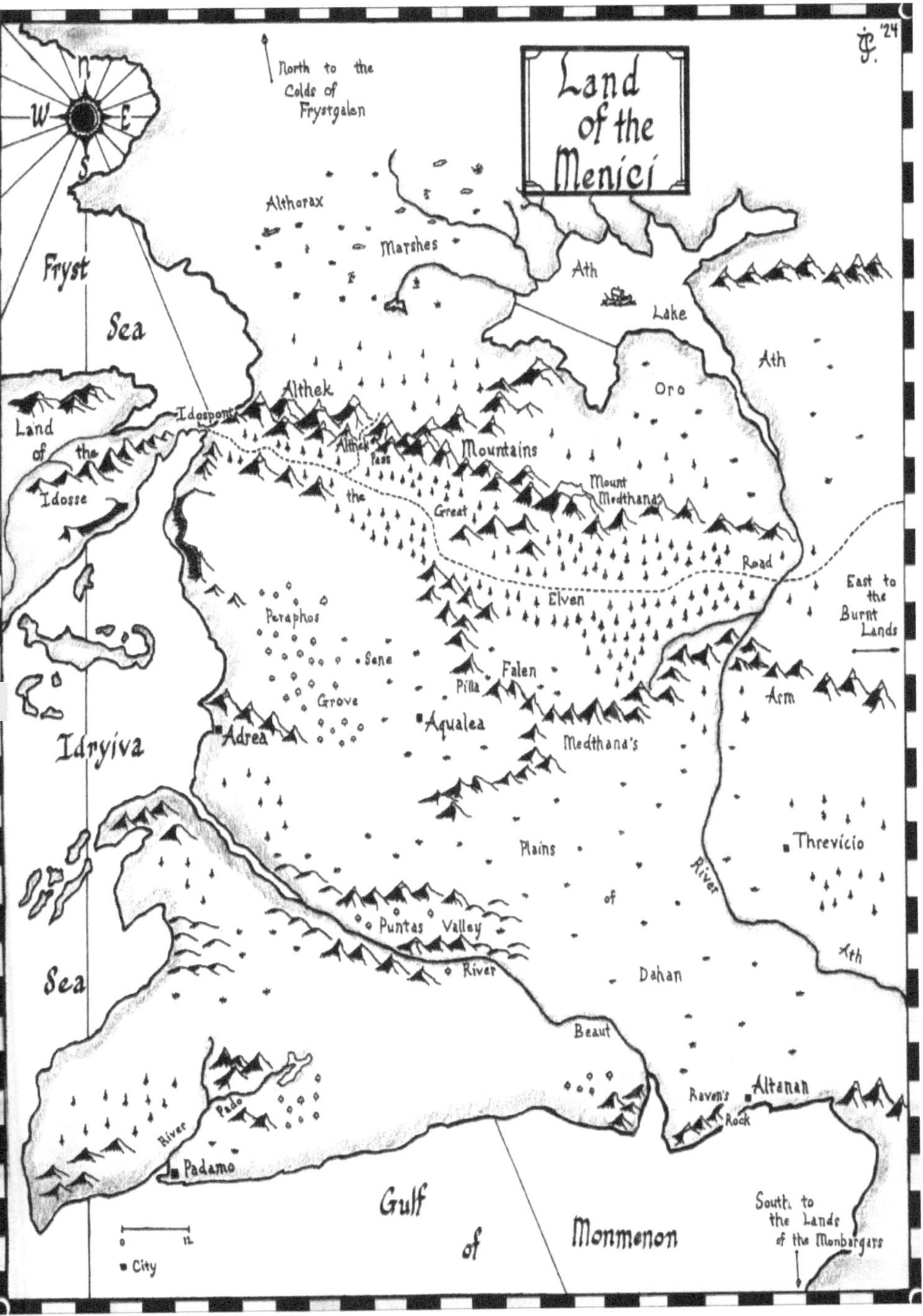

Land of the Menici
North to the Colds of Frystgalen
Althorax
Marshes
Ath Lake
Ath
Oro
Fryst Sea
Althek
Idospont
Althek Pass
Mountains
Mount Medthana
Land of the Idosse
the Great
Road
East to the Burnt Lands
Elven
Peraphos
Sene
Falen
Pilla
Arm
Grove
Aqualea
Adrea
Medthana's
Idryiva
Threvicio
Plains
of
River
Puntas Valley
River
Dahan
Ath
Sea
Beaut
Raven's Rock
Altanan
Pado
River
Padamo
Gulf of Monmenon
South to the Lands of the Monbargars
0   12
City
W N E S

1

781 After Rift

One step further and he would plummet to his death.

Morvelving was as hollow and barren as the arid land around him. After forty-three years alone in exile, he had never considered ending his life till now. He hated himself—the void in his chest pulling and consuming him. Even now, his dry tongue licked his lips, starving for the last stem of piphlid, which was sodden in his pawed palm. He craved that sweet deadening sensation just as he craved air, allowing him to forget. Forget how the piphlid had led him to watch his son, Windtail, slip from a tall oak, arms flailing for a lifesaving hold, as his small body descended into free fall. Morvelving had only watched while comatose.

His guilt had kept him from Windtail's Vhinde, the ritual that had guided Windtail's spirit to the Moon Goddess. He'd run and hid in shame. He was a slave to piphlid. It had been the final drumbeat. Executing him would have been a mercy. Worse, his tribe had titled him Morvelving: "He Who Runs Shall Mourn Alone." A punishment that marked him estranged from his people and their spirit.

The space from the cliff to the ground—welcoming.

Morvelving drew his hand nervously across his snout, looking away from the drop. Gray clouds dotted the sky as dark Celemith encroached to eclipse the sun. The daily occurrence marking midday and reminding all that the gods watched.

"Telunian, Goddess of the Moon, Matron of all Mulranei, avert your eyes." Morvelving choked.

His gaze fixed on the swollen river below, brown from upstream washing, carving around the bend. Its fullness only made his own emptiness more apparent. Morvelving's fur was damp, and the wind pushed hard against him. He shivered, not from the cold. The vast beauty and danger of the Gregalen Heights filled his eyes, yet his mind fixated on the gray shroom. Death was his only escape from his shame. Piphlid had allowed him to linger for too long. In Morvelving's mind, Windtail fell again, his cry reverberating.

Movement in the distance caught his eye. Morvelving observed dark shapes hurrying from one canyon gorge to another. They were too far to see clearly, and they moved with haste. He sniffed the air and wrinkled his nose, the scent unknown to him.

The piece of piphlid slipped from his palm. His heart froze in desperation as he saved it from being carried away by the strong wind. It crumbled against his claws-to-palm grip like his desire for death moments before. Morvelving shoved it in his mouth, sighing in elation as its bitter toxins numbed his tongue. His gut twisted with disgust, and tears welled to obscure his vision. He sobbed to dry his bleeding heart before he could feel anything.

Morvelving swung his arm against the ground, crying out, not from pain but frustration. He had to take control. In a moment of pure will, he pulled out his dagger. The dark metal stark against the tine handle, and the blade's bright edge curved like a crooked smile. His father had given it to him, and he was going to give it to Windtail . . . No, he couldn't. Morvelving sheathed the dagger.

The wind shifted from the east, offering a change. Morvelving watched a tall weed sway back and forth against the wind. Its violet crown and its green leaves and stem bristled with thorns. He was bowing to the wind like the weed. Unable to end himself, unwilling to let go of piphlid. Morvelving stood. He wanted to find more.

His upright ears twitched at a trace of sound, unnatural in the unpopulated canyon. Cries of pain and torment followed by a triumphant call. He sniffed the wind, and the scent assaulted his nose—damp fur caked in piss and blood—a minotaur. Despite himself and encouraged by the piphlid, a growl escaped from deep within his throat. Minotaurs were his people's blood enemies. He lacked the courage to take his own life, but the minotaur would not hesitate.

Halting at the cliff's edge, Morvelving surveyed the slope below from the canyon's plateau. His eyes were blinded by the boulders glistening from the rainfall. The minotaur had its quarry pinned. By the heads rotting on its bandolier, the minotaur was a young bull on its rite-of-passage hunt to prove its strength. They valued wolf-like Mulranei heads above all other races.

Morvelving leaped down to a ledge and began his descent.

The quarry was a company of dwarves, five members already slain. No wonder he hadn't recognized their scent. He had never seen dwarves before, but he had heard of a race of people who were of short stature and had long beards. Their sharpened sticks were no match for the minotaur's crude bronze armor. Desperate, the unarmed dwarves threw rocks.

As Morvelving descended the slope, the minotaur cut down a valiant dwarf. Their mournful cries were like a punch to the gut.

Morvelving landed on the rocky ground, rolling, his right ankle slamming into a boulder. Piphlid dulled the pain. Snarling, he reached the minotaur as it drew its blade from another dwarf's torso.

The crescent light of the noon's eclipse hid his approach. Using his speed and surprise, he crashed into his enemy. They fell to the ground, grappling. Morvelving clenched his jaw, his fangs sinking into the meat of the minotaur's broad neck. He shook his head, tearing and ripping, as his claws scraped against skin, leather, and bronze.

The minotaur roared in pain, kicking Morvelving off. Morvelving spat the warm clump of muscle from his mouth.

Eyes wide, the bull stumbled back. The moment passed; the minotaur trumpeted in exultation at the fight. It stomped the thin dirt with its hoof, kicking up chunks.

Morvelving returned the challenge with his own bark and growl.

Bowing its head, the minotaur charged, ignoring the dwarves scurrying out of the way and pelting it with stones.

The blow should have killed Morvelving, but his body betrayed him and fought back. Still, one horn gored his shoulder. Even the piphlid was powerless against such pain. Morvelving cried out as the impact carried him off his feet. His dagger found purchase in the minotaur's torso, and there it remained.

The young bull punched him in the jaw. Morvelving's fangs bit his tongue. A fist hit his gut, making him keel over and vomit bile. Before he could rise, a hoof collided with his torso.

Morvelving rolled twice, then hit a boulder hard, knocking the breath from him. His vision went white. The minotaur approached, its hooves scraping on stone.

The bull growled, "With your head, *mu'kunta*—"

Morvelving's vision returned. The minotaur stood over him, bronze sword in hand, reflecting the eclipse—an abyssal eye ringed with fire. Morvelving coughed up blood.

His enemy leaned close. "I'll be the envy of all bulls." Its voice was tinged with glee. "And the heifers will beg for my—"

Morvelving spat blood on the minotaur's face.

The minotaur grabbed Morvelving by the scruff of his neck, lifting him up like a coney by a butcher. Pain cascaded through him as the piphlid wore off. He whimpered and cried out despite himself. In his mind's eye, Windtail fell from the branch again, his small body breaking on the ground, echoing.

Morvelving took a labored breath, and an overwhelming scent of hope filled his nostrils. The potent emotion filled his senses. It struck him like the first light of dawn piercing the darkness. Reminding him of his life before piphlid, grief, and exile. He followed the emotion's trail, clear as day, to a dwarf with green eyes. Something tugged at Morvelving. Stronger than his desire to die. Stronger than piphlid's deadening wonder.

Drawing its sword back for a thrust to Morvelving's heart, the minotaur split its mouth into a yellow grin. Morvelving had no power to persuade the sun to rise in the west and set in the east. He couldn't change his past. The feeling of being needed by someone again was a deep pool, a chance to forget his mistakes and have purpose. This was a way to be free of his guilt. Morvelving seized it.

Morvelving grabbed the minotaur's arm. He was not a warrior among his people, but Mulranei were no stranger to the art of war. The minotaur's blade lunged for Morvelving's heart. Morvelving slapped the point away, and cold metal burned into his left shoulder. He cried in pain and defiance as he swung his arm for his dagger, still lodged in the minotaur's torso between bronze plates. His clawed fingers found the tine handle. Morvelving pulled.

The young bull cried out, staggering back.

Morvelving lashed out. The dagger slashed a dark glistening smile across the minotaur's throat. Warm blood spattered Morvelving's face as he fell to one knee and collapsed in exhaustion. As his eyes closed, the minotaur clawed at its throat, choking on its own blood. Morvelving could die now, knowing he had helped someone, if not himself.

2

———————

Morvelving's upright ears rang with the sound of Windtail colliding with the earth. He opened his eyes. "No!"

A dwarf in a ragged yellow cloak hurried away from his side. There were many dwarves sitting around him, huddled in small groups. Morvelving was in a wide cave. Bright light shone through its open mouth and around stalagmite teeth, making him squint.

He shook. Everything hurt, and cloth bandages hindered his movement. Each strip of cloth was dark red and burned like a clay kettle on shimmering coals. The blood in his head was pounding. His tongue was dry. Piphlid. He needed it. Why was he alive? He'd fought. He'd lived. Gods above, why and for what? He shuddered as another spasm of pain rippled all over.

Hope, the sweet scent of the emotion. It seemed more overwhelming than piphlid. That was why. He cursed his Mulranei sense to smell emotion. But where had the hope scent gone? Desperate to distract himself from the pain and the mad itch for piphlid, Morvelving peered at the dwarves. He had heard the elves had the whole race enslaved in their mountain halls. It had broken the alliances between the Mulranei Tribes and the Norishvarn and Mithvarn elven kingdoms. These dwarves must be fugitives.

The dwarves' scent was a churning of body stink and emotions, their distrust, worry, and determination swirling together. In each breath, step, and shuffle to ease where they sat, they were driven. Like a stone that crept down the mountain slope—over time, it would arrive at the base of the mountain. No matter the journey's longevity or hardship, they would reach their destination.

Morvelving could only speculate where that was. He could not fathom their hardships and how they had been able to escape their bondage. Shame warmed his face as he compared their plight to his own. Unlike him, their pain was not a result of their choices.

One dwarf stood near Morvelving, his face hidden by the glare of the day's light. Did they speak the Trade Tongue? He pushed to sit up, but his shoulder and leg both convulsed. He settled back, wheezing for air.

The dwarf knelt next to Morvelving to finish bandaging his wounds. His beard was gray with strands of black and brown. His emerald eyes were like polished gems set in the dark skin of his face, peppered with white freckles reminding Morvelving of the stones near the fire mountains in the Burnt Lands. Morvelving recognized those eyes as belonging to the bearer of hope and guessed the dwarf was the elder in the company. There was an aura about such elders he could smell, much like the Wiseneyes of his tribe. This dwarf was either the company's seer or leader.

"We doubted you'd wake." The dwarf spoke in High Mithvarn, her dialect polished and her voice decidedly feminine. "I am glad my doubts were unfounded."

Morvelving blinked, thrown off by his assumptions. In his understanding, beards were a distinguishing feature of men, not women. Telunian's light, or was it the other way around?

"We did what we could for your wounds," the dwarf went on, "but they will need your Mulranei magic if you wish to survive."

"You know of my people?" Even as he asked in Low Mithvarn, the heat rose to his face. They plainly did.

The dwarf scoffed. "Even deep below the earth under the whip of our masters, we have heard of the healing powers of the Mulranei."

Morvelving winced from another spasm in his leg. "My belongings," he croaked, his tongue heavy like lead. "A pouch carries a salve. Dress it on each wound." The world became dark.

When he came to, the same dwarf was sitting next to him again. The light outside the cave was brighter. Afternoon.

"It is well your accoutrements are few," she said. "I found the salve and applied as you said—" Her brows rose, eyes following his arm as he rotated and massaged his shoulder.

Morvelving sat up and leaned against the stone. His numb shoulders tingled. The bandages no longer covered his wounds. His marred body was feverish but cool as well due to the healing salve.

"Incredible," she whispered.

"What are you called?" Morvelving asked.

The dwarf stared into Morvelving's eyes, hands curled into guarded fists. "You are a stranger. You came to our aid uncalled for, but have you saved us to return us to our masters? We have escaped captivity, and every one of us would rather die before feeling the manacle snap. Tell me, who are you, and why have you aided us?"

He looked down, her distrust justified. "I didn't interfere to aid you."

"Why did you?"

Morvelving stared into those hard emerald eyes, recognizing their wisdom. If he spoke half-truths, he sensed she would continue to press him like a mother to a mischievous child. Feeling trapped by his wounds, disoriented by fatigue, and ground down by the pounding in his head from lack of piphlid, Morvelving told her. From his dependency on piphlid to his son's death and his subsequent exile. What his name meant.

Surprised and mortified by what he had just said, Morvelving cursed himself, wondering now if the dwarf had given him an elixir that made him speak. Embarrassed and not yet able to leave, he said, "My thanks for applying the salve. It only needs time to heal. You needn't stay any longer."

Icicle-shaped stones covered the ceiling. A constant drip echoed from the back of the cave. He was thankful the fur on his face hid the rising heat as he tried to forget his own words.

The dwarf watched him for a moment before turning to her folk. Morvelving ignored their whispers in their own tongue. He couldn't understand anyway. Embracing his fatigue, he fell asleep.

Upon waking, darkness enveloped him. The lack of light signified a cloudy night. Morvelving smelled the dwarves sleeping around him. He wished they had left so he wouldn't have to face them. He'd been a fool to tell them about himself.

Licking his dry tongue, Morvelving's sole thought was for piphlid. Everything was far more tolerable with it. Dim morning light began to creep into the cave.

A child fussed, making Morvelving aware of the dwarves waking around him. The one who had spoken to him yesterday was staring at him. Morvelving groaned in pain and frustration. Fools, they needed to keep moving to avoid discovery. He rolled his shoulder and slowly tested his legs. They were sore and stiff, with sharp stabs of pain, but he could move.

The sooner, the better. He wanted to begin looking for piphlid.

"Your name. It is a command, a task?"

Morvelving met her gaze and nodded. " 'He Who Runs Shall Mourn Alone.' "

"If you had been slain by the minotaur, you would have furthered your mistakes," she observed.

Morvelving blinked and looked away, grinding his teeth. He steadied himself against the stones and slowly stood. She shot a glance at his tail then assisted him when he grimaced from a painful spasm. Observing his capability to stand, she placed her hands on her hips, shook her head in disbelief, and uttered something in dwarven.

Morvelving peered down at her, wondering why she stayed. Why would any of them? He'd only helped them for his own sake—to help himself to his own death. They knew he had loved piphlid more than his son. He picked up his few possessions. Morvelving shook his head, limping to the cave entrance.

The dwarves watched his every hesitant step. A child stood, mouth agape, fair hair filling his jawline, neck crooked to gaze up at him. Morvelving was short among his people. Among the dwarves, who stood two heads shorter than humans, he was a giant.

He left them behind and quenched his thirst at a nearby river. Tall canyon walls were on either side, dirt orange and yellow, except for rugged pathways along the river's shore. White-furred goats eyed him from their cliff perches. The land was too arid for piphlid to grow. Morvelving growled to himself.

He retraced his steps to where he'd fought the minotaur. Heavy footfalls echoed off the rocks.

Morvelving faced the dwarf as she approached, her palms out in greeting. He could smell other dwarves nearby. "We should part ways."

"I'm not finished with you," she said.

Morvelving shook his head, grumbling, "I want to be."

She did speak like his tribe's Wiseneyes, confident and certain in knowledge and experience. To him, this solidified her as a seer among her kin. He stumbled down the rocky slope to where the minotaur corpse lay. Crows cawed and cursed at him as he sat down and began working on the corpse. Its hide would make a useful cloak for his travels. Thankfully, his dagger cut leather and cloth with ease, for his strength was still mending.

"My master had many names for me." The dwarf sat down across from Morvelving. "Names I shall never hear uttered again. My full name among my people is Wynthrimrathsolro. You may call me Wynthrim."

"And why have you followed me, Wynthrim?" Morvelving tossed the minotaur's bandolier and clothing aside and cut into flesh. Morvelving recognized that by giving him her name, Wynthrim was offering him her trust. He cleared his dry throat and felt the itch to fish piphlid from his belt pouch. Uncomfortable, he pretended to ignore her.

Wynthrim took a deep breath. Morvelving followed her glance to the company gathering nearby, honoring their dead who lay under small mounds of stone. "You were not meant to die, just as I'm not meant to be a slave."

Morvelving growled as he turned the minotaur corpse over. Waxy blood glazed the rocks, almost causing him to slip. "I do not wish to die now. If that is why you followed me, then rest assured, I'm content to live out my days alone."

"I understand why your throat is always dry and your hand twitches," Wynthrim said.

Morvelving's gaze met hers. He noted how she ignored his attempt to be rid of her. Wynthrim rubbed her hands and looked with sadness at her fellows, who now stood in earshot, watching them. Morvelving noticed several dwarves who had the same jittery motions as he did—subtle twitch of the hand, lips always dry.

"Our masters used many forms of persuasion to keep us docile, keep us working without revolting. Some are beyond healing." Wynthrim looked at her hands, tracing an elven hieroglyph branded there. Morvelving couldn't decipher its meaning, whether it had served as a punishment or a brutal pass for entry.

He could smell her sadness, dark like the tunnels of the mountains. He also caught the scent of her strength like the roots of the mountain holding up the summit, holding up her people. Morvelving ceased his work and listened, recognizing her wisdom. What she was offering deserved respect.

"Others have found freedom from many chains."

"How?" Morvelving croaked, betraying himself. Gods above, how could he give up piphlid now? All he had wanted was to forget.

Wynthrim answered gently, "I broke my chains, but you—you still carry yours. Face yourself, find purpose, and you'll need piphlid less and less. And you won't have to be alone."

The crows meandered close, testing Morvelving. He locked eyes with Wynthrim. What she said, he knew. His purpose was in his name. If he kept running, he would never achieve the task of his exile, and he would die alone. Face his guilt, face his responsibility for himself. Windtail hit the ground. Morvelving's stomach twisted, and he grimaced.

"While more of my kin escape bondage," Wynthrim offered, seeming to sense his discomfort, "those who are caught and returned speak of a sanctuary in the Caszark Mountains. I am more learned than some, but I don't know where these mountains lie, only that they're west and north."

Morvelving straightened his back, recognizing her offer. A kindle of hope rose in himself this time. She'd told him to find purpose and was offering a chance. So consumed by his shame, he did not see it then. Furthermore, he caught a faint scent of hope intermingled with strong patience from Wynthrim. He nodded. "Caszark. Those are the mountains beyond the highlands of Frystgalen. Your heading is accurate."

"You will guide us there."

Morvelving stared at the minotaur corpse without seeing. A crow pecked at its eye socket, then flew off. Gods above, he could use a stem of piphlid. He needed to stop running, and for better or worse, he wanted to escape. This was a chance. He began to work on the corpse in earnest.

The hope for a chance rendering him vulnerable, Morvelving agreed. "I will guide you."

"Thank you." Wynthrim stood. "We should begin our march now. We have lingered here too long."

Not quite finished with the minotaur corpse, Morvelving waved at the other dwarves. "What of your wounded?"

Wynthrim eyed Morvelving. Every dwarf spoke in unison in their own tongue: "We've endured much worse and will endure far more."

Morvelving recognized it as an intonation. "They speak with power. What did they say?"

"I'm surprised your tapered ears don't interpret the words." Wynthrim waved her hand toward his ears. Her words were warm now, unguarded.

"I can smell emotions. Intentions. Words still can deceive, and those trained can hide their emotions."

"Huh." Wynthrim's bushy brows rose. "They spoke our command, our prayer, and our belief—we endure."

Morvelving understood the meaning. He had heard the Wiseneyes sing the Song of Eorhath, the dwarven patron. How Aeputer, Lord of Gods, punished him for giving dwarves fairer beards than Aeputer's own. Daily for a hundred years, Eorhath had his skin peeled away. Every day, his godly skin would regrow. Morvelving wondered if dwarven captivity had started during Eorhath's punishment.

"Go, I will follow." Morvelving pulled the last of the hide away from the corpse, slicing away unwanted tissue. His body was stiff and sore, but the salve had done its magic. His strength was returning as he brightened to his new path.

Wynthrim watched him for a moment, then turned to her kin, urging them onward. Morvelving followed, gathering his dagger and using leather strips from the minotaur's clothing to tie the hide into a bundle. He shifted the minotaur hide under his arm, grimacing at the stench. When they camped, he would have to perform a cleansing ritual and make a contraption to dry it while he journeyed with the dwarves.

Morvelving guided them out from the deep gorges and canyon heights, across the flatlands where tall boulders stood as numerous as trees and tumbling weeds hid their movements and further west through the cacti forest of Gathor. During the days of Daetem, twilight greeted them with clouds bright orange and blue, land pink, and the horizon on fire. Storms overtook them. Floods threatened to drown them as the days of Halair grew colder. They waited in silence till Morvelving's withdrawal sickness passed. The beasts and wildmen hunted them. Morvelving put forth all his skill to keep them safe. After the first snows of Vema, he found the north passage through the Althoros Mountains and led them into the frozen wastes of Frystgalen.

There the cold seized the young and old and didn't let go. The Frystlins lent no aid. Morvelving and the dwarves crossed the highlands and looked upon the dark spires of the Caszark Mountains. Starving and freezing, the dwarves used the last of their kindling to build a fire in the hope of signaling their kin. Before night fell, their kin did discover and warmly welcome them into the dwarven haven.

———————

Morvelving shouldered his pack and clutched the minotaur cloak close. He had stayed for a fortnight too long. What they had built—hidden and fortified delves that provided water and food to harvest—impressed him. The furnaces burned as hot as their determination. He had almost become deaf from the drumming of a thousand hammers.

They were secure within their caverns. He had put forth his tracking skills to make sure there was no trace of their trail leading to the mountain.

The dwarves were gracious, and he realized that by naming him their friend, he'd become family to them, which terrified him. Every kind gesture reminded him of what he had lost.

He heard the noise of footfalls crunching in the snow behind him. Morvelving grunted. Wynthrim followed, snowflakes collecting on her braided beard. Now that she was home among her people, emerald runes had been etched on her brow and face, confirming her as the leader. She carried a long two-handed sword in both hands.

"I am leaving," Morvelving said in finality. "You may live at ease under the ground, but I cannot. I long for the light of sun and moon. I appreciate the chance you gave me; I haven't felt the urge for piphlid since we crossed Frystgalen. I—"

"I'm not here to stop you." Wynthrim stared up at him.

Morvelving clamped his mouth shut, wondering if she had guessed the real reason he wanted to leave.

"The choice has always been yours to stay." Wynthrim held out the sword. Dwarf runes on the blade glowed blue with wisps like candle smoke rising against the heavy snowfall. "Take this gift for guiding us here. My kin in bondage are forced to craft weapons and use our Ergald to strengthen them for our elven masters. This is one we reclaimed and now give to you. The bronze will not bend to breaking like other blades its length. Carry it. Let its weight be a penalty for running again."

Morvelving took the gift, feeling its balance and weight. He was running because he didn't deserve a family. A part of him wanted to leave the weapon behind, not wanting a reminder. By now he recognized and respected Wynthrim's wisdom and foresight, and refusing a gift was frowned upon by all the gods.

"Go, dwarf-friend, and may what you need find you quickly. Fare you well, Morvelving."

Wynthrim disappeared within the caverns of ice and stone. There was a Frystlin village seven days to the south. Morvelving would start there. Frystlin drink was strong, and he needed something. Haunted by her words, he navigated the snow dunes, wondering if he'd made a greater mistake by leaving.

3

––––––––––

Bitter wind tore at his cloak, bit at his ears, and stung at his eyes.

Morvelving shivered and pulled the heavy minotaur-hide cloak closer. Snowflakes twisted and dove about him like insects in the southern marsh. This was warm Eily in Frystgalen, according to the Frystlins. Elsewhere it was cold Azes, a time for blankets and tales by firelight. Still tame compared to the glacier fells further north where the dwarves now lived. Half-stepping, half-slipping on the brittle frozen earth, he corrected his footing. His paws were snug, wrapped in seal hide. A necessity, but he still wasn't used to them. He needed to find a place to sleep or build an igloo before night—what the Frystlins called "the Cold Death"—descended, seeking his life with its fractal fingers.

The possibility of freezing to death heightened his foul mood. The Frystlin drink ermuk warmed his throat and stomach but didn't reach his heart. Morvelving had almost passed the village, the wind having made the snowfall as blinding as a white blanket. He wasted no time in downing as many horns of ermuk as he could barter. It wasn't piphlid, but it was close enough.

The sky was dull gray, and the paths between igloos were lit by dim, inviting firelights. He sniffed the air. The ambience exuded peace, silence, and serenity, akin to the scent of burning jasmine on wicker. He recalled three centuries ago, when an eastern tribe had visited his own. They had burned jasmine for the Moon Dance during Hahnvi. The music and dancing were a warm memory. He sighed, his breath puffing before him like a cloud.

A subtle, disruptive scent grabbed his attention. Morvelving sniffed the air—salt and water. Indifferent, he shrugged and drank again. Nothing came to his tongue. He investigated the horn; a thin layer of ice covered the caramel-colored liquid. Grumbling, he broke it with a claw, his silver-gray fur coated with snow. He was done with the cold.

Licking his lips in satisfaction, Morvelving continued to drink the burning liquid. Perhaps he would journey to Menici or the Land of the Idosse again. It was warm in those lands. He approached a large igloo with oddments hung along the circular frame, bones covered with icicles, chittering in the wind. Soft light escaped from the delved entrance, large enough for a hunched grown man to walk through. Morvelving stooped and spoke into the opening.

"Hallo. Willing to share your fire's warmth? The Cold Death draws near, and I find myself without shelter." He spoke in Frystlin as well as he could, adding in a few words from the Trade Tongue to compensate.

The cramped igloo emitted a strong odor of humans. Morvelving heard the conversations hush.

One shouted out, "Begone, vagrant!"

Morvelving shrugged off the unnecessary rudeness with another drink of ermuk. He was a vagabond and a stranger to the Frystlins. His hand drew to his belt pouch—the itch for piphlid had frustratingly returned. The gods-damned shroom didn't grow in Frystgalen. Morvelving cursed under his breath and took another drink.

Wynthrim's words still haunted him. Why would he risk caring for someone again? He would just end up hurting them or worse. He missed Wildriver, but she hated him as much as he hated himself. He had wounded her beyond healing. Snowflakes collected on his snout as he stood motionless in the face of his memories, Wildriver's mournful cries for their son ringing in his ears. He shook his head and took a long draw of the ermuk.

He was doing the right thing by leaving the dwarves. Best not repeat the past. He wouldn't end his own life, but it was still best to be alone for the rest of his life.

Morvelving adjusted the ad hoc cloth and leather wrappings that held his bronze two-handed sword, Penalty, on his shoulder. The dwarves had clearly made it for an elf lord. Still, its length and balance suited him. He kept it covered in hide.

A fitting name for the weapon as it kept serving its purpose, reminding him that he'd run away again. The blade was long and leaf shaped. Dwarven runes had been etched on either side of the blood grooves and glowed blue with power—enchantments to keep the blade from bending or breaking like other weapons its length. The dwarves worked Ergald into their craft, but the magic was beyond Morvelving's understanding. Ergald was a telluric exchange, giving one's own blood to use Ervi's, the earth's, power. How had they imbued it into an item? He had tried to see how the process worked when he was among them, but they'd politely ushered him away from their workshops. Its cross-guard was crescent shaped, and a weighted pommel flared out at the base of the hilt, mirroring the shape of the cross-guard like a moon reflected in a dark pool. A feature that had significance for Morvelving. He still worshipped the Moon Goddess.

"Best to find a place to build a shelter," he said to himself as he surveyed the ground, satisfied Wynthrim's wish hadn't found him yet.

Morvelving heard fast footfalls on the crunchy frozen earth. He thought they would pass, but a small force hit his hock and yelped. He turned to see a small human child pushing herself up from her fall. She rubbed her head where she must have hit his leg.

Why was she running with nightfall near? Sniffing, he found the salty scent he'd smelled earlier was from the tears brimming in her eyes. She had to be less than ten winters old. Fur wrappings covered her face for warmth. Her round crimson eyes, unique to Frystlin humans, looked up at him. Those eyes were not frightened, not as most human children were when they saw a Mulranei for the first time.

Someone called from the dark. Without a word, the girl crawled under him and held his leg. Morvelving's heart skipped a beat. Windtail had often resorted to the same behavior when he'd felt scared. Morvelving remained still, stunned.

Five Frystlin men stopped in front of him, shouting and pointing at the girl, breath clouding about their faces. Their blue-tinted skin wrinkled under their furrowed brows. Morvelving blinked away his grief, shame, and lethargy. The men's words pounded his ears like a trumpet. He smelled their scent of anger and greed—unmistakable, like smoke in the wind, a warning of wildfire.

"Wolf-kin, hand over the girl," one demanded, quickly covering his mouth with fur wrappings. His gloved hand eased onto the handle of his dagger. "She runs from her masters."

"Why would she do that?" Morvelving questioned. He licked his lips, his tongue wetting the icicles that hung from his whiskers. Warmth filled him with his growing anger, making him sound far bolder than he felt. "I smell her fear and your hate. What has she done to you?"

Another man spat, the spittle freezing before it hit the ground. A ridiculous gesture, for he had to unwrap and rewrap his fur hood to stave off the cold.

"She's our *salvariyok*," he said, looking back and forth to his friends—

who gave him reassuring shrugs. "Prize claimed after we defeated her tribe in raid. You have no right to meddle in Frystlin affairs, dog."

"Dog? And prize!" Morvelving said, snout quivering to tease his fangs and show his anger. Humans had called him many names, but the stench of their cruelty, as feces left in the sunlight, clung in his nostrils. He knew the Frystlin tribes raided each other to remove competition for rare resources, but now he was seeing it before him, feeling the child's desperate grip on his leg, and hearing her rapid heartbeat. While he couldn't alter their way of life, he could still make a difference to the child.

"You insult my people, human. Enough reason alone for me to seek comeuppance. I smell your intent for the child, and it sickens me. By the Moon Goddess, this girl is under the protection of Her silver light and my fang and claw."

"Have it your way, mongrel."

The men drew their antler knives, edged with sharp bronze.

Morvelving stood still. Human courage often made them foolish and brazen. He considered removing Penalty from its wrappings. He didn't need the bronze blade.

The first man leaped at him, dagger poised to stab him in the chest. Morvelving stepped aside—careful to keep the girl under his wide stance—grabbed the man's arm, and twisted.

A muted snap followed by an agonizing scream broke the stillness. Morvelving punched him in the face, sending him to the frozen earth.

The next attacker, Morvelving kicked in the gut and kneed in the face, blood freezing as it sprayed out from the man's nose.

For the third, he used his hide cloak to catch a thrusting dagger. Then he twisted and slashed his own claws across the man's face. The man screamed, "My eye! My eye!"

Morvelving turned. Two men tackled him to the ground. His hide tunic hindered the quick dagger stabs, but he felt warm pain. Too close. He twisted, untangling himself and ensnaring one man's throat in an armlock. They didn't wrestle like Mulranei—their human limbs were too short and weak. He pinned the other man's throat between his knee and hock. They hissed and choked, limbs flailing. Morvelving released them both when they became unconscious.

Standing, Morvelving looked back to the girl. She was gone. A moment of panic, then he heard footfalls and smelled desperation and fear, unmistakable, like rotting flesh. He turned. The first man had her cornered where two igloos met, his broken arm limp at his side, dagger in the other. The fool believed Morvelving was occupied. Morvelving pulled the hide-wrapping off Penalty as he sprang to the girl's aid. Four leaping steps.

By the glow of Penalty's runes, the man turned and understood his mistake. Morvelving struck him down.

The girl just sighed in relief, ignoring the steam rising from the growing dark pool before her feet. Clearly, she was no stranger to violence. Morvelving considered that her own family could have been slain before her eyes. Whimpering at the sad thought, he wiped the blood from Penalty on the dead man.

"You can't stay in the village, girl," Morvelving spoke softly, looking down at her with his ears flattened to show himself as no threat. "Come along."

She fixed her eyes on him, unblinking, and tilted her head sideways. Morvelving pondered for a moment; had he said the wrong words? "You need to get away before the whole village is after us. Are you coming with me?" he asked, speaking again in the Trade Tongue as he gestured for them to leave.

He extended his hand. The wounded men were groaning and waking from their beating. Soon they would call out, and Morvelving wanted to be gone and burrowed in shelter before nightfall.

She examined his paw-like hand, with black claws at the fingertips, rough pads between knuckles, and then placed her own small hand, covered in a fingerless fur mitten, on top.

Morvelving led her out of the village without hesitation.

With Penalty tucked in his armpit, Morvelving rummaged through his pack for his healing salve. Thankfully, he had made more. The wounds on his side ached, and he could feel the warm blood cooling. Hyperaware of the steady, quick footfalls that followed him, he glanced back. The girl looked up at him, tugging her hands behind her back. What was she doing? Only when something brushed his tail did he know. She was trying to grab it.

"Gods above," he swore under his breath. Morvelving did not know how to explain to a human child how rude that was. He felt her mittens tugging on his tail.

"Ah! No. No, thank you," he said, turning and shaking his head. The girl blinked once. She was young, but he saw her watching him speak. He considered having her go first, but she was using his pawprints in the snow to navigate. He beckoned her to follow.

Morvelving found the salve and shouldered Penalty and his pack. He applied the balm to the last of his wounds. Satisfied, he wrapped his cloak about himself. The air became bitter and cold, with the snow falling leisurely. He sniffed and surveyed the snowy flats. They had distanced themselves from the village.

"We must build a shelter and quickly," he said to the girl. She watched him without speaking. Morvelving didn't wait and began to burrow into a snowdrift.

Survival in Frystgalen was, to put it lightly, difficult, and he had quickly learned how to build into and compact the snow like the Frystlins. He made it wide enough for himself and the child and a firepit. The chimney for smoke was difficult to make, but he managed.

As he rose, the cold hit him like a physical barrier, like slamming an open palm on a water's surface. Morvelving shuddered, grabbed his pack and Penalty, and hurried into the burrow. Ice blocked his nose, and his tongue felt numb. He fished out his flint and kindling, thankful he had gathered wood the day before.

It took four strokes to coax out a spark, and the kindling caught. Before long, the burrow was lit and warmed by the crackling flames. Morvelving blocked the entry with his pack and lay Penalty behind him. His dagger was a better defense against an intruder in the tight space.

With the burrow warm and bright, Morvelving focused on the child. She was hugging her legs, her crimson eyes watching him, a few loose strands of white hair hanging over one. She had taken off her mittens, her hands' pale blue skin pinkish from the warmth of the flame.

He had seen humans with many features. Frystlin features were more pronounced—bluish skin, red eyes, and pale hair. He assumed other humans found it unsettling—why Frystlins were a rare sight in warmer lands.

The child raised her head. She had taken off her fur head wrappings, blue cheeks a rosy tint. She sniffled. Not from sadness. Morvelving smelled her emotion—curiosity. Like a familiar itch that he couldn't quite reach.

"What are you called?" he asked.

Her brow furrowed. Her eyes were on his mouth. Morvelving checked his Frystlin tongue and spoke again. Still no response. He spoke in the Trade Tongue. She continued to look at him, confused.

He had seen human children speak with fluidity at her age. She couldn't understand, apparently, so he pointed at himself and spoke his name.

The child pointed at him, then made quick signals with her hands. Now he was curious. He motioned at her hands and shrugged. "Why are you making those signals?"

She looked at him like he was speaking gibberish. The child crawled closer to him. Morvelving fussed over the fringes of her coat that had almost brushed into the fire.

She opened her mouth and pointed. She had no tongue. A precise severing with a practiced hand and a sharp blade. The maim had been healed, but its recent nature was apparent. His ears drooped. Nose tickled from tears that brimmed his eyes. A desolate place in the Darken Depths awaited those who would mutilate a child.

"You cannot speak, but you can hear me?" he asked, pointing at his ear. The child pointed at her ear. He nodded, happy to make progress in communicating.

The child shook her head.

"Blessed Goddess." Morvelving frowned. He watched her face droop. "Do you know your runes?" he asked and drew the Trade Runes in the snow with his pointer claw.

The child noticed his movement and her face lit up, which warmed him more than the flames a handbreadth away. She made a croaking gasp as she hurried to see what he was drawing.

She watched him draw the lines. Morvelving introduced himself and asked her name. She sat up to draw in the snow. Morvelving leaned over, fascinated. She wrote her runes in haste, the lines often blending, but he could read them.

"Nippiktua," he said aloud, after reading what she drew, and pointing at her. Seeing his mouth move, she nodded and pointed at him, then made some quick hand signals. Morvelving mimicked her signals.

Nippiktua beamed and, with fervor, made intricate signs with her hands and fingers again. Morvelving didn't understand. He put up his hand to stop her.

"I do not understand," he said, waving his hands palm up. She scowled at him. *Feisty,* he thought, amused, and was amazed she was already reading his lips.

The child drew in the snow again. Morvelving looked at the runes: *Hungry.*

"Oh." He turned and fished out the pouch with the dried seal meat from his pack. He'd been so focused on the child he had forgotten hearth courtesy. "Here we are. There isn't much—"

Morvelving stopped himself. She couldn't hear him. He placed the pouch in front of the child. It had frozen. After removing the wrapping, he placed the meat near the fire.

They watched the ice melt in the stillness. Morvelving found the child's patience impressive, even though her stomach sounded like a distant avalanche. She stole a quick glance at him, twiddling her thumbs.

Nippiktua walked up to him. He was sitting cross-legged; she stood at the height of his shoulder. He side-eyed her and twitched his right ear. The girl only looked up at him.

Without warning, she reached up and ruffled the dark fur on the back of his neck. An action he had seen humans do to their pets. Morvelving sneezed his displeasure and yawned to show her his impatience. She didn't stop. He shook his head and waved for her to sit down.

She finally understood.

The meat had thawed. Morvelving gave her a piece. The child tore at it with abandon. While she made war on her dinner, Morvelving drew in the snow, asking, *Do you have any family?*

She read the runes but continued to eat. He was happy to wait. Though he was worried he had asked too much of her. Frystgalen was a brutal land and bred hard people. Even the night was so cold it would kill him in minutes. A creeping dread slithered up his spine. He had no clue how to take care of a human child. He shouldn't care for any child. The last one, his child. He—

Nippiktua wrote in the snow, her mouth still full of the last bite. No. No family. Fought the Qilatuuga when they attacked again. I tried to run like Qim, Mik, and Immit. But my legs are too short. Qilatuuga caught me.

Her eyes showed no emotion as she recalled the death of her family. Morvelving guessed that, sadly, it wasn't bravery. Killing and death were common in her life. Drooping his ears, he wrote, *I am sorry. Qim, Mik, and Immit are family?*

Nippiktua shook her head and drew. No, they are the sled dogs. And smart to run and live.

Morvelving blinked, astounded at what she focused on. She wasn't a stranger to death or murder and found running away to survive smarter than fighting. Morvelving inquired, *Is that why you ran in the village?*

Nippiktua nodded. He smelled sorrow around her though. Like charred trees soaked by heavy rainfall. Hoping to change the subject and distract himself from the rising dread within his chest, he wrote, *Will you teach me your hand symbols?*

She frowned at the runes. Looking up at him, Nippiktua furrowed her brows. Then gave a sigh of resignation. Nippiktua began right away with finger motions in one hand.

Morvelving mastered them with diligence. His people understood patterns and had learned many secrets and knowledge of life from the Moon Goddess when she had walked in the woods with them. Long ago, when the world had been young. Tribal Wiseneyes had then taught the young.

After a time, he noticed Nippiktua's eyelids drooping.

"Sleep?" he signed. Her face lit up at his successful sign and nodded. *"Tomorrow,"* he signed, slow and deliberate. Making sure he got the signals right. *"I leave south. From Frystgalen. You come with?"*

What was he doing?

Before he could change his mind, she jumped up and ruffled the flat of his head—like he had seen humans do to their canine companions— and nodded with enthusiasm.

Morvelving tolerated the offense. He took hold of her small arm. She looked at him confused, stared at his drawn-back ears. He shook his head. Nippiktua shrugged.

She signed. Her movements were too quick. Morvelving waved for her to slow down. Nippiktua humphed but slowed her signs. *"Where south?"*

Unsure whether he would make the correct symbols, he wrote in the snow, Menici or Idosse. You can't stay in Frystgalen. I am an exile. I don't have a home. I must continue to roam. It will be a hard journey. But I'll find you a safe home.

"I'm ready," she signed, standing up.

Morvelving laughed at her promptness then signed back, *"Sleep first."*

Nippiktua yawned in agreement and lay down next to him, drawing near. Just as Windtail used to. Morvelving held back the lump in his throat and sniffled at the tickle that came up from the constriction in his heart to his nose.

Afraid of waking Nippiktua and struck by growing panic, Morvelving took deep, slow breaths. It didn't work. This was not happening. The space was shrinking, too small—the walls were closing in. His breathing became rapid. She looked to him for care. He feared she would learn why that was a terrible idea. He could not do this. He had to leave, but he remained motionless.

Morvelving forced himself to breathe against the invisible restraints that sought to constrict his chest. He glanced down at the human child, sleeping unaware of the coward next to her. He couldn't go back on his word. He was helping her find a home. Morvelving had to make sure she lived till then. He couldn't abandon her.

"Goddess guide me," he muttered as he seethed. He couldn't close his eyes for fear of seeing Windtail fall again. The dancing flames filled his eyes as he fought to remain still and not flee. He pleaded to the Goddess in vain.

Morvelving flinched when the child moved in her sleep. With his vision drawn away from the flames, he noticed them: Dae, spirits of panic and fear, sickly green and yellow shapes shifting like wisps of smoke dancing back and forth, reveling in his dismay. They were harmless, except as a visible reminder of his state. Morvelving took another deep breath, trying to gain his Ikigai, peace of self.

An idea came to him. Morvelving pulled the disheveled goose feather from the braid behind his ear, fished out the pouch of healing salve, and smeared a tiny portion of the salve along the feather. He tossed it into the fire and began to quietly hum the Wajpheni, the Dance of Grass and Wind, as the acrid scent clouded his nose and stung his eyes. A means to call the Moon Goddess to him for strength and wisdom. It wasn't the full ritual, but he hoped Telunian would show mercy.

The warm space of the igloo became blurred in Morvelving's vision as he drifted into rhythm. He felt the spirits of his ancestors look upon him and then turn away, his guilt laid bare, and Telunian's light veiled by more than the snow den he sat in. Still, he hummed the chant and hoped, till the aroma of the healing salve dissipated. No aid had come. The weight of his exile made his shoulders slump.

Sparks flew from the fire and landed on a shape across from Morvelving. He braced to stand and defend himself. The shape shifted with the dance of the flame that burned between them, but it mimicked the aspect of a small stout creature. Once his shock subsided, he recognized it as a Dae of the Night, which seemed to soak the light of the fire to form a shimmering semblance akin to a raccoon. With each flicker of the flames, the Dae would disappear and reappear.

The Dae of the Night had aided Telunian in her works when the world was young. They were rarely seen, only glimpses under the light of the moon. They were drawn to where the Goddess set her gaze, which gave Morvelving hope. But they also fed on the power of the Fates as they tightened their grip on a thread of a life, which made him shake in fear.

Standing on its hind legs and sniffing the air, the Dae looked down at Nippiktua and then met Morvelving's stare. "He who mourns shall die alone." The mouth remained motionless, yet the words were sharp like frightful howls of the night.

Morvelving swallowed. "Does the Goddess speak?"

Only dark pools for eyes remained as the fire dimmed. Morvelving stoked the fire and the Dae reappeared.

"No." Its chuckle like a branch snapping in the silence. "But they see. Goddesses. Gods. And the Fates more."

His heart drummed in his ears.

"They see you, hold your immortal thread, but hers . . . " The Dae set its eyes upon the sleeping child. "Her short mortal ribbon warms their timeless hands. The Fates cackle with glee at the sorrow and doom that await upon her path."

Morvelving gazed down at Nippiktua with wonder and terror. She slept in blissful peace. Was the Dae speaking the truth or was it drunk on its own cravings? Even now it seemed to sway back and forth as if in a trance. Morvelving recalled Wynthrim's words. Had she seen this? Face himself and find purpose—no more piphlid.

"What must I do?"

The Dae of the Night swayed and made a sound like a tree bending to the wind. "What can you do?" The spirit gave a dark laugh. "Flee, and her doom is decided. Stay, and her doom will be decided tomorrow or after she is long dead. The threads change and slip from the Fates' fingers, but they always find those lost threads again."

Sudden pain in his leg made him blink and release his clenched fists. Morvelving examined the glistening liquid on his pointer claw. The Dae was gone, and the fire needed more kindling. He added more as his heart eased, his thoughts on the Dae's words. Could he trust the words of a spirit drunk on the Fates' will? Morvelving was now a part of a dangerous path. He saw no outcome where he would not suffer.

What about the child? Should she suffer for his own cowardice? No. Morvelving reached into his mind and held onto his actions in the village, how he'd protected Nippiktua. He was able and therefore he should. He'd said he would find her a home. Now he had to find a home that was both reclusive and hidden in hopes that the Fates would forget her till she was older.

They always find those lost threads again, the Dae of the Night had said.

Gods above. Morvelving licked his dry lips—the thought of piphlid was tantalizing. In his heart, he knew if he took piphlid again, it wouldn't be Windtail falling but the child sleeping peacefully next to him. He gave out a humorless chuckle. Wynthrim had cursed him with what he needed. What was worse was he couldn't run away this time. The thought of the child waking to find herself alone kept him rooted next to the fire as he prepared himself for the journey that lay ahead.

4

___

A small poke to his nose woke him. Morvelving sat up, still half asleep. The child was looking at him wide-eyed, with her pointer finger still aimed at his face.

It was morning, just before sunrise. He sniffed the air and immediately regretted it, for a foul stench assaulted his nose. The smell came from within the igloo—a tiny mound of snow at the far end. Morvelving waved his hand in front of his nose. Disgusting little creature. Do all humans defecate where they sleep? He shook off his sleep and started to work the ice off the side of his pack that was exposed to the outside. With the entrance no longer blocked, cold air crawled into the igloo.

The child began putting on her coat, head wrappings, and mittens with due diligence.

Initial shock gone, Morvelving thought it better that she had defecated inside rather than roaming outside. They were not far from the village. Once he rescued his pack from the ice, he began to burrow out of the igloo.

The morning was a dark blue, the air sharp and clear, refreshing from the stench of the igloo. Morvelving took a deep breath. There was a human child looking to him to find her a safe home. He wouldn't repeat his past—he wouldn't. Worse, the Fates were intent on her life.

"Gods above." Morvelving spat. The spittle froze midair. First, they needed to travel south from Frystgalen. Nippiktua struggled out of the igloo, wiped the snow from her mittens, and met his gaze.

"I'm . . ." Nippiktua signed, but Morvelving didn't catch her quick hand signals. He took a moment to remember the right signal and asked, *"What?"*

The child motioned at her stomach and pointed at her mouth.

"We'll eat later, we must press on. Our—" Morvelving stopped himself and slowly signed, making sure he formed them correctly. *"Here not safe. Food later."*

He ignored the growing scent of frustration emanating from her and sniffed the air. No other human but her. Evidently, the Frystlins who'd fought him last night either deemed her not worth the effort anymore or presumed she was dead.

A herd of caribou had passed. Morvelving waved for Nippiktua to follow and began to move south. If he stayed focused, he wouldn't have to think about his growing anxiety. They had to leave before a hunting party came after them.

As Morvelving trod through the snow, aware of the child jumping from one pawprint to the next, he knew he couldn't outrun the Fates or hide her from them. He would have to find a human settlement hidden from the great events of nations where she could thrive. The Land of the Idosse was the furthest west. Morvelving nodded to himself. When he had last journeyed on that rocky peninsula a century and a half ago, the humans had quiet fishing communities. The journey would be long but quiet. There were vast unoccupied lands between them and the Land of the Idosse. If they kept this pace, they—

Morvelving's left ear twitched back. The child was no longer following him. He spun around and found Nippiktua lying face down in the snow. His heart jumped to his throat as he hurried over.

He lifted her up with ease to find her crying. *"What is wrong? Are you hurt?"* Morvelving didn't understand. They had only walked for several hours. Had his pace been too fast?

"Are you hurt?" he signed, then looked her over for injuries. Nippiktua shook her head, swatted at his hands, and pointed at her stomach.

Morvelving stared, stunned. All of this because she was hungry. He could smell her anxiety and sweat from the exertion, and his ears dropped in embarrassment. Even during drought, Mulranei children suffered in silent resolution. He fished out food from his pack and gave some to her. She sniffled and began to eat. Morvelving vowed to be more attentive. For them to survive the journey ahead, he'd need to do more than just guide her—he'd need to care for her too. This time, Morvelving made sure Nippiktua had her fill. Only when he was certain she was fully recovered did they stand to restart their longer journey south once more.

———

Over the next several months, they crossed the snow dunes in the slowest manner Morvelving had ever traveled. Nippiktua stopped frequently—either out of curiosity or necessity—needed food regularly, and was arduous to communicate with. Morvelving found he had to rush in front of her to warn her of any danger.

Still, she was quick and eager to learn and began to read his lips, even started to recognize Mulranei facial expressions. She taught him where to hunt for seals when their journey led to the icy shores. Morvelving felt the Eyes of the Fates upon his back whenever the world seemed to take note of their travel. An avalanche waited to erupt until just after they'd treaded silently through a pass. A crow or raven always seemed to find them despite the cold waste. No doubt sending word to the Eyes of the Fates, the raven brothers, Felren and Rnudfel. He was relieved when the snows relinquished to plains, and they finally reached the forests at the western foothills of the Althoros Mountains.

Rain blanketed the forest. The tall pines offered sporadic shelter from the common Ruech deluge. Morvelving shook out his fur again, his pack and Penalty attempting to fall from his shoulder. He always hated the wet season. Nippiktua carried her coat under her arm. Her wet hair clung to her scalp, and her blue skin glistened from thousands of rain droplets.

The warmth of the southwestern lowlands of the Althoros Mountains was a shock to her at first. They'd had to flee the mountains, for a great fire had spread after a storm. Morvelving had needed to carry Nippiktua as he'd run from the raging flames. Even afterward, his hackles remained standing, and he couldn't escape the feeling the Fates were trying to flush Nippiktua out of hiding—the thought made him sneeze a tickle out his nose.

Nippiktua glanced up at him sharply.

"Stay close to me," he signed to her.

Nippiktua shook her head. *"Not that. This."* She corrected his hand signal.

Morvelving scowled. *"I did."*

He kept mimicking her motions. Satisfied, the child pointed to the community tucked in the wooded valley near a mountain river just down the hill.

"Yes, stay close. They smell and look friendly, but you can never be too sure." Morvelving had followed the scent of humans for the past several days, and it had led them here. The small village surrounded an old

stone temple. He guessed it was a priestly community. Not the ones who'd built the temple. The stonework—intricate, with faded statues of the gods on the crown and roof—were designs Morvelving had seen in elven architecture. These villagers had no defenses, and the only tools he had seen were for managing their crops. Clearly, the community had found the temple and, seeing it abandoned, made it their refuge.

His tall ears picked up the talk. Morvelving recognized several eastern dialects. These people came from the east across Middenfaer. He recognized Lindarcan and Hedressen, and he thought he even heard Gaeltic as well. If so, they had journeyed across many perils to find a home far from the dangers of the world. This community may be exactly what he was looking for.

A drum beat twice, and the villagers began to trickle toward the temple, the children hurrying to their places next to family. Morvelving decided to announce their presence now so as not to alarm anyone.

He motioned to Nippiktua to follow. She hesitated, nibbling on her fingernails. Morvelving encouraged her again, and then she followed, raising her hand for him to hold. It was his turn to stall. No doubt she was nervous. There was no harm in helping ease her nerves.

As they made their way down the muddy slope, orange from last season's fallen pine needles, Morvelving began to feel hopeful. He had made it far with the child without incident, besides the ominous signs, and his own dread that he would turn around to find her falling from—

Morvelving focused ahead. First, he had to be sure this place would be a good home for her. Already, the villagers were talking happily among themselves and passing wooden bowls of steaming food. He had to be tactful, to not alarm them. Mulranei were no strangers to the eastern peoples, but a stranger unannounced was always a surprise.

A fence surrounded the small village, not for protection but for blackberries. Morvelving stood at a gap in the fence where he was visible to those gathering. Nippiktua hid behind him.

"Greetings and the gods' blessing!" Morvelving called in the Trade Tongue, raising his hands, black palms out.

The villagers all fell silent and faced him in shock. Women hid their children behind them, and the men walked out in front. Their long tunics were weatherworn but sturdy. They all carried the characteristics of their people. Tall and pale Lindarcans. Short and brown freckle-faced Hedressens. Pale and stocky Gaeltics with matted hair stacked in braids and forked beards.

Their elder, a hunched lean man with a few strands of white hair clinging to his bald scalp, raised his hand and replied, "Greetings! What do you seek? We have no riches."

"Only shelter for the night and food for myself and my ward, if you are willing. That is all, the Moon Goddess as my witness." They had no reason to trust Morvelving, except for the reputation of the Mulranei—he was confident they had interacted with his kin since the tribes were more populous in the east. He was ready for their rejection despite the laws of hospitality praised by the gods.

The elder consulted with the others. While they talked, Morvelving noticed an odd trinket hanging behind them above the temple's entrance. Where had he seen that before? It was the Runic Ring but with several convex lines made with laced bone and a human skull at the center. His stomach dropped with recognition. He had no fear of being turned away, for he now wanted them to.

"You are welcome to our shelter and food for a night," the elder said.

Morvelving swallowed. They were cultists of the Dormant Goddess, Drudan. Harmless to him and Nippiktua. But they lived to sacrifice themselves in an Ergald ritual to awaken Drudan.

Leaving Nippiktua here was no longer an option. He sighed. The odds were not in his favor, even before he'd promised to find a home for the child. Still, warm food and shelter for one night would be a blessing. "My ward and I thank you." Morvelving motioned for Nippiktua to step out from behind him. "I am—"

The villagers gasped and immediately took a step back. Nippiktua had stepped out from behind Morvelving. His ears drooped, and he frowned.

"What is that? A Dae possessing a child. Begone! Before it curses our children and crops!" the elder cried, caution replaced with horror and contempt. The men and women quickly filled their hands with stones and sticks.

Morvelving gave a sad whine. By the scowl on her face, Nippiktua had read their lips. Their fear was born of ignorance without regard for the hurt they caused the child, which made Morvelving very angry. Not to mention going back on their word. He stepped in front of Nippiktua and showed his fangs.

They all took another step back.

"She is not a Dae. She is a Frystlin child."

"Lies! He's been corrupted by Nameless!" the elder cried. Morvelving sneezed from the overwhelming scent of their fear.

"We'll be on our way then," he snarled, waving for Nippiktua to retrace their steps. "I have no desire to share bread with fools."

"You are the fool to harbor a Dae-child!"

Morvelving followed Nippiktua as she stomped away, his senses tuned toward the villagers, monitoring to see if they'd give chase. Their angry talk behind him was incoherent, and they thankfully left him and Nippiktua alone. Morvelving focused now on Nippiktua.

The child was making splashes of mud with each step, reasonably upset. Morvelving waited for Nippiktua's anger to subside. It didn't take long. Walking so forcefully tired her quickly. By the time the rain had calmed to a drizzle, she had calmed as well.

"Let's rest here." Morvelving motioned toward a wide pine tree, its eaves able to keep patches of ground dry.

Nippiktua sat down heavily. Morvelving handed her dry meat and berries, not warm stew with the comfort of a roof overhead. But it had to suffice. Morvelving set the waterskin down, still angry with the cultists rejecting them out of fear. He hurt for Nippiktua. It wasn't fair for her, but anywhere beyond Frystgalen, other humans would judge her for her differences out of fear and ignorance. It was his fault, hoping he had found a place for her to stay.

"Those people didn't know you and spoke in fear," Morvelving signed once the child was finished eating. *"Do not take what they said to heart."*

Nippiktua scowled.

"Are my signals correct?" Morvelving grunted when she nodded. Waiting for her to sign something, he checked if water had gotten through Penalty's wrappings. She watched him till he was done.

"Can I curse children and crops?"

Morvelving eyed her suspiciously. By her stern look, she was serious.

"Gods above, no." Morvelving turned to fully face her. *"They said that because they didn't know you are like them, just with different features. You're Frystlin. The colds of the north turned your skin bluish, and being closer to the sun, your eyes became red and your hair white. Humans in the south have black skin. Did you know this?"*

Nippiktua shook her head.

"But they are human. There are differences among my people as well. The tribes far in the east are shorter and faster, their fur copper and brown. In

the vast forest of Tyshr, where the trees are white and their leaves are orange all season, the southern tribes have stubby snouts and short tails."

"So . . . " Nippiktua considered her words. "We should go back and tell them."

Morvelving smiled at the thought. "People that let their fear dictate their lives are difficult to persuade. I doubt they'd listen. It is best to learn to not let people's fear rule you."

"How?"

"Do you think you are a Dae who curses children and crops?"

"I could be!" Nippiktua signed enthusiastically.

Morvelving scowled. That wasn't the answer he'd expected. He couldn't tell if she was being playful. "Uh, well, Dae are spirits of life, so you aren't one."

Now she looked sad. Morvelving sighed. What was he doing? "Gods above," he muttered aloud. He stood up and shook, pine needles cascading from his fur and trousers. "I mean you are you, and don't let what other people think of you change that. Now, on your feet. I'd like to find a good place to camp while we wait for spring."

Nippiktua sprang to her feet. "Where are we going?"

"Once the snows melt during Prila—" Morvelving pondered the correct hand signals. "—we'll travel south and west away from the Althoros Mountains and the vast unnamed lands, down the coastal path around the Althorax Marshes, and through the Althek Pass to the Land of the Idosse. You should rest to gather your strength. The journey will be long. A year or a year and a half before we reach the Idospont."

"Why are we going there?" Nippiktua had to hurry to get in front of Morvelving so he could see her signs.

"It's a quiet land, far from great events. I promised I'd find you a home, and . . ." He paused, not wanting to tell her how the Fates had marked her. Best she found out when she was older.

"Will you stay? When you find me a home?"

The question unbalanced Morvelving for a moment. *"For a time, yes, but I am an exile. I can't stay in one place too long."*

That answer seemed to please her—at least, she watched her feet without further questions. Morvelving set his mind to the long journey ahead with the human child. He flinched when she stomped on another dry branch. One thing was paramount: he had to teach her how to walk quietly in the woods.

5

―――――――

783 After Rift

Together a year and a half, and Morvelving was no more confident he'd find a home for Nippiktua than on their first day together. He had made mistakes and still couldn't believe the child had stayed alive, even flourished, in his care.

"*No!*" Morvelving hurried over to Nippiktua.

She was attempting to pocket several olives while the shopkeeper was busy with a customer. His sudden movement drew many eyes as he stopped her.

A Frystlin girl and a Mulranei were hard to miss among the stocky Lesgossan people with their sturdy legs, light brown skin, and black curly hair. They liked to hang tassels with beads and metal ornaments in their hair and beards, which added a humming clatter like a beehive to the resounding bargaining calls in the busy market.

The child continued to act as if she had done nothing wrong. "*Why are we staying in this smelly city?*"

"*This city is Lesgos, and we're here because it's safe,*" Morvelving signed while leading her through the bustle of the market and around a large well and fountain. At least, he hoped it would be safe. "*The Land of the Idosse isn't the quiet land of fishing villages I remember from a century ago. It's why I had to barter passage as a mercenary to get here, remember?"*

Nippiktua nodded. *"Yes, but why did we have to come here instead of staying at Thressea and Ugris?"*

"Because they are at war, and it's best to avoid those."

The market was a wide space on the eastern end of the city, surrounded by high stone pillars that supported roofs over the more expensive shops. Banners of all shapes fluttered in the wind. Their orange, purple, blue, and yellow fabrics brightly displayed the runes that named the owner and wares of each shop. The Idosse people built their cities and towns around a structure they called the Ancheas, a stone amphitheater that usually had a well at its center. In this case, a stone fountain stood in the center instead. It was a place where everyone gathered to fetch water, hear heralds or proclamations, or merely converse with neighbors.

He weaved through the crowd. People in dirty white tunics stepped out of his way while others in rich tunics of green and orange trimmed with gold seemed to expect the very earth to move if it were in their way.

A Kerykoros waved his sweaty arms as he stood on the stone platform near the Ancheas. "Muster called! The council votes for immediate action against the Grece invaders. And lo! War against the Makoidake Pella, who continue to raid along the River Tailn. Remember, good citizens, cast your vote whether the traitor philosopher, Sokrathese, be flogged or—"

Morvelving growled in his throat and tuned out the rest. This was the fourth day of such news. He had gathered that the Lesgossans were responsible for the war with the Makoidake Pella. Not as alarming as the rumors of a draekurm sighted flying south a year ago. When he'd heard, he had almost turned around for the eastern road, but no other news had reached him. There was no way to know whether the draekurm remained in Idosse lands.

Nippiktua ran ahead of him to sign, *"Are we going to see Thnossos again?"*

"Yes, I want to see what he knows about the rumors of disease spreading in the southeastern quarter."

Thnossos was the leader of a community Morvelving had never seen among humans before. They housed people from every part of the world and cared for each other equally.

As they passed under the gatehouse that led away from the market toward the southeastern quarter, Morvelving whimpered in dismay. He could already smell the decay. Thankfully, Nippiktua followed close behind. It only took them an hour to find Thnossos.

"It is true, gods above," Thnossos answered Morvelving's inquiry as he encouraged several children to move along. A soft-spoken and kind middle-aged man, Thnossos had introduced himself and helped Morvelving and Nippiktua on their first day in the city. "The city watch is vacating those near the sick as we speak. I fear it will spread regardless."

Morvelving sneezed out his frustration, making Thnossos give him a skeptical look. This was not good.

"Of course, the child is welcome to stay," Thnossos offered. "As you've seen, there are several Frystlin families in our community. She will be welcome and loved, even with her aptitude for oddness."

Morvelving grunted and even now could smell and hear the pack of stray dogs. Somehow, Nippiktua had gained the loyalty of the pack. They kept their distance though. One was peeking at them from down the alleyway. The Idosse liked their buildings made of stone and wood, but clay was more abundant in the poorer quarters.

The dog sniffed the wall, noticed Morvelving's stare, and scurried away.

Nippiktua poked his leg. *"You shouldn't scare them away."*

"You shouldn't have . . . whatever you did."

"They were hungry! I fed them."

Morvelving grunted. That was nice of her.

"I wanted to make friends, especially if you were going to leave me here."

Morvelving wasn't expecting something to get caught in his throat. He cleared it. *"I'm not leaving you here. Pay attention."*

He couldn't leave her here with a disease beginning to spread, and being in a city during a war was often either the safest or worst place to be. Morvelving saw the Fates' will in the wars and now in the disease. He wanted to believe these events were just the nature of humans. Perhaps the Fates' designs for Nippiktua only spurred them on.

"Thank you for your kindness and help, Thnossos," Morvelving said. "I fear the risk of disease, and I cannot leave the child here."

Nippiktua jumped up and down in excitement.

"That is probably wise." Thnossos smirked at the child. "She appears happy about it."

"Huh." Morvelving scratched the itch behind his ear. She continued to resist his efforts to find a place for her and was always happy to move on.

Before he could inquire why she was excited, Thnossos said, "Mulranei are renowned for their skills of healing. Any wisdom to halt the spread of this disease?"

Morvelving's ears flattened. Without knowing what sickness was spreading, he could cause more harm than good. He knew how to make his healing salve and other oddments to mend ailments of the body, but he didn't understand the cause, especially with humans.

"Boil your water, clean out the latrines, and defecate outside the city." General practices would have to do. "Gods be with you, Thnossos."

He waved for Nippiktua to follow and watched her skip ahead of him.

"Where are we off to next?" the girl asked.

"The Plains of Makoidake. The people are nomadic, live in tents." At least, that was how they'd lived the last time Morvelving had journeyed through these lands.

"Are their tents as smelly as cities?"

He shook his head. *"I don't know."*

Nippiktua tried to get one of the stray dogs to follow them.

Morvelving growled in his throat at it, which made the dog flee. *"They can't follow us."*

"You didn't have to be mean." Nippiktua scowled up at him.

Morvelving shrugged his shoulders. He didn't want to argue with her over this. Every time he wondered if he had found a place for her, something out of his control would happen. Cultists, war, and now disease. How much of a fool was he being for trying to hide her from the Fates' machinations?

———————

Water soaked Nippiktua's feet, adding to the brown mud cooling and tickling her. She smiled down at her wiggling toes. If she'd gone shoeless in her homeland, her toes would have turned black from the cold and needed to be cut off. She didn't need to bundle up at night in the Makoidake plains. Even now, the sun warmed her wet arms as she pushed the bloodied tunic into the wash bin. More pink water spilled out.

As she squeezed the water from the tunic and hung it to dry,

Nippiktua gave a grumpy sigh. She missed walking through woods and grass with Morvelving. Doing all this work—cleaning and fetching wood or whatever grown-ups told her to do—was bad for her. She needed to run and inspect wildflowers for Dae. She was tired of Morvelving thinking she wanted a people to be among and call home.

"The cities here have too many comings and goings, wars and diseases," Morvelving had signed when they had been approaching the Makoidake Pella camp. *"I'm hoping these people will be better for you. They live like Frystlins, nomadic, never staying in one place. You'll be able to grow with them among the open plains."*

Nippiktua still disagreed. The Pella weren't like her people at all. They didn't know how to hunt for seals or build igloos. She didn't want them to be like her people. She didn't want to be Frystlin.

"I want to be Mulranei," she had told Morvelving. His ears had flicked about then; she hadn't understood what it meant.

Morvelving had scratched his neck. Nippiktua recognized that as him being thoughtful.

"Nippi, I am an exile. I can't—I shouldn't have you accompanying me. You should remain among your people. It's what I promised to do when we met and what I've been trying to do for you these last two years. I know it hasn't worked because I haven't found somewhere safe. The Pella haven't changed their way of life since I was in these lands a century ago. You'll be safe and able to grow hidden from the Fates."

Nippiktua remembered her chest hurting then, and it hurt now, thinking about it. She didn't understand it, which made her angry. Morvelving grumbled a lot about Fates when he thought she wasn't looking, and he wasn't happy to leave the smelly, swollen city. That was two fortnights ago. Nippiktua wasn't entirely sure. Many days and nights.

She was happy to have left the city of Lesgos, though she missed the pack of street dogs. The Pella grown-ups expected another battle to take place today following yesterday's confrontation. Fluff had left at sunrise with all the warriors. She wasn't sure he liked her nickname for him. She smiled to herself; he really didn't have a choice. Besides, he was fluffy. It fit.

When the Pella people had welcomed them, Fluff had told her, *"I need to help them against the raids. This means I'll have to leave you with them. Listen to those older than you and try to make friends."*

Nippiktua had tried.

Someone poked her arm. Nippiktua recoiled, baring her teeth like Fluff often did, mistakenly assuming it was Chub and Thin, the notorious troublemakers in the camp who liked to yank her hair.

Instead, it was Bossie.

When she and Fluff joined the camp to find her a new home, Bossie wouldn't leave Nippiktua alone. Making sure she was working instead of doing fun things like eating food that wasn't for her, climbing, and playing games with the other children. She only listened because Fluff was coming back.

"You're a wild child," Bossie said. Nippiktua was cornered, so she had nothing better to do than read Bossie's lips. "It ain't right that Morvelving's caring for you, gods above. Not natural. Good sense for him to come here. Now, there's plenty that needs doing. Idle hands are offerings to Kragius, and we don't need the god of mischief about now."

Nippiktua doubted the god wanted her hands. They wanted fat seals or cute white foxes bled out on their altars. She frowned back at Bossie's scowl.

"We don't show our teeth like animals," Bossie was saying. Nippiktua followed her lips, grimacing. The woman had something green stuck in her teeth. "Battle's over or never happened. Regardless, the men are coming back. It is proper—"

She didn't wait for Bossie to finish. The battle's end meant Morvelving was returning. Nippiktua dodged through lumbering adults, firepits with cauldrons steaming with the midday stew, old men dropping their hammers and the weapons they sought to mend, and other children who gave her space and fearful glances. She knew her skin and eyes scared them—not as bad as those hermits by the stone temple. Morvelving said people were afraid of what was different to them. She wasn't afraid; she was eight.

The other kids, Idosse peoples, had light brown skin and dark curly hair. Most had brown or gray eyes. She'd seen two different babies that had green eyes! Nippiktua hadn't been able to get close to them, as the mother had gestured for her to stay back. Which was silly. Nippiktua was great with babies. She had stuffed snow in her baby brother's mouth when he would not stop crying. The reminder he was gone made her feel queasy, so she distracted herself.

Movement caught her eye. Two boys were waving at her. Chub and Thin. Their mouths moved and pointed at her, but she didn't need to read their lips to know what taunts they were saying: bluebutt, whitebush, and pinkeye. She didn't know what any of them meant, which made her hate them more.

The boys were sitting on a large sled, the kind pulled by the fat caribou Morvelving had said were called oxen. Instead of blades, the sled had four wheels. Wheels. Ridiculous. Still, there wasn't any snow, so perhaps they knew what they were doing.

Thin jumped down from the cart. His dirty blue tunic was black now. He was so bony that Nippiktua guessed the tunic could hold three Thins.

"Goin' to find your dog? They put him in the front, I hear. Where the fightin's bad," Thin said. Nippiktua clenched her fists.

Chub missed his step off the cart and tumbled to the ground. Nippiktua laughed, her throat vibrating and nose choking.

Thin and Chub seemed angry, so Nippiktua ran, confident she could outrun Chub. Thin? She wasn't so sure. She ran around two women. Something pulled at her tunic. She twisted free, running into a wooden barrel and almost knocking it over. Other people now turned her way and shouted, shaking their fingers at her with contempt. Fingers wouldn't stop her from outrunning Thin.

Nippiktua slipped and skipped through the mud outside of the camp. The road led down a hill with an old oak toward a wooded ravine. A stream flowed under those trees. Warriors emerged from the woods and continued into a vast field. Bronze spears gleamed in the sun like torches. Some men held painted shields aloft, waving. Others dragged their slack limbs along, uncaring. Some carried stretchers. Men stood shoulder to shoulder, supporting the wounded.

Air brushed by Nippiktua's ear. She picked up speed as she glanced back. Thin was right there, face sweaty and distorted. He must have missed her by a finger's length. Nippiktua ran for the withered oak.

She scampered up the tree, dry bark scraping bare feet. Nippiktua grabbed a branch with both hands. Pulling with all her strength, gritting her teeth, Nippiktua pulled herself up. Fingers tried to grab her right ankle. She kicked, eluding any vise, rolled onto the branch, and crawled to the center, ready to kick at Chub and Thin as they climbed up.

Morvelving stood there. She was at eye level with him. Nippiktua thought she was high up. Evidently not *that* high. She had grown accustomed to the wolf's face. The black fur around his face was peppered with silver streaks, fur shifting to white where the bronze cuirass met his neck. One ear was tilted while the other remained straight. He tucked his long tongue into his snout and looked at her with his big brown eyes. She knew that expression meant he was concerned and curious. The wolf people, Mulranei, were hard to read for humans. Good thing she was smartest.

Glancing toward the camp, Morvelving tucked Penalty under his arm. Dark lines of blood decorated the long bronze blade. Near the hilt, fierce blue runes that she couldn't read glowed bright with tendrils of mist. The movement made the mist trail off the blade like candle smoke.

"Are you well?" Fluff signed to her.

Nippiktua watched Thin and Chub running back to the camp. She smiled, relieved, and signed back, *"Yes! I'm glad you're back, Fluff. If you hadn't, Bossie would never have left me alone."*

"Those boys didn't hurt you, did they, Nippi?"

Nippiktua smiled at his shortened name for her. He'd started calling her that recently. It made her feel important to him. She hated it when her siblings had called her Nip-Nip. Not hiding her triumph and the warmth she felt at Fluff's concern for her, Nippiktua signed, *"Pfft, no. They couldn't catch me."*

Morvelving's tongue hung lax to the side of his snout. Nippiktua was glad he was relaxed now.

"Come. Down you go. Why were they chasing you?" he signed, holding out his arm like a tree branch.

The fur was wet around the bronze vambrace on his forearm. Nippiktua stood and jumped off the branch, laughing as she caught his arm and swung until Morvelving set her on her feet.

Walking alongside him, Nippiktua answered, *"I laughed at Chub when he slipped and fell. His face looked funny."*

His upright ears twitched back. Nippiktua couldn't remember if that meant he was questioning what she said. He was strolling, so she could easily walk with him. She had to take three steps for every one he took. Warriors were making their way to the camp, their families greeting them. Nippiktua watched, fascinated by how people's faces distorted when making expressions of joy or sadness. She wondered what their cries sounded like.

She blinked, noticing now that Morvelving was signing to her. *"Was Chub injured?"*

"What? No. At least, I don't think so. I mean, Chub looked like . . . Well, Chub." Nippiktua was satisfied that Fluff had accepted her names for the two boys.

With his ears to the side, Morvelving turned his attention to the people gathering near the muddy road outside the camp. She knew that meant he was considering something. Fluff thought about a lot of things for a *long* time. She focused on walking all important, with her chin up and steps wide, now that Bossie couldn't tell her what to do.

The only person she allowed to tell her what to do was Fluff. He'd said he would find her a safe home, but the truth was she was happy wandering the lands with him.

Morvelving's mouth was dry. The battle had been hard and short. Wounds on his left arm and leg burned. In contrast, the blood trickling down his leg was cool and tickled enough to almost distract him from the pain.

Seeing Nippi chased out of the camp made him more uncomfortable than he was willing to admit. He had reopened the cut on his thigh rushing to her. He was tired. He had tried to find a place where Nippi would be safe and feel at home, but the Land of the Idosse had changed significantly since the last time he had journeyed here. Granted, the last time was a century and a half ago. He couldn't bring himself to leave her in Lesgos with an outbreak of disease. He was beginning to believe his promise was futile against the will of the Fates. All of which was moot compared to caring for the child. Exhausting, but rewarding. He wasn't alone.

Unfortunately, the Idosse towns and villages were no different: under constant threat of being plundered and burned. So, they traveled. Wherever they were, he kept teaching Nippi many skills to survive. She was slow to learn, until she decided she wanted to. Two summers in each other's company, and he felt a decade older. Even when he had watched over all his tribe's pups during Wanhatica, he didn't feel so stretched.

The Makoidake Pella tribe had been welcoming to him and Nippi. The Plains of Makoidake was a wide land with rolling hills and deep ravines. There were no stone cities, making it less of a target for boundary wars that were a pandemic among the Idosse city-states. Nippi had assimilated into the Pella tribe well enough for him to begin to hope this great risk was almost past him.

Nippi was skipping alongside him, making her white hair—tangled like brambles in a deserted garden—sway back and forth. She wore a simple tunic, its edges fringed, and her scabbed knees showed how often she scurried with abandon for curiosity's sake. She absentmindedly plucked at a loose thread. Morvelving swallowed the lump in his throat. He had begun to appreciate her presence and feel a sense of purpose beyond his exile. He felt caught in a thistle bush.

Soldiers embraced their loved ones. Exhalations for the safe and mourning cries for the lost filled the camp in an uproar. Morvelving drew in a deep breath. A short battle but terrible as any.

He had placed Nippi in the care of the tribe—while he helped them with skirmishes against Lesgossan raiders. He was afraid he'd given them too much trust. After tapping Nippi's shoulder so she would look up at him, Morvelving signed, *"Who is Bossie? Will you point her out?"*

Nippi nodded. *"Bossie is her."*

She pointed at the woman fretting over the two boys who had chased Nippi. Her hair was graying, her shoulders square, and her skin leathery. A lifetime of hard labor and turmoil. Life was tough for the Makoidake on the plains of the central Idosse lands. Morvelving tuned his ears to them and sniffed. The air blew from his back, hindering him from smelling their emotions. But he could hear them as they drew near.

"She tripped me!"

"And kicked my face!"

Spotting him, the woman pinched both shouting boys on their arms. They squealed. The woman commanded, "Begone, both of you."

Bossie, Morvelving concluded, was a fitting name for the woman. She pointed her finger at him. "It ain't right or proper or natural, Mulranei, for you to harbor the child. She is wild, tries to bite the other children. Among our tribe, she will learn to be like her kind."

Her outburst drew the eyes of others. Morvelving's ears drew back, but he kept his initial anger in check. She didn't understand he was trying to find Nippi a place among her kin. He glanced down at Nippi.

Nippi sighed. *"I didn't bite anyone! I only show my teeth like you did with that big cat and that boar and those robbers."*

"I didn't think you'd bite anyone," Morvelving signed, reassuring her. *"We'll talk later about why I show my teeth."*

Nippi crossed her arms and glared at Bossie.

Morvelving eyed Bossie. "I care for the child. No one else was doing so when I found her. I swore to the Moon Goddess that I'd find her a home." Saying it out loud scared him. Terrified of making the same mistake, he hadn't even attempted to search for piphlid in the wild. Thinking of it, his mouth was suddenly dry. Longing. And now, this close to meeting his promise, he didn't want a disagreement. "You and I both want the child to have a home among her own kind."

Nippi threw her hands to her hips. Morvelving scowled.

Several of the men and their captain approached. He recognized the captain—Thersandra, bloodied from the battle. Thersandra and her men stood at the back as more women drew to Bossie's side.

"Why pester the Mulranei, Lesaphene?" said the man who bore the Makoidake Pella's carnyx, a trumpet whose harrowing sound still rang in Morvelving's ears. He held an honorary role, so the crowd listened to him. "He kept the centaur mercenaries from our flank. Saved many warriors. Family members stand here now due to his aid."

"I do not challenge his courage or aid," Lesaphene said.

Not Bossie, Morvelving thought. Nippi and her nicknames.

"I praise him for it," Lesaphene continued. "Truly, the Mulranei has gained honor and reward among the Makoidake Pella. Still. Your kind shouldn't care for our own. The girl is dirty, wild. She doesn't know how to be among us. You've done too much damage. Her time here will be hard, but it will be for the best."

Other women around her voiced their agreement. Morvelving smelled their concern. It lingered and overwhelmed him like a skunk's spew. The strength of it made him agree with them: he had spent too much time with the child. He had no right or reason to be the one caring for Nippi. And he understood Lesaphene more than she realized. Morvelving could smell the scent of stress coming off her like smoke from overcooked meat. She'd kept track of and cared for Nippi while he'd been fighting. He knew how difficult Nippi could be. The Fates continued to play their game. Of one thing, he was confident: he would have to make sure Lesaphene wasn't the one watching over Nippi.

Morvelving had fretted these past months about Nippi's ability to live among her own kind. She was in between two worlds: her own had been destroyed, and his had welcomed her. The life of an exile. Then there was Windtail, his son, who he . . .

Morvelving shifted his thoughts. Unwilling to open the door to his shame and pain. He knew he shouldn't be the one to care for her, and he had pretended for too long. Lesaphene was talking with those present, reaffirming and arguing. Morvelving looked among the humans, his nose overwhelmed with the scent of all their emotions. He sneezed.

"I understand," Morvelving said. Silence fell. Lesaphene eyed him. "You speak as if I have a choice. Nippiktua chose to come with me away from Frystgalen, where her tribe and family were killed. It was her decision. I came to your tribe with the intention of finding a home for her among your people. We have traveled far to find one. But it is her decision, as it was at the start." He spoke the words before he'd fully considered them. What if she chose to stay with him? She wouldn't. And if she stayed among the Pella, would the Fates become bored? His own uncertainty made his stomach churn. Was this what he wanted, or was he playing into their designs?

"She is only a child!"

"Quiet, Lesaphene," Thersandra said, as commanding and stoic as she was in battle. She stepped between Lesaphene and Morvelving. "The Mulranei speaks true. She is a child, but he made a promise. Be honored that he has found the Makoidake Pella worthy to care for the child and raise her to be Pella. And do our own children not choose to fetch water in the night when the old are thirsty, despite the lions that lurk nearby? I understand your concern. It is true—the child needs to be taught and cared for properly—but she can and should choose."

"How do we know she speaks for herself?" Lesaphene demanded, the women behind her nodding in affirmation.

Thersandra nodded, turning to Morvelving. "That is a fair point. She can't speak for herself."

"Nippiktua knows her runes," Morvelving admitted, dazed by how quickly change was happening and needing to fight to stay standing. "She can write in the Trade Tongue. Use runes to explain your proposal to her. I will not intervene."

Satisfied, Lesaphene nodded and called for parchment or clay to be brought forward. Morvelving felt abruptly dizzy. Was it the blood loss or Nippi's potential departure? Did she want to stay? Morvelving peered at Nippi. She was watching Lesaphene with arms crossed and a dirty scowl. Despite his failures and flaws, with her in his life, he could be better. Not make the same mistakes. If she was with him, the chances were high. Either way, dread filled him, and the Dae of the Night's warning that the Fates loved him was proof enough. This was for the best.

Thersandra took the presented parchment. One side displayed a list of items, but the other was blank and serviceable. The captain used a shield as a table, drawing runes with a piece of charcoal to inform Nippi she was welcome to stay with the Makoidake Pella. They would count her as one of them if she chose to stay, and she wouldn't have to be with Morvelving if she didn't want to. Morvelving would make sure Thersandra oversaw her care. He didn't trust Lesaphene.

Nippi read the runes. Looking up at Morvelving with a questioning gaze, she took a deep inhale, knuckles white from her clenched fists. Morvelving's heart skipped a beat—smelling her anger and frustration.

Nippi vigorously shook her head and ran, slipping by three attempts to stop her, and raced out of the camp and down the hill to the woods.

6

Morvelving stood motionless, stunned that he had hurt Nippi and that she had run away so quickly.

"I think this resolves the whole dilemma," Thersandra said, dirty hands on her hips, clearly tired. She hushed Lesaphene with several dismissive gestures and a volley of decisive words in their own tongue. "Perhaps, Morvelving, the home you seek for her, she has already found."

Morvelving hurried into the camp and tore down his tent with haste, driven by relief and terror. His and Nippi's belongings fit in one bag, which he slung over his shoulder. No time to carefully apply the healing salve to his wounds. He licked the minor wounds and bound the cut on his thigh. No one hindered him as he left the camp.

"Mulranei!"

Thersandra jogged after him. Morvelving halted. Nippi's scent was clear. She was not far. He waited for the captain, slowing his breath.

"Be quick, captain," Morvelving said, regretting the tinge of anger in his voice. He was angry with himself, not her. He added more calmly, "What you said earlier . . . You are right. I was blind to it by my own— I'm going after the child."

"As you should! Gods above, here." Thersandra tossed a small pouch at him. Morvelving caught it, feeling and hearing the dry clicking of drakma. "As agreed."

"Farewell, and thank you for helping me back there."

Thersandra shrugged and waved as she turned back to her people.

Morvelving paid no more heed to the Makoidake Pella. Intent on Nippi's scent, he followed her footprints into the grass. They led to the woods and a river there. He no longer heard her hurrying through the underbrush. Perhaps she was hiding. Morvelving sighed.

The initial shock of her running away was gone. He recognized her actions for what they were. Windtail had tried to hide, to be alone, when he was upset. Nippi required a great distance, it seemed. By her scent, he could determine she was not far beyond the lethargic river.

Her footprints ended. He stopped, scratched his neck, and sniffed the air. "Well, Eorhath's beard," he said, shaking his head. Warm pride filled his chest. She was using skills he had taught her. Morvelving lifted what looked like a fallen branch. Her footprint was underneath. Now he wondered what else she had learned.

Sure enough, she had not crossed the shallow river in one crossing. Using what he'd taught her to mask her scent, she had waded downriver. Morvelving noticed clouds of disturbed water. He studied the bank for signs of where she'd left the river. A large smear in the mud where she must have slipped gave away her direction. Morvelving struggled to shuffle up the bank. His wounds made it difficult, and the exposed tree roots that hung out like gnarly fingers hindered his way.

Birdsong filled his ears, and squirrels scampered from branch to branch. Nippi had hidden her prints. Morvelving followed her scent, a conglomeration of smells: salt from her tears, anger like charcoaled bread, and sadness like the earthy mud clinging to his feet.

She was hiding between two spruces, where their roots twisted and maneuvered over one another. Without her sniffles and scent, Morvelving would have overlooked her, as she had concealed her presence. He smiled with pride.

Morvelving took extra care to keep himself visible as he approached, not wanting to startle the child.

Nippi's head jerked up. Her red pupils were bright in the shade of the woods. She crossed her arms and turned away from him.

That hurt. Morvelving breathed deeply, acknowledging his responsibility for his own mistake. He deserved it for being so blind to what was in front of him, searching for a home for her when she had decided he was her home. His chest swelled with pride. And worry. Morvelving set Penalty and his pack down and sat on a dry patch of earth. He would wait for Nippi to approach him. The wood was peaceful, and he focused on it to calm his own anxiety.

Morvelving had applied the healing salve to his wounds, cleaned Penalty and his cuirass, and welcomed the sun beginning its descent into the west with the jovial song *Away West* before Nippi turned and stomped over to him. She plunked herself beside him as he finished the last note. He caught distant howls adding to his song as he handed dried fruit and jerky to Nippi. He waited by building a fire while she ate.

Once the flames were steady, the embers bright, and the sky filled with streaks of red and orange, Nippi turned sharply and signed to Morvelving.

"Why do you want to get rid of me?"

Morvelving shook his head, fighting back the tickle in his nose and eyes. *"I—I told you I'd find you a home—"*

"I don't want a home! I want to be a Mulranei like you."

Morvelving smiled, then took a deep breath. *"I thought it would be best for you to be with your own kind. I was mistaken."*

Unbidden, Windtail's body falling, limbs flailing, played in his mind. The Dae's warning about the Fates' intent for her. Gods, he was mistaken about many things. His hand jerked to his belt. One chew of piphlid would dampen it. He forced his hand to his side and suppressed his frustration that he still longed for the shroom.

"Yes," Nippi signed. *"You are wrong. I don't want to live with them."*

Once again, relief and panic filled Morvelving in equal measure. This was what Wynthrim had meant by giving himself a chance. Whether he liked it or not, Nippiktua wanted to be with him. So, he had to be better for her than he had been for Windtail. He couldn't hide her from the will of the Fates. He had to face their designs with her.

Morvelving cleared his throat.

"Very well, we'll stick together." Morvelving involuntarily whimpered and exhaled. Telunian's light. He was resolved. Their threads were set in the hands of the Fates, and by her choice, he was the home he'd promised her. His mind drifted to where they could go. As an exile, he couldn't return to his people, but living in the wild was something he could do.

Nippi watched him for some time, then eased her posture and sat closer, satisfied with his answer.

Once his nerves settled, Morvelving eyed Nippi. *"Next time, don't run away when you are angry. It could be dangerous. Use your voice."*

Nippi crossed her arms.

"Sorry, use your hands." Nippi gave a curt nod. Morvelving added, *"You were fortunate I found you. I saw signs of jackals."*

"I knew you'd find me."

"You thought I needed the exercise with my wounded leg?" Morvelving smirked.

Nippi shook her head, her face skewed in confusion. *"What? No, you are the best tracker."*

"I've had centuries to practice." Morvelving pointed back toward the hill. *"You covered your trail well."*

The child held her chin up. *"I can run fast too! Climb faster and hide my trail. When do I get a dagger?"*

Morvelving choked on a piece of dried fruit. He washed it down with a drink from his waterskin. Gods above, Nippi with a dagger. He chuckled. It reminded him of what she'd said back at the human camp, how she'd showed her teeth like him. She was still waiting for him to answer. He signed, *"You might have a dagger if you weren't grinning your teeth at everyone."*

Nippi stared at him for a moment, calculating.

Before she could ask anything else, Morvelving added, *"You and I are different people. We communicate in different ways. I show my fangs to indicate that I'm angry or uncomfortable, like with the lion, you remember? Good. I was telling him he'd regret enforcing his territory. That's only with an animal. My people have entirely different motives for aggression. Humans, well . . . "*

He thought about the Frystlin men who were after Nippi. Their sneers, their gritted teeth during their fight. Morvelving recalled how the Makoidake Pella fighters during the battle had similar expressions. At a loss, he continued, *"Humans show their teeth for different reasons."*

"That makes no sense," Nippi signed, and Morvelving agreed with her. He let out a deep sigh, overwhelmed by sudden fatigue from the day.

"Just don't bite people," Morvelving signed, giving up, then considered. *"Unless they are trying to hurt you."* Wildriver had excelled at explaining things to Windtail. At the recollection, his mood fell like the sun now descended beyond the horizon.

The woods darkened into shadow. He glanced at Nippi. She waited for him to continue speaking.

He sought an itch behind his ear, then signed, *"Watch before acting. See what someone wants before showing your teeth. Sometimes people can surprise you. First, determine what they want. Look at their body language. Are they tense? Standing to the side? Backing away from you or giving you space? They shouldn't touch you without your permission."*

"So . . . if they touch me, I bite them?" Nippi interrupted.

Morvelving grunted. Gods above, how to explain? He scowled at her, wondering if she was purposely being difficult. Many emotions clung to her like smoke with no chimney. Discerning the scent alone was challenging. Mulranei were better at tuning their emotions.

"At least shake your head at them first, and if they don't listen, then yes." Morvelving shrugged. Nippi nodded and thankfully refrained from asking another question. He was tired.

Wincing, Morvelving removed the bandages from his wounds. Nippi took her blanket from their pack and lay down, using an exposed root for a pillow.

"Where are we going next?" she asked.

"The city of Thypan," Morvelving answered. *"We'll gather supplies and hear about any contracts."* He was still working out what to do next.

That seemed to satisfy Nippi, for she turned on her side and closed her eyes. He took the moments before falling asleep to consider his course of action. Gather enough drakma to make their way to the land of Srel, a sparsely inhabited land he had explored centuries ago. Like the Land of the Idosse, a lot can change. A risk he would have to take. Unfortunately, he realized that becoming a mercenary fighter was the quickest way to make drakma. Often, he would do scouting, or the battle wouldn't happen at all. Today was the exception. He didn't like it, especially having to fight centaurs. There had been two of them. He shook the memory out of his mind.

On their way to the plains, he had laid eyes on the Olykis Mountains. The foothills were rugged and uninhabited. Perhaps there was no need to travel far, and the Fates worked best through the lives of humans and other races. If he and Nippi could live their lives in solitude, there was a chance, a small hope, they could hide.

A crow landed on the branch above Nippi, cawing and picking at its wing.

Morvelving froze, staring. *How did they always find Nippi?* he thought. The crow was at peace, but he knew they were clever creatures. Was it acting nonchalant only to report its findings to Felren and Rnudfel?

He picked up a piece of kindling and threw it to scare the crow away.

The kindling flew past the crow's head. It ruffled its feathers and cawed, noises to human ears, but Morvelving understood the crow shouted at him, "Vermin! Nuts for brains."

"Begone, there's nothing here to tell the Fates," Morvelving growled under his breath.

The crow flew away, its cackles saying, "Mad, wolfkin! Rude."

Morvelving scowled. Perhaps he'd been wrong about that crow. Heat rose to his face—he'd been rude to the crow.

With a wide yawn, Morvelving walked under the light of the stars. He marked a large radius around their camp, a boundary animals obeyed. Most humans he could hear approaching, even in his sleep. He imagined the knowing smirk on Wynthrim's face if she could see him now. If his fear of repeating his mistakes hadn't ruled him, a lot would have been different. After meditating to hold back the growing apprehension, Morvelving fell asleep, attentive to the noises of the night.

7

———————

The afternoon sun was warm on his head now that the midday eclipse had passed. Morvelving had bundled his cloak with Penalty and his pack, the contents shifting and the cuirass making it difficult to carry them under his arm. Nippi was hustling from one curiosity to the next. More comfortable in the woods off track than on the road, Morvelving led them southeast to Thypan.

As with other Idosse city-states, it functioned as a port city. It rested snugly between River Togis and Serpres, along the shores of the Idryiva Sea. They crossed over the Daespine Mountains and hired a ferry across River Togis before dawn.

Tall spruce and pine trees hid most of the city from sight. Judging by their pace and the glimpses of the city's stone walls, Morvelving realized it would take another hour to reach its gates by walking down the sloping land. He could no longer hear Nippi's loud footfalls.

"Hmm," he grumbled, knowing this meant something must have drawn her to investigate. Her scent was near, and he could hear her breathing. Stepping around a wide pine, Morvelving found Nippi examining an anthill. She lifted her foot to step on it.

Morvelving rushed into her line of sight. *"Best to leave them be,"* he signed as best he could while balancing the pack and equipment on his hip. Morvelving set them down. Thankfully, Nippi set her foot down too.

"What are they?" she asked, stooping so her nose was inches from the busy insects, her eyes trying to track the myriad movements.

Nippi looked at him when he signed, *"Ants. There are thousands within that colony, perhaps more."*

"Why can't I step on it?"

"Well, it would be rude and unnecessary." Morvelving pointed at all the lines of ants moving in and out. *"They labored tirelessly to shelter their queen. Now, come along. We're almost to the city."*

Nippi continued to stare at the ants. Morvelving shrugged and hefted the pack over his shoulder. The cuirass hit a branch. The clang made him flinch and caused a flock of birds to disperse from the leaves above. With Penalty wrapped in the minotaur cloak, he carried it by the blade. He planned to acquire a proper harness for it in the city.

A scream erupted behind him. Morvelving squinted his eyes shut to let the ringing in his ears pass as Nippi caught up to him, stomping and swatting at her leg. She had stepped on the anthill. Once the ants were gone from her leg, she deliberately avoided looking at him. Morvelving smirked and followed.

They joined the road to Thypan's gates without further incident. A stream of people passed into the city, laden with goods or pulling squat carts. Morvelving was wondering how overwhelmed the gate's guards must be when Nippi hurried off the road and looked under a stone. She picked up something white and earthen brown. Morvelving paid no mind till she lifted it up for him to see.

He froze. Nippi had one piphlid in her hand. Unbelieving, Morvelving looked back at the boulder where Nippi had found it. An ideal environment for the shroom to grow. Its earthen scent filled his nose. Already, his mouth was dry, and the desperate urge filled him. How did Nippi know he wanted it? She couldn't—she was only showing him what she'd found. Morvelving extended his free hand, hoping she didn't notice how it shook.

Her expression became flat, but she put the shroom in his palm. Morvelving stuffed it in his belt pouch, ignoring the warning drums beating in his mind.

"What is it, Fluff?" Nippi asked.

Morvelving licked his lips. *"A mushroom. It's poisonous, but the right amount has many uses."*

"Should I go pick more?" Nippi started walking back.

Morvelving shuffled into her way. *"No, no. One is enough."* He directed her back to the city. His complete focus was on the piphlid in his belt pouch. How could he keep it? The root of his shame. He didn't need it. He never had. Yet, even in that conclusion, he felt embarrassed about stooping so low as to lie to Nippi. Abruptly hot, Morvelving panted. The cobbled road became his entire focus. Everything else blurred. Windtail falling. The fault lay with him. A crushing weight from within. A release—he needed to escape the feeling. A small bite wouldn't do any harm. He—

Nippi poked his leg.

Morvelving looked down, stunned. The piphlid was in his hand again, its soft crown crushed. He couldn't tell if Nippi had noticed.

"When are we going to celebrate my sanitja?*"*

Morvelving's ears drooped in confusion. "Your what? I don't understand," he said. Realizing he'd spoken aloud and hesitant to sign with the piphlid in his hand, Morvelving pointed to the city. Nippi looked, her brow furrowed. His arm felt like lead, but with a great effort, he tossed the piphlid under a fern along the road. At least, he did that in his mind. He fit the shroom into his belt pouch.

Nippi threw her palms out. *"What?"*

"Never mind," Morvelving signed, his chest no longer constricting. *"What's your . . . I didn't catch that."*

"My **sanitja** *is today. The day I was born, my* amua—*my mother says it is to be celebrated with giving and dancing. All my siblings had their* sanitja, *but you missed one."*

Morvelving scratched the tickle behind his ear. This was completely new to him. He eyed Nippi, suspecting that she was making this up. Mulranei celebrated when a child was born, showering the mother with gifts and praise, but they did not celebrate that child every year on that date. Seemed excessive. Of course, mortals often did many things more consistently.

"Giving and dancing are wonderful. We can dance by firelight when we camp tonight, and I'll give you food. Why are you telling me now, Nippi?" Morvelving asked, moving for them to continue their way to the city.

"I thought you knew and were going to surprise me."

"Surprise you?" And give her a heart attack? He wasn't sure her meaning of a surprise was the same as his.

"Yes, with a gift."

"Now a gift." Morvelving furrowed his brow, becoming more lost, and concluded she was making it up. *"I thought we were supposed to be giving?"*

"No!" Nippi skipped in frustration. *"You're supposed to give me something."*

"Ah." Morvelving tugged at the tuft of fur on his snout in thought. *"Strange custom."*

Thypan's main gate bustled with activity. Locals streamed in and out. A shepherd clicked his tongue to drive his goats on. The guards eyed Morvelving longer than the other passersby but did not stop him. The city was awash with the stench of feces, fish, and tar. His ears resonated with the whine of gulls, the cries of merchants, and the ballads of everyday life. Nippi's *sanitja* left his mind.

In the artisan quarter, Morvelving located a Leatherman willing to create a belt and harness for Penalty. He paid the man and acquired several wrapped pies while they waited. The Thypanei called the pie *tzagy*.

He ate the wrap filled with spiced goat meat and cheese while watching Nippi communicate with several street urchins by drawing in the dirt. She had devoured her food and was now suffering from hiccups. The urchins summoned an older child, who read the runes drawn in the dirt. They ran off.

When Nippi sat next to Morvelving, he asked, *"What did you tell them?"*

"That it's my sanitja.*"*

Morvelving swallowed his last bite and chewed on her words. Before he could inquire further, the party of children returned, all bearing many oddments and trinkets. They offered them to Nippi with smiles and excitement.

"I found this under the old bridge. It doesn't smell like fish anymore." One boy handed Nippi some bauble. Morvelving couldn't discern its function.

"This shell from the Idryiva will give you luck," the older girl said. "I hope this helps you celebrate your born day."

Nippi took each item with a smile on her face. Morvelving had seen enough.

"Wait a moment," he said, standing with his hands on his hips. The urchins took a hesitant step back. "What's this all about?"

The children shouted, "Gifts!"

"It's her born day."

"You forgot!"

Morvelving waved his palm out to cease the accusations. The Leatherman chuckled from his seat as he completed his work. He didn't offer any help. Morvelving licked his lips. "That is well and good, but—"

"Meanie! You're a bad wolf," the little boy protested, pointing his finger up at him.

Morvelving sneezed away the bold scent of courage emitting from the boy. He glanced down at Nippi.

"Nippi, these children have nothing, and you are asking them to give away things of value," Morvelving signed with haste.

Nippi shrugged, palms out. Maybe or maybe not. The three trinkets lay at her feet. Morvelving sighed.

"Thank you for your gifts. Here." He tossed two drakma to the elder girl. "Now go!"

"Ha, after that offering, best leave the city, or you'll have all the urchins following you by the evening," the Leatherman said, laying out the belt and harness. "Untie this here and you can hoist the sword by your hip or keep it as is."

Morvelving nodded. Satisfied, he thanked the Leatherman and waved for Nippi to follow him. After a few more stops for rations, they left Thypan without delay. Morvelving didn't want to stay longer for news fearing the Leatherman's words would come true.

"Why don't you want me to receive gifts?" Nippi asked as they passed under the shade of the northern gatehouse.

"That's . . . " Morvelving grunted. How was he going to explain? This was a human custom he was unfamiliar with. He was fond of the idea. But he didn't understand why Nippi was telling everyone, especially the downtrodden children. *"I want to celebrate your* sanitja. *We are going to tonight, and I will make you a gift. What you did with the kids*

wasn't wrong. But consider, Nippi: they are poor, potentially orphaned. Still, they were gracious enough to give you trinkets that were valuable to them."

Nippi looked down at the trinkets she held to her torso. *"I shouldn't have accepted them?"* she signed unsteadily, nearly dropping the shell.

"No." Morvelving set down his pack and motioned for her to put the gifts there. She kept the seashell in hand. "Now, I'm confusing myself," he grumbled to himself. When he stood, he noticed Nippi watching him, brows furrowed.

"How about this? I won't forget today . . . You sure it's a specific day?"

Nippi's hands went to her hips.

Morvelving chuckled. *"It's today. I believe you and will remember."* He stole a brief glance to find the placement of the sun and moon in the blue sky. Dark Celemith was following the sun closely. He sniffed the air and accounted for the empty grain fields in Makoidake. The season of Perseph was near. He guessed it was the second-to-last or last day of the warm days of Eilv.

Nippi was humming in satisfaction.

"But," he added before he lost her attention, *"no more telling people only to receive gifts. Deal?"*

Nippi cupped her chin in thought and then shook his extended hand with enthusiasm.

———————

The western horizon was pink fish scales and darkening depths of gray beyond the black inland ridges. To the east, the Idryiva Sea glistened like a deep emerald blanket woven with silver thread. The air cool, refreshing. When twilight, a feast of color before the Moon and her silver light, reigned.

Nippi yawned. Morvelving kept his attention on the firelight ahead and the gentle noise of several men talking around it. He smelled contentment, roasting coney, and ale. Their shapes were barely visible. One man stood watch while the other three sat near the fire. One reason he traveled off roads was to avoid these chance meetings. The terrain between the Daespine Mountains and the Idryiva Sea was bare and rough, with sparse trees and torn rocky soil. One misstep could cause a rockslide.

These men had claimed the only wide flat area Morvelving could see. To continue in the growing darkness could be fatal, and the men didn't make him uneasy. Nippi was on the verge of falling asleep standing up.

"Greetings, travelers," Morvelving called ahead.

They instantly became silent. The one on watch unfolded his arms. They whispered to each other.

"*Eiso*, friend. The light fades. It is ill luck to travel now. Come and share our fire." Their dialect differed from that of other Idosse. Morvelving guessed they were from further south, perhaps Old Aphoeria or Danare. "The coney is near roasted."

"That's well. The land is rough here, and there has been no pleasant place to camp," Morvelving said, motioning for Nippi to follow him.

"Gods above, you speak true. We'd almost succumbed to despair when we found this enclave. We—"

Startled, they glanced up at Morvelving. And then down at Nippi, flummoxed.

One man pointed at Nippi. "A Dae!"

The other older man slapped him. "Aethra's tits, man. She's a Frystlin."

"A wha—"

"*Advei*, shush. Sorry, friend. I never . . ."

The watcher spoke, but everyone else fell silent. His hand had involuntarily gone to his dagger at his side, but he relaxed. The others stood. Each had dark hair, short on top and long behind the ear, that rested on their shoulders. Long beards that touched their poor tunics. Their equipment, in contrast, shone brightly. Shields, spears, short swords, helmets, and greaves. They were mercenaries and eyed Penalty with interest.

"I hope we are still welcome at your fire," Morvelving ventured to say.

"*Eiso*, Mulranei, we'd be honored. I am Alkythes."

"Gartios, at your service." Gartios was the one on watch. He pointed to the other two. "Therthpharn, who doesn't know a Dae from a child, and Boraclides."

Morvelving bowed his head and motioned to Nippi. "Nippiktua of Frystgalen. I am—"

"Aeputer's cock, you're the Morpheltheng," Therthpharn bleated, pointing at Morvelving. "The Mulranei mercenary, the Sword of Morning. They say he—"

"Quiet, Therthpharn, you—"

"He has the sword too," Therthpharn continued. "I heard someone say it was crafted by creatures of the mountains and enchanted with elven Ergald."

"Will you let him speak, Therthpharn! Of course, he's what you think. Don't know many Mulranei in these parts, eh? Now hush," Gartios said before turning to Morvelving. "Sorry, friend. Please sit. Some ale?"

Morvelving took the ale skin.

"We travel north to Eugrator."

Nippi plopped down, sleepy. Morvelving took a drink. "Thank you. That is far to travel."

"*Eiso,* you're right." Gartios sat down. "The ruler of Ugris is gathering mercenaries. Local trouble. We're hoping to join a larger band there."

Morvelving set his pack and Penalty down next to him. He noticed all their eyes on the sword. "Therthpharn is right. I have fought as a mercenary before. I'm called Morvelving." He exaggerated the pronunciation in the Trade Tongue.

Gartios nodded. Boraclides and Therthpharn curled their lips, mimicking the sound. Alkythes cut up the four coneys and held out portions. Nippi took ravenous mouthfuls, grease running down her chin. Morvelving ate with less abandon. The younger man, Therthpharn, was still mouthing Morvelving's name. The scent of his curiosity was like an insect floating above Morvelving's ear.

"How long are you taking the north road?" Alkythes asked after taking a dredge of ale.

"Is there a reason I shouldn't?"

Gartios nodded. "We heard tell in Inthia—there's a band of centaur brigands raiding the road to Agrothica."

"Agrothica's Plutriach has a list of bounties, one to be rid of them," Boraclides offered. "Didn't say their heads, just 'be rid' of them."

"Yeah? Well, I value my head on my shoulders, Aethra's tits," Gartios said, glancing back at Morvelving. "We're heading through Makoidake."

Morvelving nodded. "A wise course of action. Many centaurs deal less and less with humans."

Nippi tapped Morvelving on the arm and signed when he glanced down at her. *"What's a 'list'?"*

She must have been reading Boraclides's lips. Morvelving signed, *"A group of things: items or tasks you keep, either on parchment or in your mind, so you don't forget that you need to do them."*

Her eyes widened in shock as if she had an idea, which worried Morvelving. He was about to inquire about it when Alkythes asked, "You think you'll treat with them?"

Turning his attention back to the four men, Morvelving shrugged. "I may, if the Agrothican Plutriach has a bounty. The road—"

"What does your name mean? Why do they call you the *Sword of Morning*?" Therthpharn interrupted, giving into his curiosity.

Morvelving waved his hand, dismissing the older men, who were about to scold the younger. Therthpharn was being nosy, but Morvelving was tired of them shutting him down, and he wanted to correct this rumor. He had heard some Makoidake Pella whispering about it.

"In the Trade Tongue, it means *mourning*." He didn't feel like explaining its full meaning.

Therthpharn blinked in confusion. "Sorry, I thought that's what I said."

"He said '*mourning*,' to grieve. Aeputer save us from ignorant boys," Alkythes said, chuckling.

"*Eiso*, no, he meant '*morning*,' " Boraclides added.

Gartios struck his hand to his forehead. Amused, Morvelving pointed. "Alkythes is right. Names are used to define individuals among my people, but they are also a guide and inspiration to help us reach our full potential. With my exile, they took away my name and gave me the name Morvelving. It both defines me and gives me a duty to fulfill."

"Why were you ex—"

Gartios silenced Therthpharn by slapping his shoulder and said, "Kragius's mischief, boy, it's rude to pry."

Morvelving let them argue among themselves. He had noticed Nippi watching him while he spoke. *"Are you trying to read my lips?"* he asked her.

She nodded. *"I understood some of what you said. I'm getting better at it. Your lips move funny."*

Morvelving mischievously crooked his brow at her. But she yawned. He fished a blanket out of the pack and handed it to her. Nippi was soon asleep.

"I will take watch, if that's agreeable?" he asked the four mercenaries. They exchanged glances before Gartios nodded, saying, *"Eiso,* we thank you. I shall sleep easy with a Mulranei on guard."

Morvelving was thankful they didn't bring up the fact that he couldn't trust them.

"No one will believe me if I tell them," Therthpharn said, shaking his head. "My *nane* used to put me and my siblings to sleep with the Song of Ivalin. Were you there in the beginning when the Mulranei found the first men far in the east?"

Morvelving chuckled, pleased to hear humans still knew the tale. He shook his head. "No, I was born after the First Rift. Sharpnose, who found Ivalin, I know. Her tribe visited mine centuries ago for the Wajpheni."

"Aeputer's brow, that's something to ponder," Boraclides mumbled. "The stars are bright, and I shall sleep."

The three others followed Boraclides's lead. Though Alkythes stayed awake for two hours, then subtly kicked Gartios awake. Morvelving didn't mind. They didn't trust him completely either.

Soon Morvelving sat with the soft crackle of the fire and the noises of the night as company. He looked up at the silver moon on the horizon and considered the ages past. How sad Sharpnose had been when she'd sung *The Lay of Ivalin* during the Wajpheni, remembering her long dead friend. Morvelving glanced down at Nippi, sleeping peacefully, and pondered his own similarities to the story. Nippi was mortal and would die of old age just as Ivalin had. He pushed the thought out of his mind and put himself in a practiced state of meditation so he could rest and still be aware.

8

"It is time we left Theba," Morvelving signed to Nippi.

Nippi's eyes diverted from reading his hand signs. Her nose twitched in a short grimace. *"No,"* she signed, shaking her head. She gave a wry smile and pointed across the bustling market of the town of Theba to the bakery.

"Nippi," he signed, slowing his signs to emphasize his impatience as he looked to where she pointed. He adjusted his pack to keep it from chafing his armpit. He had noticed no signs that the Fates still had their will bent on Nippi. Which gave him unreasonable urgency.

Morvelving gave a resigned grunt as she crossed over to the bakery. Not enough urgency for him to rush the child. He followed, loosening the collar of his minotaur cloak from pulling against his neck and putting the Fates out of his mind. The bakery was a rectangular building nestled into the slope of a large hill, and its front boasted a large window that allowed passersby a view inside. Steady plumes of smoke billowed from the chimney. Even from the street, several bakers were visible as they worked the dough, their hands chalk white with flour. The cakes were on display atop a wooden plank alongside several loaves of bread, steam rising from their brown crusts.

Morvelving reflexively licked his lips at the decadent scent. Humans prepared delicious food, which was usually healthier for Nippi as well.

At least, that's what she told him. He followed Nippi, catching up to her in three strides.

They were in Theba to gather supplies, enough to reach Thressea in the north of the Idosse lands. Theba residents stole glances at him and Nippi as they passed. He heard their hushed whispers, noted their curiosity, wonder, and even contempt. The scent of their reactions battered his nose. He looked over to the bearer of one of the more acrid smells. The old woman averted her gaze, returning to her needlework while she assessed the other people passing by. He understood they couldn't help it. To untraveled humans, he looked like a wolf standing on its hind legs following a bizarre-looking human child through their peaceful city.

The Thebans were more distrustful than the Thypanei had been, and far more than Gartios, Therthpharn, Boraclides, and Alkythes. They had parted ways with the four mercenaries with the rise of the sun five days ago. He missed their hospitality and ease with strangers.

He met Nippi's imploring round eyes as she stood near the steaming pies. She was an artisan at beggary. Denying her was difficult.

"*Fine,*" he signed. They hadn't had fresh baked food since their stay in Agrothica two days ago. A long time for Nippi. The Plutriach had paid him well for freeing the city from the centaur band. It had not been a gang of outlaws but a family of centaurs that had been chased off their land in the Olykis Mountains. Morvelving had offered them the bounty if they quit their thievery. They had accepted when he returned the drakma. Morvelving had no qualms about exploiting the Plutriach's wealth.

Nippi's toothy grin was triumphant as they approached the open awning of the bakery.

"Two cakes, please," he said to the baker, whose back was to him.

Turning, the man squealed like a pig escaping a slaughterhouse. Morvelving took the attack in patient silence. Though rare, he was used to overreactions. The mercenaries on the road had handled themselves far better.

The baker held his hand on his chest and said, "My apologies, Mulranei. I thought you were a Kukran."

Morvelving's lip trembled, and his ears pulled back at the insult. He forced a growl back down his throat. To the untrained eye, he could easily be mistaken for a Kukran.

"Far better for you," Morvelving said. "If I were, you'd be dead."

"Of course, sorry. I dreamed of one last night."

"Nightmare, you mean."

"Yes, you're right. Please, take two for the price of one," the baker offered, "for my mistake." Now Morvelving felt a tinge of guilt.

"Thanks." Morvelving didn't feel guilty enough to decline. He held the cakes out to Nippi, who took them with glee. He pulled out two drakma from the leather pouch on his belt and held out his paw with the copper coins. The baker hesitated, eyeing the black claws at the end of each finger and the rough pads on his digits and palm.

After considering for a moment, Morvelving asked, "Has a Kukran been sighted near Theba?" Despite being exiled from his tribe, he was still Mulranei. If a Kukran raged nearby, he was honor-bound to hunt them down, something he wouldn't want to do with Nippi under his care.

"Gods above, no. A wanderer drank at the tavern I frequent." The baker took the two coins, shaking his head. "He told a harrowing tale from Elg Narsh yesterday. That is all."

Morvelving nodded. "A fair day to you."

He didn't feel obligated to prove his Mulranei heritage to every person who mistook him for a Kukran. Mulranei who forsook the Moon Goddess for the fallen god, Nameless, became Kukran. Bedeviled through Nameless's influence, their poisonous bite cursed their victims to become ravenous beasts who transformed into Kukran under the moonlight—an additional insult to the Moon Goddess.

"That was silly. He was terrified of you," Nippi signed when Morvelving took the pies from her. She had taken a bite from both. "Little *dilyinei,"* Morvelving grumbled to himself. He took a bite of the delightful pie. The crust must have had honey drizzled on it.

"Good thing he hasn't seen you with your tail pulled. You're really scary then," Nippi signed.

That had been an embarrassing moment. One he wished she hadn't seen. Morvelving didn't appreciate being reminded of it again. They had used a goat path to cross over the Olykis Mountains when a guisharpy, a witless creature, had flown by and grabbed his tail. The flying fiend had suffered the consequences of its cruel prank.

"I had hoped you'd forgotten," Morvelving signed as Nippi ate her pie. She grinned triumphantly.

They hiked to the higher half of Theba that overlooked the flat tiled roofs and river dock. Morvelving considered whether he had everything: a new green tunic and sandals for Nippi, food for the journey, fresh blankets, and a small leather-bound pack. Nippi needed to carry some of the weight. He looked down at her. She would also need to learn to defend herself soon. Though growing steadily, she remained small and fragile. He had taught Windtail many defense and hunting skills much earlier. Humans were . . . odd.

A boy ran past him, almost knocking into Morvelving. Turning around, the boy called back to someone behind Morvelving. "Hurry! He's started speaking at the Ancheas."

A second boy bumped into Morvelving's leg and almost stumbled over into the dirt. The kid recovered his balance and continued after his friend, calling behind, "Sorry!"

Morvelving humphed at their rudeness. He sniffed after them. A scent of fracas loomed ahead.

People abandoned their tasks, closed shops, and hurried toward the Ancheas.

"A Kerykoros from Phoithese," Morvelving overheard a man saying. "I thought it was destroyed by a draekurm."

"Captured, I heard. Gods help them."

Nippi stood in his way. *"What is it, Fluff? You have your grumpy face."* He was impressed by how well she understood his expressions.

"A messenger from the city of Phoithese. Come, let's go see," Morvelving signed, concerned to learn the draekurm hadn't passed over the peninsula. He brushed pie crumbs from his muzzle and took Nippi's hand. Nippi smiled and ran to keep up.

If a draekurm had destroyed the city of Phoithese—calamity like this warranted all ears to listen. The Wiseneyes of his tribe sang of great creatures who held the stars from the world. Unlike those noble dragons of legend, draekurm were fell creatures—devious at best and cruel by nature. He had never seen one, only the destruction they could cause. In the first wars between elves and Nameless, when he'd only been a pup, his tribe had aided the wounded after a terrible battle. An entire valley scorched and the fortress destroyed, along with the mountain behind it.

The Ancheas was a short walk down a zigzagging pathway. Stone and wood benches encircled a well at the center. A large wooden board stood along the rock wall. Nailed parchments danced back and forth in the breeze. In his time among the Idosse, Morvelving had seen plenty of heralds go to the town or city's Ancheas to proclaim a king's law or announce nearby events. The well, half-built and carved into the nearby mountain slope, provided shade for those fetching water. Stone benches stood along the rocky wall. Several stone buildings stood at the corners of the semicircle. The crowd was filled with listeners and passersby who moved slowly through the area.

Seven men in travel-worn clothes stood near the well. They were all lean. Some had scars on their limbs—both lacerations and burns. Nothing compared to the seated man. His face was sharp, his scalp bald, and his sunken eyes surveyed the crowd like a hawk hunting for prey. Though his tunic was poor like his followers', he was clearly their leader. The staff in his hand was chipped, the bottom half charred. A detail Morvelving fixated on yet could not decipher why. The man held it poised as both a support and a weapon.

Nippi tapped Morvelving's hock several times. He looked down at her.

"I can't see," she signed then raised her arms up to him.

Morvelving doubted even Acraces, god of war and strife, could deny the gesture. He picked her up and placed her on his left shoulder. The movement gained him inquiring looks from the crowd and envicus stares from two nearby children. Nippi had the best view. She leaned slightly into him, put her arm around the back of his neck, and fiddled with his fur.

The leader of the Phoithesens maintained his gaze, tempering the crowd to silence. He emitted a throaty cough to clear his throat and spoke, his voice astonishingly loud, pronouncing his words with eloquence.

"I am Sophokis, Kerykoros for the city of Phoithese, and I tell you being surprised by violence is best." Sophokis ignored the perturbed stares and hushed talk of the crowd and continued. "To live in peace is far better, but if I had a choice, I'd rather choose to be surprised."

He paused for effect, as the spectacular speakers Morvelving had listened to had done. The crowd consumed the quiet portion in rapt attention.

Nippi tapped twice on Morvelving's shoulder.

"I can't read his lips from here."

"Watch my hands." Morvelving began translating for her. Several listeners eyed him with perturbed scowls.

"It would be best to not see the attack coming." Sophokis pronounced each word clearly, with passion. "For the attack to come so swift that the fear, the panic, and the pain could not exist. Yet all who suffer such violence are dead, so who can truly tell what's better? What I can tell you is this: fear consumed me completely that day, leaving me powerless. Panic was all I had—raw, unfettered panic. That's how it was that day, I tell you true. The day the draekurm passed Mount Kydos and swooped over Phoithese, my beloved city. It was no surprise. Yes! The runners and rumors speak true! Yes! Phoithese was indeed attacked by the dread winged beast!"

Sophokis took a deep breath. "It was a clear day, not a cloud in sight. Phoithese's white and painted stones glimmered in the sunlight. Fields and forests flourished rich and green till they ceased at Mount Kydos's bald crown. The sunlight glittered off the River Serpres. On that dreadful day, I was in the market. The young women were pressing wine, their laughter music—like birdsong in the meadow.

"A black line marred the sky, at first appearing only on the horizon northeast of Mount Kydos. It was too high to be any bird; even the guisharpies nesting on Kydos's peak cannot soar so high. I did not understand what it was. A sentry had sighted it and set the bells ringing, but it was too late."

Sophokis shook his head. The pause gave Morvelving time to catch up with his interpretation for Nippi. He was as intent as the crowd to hear what had happened.

"Draekurm. You couldn't hear it; only see your doom in the great span of wings. The dreadful shape grew as it drew near. Black became sharp jade, its eyes like twin blue stars. Everyone ran in panic. A few brave souls climbed Phoithese's walls with bows in hand. It was of no use. Its scales are harder than our best-forged bronze. When it first passed over the city, the air boomed and cracked as if a great western storm had moved in from the sea. It was faster than a diving eagle. It circled the city again and again." Sophokis bowed his head and shook, as if to rid himself of the memory. "That was when I wished it had been a surprise. I would be dead and would tell this tale in Celemith after crossing the Emerald Rift. Alas, I lived."

The speaker stopped. As Morvelving continued to sign for Nippi, he noticed Sophokis's eyes remained on them. Morvelving didn't like how long he lingered.

Those gathered forgot their errands. The men shook their heads in commiseration. The women half listened as they diligently went about their tasks.

"I lived," said Sophokis, gesturing at himself. "There was no hope for my city. The draekurm swooped down. The air shimmered then exploded in flame, consuming everything it touched. I still hear the screams."

"After three destructive swoops, the draekurm then landed. And I tell you the truth, Aeputer as my witness: the draekurm doused its own flames with an extravagant Runic Ring drawn with its own blood, as the Crafters of Ivalin do. The very flames that licked thirstily upon the city dissipated!"

"It did what?" Nippi asked.

Thankfully, the speaker waited until the crowd quieted down again. Morvelving was able to answer Nippi. *"It used Ergald."*

"What is that?"

Morvelving scrutinized her with a puzzled expression. He could have sworn he had told her about Ergald before. Sophokis was about to speak once more. Morvelving signed with haste. *"The draekurm used the powers beneath the earth. I'll tell you more later."*

"She spoke then," Sophokis resumed. "Her voice was thunderous and seductive. All were in silent shock. 'I am Orrothix,' she said. 'All lands below Mount Kydos are mine. I have destroyed and restored. Tribute I require: a tenth of your wealth annually and all your firstborns brought before me once every decade. I shall hold these lands. You will prosper under my gaze. For your grievances, I will listen only to one who cannot speak and speak only with one who cannot hear.'

"You can imagine the horror at her demands. The entire city looked upon the tyrant as she spoke of our doom. We were to be captives, to live in fear, bound to the whims of a monster. And who can answer the riddle? Who can listen yet cannot hear? Who can speak and yet cannot? Already, many have sought the summit of Kydos to deal with the beast—many warriors and even the Crafters of Ivalin—but none have returned. And the powerful Mithvarn have ignored our pleas. Can you imagine giving your firstborn to fatten the draekurm? Who has that strength?"

Morvelving's hands froze. Orrothix's words were ringing in his ears. "Gods above," he gasped. The draekurm wanted Nippi. Or someone like her. It made little sense. They'd had no dealings with Orrothix. What was her purpose? His mind raced. The Fates had spun their web.

He ignored Nippi's finger poking him, asking him to continue to sign for her. Was this a cruel trick? Draekurm were known to do such things. He latched onto that thought. Orrothix was toying with the Phoithesens, giving them false hope. It had nothing to do with Nippi and the Fates.

Regardless, they needed to leave. Sophokis and his followers would see it the same way. He could already hear the speaker detailing the rewards the Phoithesens would pay to anyone who provided a solution to the beast's terrible riddle.

Despite Nippi's silent protest, Morvelving put her back on her feet. *"We are going now,"* he signed.

"No, I want to know the rest of the story," Nippi signed back, still trying to see Sophokis speak.

"Nippi!" Morvelving slowed his signing to emphasize that this wasn't up for debate, though by now she knew how to read his body language. She would know what him sniffing with his ears bent back meant. She pouted but took his hand. Morvelving didn't hurry from the crowd. He walked at a calm pace until he found cover behind one of the shop stands. From there, he picked up speed, Nippi skipping alongside his long strides.

"Sophokis was talking about you. If they know you're deaf and tongueless, they'll take you to Orrothix," Morvelving explained, slowing his steps now that they were away from the Ancheas.

"That's silly, Fluff."

He gave her the stink eye.

She ignored him, *"The draekurm wants one of them. Besides, I'm eight, I can take care of myself. And you'll stop them."* Nippi paused in thought. *"Though talking to a draekurm is on my list now. It could tell me what flying is like!"*

Morvelving grumbled. "This list again." The invention of her list continued to confound him. He didn't know when she'd picked up the idea, but ever since Thypan, she'd put herself in silly and often life-threatening situations. On their way to Theba two days ago, he'd had to apologize to an old badger. Nippi had wanted to see its burrow. Then she had tried to join the Dae-ish Thurstice Festival dance. He was amazed she had sensed their presence to begin with.

"I advise you to remove draekurm from your list," Morvelving signed to her as they slipped out of sight of the Ancheas. *"Or cast the whole thing aside."*

They retraced their steps through the zigzagged pathways. Uphill from the Ancheas, he could still hear Sophokis speaking below. Square stone and brick homes blocked the view. For a town of its size, Theba was still busy with traffic. Men and women gave him and Nippi a wide berth as they walked by. The townsfolk moved over as if brushing against the strangers would bring them harm. They pushed their backs against the surrounding crates of local bilo fruit grown in flat mud pads along the slopes. Farmers observed the commotion keenly as they eagerly sold their wares. Morvelving had to force his hand from reaching for the piphlid again. Of all the times to be aware of his urge. He growled at himself for having kept the wretched shroom.

Morvelving smelled haste and desperation behind them. Like an overripe lemon molding in seawater. It made him nervous. Glancing back, he noticed a farmer standing with crossed arms and glaring at Morvelving. Everything was as it should be.

"What are you doing, Fluff?"

Morvelving rumbled in his throat. *"I'm checking everything. Here, take your pack."*

"But—"

"Yes, you will share our burdens."

"This is slavery. I'm no dwarf."

Morvelving released a low whine, impatient. An old woman carrying a basket full of clothes observed them with interest, grunted, and walked on.

"That is poor humor, Nippi. It is not the dwarves' choice."

Nippi rolled her eyes after reading his lips. Her talents were improving: she was better at both reading lips and rolling her eyes. She took the pack. *"Where are we going?"*

"Land of the Menici first. If Orrothix is after you, we need to leave this land with haste. I fear we need to distance ourselves from the Idosse." Morvelving adjusted his own pack and Penalty on his back.

"You're really worried about the draekurm?" Nippi put her hands on her hips after signing. A scent, sharp and fresh, tickled his nose. Like newly unearthed dirt. Morvelving peered down the path behind them. A group of men came into view around the bend. He instantly recognized them.

"Mulranei, please—a moment!"

Morvelving dropped his ears and curled his lips. Sophokis approached with seven men accompanying him. Their cloth as poor as their scent. They stopped in their tracks when they saw Morvelving's fangs. The men wore emotionless expressions as they observed Sophokis and Morvelving. Their smell was a strange medley of trepidation and determination. Like a craftsman sawing urine-soaked wood. Several of them had spears. Nippi sidestepped behind Morvelving.

"Peace. On Aeputer's brow, I mean you no harm," Sophokis said, one hand raised in greeting. Morvelving smelled the lie, like mold hidden beneath a green leaf. His promise was only meant for Morvelving—not Nippi.

Before they could speak more lies, Morvelving stated, "The harm you carry and cause reeks from you like a rot. I know what you seek. You will not find it here. I suggest you go back to Phoithese and flee from the draekurm's land."

Sophokis shook his head, ignoring Morvelving and pointing at Nippi. "She can't hear? I saw you making hand signs. I've seen Apothurgeons do the same for the deaf. She can't speak either. Say something, girl. No? She is the answer to the riddle. We found others, only deaf or mute, never both. Orrothix will commune with her. She can plead for the freedom of Phoithese." He took an eager step forward, leaning heavily on his staff, still looking at Nippi.

"You are foolish to think Orrothix will honor her own riddle," Morvelving said with a snarl, forcing Sophokis to look at him. Several of the accompanying younger men took a hesitant step back. Morvelving snorted at their pitiful attempt at intimidation by numbers. They lacked any warriors. His ear twitched at the slight shuffle of dirt behind the stone and tiled buildings. The number of men had increased. He could handle the ones before him, but any more would overwhelm him.

He hid his discovery by adding, "Draekurm do not bind themselves to such Dae legends. It is best to wait until she tires of her own game and slumbers."

Sophokis shook his head in shock. Morvelving licked his lips. The smell of defiance tasted acrid. "You will turn from those in need, Mulranei? Do not your people follow Telunian's teachings—"

Morvelving barked, cutting Sophokis's words short. His fangs fully revealed and his hackles bristling. The men stumbled back, one tripping on his own foot and falling on his rump. Their fear smelled good to him. Their threat to Nippi and their insolence at speaking the Moon Goddess's name made Morvelving ready. He would not succumb to their twisted logic.

"Your arrogance in thinking that you understand the Moon Goddess's teachings is enough for me to draw my blade. Your naivete in presuming that Orrothix would bother to listen to you, even if you sacrificed a hundred children to her, tells me to turn my back. You understand very little, and your own self-pity blinds you." He spat on the cobbled stones. Mad that he had been consumed by self-pity not long ago. Which made him angrier. "I am Morvelving, exile. I have no tribe. I remain under the Moon Goddess's silver light with this child under my protection. I will not hesitate to kill any of you. Do not follow."

Morvelving walked away. It burned his heart that Sophokis would try to manipulate him with the Moon Goddess's teaching.

Sophokis shouted, "Hundreds of children have already been sacrificed to the tyrant! What's one life before the lives of many! I tried to reason!"

Morvelving ignored him. He had ears for the quick movements on either side of the pathway. A man on his right stepped out from behind a stack of crates, holding his breath, and threw a weighted fishing net to catch them.

Simultaneously, men to his left also did the same.

Morvelving scooped Nippi up, prompting her to gasp. He ran ahead, the nets catching air. Penalty, wrapped in cloth, banged against his legs, and his pack bounced as he weaved away from a spear thrust.

Four men barred the small pathway ahead. The residents nearby ran into their homes. With Nippi in one arm, Morvelving didn't like his odds. Two men wielded spears while the other two carried clubs.

With men chasing him from behind, he had no time to weigh his options. Morvelving charged at the four men. They braced. Before getting in range of their spears, he darted left and leaped up to the nearest building. He grabbed the roof's edge with his left hand, pushing off the wall and swinging his legs up. Thankfully, the people of Theba built their buildings with flat roofs. Morvelving rushed and promptly leaped to the next building.

"Get him!"

An aggressive whistle hissed in his ear as he jumped to the next small house. A weighted rope tangled around his right leg as another object slammed into his other leg, making him stumble and crash into the plaster of a chimney. Morvelving reflexively turned so Nippi wasn't crushed. Penalty's hilt scraped against the back of his bronze cuirass. Snarling, he untangled himself and checked on Nippi. Wiping dust from her face, she looked up at him wide-eyed and pointed behind him.

Morvelving glanced back to see a man climbing onto the roof, his teeth clenched in exertion. The man's eyes widened in fear as he glanced up. Morvelving rushed the man, kicked his legs out from under him, and pushed him off the roof. From his vantage point, Morvelving saw the other men swarming toward the building. He gave a short growl before turning back to Nippi.

She was ready for him to pick her up this time. Nippi clung tight to his chest. He held her close. He leaped to the next building. The roof gave way under his right foot as he landed, making him stumble forward. A rush of air and a soft hum announced a thrown spear that missed his head by a finger's length.

He couldn't trust the integrity of the rooftops for their escape. The edge of town lay above them on the last stretch of the zigzag pathway.

Their pursuers called out encouragement to one another.

"Cut them off! They have no escape."

"Surround the last house!"

Nippi's small hands held tight to his fur, pinching him painfully. Morvelving kept holding her close. The Phoithesen gang was thorough in surrounding him. Locals shouted and cursed at the gang but did not hinder them.

A spearman stepped into view and threw his spear. Morvelving leaned aside and caught the shaft and threw it back at its former wielder, who dove out of the way with a shriek.

The riposte gave him time to spot their escape route—a rock ledge within reach. He ran to the building's edge and jumped off. He grabbed hold of it, his claws digging into the dirt and loose stone. His pawed feet found purchase, and he leaped up, reaching a higher ledge. Morvelving heard a sharp clang under him just as he reached the ledge. The spear narrowly missed its mark, the timbre of bronze ringing.

Morvelving lifted himself up with Nippi still holding on tight. He swung his legs up as his pack and sword hit the rough stone and dirt with a clang. It was too awkward with Nippi clinging to him.

"Go up and around!" he cried, aware Nippi was watching him. Nippi climbed up him onto the ledge to let Morvelving finish clambering up.

"*They're hurrying up this way,*" she signed with haste in front of his face, her finger flicking his snout with her hurried movements.

Morvelving grunted and nodded as he stood. Several men with spears were rushing up the path. He and Nippi stood on the ledge, hidden by a small stone house. From a window across the gap, an old man glared at him with contempt before abruptly closing the shutter.

Nippi turned to Morvelving, waiting. Morvelving saw one of the Phoithesens closing in. He barked several times, making the man hesitate. At that moment, Morvelving hurried out onto the path away from the rock ledge, Nippi in his arms. The way was open, and he could effortlessly outrun the humans. He sprinted in a serpentine path to evade desperate spear throws. One thudded into the earth far behind him.

The men's shouts dwindled. His chest heaved, and the wind cooled his tongue as it dangled out the side of his snout. Morvelving looked back several times to check if they were being pursued. The dirt track was empty save for the lingering dust he had kicked up. Theba was no longer visible behind the rolling hills.

9

———————

He maintained his pace for a quarter league. Nippi was restless as she clung to him and fidgeted, making it difficult to keep his pace, and his legs were becoming bruised from the sword on his back. Morvelving halted and set Nippi down.

"Are you hurt?" Morvelving signed to her.

She shook her head. *"They really thought the draekurm would listen to me,"* she signed, unbelieving.

"They believe it, which makes them unreasonable. Follow me," Morvelving signed.

She obeyed without argument. He led her into the forest of tall oaks, sycamores, and old willows. Away from the roads, he could hide their tracks and set an ambush for any pursuers.

Nippi kept up with plucky determination, her rapid footfalls crunching on every dry leaf, disturbing the silence. The road was no longer in view. Oak and carob trees clung to the slope, their leaves shading all below from sunlight. Their knotting roots gripped around boulders, seeking nourishment from the dirt beneath. Morvelving's thoughts lingered on Sophokis's words. He had a distorted understanding of what it meant to sacrifice for the well-being of fellow mortals. He wasn't wrong, nor was he right. The Phoithesens, according to their own tale, could have abandoned their city. Left Orrothix the spoils and found a new home for themselves. Perhaps they had chosen to stay due to the fear of only leaving one danger for another—neighboring cities were rarely, if ever, on peaceful terms.

Nippi skipped ahead of Morvelving to sign up at him, *"That was close. I didn't know you could run so fast. One day, I will run as fast as you."*

His stomach fluttered. Morvelving decided not to tell her she was physically incapable just yet.

"You will run faster one day," he signed. *"You'll have to work at it though. Your body must be taught."*

Morvelving felt a sudden surge of confidence as he watched her swing aimlessly at shrubs. He had successfully carried her out of harm's way. His shoulders felt light despite the weight of his pack.

Small birds dove and circled among the branches of a fig tree. Morvelving glanced back the way they had come. He could hear the faintest trespass of humans. The footfalls were not urgent. It mattered little to him whether he traveled on roads or through the wilderness, though he preferred the wild. Morvelving could find his way by the position of the sun or stars, by scent, and by sight.

"Why can't we help them?" Nippi signed after skipping ahead of him again. Morvelving focused on her. *"If Orrothix wants someone to talk to, I can do it. We can talk about flying. Maybe Orrothix will teach me. I want to ride on your shoulders."*

Nippi raised her arms. Morvelving sniffled and gave a brief whine but indulged her again. Once on his shoulder, she scratched behind his ear. Another form of affection humans showed their pets. He assumed she did it for her own comfort, so he allowed it.

The moment gave him time to consider her words, which stemmed from ignorance. She had never seen a draekurm, and he hoped she never would. Morvelving was not as knowledgeable as a Wiseneye, but he still had a responsibility to share his knowledge with her. Telling her about draekurm was long overdue. He took a calming breath and yawned. Her little fingers massaging his ear *did* feel nice.

He hurried down a short slope. A fox scurried across their path and disappeared under some shrubs.

"Nippi," Morvelving signed. *"Draekurm are the Children of Nameless, the god who remains and broke the Rift Law. They are devious, selfish, and destructive. Like Nameless, they believe themselves superior to the laws of peoples and nature. Orrothix doesn't want to talk. She gave the Phoithesens false hope. She's playing with them as a cat would with a mouse."*

Nippi remained still and gave a small grunt. She tapped him three times, the signal she wanted off his shoulders. He put her down.

Morvelving caught the scent of deer among the woods. And Nippi's emotions—an alliance of indifference, confusion, and more. Like a soup with too many ingredients. He distracted himself with the sounds of the woods. A city of beavers was active in a river further south. A distant screech from a guisharpy echoed from the mountain ridge.

They walked north toward the Idospont. The Land of the Idosse was no longer safe. He had been a fool. The Fates had found Nippi and cast their web. A ship would be faster, but he had no love for great bodies of water, and the Idryiva Sea was treacherous in midsummer. They could remain in the Land of the Menici, known as the Land of Three Kings. The land offered wealth and a desirable winter haven. But would it be far enough?

Sudden footfalls on dry leaves made Morvelving pivot swiftly. Nippi had darted away from him. She was inspecting a wildflower in bloom. Morvelving sighed, admitting he was on edge. The Phoithesens were still after them. They were safe for now, as long as they kept moving. He sniffed the air for anything amiss: wilderness—peace.

Nippi sniffed at the flower, twiddled with the petals, and jumped back from a bug that flew out of it.

In the human world, it would be normal for others to sacrifice one to save themselves. Though she had already seen the results of that brutal outlook firsthand—her family murdered and her taken. Such human behavior was why the Moon Goddess hid behind clouds at night. Morvelving had seen love among her people as well. Nippi was missing out on that.

She saw him watching and smiled. Morvelving grinned as she caught back up to him.

"When will you give me my sanitja?*"*

Morvelving smiled. He had something in mind. *"Soon. Be patient."*

———————

Nippiktua scowled up at Morvelving's dark brown eyes as she walked alongside him under the shade of the forest. She wouldn't show that she was eager. Surprise gifts were the best! He often worried too much that she missed her people. She did not. She enjoyed being with Fluff.

"You are terrified of the draekurm?" she asked, still curious about what he had said. Nippiktua realized she had never seen him scared, or maybe she didn't recognize the expression. Understanding Fluff's emotions was often difficult. Fortunately, she was smart and had figured out how he expressed his feelings. More often than not.

"It is wise to be afraid of a draekurm."

Nippiktua shrugged. *"Many fear you, but you're scared. You're confusing. Is that why you use Penalty?"* She pointed at the long sword across his back.

Morvelving looked thoughtful. Nippiktua wondered if she had outwitted him.

He signed, *"There's a difference between fear and respect. Though they often feel the same. I fear the draekurm because I respect their ease in rendering destruction. That is sensible. Humans feel the same for Mulranei, though for different reasons, I suppose."*

Nippiktua pretended to be asleep by clasping her hands to the side of her head and leaning over so Fluff could see her. Fluff reached out and tickled her ear. She smiled and ran out of reach.

These little games gave her time to think about his words. All of it made sense. Fluff feared the draekurm because it was better at killing than he was. But being good at killing didn't make Fluff bad. She was sure Fluff was good and respected him. He had bought her pies and was planning a gift for her *sanitja*. More importantly, he had followed her when she had run away and had told her she could stay with him.

The days passed as they should: uneventfully. Morvelving had used the wilds to escape human eyes before, during his exile. Far easier to hear pursuers in the wilderness. Most humans didn't know how to traverse among the trees. The Mulranei's ability to move silently and be aware of their surroundings was unmatched.

Morvelving sat with his legs crossed, knees out, and his hocks under his thigh as he skillfully whittled a fine piece of yew. Nippi was pacing back and forth, fidgeting with the already frayed ends of her new green tunic. He smirked, remembering the first time she reacted to his legs crossed. She had tried to mimic him but realized quickly she was missing joints.

Nippi had already finished the string for her bow. Eager for her *sanitja*. He had hoped the task would occupy her attention for longer. They were three days past Theba and one day from the city of Thressea and the Idospont crossing. Sophokis may have sent runners to each city-state to spread the word across Idosse and set a bounty. If so, they needed to avoid cities. He was already considering changing their path to confuse any pursuers. Perhaps they should linger in the Ykris Mountains before crossing the Idospont.

Nippi wasn't good at hunting or keeping silent in the woods. Her best sense was her sight, so a bow should be a reasonable fit for her. She had asked for a dagger again. Though at first she had resisted carrying her own pack, Nippi hadn't complained since. What a marvel that youngsters of all races desired so much to be helpful. How could he teach her to be quicker and quieter in the forests?

Nippi stood in front of him. *"Is it done yet?"*

Morvelving replied aloud so he could keep working and gauge how well she could read his lips. "No."

"When will it be ready?"

"When it is," he said, sniffing and snorting at her impatience. She continued to watch him speak. "If you rush the making of a tool, it will not work as well and will betray you."

Nippi threw herself on the ground with an impatient groan. Morvelving did not find it impressive. He persisted, consciously ignoring her fit, confident she would find something to do.

Nippiktua eyed Fluff. His ears were back, but he didn't react further to her show. She stood with a dissatisfied grunt and began to pout. There was nothing to occupy her mind. The sun was rising toward midday. Celemith followed close behind, casting weird shadows upon the forest floor as its dark form crept to eclipse the sun. Her parents would have said, "The gods watch. Behave now or they'll be displeased." Of course, they had only said that when *they* had needed her to behave.

Yesterday, she had seen a river near their shelter under the roots of a large oak. A dip would be nice. Water felt amazing when it wasn't painfully cold like the water in Frystgalen. She watched the precise movement of Fluff's knife carving the wood. If she weren't so bored, it would have been enjoyable.

Nippiktua blew raspberries. Fluff eyed her with one ear reclined back, perturbed by her disturbance.

"I'm going to the stream," she signed, pointing to where she had seen it yesterday.

He set the wood and knife down. Fluff yawned, showing all his fangs. It made him look funny. And scary—all those teeth. She understood what his expression meant: he was annoyed and even a little stressed. Fluff cared about her. Nippiktua only wished he would trust her more. She still believed they should have helped Sophokis with his draekurm dilemma. She had seen Fluff help people with lesser problems before. Her *amua* had told her fire-night stories about draekurm guarding towers and talking with princesses. She wanted to talk with draekurm as well.

"What? It's not like you wouldn't smell or hear if anything happens." She insisted on the fact, for it was undeniably true. She had attempted various mischievous acts in the past—vanishing out of his sight or trying anything that promised amusement. Fluff was always aware of what she was doing or where she was. Sometimes she got away with stuff on her list, like the tumble-bush race and the badger home. Fluff had been mad about that. She wondered if he had been made an outcast for being so boring.

"Very well. Remember to signal if anything happens." Fluff went back to his craft.

Nippiktua jumped up in the air with a smile. She tugged on the hollow piece of wood Fluff had made for her, which was tied around her neck. If anything happened, she was to blow into it. Apparently, Fluff could hear the sound from miles away.

She gave him a hug, his fur tickling her face, and kissed his snout. Nippiktua was off. She ran as fast as her feet could carry her. She imagined herself a Mulranei with blue fur, moving like the wind among the trees. A fierce huntress that boys like Chub and Thin wouldn't tease.

Although the stream wasn't wide, it was deep enough for her to swim in. Nippiktua pulled off her sandals and tunic. The water was cool, the sun warm on her back despite the half eclipse, and the pebbles smooth beneath her feet. She plunged beneath the surface.

Refreshed, she pushed her tangled hair back and surveyed the heavy woodlands around her. Fowl were bathing further upstream. Her presence perturbed a badger, but it stomped irritably downstream. A beaver sauntered right by her with sticks in its mouth. She began collecting pebbles with interesting patterns and stacking them. Her favorite was one with vibrant green swirly patterns.

She was holding fourteen stones cradled against her stomach when she saw a pebble with emerald patterns and black stripes running through it. She used her free hand to pick it up. The sun's warmth faded from her back. A broad shadow with a crown of spikes fell over her. Her heart quickened. She dropped the pebbles and frantically clawed at her throat for Fluff's whistle.

A giant Stag stood before her, looking at her with bright golden eyes—blazing and as deep as the sea. Its fur was dark as night, and its crown of antlers silver with burnished white tips. One length of the antlers held a perched raven. The bird tilted its head, its black bead-like eyes looking at her and blinking once. It opened its beak wide, and then it flew away.

Nippiktua took several steps back. She had read the lips of peddlers speaking about Stags, how seeing one meant the gods were watching you, for better or for worse.

Nippiktua held the Stag's golden gaze. She realized she was being rude. She moved quickly to bow low and almost lost her balance. If a god was watching, she needed to be on her best behavior. When she rose, the Stag was drinking water, oblivious to her presence. She smiled to herself, pleased. Perhaps the gods didn't watch important girls. Leaving the stream, she dried her pebbles and put on her tunic.

The Stag continued to drink and splash in the stream. Nippiktua marveled at how dark its fur was, the light casting a silver sheen on its back. Morvelving walked up and stood next to her, and she pointed at the Stag, smiling. His mouth was closed, and his ears were straight up. She knew *that* face. This was one of his more serious moods.

Morvelving couldn't believe the scent when he first smelled it. Like the coolness of air before a rainstorm. He would have usually ignored it. Stags were best left to their own path. Yet Nippi was staying near it, and he saw a raven fly away to the east, which worried him. Stags were the eyes and messengers of the now-dormant Goddess Drudan. The Mulranei had many mourning songs for her tale. To create the world, Drudan had infused a significant portion of her power into the lands of Ervi, an act that had caused her to lose her sanity and fail to cross the Rift to Celemith. Now her heralds roamed the land, hunted by humans. Morvelving had stumbled upon a few people cursed by a Stag's bewitching glare—called Drudan's Gaze by those who had seen its effects. Those cursed aimlessly roamed the earth, their bodies marred by self-inflicted wounds, eyes not seeing, expressionless. He was relieved to find Nippi untouched. Her smile when she noticed him warmed his heart.

The Stag's gaze remained on him as he approached.

Morvelving bowed to Drudan's servant.

Surprisingly, it returned the bow with a slight tilt of its head. Morvelving removed some hare bones and obsidian shards from his pocket. He had been planning to use them as decor on Nippi's bow, but they would serve a higher purpose as an offering to Drudan. After placing them on a smooth stone above the water's currents, Morvelving stepped back and sat down next to Nippi.

A moment later, the Stag stepped toward the offering and lowered its head so that its nose was touching the pieces.

Nippi clasped her hand over her mouth. Morvelving watched her marvel as the Stag bit down on the obsidian, the black stone turning to dust between its molars.

Nippi pointed and signed at Morvelving, *"Is that Ergald?"*

Morvelving winced. He had said he would tell her about Ergald. He may not have the time now. Perhaps enough for part of a lesson.

"No," he answered. *"The Stag is using its Eifgald, its power. I offered small trinkets of value to the Goddess Drudan. The Stag is doing his part and accepting the offerings. They are wonderful creatures. Even guided my people when the earth was young and unpredictable."*

He then noticed several scars on its hindquarters and could smell pain over the Stag like a cloudy haze.

"Drudan's servant, can I offer you healing?" Morvelving asked. The Stag stared unblinkingly back at him.

After reading his lips, Nippi tapped his leg. *"Is the good Stag hurt?"*

He nodded. Her eyes indicated that she expected him to help the Stag. Though he'd been doubtful at first, Morvelving's determination grew.

The Stag shook itself and looked away from him. A clear sign it rejected his offer.

Morvelving's ears drooped. *"Not physically, it seems,"* he signed. Could it know the reason for his exile? How would the Stag know such a thing? His stomach sank as if a heavy stone weighed it down. Since the Stag had accepted the offering, he'd hoped that the Goddess would have spoken. Yet the Stag had taken the offering out of instinct and its own volition. This wasn't a chance encounter. Even dormant, Drudan sought Nippi and what the Fates had in store for her and set her will upon the child. Morvelving's ears flattened.

He nudged Nippi, and her wide red eyes regarded him.

"It's time we were on our way. We shouldn't pester the Stag any longer. Here," he said, handing her the smaller pack. It contained a few of her belongings and the pieces for her bow. She put it on all while watching the Stag walk away. Morvelving shouldered his own pack with Penalty and his harness and was about to walk away when Nippi tapped him on his hock. She held up an emerald stone.

"It's beautiful," he signed. She turned and immediately picked up ten pebbles with both hands. Morvelving drooped one ear and snorted. *"Those are nice. Are you bringing them all?"*

She smiled. Morvelving yawned in impatience. "That's too many. Pick two so you can pocket them."

Nippi pouted but promptly saw sense. She picked two green ones and ran off ahead back to their camp. Morvelving glanced back at the Stag, who was watching them. He waited a moment in the hope that Drudan would speak. The Stag only stared, motionless in the eclipse's odd light. He caught up to Nippi.

Though he knew a road was close, he had no problem with Nippi skipping ahead. The sound of birdsong filled the air, and there was a distinct absence of human scent. A flock of waterfowl flew overhead, mocking Morvelving and Nippi's inability to fly. He wanted to bark at their rudeness, but they swiftly passed by.

At their current pace, it would take them two days to reach the Idospont. He offered a brief prayer to the Moon Goddess that Orrothix's riddle wouldn't catch up with them. He couldn't afford to worry about the draekurm.

The Stag had been a blessing, unlike the raven. That raven—the one that had flown over Nippi and the Stag—had been an omen. The Fates had two eyes: Felren and Rnudfel. A shiver ran down his back. He could be wrong, as he had been with the crow the night Nippi had run away.

He had gained no guidance from Drudan, only the knowledge that she was moving for or against the dreaded Crones. Two entities vying for Nippi. The Fates' will moved, and Drudan watched. He feared protecting her was beyond his control. The idea of anything happening to her terrified him, for both Nippi's and his own sake.

Orrothix might be aware of Nippi because of the Fates' interest in her. Morvelving shook his head. The draekurm had cunningly devised the riddle to divert the Phoithesens' attention. No tale or song mentioned the Fates communicating directly with mortals or immortals on Ervi. Still, what did Orrothix want from one city-state? Morvelving believed it to be a petty ambition. Immortality had a toll. The ancient Wiseneyes had demonstrated this. Alive since the dawn of time, they would often leave the tribe to pass into death, and the entire tribe would sing a Vhinde, letting their spirits run in the woods once more, until a Rift where their spirit would return to Telunian's embrace.

Draekurm were similar. The larger ones usually founded crypts and embedded them with mighty runes so no one could disturb their eternal slumber. Orrothix could be preparing her own tomb while still pursuing power, dancing between her two instincts to seek rest and domination. Morvelving also had doubts about that. Draekurm desired power and dominance; he didn't know of any that had chosen eternal sleep.

His neck fur bristled. He'd felt it, a tickle as if a feather had lightly brushed his ear. He checked his senses. There was nothing. Only his own thoughts. The worry made his hand twitch for the piphlid.

Morvelving grumbled with frustration and focused on what Nippi was doing.

She was trying to stick a wildflower into the long tufts of fur around his elbow. When she succeeded, she smiled up at him and tugged at his arm, asking him to swing her.

How could he resist? Morvelving held her tight and lifted her up, swinging her forward and back with his strides. Her legs kicked out in the air, and her laughter filled the woods. The disturbance caused squirrels to chirp aggressively. Morvelving ignored their crass words.

He knew he should throw the piphlid away. Part of him kept it as proof that it no longer held power over him. His shame didn't weigh as heavily on him when he focused on Nippi. He wouldn't run away ever again. Perhaps one day he could even return to his tribe and prove to them he was Morvelving no longer. But not now, not for a long time.

10

Nippiktua had succeeded in the impossible. She, the Mistress of Words, had convinced Fluff the Stubborn to take her on a hunt. He had said they were a day's walk from the crossing to Menici and needed to hunt for food.

She kept her breathing calm, despite her excitement. She could feel Fluff's heart thumping fast. Every inch of her taut and ready. The smell of his wet fur filled her nose. Dew covered the brush, as the morning sun had not yet reached it. The gorge extended into the distance, becoming darker and cooler the further they went.

Her lips were being tickle tortured by his fur as she tried to see their quarry. The harness crisscrossed around Fluff's torso, securing her legs to his back. He had left shiny Penalty behind at the camp with their other equipment. He only had his black dagger. Fluff wanted her to stay low, but she couldn't help watching.

They were stalking a deer with a big crown. The Stag they'd encountered the previous day dwarfed it in size, its brown fur merging with the shadows. Nippiktua counted the crown's ends: eight points. Fluff's right ear twitched. She knew that signal!

The time was nearing. Fluff crept toward the deer with painful slowness. Fluff abruptly tensed. He was about to pounce! One of his hairs went up her nose! Way up, oh no!

She sneezed. Her forehead hit Fluff's shoulder hard, making small lights cripple her vision.

The deer bolted, and Nippiktua was almost flung from the straps as Fluff ran after it.

Trees and bushes were a blur. Nippiktua had never run so fast! Her hair pulled at her scalp as she kept her head down. She stole glances at the chase as often as she could manage with the quick turns.

Morvelving was remarkably swift, faster than Nippiktua could have imagined. Though the deer was just barely faster, it stayed ahead. It weaved among brush and trees like water through fishnets.

Fluff leaped over a fallen tree, using a branch to propel himself further, and Nippiktua gasped at the moment of weightlessness. Her head smacked against Fluff's backbone from the jolt when they landed. It didn't matter. Nippiktua watched in awe as he gained on the deer. It darted and weaved. Fluff dove when it tried to dart left again.

His jaws clasped around the deer's neck. His fur covered her eyes as he stumbled, controlling his speed and the thrashing deer. After a moment the deer's life passed, and Fluff delicately placed the limp carcass on the ground. The air smelled cool, with a tinge of metal. She hadn't realized how tense she was till then. Her arms and legs ached, and her head felt bruised. It didn't matter. Her heart tried to beat out of her chest. She would be as fast as Morvelving one day. After that, she had to be.

Fluff unbound her. Nippiktua stumbled to her feet. Once her balance returned, she danced, leaping for the sky. With every step, the gentle pressure of her feet against the cool moss released a unique, earthy smell. Upon spinning around to check Fluff's reaction, she abruptly stopped. He was watching her with patience, ears forward and long tongue dangling while he was panting to catch his breath, sitting cross-legged next to the deer. He motioned for her to sit.

Nippiktua sat down, feeling confused. He wasn't happy.

"*Nippi*," Fluff signed. "*It is good for you to rejoice in our successful hunt. Though the spirits do not understand your expression, it is more gloating than thankfulness.*"

He waited for her to nod her understanding. Nippiktua shrugged.

"*They understand a quick kill. The deer didn't suffer,*" Fluff signed, pointing at his bite marks. "*We must use everything of the deer, let nothing go to waste. If we can't do so, we must make the Runic Ring of branches. Pay attention. This is your first Ergald lesson. See, like this.*"

Nippiktua watched with greater fascination as Fluff broke small dead branches and made the Runic Ring—a circle surrounding a triangle and three convex lines.

"*This action signifies to the spirits that you have returned the remains to the Ervi, replenishing life. Feeding the plants and other animals. One day, we will die, and our bodies will enrich the land. This is the Song of Life. Telunian created it, and Drudan imbued it into the very veins of Ervi. It's an exchange, blood for blood. Do you understand?*"

"I think so." Nippiktua focused hard on his words. "*We kill for food and farm the land, but when we die, we give back. But how is this magic? How—*"

Fluff held up his paw's black palm. Nippiktua waited. He pointed at the Runic Ring.

"*The ring shows the path of the song. Here, life. Here, death. Here, the telluric exchange—to give and command. Here—the warning.*"

Their eyes locked. The dark center of his eyes shone silver like two full moons. Beneath her, the ground trembled as the branches swayed in a sudden breeze. Nippiktua gasped.

"*Drudan's warning: balance or be bled, your soul damned. What happens when Frystlins kill all the seals from the sea instead of only the ones they need?*"

Nippiktua shook her head at the ridiculous question. *"They wouldn't. That would mean no seals to hunt for food. Then the tribes would starve."*

Fluff nodded. His eyes were no longer burnished silver. Nippiktua wanted to ask him why his eyes had turned silver, but he continued. *"It is the same with the magic of Ergald. If abused, it will destroy you and the Eifgald, power of Ervi. That is why you shouldn't use it."*

"I don't know how." Nippiktua shrugged, hoping he would explain.

"Good."

"But how—"

"When you understand the consequences, I will tell you how," Fluff signed, his ears flat. Meaning she would not get her way.

That wasn't fair. He could tell her *something* about Ergald. What if she needed to use it to fly or run fast? She crossed her arms and glared up at Fluff.

"Now," he signed, ignoring her, *"we will take the carcass back to camp. There, I will take everything we need and bury the rest."*

"Can I help?" she asked, hoping to placate him so he would tell her what she wanted. Fluff smiled, a combination of his tongue out, panting, ears flexing back and forth, and a wink from his left eye.

"Yes." Fluff stood. He sniffed the air and licked his lips. Nippiktua sniffed too, but all she smelled was the damp ground and blood from the deer. *"First, we must give thanks to Osideyos, God of the Hunt, and Medithera, Goddess of Critters. Watch."*

Fluff shuffled his hind paws back and forth in small steps. He spun, his arms slack and head bowed, then threw his arms up. A dance! Ergald could wait for dancing.

Nippi stood and began to mimic Fluff's movements. The rhythms and steps came to her quickly, as her people had done something similar after a successful seal hunt. She smiled as Fluff moved faster and faster.

Her little legs were not as quick as his, but she would not let the gods think she wasn't willing to try.

Fluff came to an immediate halt and lifted his nose to the sky, chest exhaling. Nippiktua knew he was howling. She stood and watched, wishing she could hear the sound he made. She could feel it, the vibrations tickling her gooseflesh. Fluff finished.

"Great work," he signed. *"The gods and spirits are pleased, and the deer is honored. Come, let's go back to camp."*

He picked up the deer and offered to lift her onto his shoulder. Nippiktua shook her head and started walking. She wanted to be close to the ground.

A chipmunk scurried across her path, and a snake lay in the sun. She watched them with interest as Fluff walked by. There was a plant with red berries, which she knew were poisonous. The advantage of having Fluff around was that she knew what was edible and what was not.

The sun was starting to sneak its way into the gorge. Beams of light glowed in the forest gloom. They were almost at their camp. Walking among the bushes made Nippiktua's legs wet. Her attention was drawn to some unfamiliar purple flowers.

Fluff rushed in front of her. She eyed him, questioning. He was looking ahead at the heavy bushes with thick brown leaves and moss. Fluff's lips were quivering, which she knew meant there was trouble. She noticed the smell then, the heavy, pungent smell of urine. She wrinkled her nose.

She began to wonder why they didn't just continue when the big brown bush moved. Nippiktua grabbed Fluff's leg tight, staring wide-eyed at the massive bear. It stood on its hind legs, mouth open wide. She felt the ground shake from its roar. It had several arrows sticking out from its shoulders, and its left eye bore a vicious scar.

The bear kept roaring. Nippiktua held tight to Fluff. She had seen the big white bears in her homeland and the hunters dead from their attacks. She looked up at Fluff, his features now terrifying. He bared his teeth and bristled his mane to sharpness. By the movement of his snout, she knew he was barking at the bear.

Nippiktua breathed again when the bear backed away, deciding Fluff was too much to contend with. She gladly allowed Fluff to lift her up. She put her legs over his shoulders on either side of his head and pushed down his bristled fur. There was no need to discuss what had happened.

The bear had challenged them, and Fluff had been too scary for it. She patted his head twice. His ears flicked back once, but he kept his focus on the forest.

Back at camp—an alcove wedged into the rocks—Nippiktua felt relieved. Sometimes the forest was scary, and she often wondered if it would be less so if she could hear.

Her knapsack and blanket lay near the small fire, now reduced to ashes. Feeling a sudden chill, she hurried over to the blanket and wrapped herself in its warm folds. Fluff had set down the deer and put his dagger next to it. He grabbed Penalty from under a thorny berry bush, along with his knapsack and cuirass. All covered by the minotaur-hide cloak. Nippiktua had never seen a minotaur, only knew the stories about the bloodthirsty bovines.

Fluff pulled out his short skinning knife. He had shuffled out the other tools and equipment. They were primarily items he had gathered over time—wooden utensils, a wooden bowl, and a bone with tough fur at the end for cleaning teeth. Among the pile were an extra cloth, a few dull items, and some bottles of liquid. Fluff never told her what they contained. One was dark while the other had a bluish hue. She didn't mind, for she kept things from Fluff too. Like her list, which reminded her to remove "gather honey with a bear." They seemed grumpy and stinky. She was still happy with herself for following those mercenaries' advice about lists.

Nippiktua pulled her blanket back and started signaling to Fluff. *"Why did the bear challenge us? Was it for the deer?"*

Fluff looked up at her, and his left lip got caught on his fang, making him look like a squirrel with a nut in its cheek. Nippiktua smiled.

Fluff signed back to her. His signing had improved—she was an impressive teacher. *"Old Boru was making sure we weren't a threat."*

"You know him?"

"No," Fluff signed patiently. *"He introduced himself. We surprised him, you see. His nose and eyes aren't as good as they used to be."*

"It didn't look like you were happy with him . . . "

"I wasn't," Fluff said. *"He was rude; the forest isn't his to sheriff. I had to assert myself and not let him bully me. That is an example of when to show your teeth. Now"*—he pointed at the deer—*"I am going to tend to the deer. You've seen me do this with rabbits, but only watch to learn. If you don't want to, you don't have to."*

"I want to know," Nippiktua signed, determined to be brave. She didn't enjoy watching him tend to rabbits. They were cute. The deer reminded her of her family hunting in Frystgalen.

Fluff nodded. *"Pay attention to the process, not what it brings."*

He picked up his skinning knife. Nippiktua watched his paws move with a smooth, practiced rhythm as he removed the hide. There was a minimal amount of blood, and the smell was peculiar. She couldn't place it. She'd thought it would be stickier.

She averted her gaze as Fluff decapitated it. Then she didn't feel well when he opened the abdomen. She had always arrived after her tribe had finished butchering the seal to collect fat or oil with her mother.

Fluff must have sensed her discomfort. He now started talking, so she focused on watching his mouth.

"It's right to use everything you can from a hunt," Fluff said as he worked. "Medithera first taught the Wiseneyes how to do so when the sun was young, so we may respect her creations even when we need them to survive. Telunian, with her silver light, taught the Song of Life, as I mentioned earlier. Taking any life has a toll on the soul, and so if it's for survival, it is proper to honor the spirit of what was taken."

"Have you seen the gods?" Nippiktua asked. She now added "meet a god" to her list.

"No, I was born three centuries after the First Rift," Fluff said, shaking his head. She struggled to grasp the meaning behind his words, pondering the significance of *first* and *rift* and their nature and timing.

"I feel the presence of the gods in their creations though," Fluff continued. "Did you feel their presence with the Stag?"

Nippiktua shook her head. *"I know one was watching because of the raven. 'Dark wings, god's eye, beware,' my* amua *used to say. I only heard about the Stags and what you told me."*

He froze and stared at her signing. "You saw the raven with the Stag?"

"Yes. Is something wrong?"

"Not exactly. Ravens do not spy for the gods. The brothers, Felren and Rnudfel, are the Eyes of the Fates. They are giant ravens, but they enlist the help of others to report to them."

Fluff didn't look happy, but he shook his head and continued his work on the deer, saying, "Stags used to be heralds for Drudan. If the goddess is bending her will, she would know who we are through the Stag's eyes. But now, Stags are more akin to this deer." His ears drooped, showing his sadness.

Nippiktua eyed the branches above for any ravens.

"Fluff, what is the Rift?" Nippiktua signed. She knew it was meant to occur. An emerald and black bridge that allowed the spirits of the dead to cross into Celemith. But she didn't understand it.

She watched his chest take a deep breath.

Fluff began organizing the cut venison, taking a moment before saying aloud, "After the dawn of time and the forming of Ervi—and after the gods had populated Ervi with their children—the Fates tightened their threads, for even the gods' golden weaves were held between the fingers of the eternal Crones. Forced to abandon their children's lives to the Fates, the gods created the Rift. At the turn of each century, the Emerald Rift bridges Ervi and Celemith together, allowing the spirits of the fallen to cross into Celemith to each god's respective halls. The First Rift was seven hundred eighty-three years ago."

Nippiktua watched his lips with rapt attention. *"You believe the Fates are watching me because of the raven?"* She felt a chill on her back. Her mother had never talked about the Fates. To command the gods, they must be truly terrifying.

"For a reason I can't fathom, the Fates are watching you, us. I don't understand, since you're only a silly girl," Fluff said with a smirk.

"I'm the only Nippiktua, and don't you forget it." She shook her pointer finger at Fluff. He chuckled and went back to work.

Nippiktua thought about gods, Fates, and the Rift. Every hundred years—that was ten years, ten times over! And she was only eight.

"Fluff, how many have you seen?" she asked.

"How many what?"

"Rifts."

"Four," Fluff said. The deer was now pieces of meat and organs. He was working on the bones now.

"You're old," Nippiktua signaled, amazed, and laughed, happy to tease him.

"I am still a very young Mulranei, thank you, Nippi," Fluff said, smiling—mouth open and tongue flapping to the right side as he winked with his left eyelid. She crossed her arms, unbelieving. He eyed her, and his nose vibrated, snorting at her. She felt the spittle and looked away, giggling and wiping her face.

"I'll call you Puppy Fluff now," she teased, regretting it immediately. Fluff dropped what he was doing and stared at her, ears up, mouth closed—serious. She put her hands up.

Fluff smiled. "Funny, Nippi. But inappropriate," he said, and resumed his work.

"Sorry," she signed, genuinely. Nippiktua knew he was sensitive about only using human terms to refer to himself and other Mulranei.

"Thank you, Nippi. You were good on the hunt," Fluff said.

She leaned against one of the smooth rocks near the fire, her heart swelling with pride. The day had been satisfying. Her mind replayed the hunt as she leaned back against the rock wall. The comfortable coolness of the rock and the smell of damp earth wooed her to sleep. She was fast again, in her dream, running in the woods.

11

Morvelving stood behind Nippi, arms crossed, watching her.

They were camped a two hour walk from the Idos Road to the Idospont. The road connecting the Land of the Idosse to the continent of Bregalen had been laboriously carved through the sharp hills of the mountainous pass. Tree branches above danced in the sea wind. They had made good time and remained undiscovered. Morvelving wanted to give Nippi time to practice with the bow he had made for her. He had carved a circle on a fir tree ten yards ahead to serve as a target. Salt was heavy in the air, and Morvelving could already hear the whining calls of seabirds nearby. Clouds hung low, but not low enough to fog his vision.

Nippi was wearing her green tunic, acquired in Theba, with wildflowers embroidered on the hem. The belt wrapped around her waist wrinkled the tunic, and the clash of its color with her light blue skin confounded his eyes.

Morvelving had got her to hide while he had bartered with a wandering merchant. The trader had haggled as if his life depended on it, but Morvelving had been able to trade the deer pelt, bones, and venison for assorted supplies—fletching for the arrows, nuts, and dried meat.

He watched closely as Nippi pulled back on the bow. He had made it for her size and weight, which made it useless as a hunting tool. He wanted her to learn and develop skills first. With the Fates, and even

Drudan, keen on her life, she would need to know how to survive and defend herself. So, he would teach her, no matter how unsure he was of it being the wisest choice.

Morvelving noted that she breathed in too soon and was pulling back too much. She was too eager to receive instructions and had insisted on starting with practice shots. Morvelving had been reluctant to say *no* after giving her the bow for her *sanitja*.

Nippi relaxed the draw. Her head down, visibly frustrated—she couldn't do it. Morvelving was proud of her for not releasing the arrow. Windtail had let loose on his first attempt. The arrow had been lost, and he had cut his arm on the string.

Morvelving stepped in front of her so she could see him.

"Good, you kept the arrow," he signed, giving her a reassuring expression—tossing his nose up and down and finishing with a head tilt. *"Move your lead foot and your shoulders like so."* He showed her what he meant after signing—her left foot pointed at the target, shoulders square with her hips. *"Only turn your neck to look. Draw from your shoulders with an intake of breath. Try without the arrow."*

Nippi did as instructed. She pulled back, seeming surprised to discover strength she'd never known she had. She looked up at him with a wide grin. Morvelving sniffed and barked. Her arm was shaking like a tall tree's branches in the wind, but her form was straight with proper structure.

"Good, Nippi, you can relax," Morvelving signed, watching her, giving her time to respond. She set down the bow and shook out her arms.

"That's hard," she said.

"It will become easier the more you practice," Morvelving signed, pointing at the fir tree with the carved circle. *"Now try to drive the arrow into the center. Remember, breathe in with the draw and release the arrow with an exhale."*

He showed her what he meant. She observed with intent, trusting him now. He stood with his left paw-foot and paw-hand pointed at the target. Then he inhaled, pretending to draw, and exhaled while releasing his three fingers holding the imaginary bowstring. He encouraged her to mimic him.

"Good. Now notch your arrow." Morvelving stood back and watched Nippi. Nippi checked her stance twice, drew the bow, and relaxed, testing the draw again. Her lips crooking to the left, she took a deep breath to prepare herself. Her face was a picture of stern concentration.

Morvelving held his breath, wishing for her to succeed. Hoping he hadn't taught her too hastily. With Windtail, he had needed to repeat his instructions often, but the little pup had had a distinct personality—eager to listen. Nippi was headstrong, only paid attention when necessary.

Nippi inhaled and drew back, pulling the arrow to her cheek as he had told her to. She didn't hold it for long and released it with an exhale. The arrow flew straight and stuck into the tree below the circle. She looked at him, disappointed. Morvelving shook his hands up to show his excitement for her.

She pointed and signed, tucking the bow in her armpit. *"I missed. I was looking right at the circle."*

"It takes practice, Nippi," Morvelving encouraged. *"Try again. Remember, the arrow shaft is below your eyes. Consider that when aiming."*

Nippi nodded and tried again.

She missed the tree on the second attempt and hit it outside the target on the third. Morvelving collected the arrows.

"Well, keep trying." Morvelving placed the arrows by her feet.

Nippi notched another arrow, drew, and released. It wedged itself into the tree just within the circle. Nippi jumped up and down in her excitement, yelling out.

Morvelving added baying to her sounds, raising his arms so she could see his excitement. Nippi started dancing in triumph. He laughed and joined her in her merriment, the critters nearby their only audience.

Breathless from her dancing, Nippi stumbled over to her bow. Morvelving watched her pick up the arrows in earnest.

With difficulty, Nippi signed, *"I want to practice more!"*

"Well, it is your bow, and you should practice every day to become proficient. I will set up our camp for the night." Morvelving's chest swelled with pride and relief. He had worried that she wouldn't like her gift. He saw now that had been foolish.

They were a safe distance from the road, and the cavernous land, with its deep ravines and tall forest, was to their advantage. He set up a pit for a fire to limit the smoke. Already, the sun had fallen behind the Ykris Mountains, giving each summit a crown of fire.

When he turned back to Nippi, she was braced against the tree, pulling at the arrow to free it. Morvelving stifled a chuckle and hurried over before she broke the arrow.

He tapped her shoulder, taking a patient breath. Nippi's blue skin was flushed with exertion. He showed her how to pull it out, placing her hand on the trunk and the other on the arrow.

"Now pull," he said and signed simultaneously.

Nippi yanked the arrow out with so much force she stumbled back, triumphant again.

"Come along, twilight is here. Let's eat and rest." Morvelving gently took the bow and arrows from Nippi. She nodded in tired resignation but still raced him to the camp after he had made sure to hide any evidence of their presence.

Morvelving massaged the sumac and sage he had collected into two cuts of venison and slowly cooked them over the fire. The spit and sizzle from the grease were the only noises between them. Nippi lay on her stomach, hands pressed against her cheeks, content to watch. An owl perched upon a tree above, perturbed by the light of the fire.

They ate in peace.

Morvelving chuckled when Nippi grimaced as she bit into the folded nettle leaf he had handed her. *"They are better with berries."*

"My arms feel like seal fat, and my back is warm." Nippi shook out her arms.

"That means you practiced well." Morvelving smiled. *"Over time, and with more daily practice, it will become easier and your body stronger."*

"Like running a lot makes you faster!"

Morvelving nodded. In the quiet of the growing darkness and with a full stomach, he leaned back against a cold boulder and sighed in contentment. Tomorrow they would pass over the Idospont and leave the Land of the Idosse.

Nippi found her blanket and lay down to sleep. After a loud and impressive yawn, she signed, *"Thank you for the bow."* The child yawned again, eyes closing as she curled into a ball. *"And for being the best Mulranei I know."*

Something in his throat tried to choke him, and his eyes stung. Morvelving ran his finger across his nose and cleared his throat. "How about that?" he said with a chuckle. He was the only Mulranei she knew. A far and hard journey they had traveled together. Morvelving had kept his promise and succeeded in his new one. Orrothix's riddle was behind them, and he would keep to the wilds after crossing the Idospont. He doubted any man, especially Sophokis, could track him or have the reach to set cities on a watch.

Warmed by the fire and protected by the land, for the first time since taking Nippi under his care, Morvelving felt he had slipped from the

Fates' eyes. He hadn't seen a crow or raven. The wandering merchant had been heading east, away from Phoithese, and had known nothing about any bounty for Nippi. His ears twitched to catch any sound in the woods to warn him of trouble: nothing. He sniffed the soft breeze that carried the scents of critters and pine trees north: nothing. Morvelving longed to be more comfortable.

He removed his belt and froze—the piphlid had fallen from its pouch. Morvelving held it in his palm, barely visible as the fire's embers dimmed. Now shriveled and dry, its effects would be diminished. No human tracker would be able to find them—Morvelving had made sure of it. But still, he didn't need to take it. Nippi would surely notice him acting differently and wonder why. He pocketed the piphlid.

His mind remained on the pouch that held the shroom. A nasty root delved into his hip. Piphlid would certainly help him find some needed rest.

Morvelving chewed the dry piphlid, surprised and unsure how it had got into his mouth, but he was instantly reveling in its noxious sensations. Every part of him eased into the ground where he lay, and he strayed into a captivating sleep that cocooned him in pleasant dreams bereft of all worry.

His world was shaking. Morvelving jolted awake, knocking Nippi away from him. She stumbled back with a shocked scream that evolved into grunting.

"You big sleepyhead. I had to shake you awake," Nippi signed after brushing dirt from her tunic. *"I had to make my own food too. What?"*

Morvelving wiped the sleep from his eyes. His stiff body moved as slowly as the realization that hit him. Already, he longed for it, needed it. Piphlid. "Gods above and below," he groaned. His head felt like it was on the receiving end of a battering ram. Shaking away his disorientation,

Morvelving attuned to his senses. Everything was fine. Nippi was here, looking at him expectantly. There was no immediate danger . . .

"Gather your things," Morvelving signed as he stood in a flurry of motion. Nippi jumped back in shock for the second time. *"And quietly."*

The woods around them were silent, and the air was taut as a drawn bowstring. Morvelving's hackles rose. Every one of his waking senses was telling him something or someone was near, with intentions for him and Nippi.

"Gods-damned, thrice-cursed coward," he hissed at his own complacency and fought against the piphlid's remaining lethargic effects. His nose felt numb, hindering him.

Morvelving tried to determine what was near them while he methodically shouldered his pack and unwrapped Penalty. Upon seeing him unsheathe the long sword, Nippi seemed to recognize his urgency and hurried to pick up her things. There was no scent that gave him a hint. Morvelving's grip tightened on Penalty.

He turned to Nippi. *"Quiet. Follow me."*

Once they were away from their camp, Morvelving half froze, slowly setting his foot down. Thirty strides ahead, a centaur stepped from his hiding place and faced Morvelving. Nippi placed her hand on his hock. He kept Penalty pointed down across his front, poised to strike or guard.

The centaur stood silent, his fur and hair dark. Morvelving tensed, eyeing the spear the centaur held and the bow and quiver strapped to his back. Morvelving growled when others began to show themselves. They were not close, but they had fully surrounded him and Nippi. Their limbs were strong, visible under the fur that covered most of their bodies, except for patches on the human torso and face. Heavy beards and wild manes shrouded their faces. They must have found his trail and closed in while he had deeply slept in the piphlid's embrace. Morvelving was a fool, tramping about like a giant bear drunk on fermented honey. This was a fight he couldn't win.

The one facing Morvelving spoke. "Mulranei, peace. The stars shone to show us your hunter paws crossing north. We have looked for you." The centaur's heavy black beard and mane dominated his visage, dwarfing the pale face. His large hands held an osage-wood spear across his strongly defined chest. He gave a slight nod, unsettling Morvelving with his glazed white eyes. People commonly mistook their white eyes as a sign of blindness, but it was an attribute of their species. The feature enabled them to read the stars, at least according to his tribe's Wiseneyes.

"Though rare are Telunian's worshippers in the rocky lands of Idosse," the centaur continued, his eyes lingering on Morvelving's hand on Penalty, "we have heard of you who the human sellswords call 'Sword of Mourning.' I am called Keissus, and I ask a moment for you to hear what our Kazar proposes."

Morvelving released his breath but remained ready with Penalty. If they wanted him or Nippi dead, they would have killed them already.

"It appears I don't have much of a choice," Morvelving growled.

"You do not." A smirk played on Keissus's lips. "But the outcome is your choice. The stars as my witness, no harm will come to you while you are willing to talk and comply. I've offered my name, yet you haven't yours."

Keissus eyed Nippi curiously, then looked back at him. Morvelving stole glances at the other centaurs—their hands tight on spear shafts, their arrows notched. They were ready.

They had to be from the powerful tribe in Eugrator that Morvelving had heard had ties to the human city of Ugris. Keissus must have come from there, and their leader was taking a risk by sending them into Thressean lands.

Morvelving held back the scoff in his throat. Expecting him to follow laws of courtesy when they had clearly meant to surprise and capture him and Nippi. He could trust Keissus to keep his word, at least, since he had invoked what centaurs worship. Morvelving had to let this play out—he had no other choice.

"I am Morvelving," he called out. "And this is Nippiktua. What's your Kazar's proposition?"

With formal courtesy complete—which was evidently important to the centaur—Keissus visibly eased, stomping on the ground. He spoke, his voice confident. "Morvelving and Nippiktua. My people, the Roxanar, live peacefully among the Idosse in the Eugra Valley. We trade with the Idosse peoples and defend their borders when they're attacked. There is trouble though. The old fair king has perished, and his son is . . . " Keissus paused, his hooves shifting and his hand resting upon his chin in thought. He shook his head, seeming to give up on his first thought, and continued. " . . . a colt who hasn't found his hooves, yet believes he has. We have sought a new alliance to live peacefully, as is fitting and as is traditional. Yet the young king sends us away while still expecting trade, demanding prices. How can we trade if no formal alliance and deal has been made? Already, heralds from other human kingdoms are calling us to move to their lands. We can't leave our lands where our foremothers are buried."

Keissus gazed fixedly at Morvelving. Morvelving held back his frustration at Keissus's conversational tone. So, they wanted him at the negotiations to sense if the young king meant to betray them. All the effort made by the Roxanar to find him for the alleged negotiations was fitting for centaurs, who were known to go to great lengths to achieve their ends. Unlike the Mulranei, who formed civilizations and societies, or the minotaurs, who created their warmongering roving clans, the centaurs lingered in the wild. They avoided Mulranei, and when elves and men had come into the lands, the centaurs had fought them. The wars had been terrible, and in the end, the elven and human societies had forced the centaurs to give up lands they deemed their own. Now, too weak in numbers to combat humans, they made complicated treaties and trade agreements that were held by a thread, often broken as quickly as they were made. It seemed the Roxanar had found a hard balance.

It didn't explain why they would go to such great lengths to find him. Morvelving tried determining anything by their scent. Keissus and the other centaurs were guarded. He feared they also knew of the Phoithesens' pursuit of Nippi.

"Our path leads east. I cannot accompany you to—"

"If you refuse, we will kill you and take the child to the Phoithese." Keissus held his spear with both hands. "If you comply, our Kazar will ignore the bounty and plea of the Phoithesens."

Morvelving held back from barking and took a deep breath. Once again, he surveyed the centaurs surrounding him and Nippi.

Seeing him eye them in turn, they drew back their bows and readied their spears.

He saw no avenue of escape. Morvelving's shoulders drooped. He'd put his guard down. The allure of piphlid had won again. Was this the moment when Nippi would fall instead of Windtail? Morvelving took a deep breath and held up his head. No, he may have repeated his mistake, but the result wouldn't be the same—not while he breathed. He wouldn't let guilt and regret hold him hostage this time. He had no choice but to accompany Keissus to the Roxanar lands.

Morvelving instinctively yawned in distress, ending it with a brief whine. "I have no choice but to accompany you." Only centaurs would go to such grand lengths for a small task. The Kazar must be ambitious, and he was sure the centaur leader had more plans for him and Nippi than Keissus had told them. A piece of the puzzle was missing. Morvelving doubted Keissus would reveal it.

Keissus gave a curt nod. "We know the wise Mulranei have long shed their fur of politics. In the past, the Roxanar would not have dealt in words, as I'm sure you know. The new age dawns, and the stars are veiled. We must barter to survive on our own land." Keissus was angry now. Morvelving could smell it. There was bitterness in his words. The Roxanar had made many demeaning concessions to survive. The young king, on purpose and in ignorance, had further poured insults upon the Roxanar.

Keissus recovered, his anger melting into melancholy, and now looked Morvelving in the eye. "Your presence will help the Kazar make her decisions. The stars do not lie, and Mulranei smell ill intent."

For all the good it did me, Morvelving cursed to himself and asked, "Should I expect hospitality for myself and my ward?"

Keissus bowed his head low and nodded. "Yes. We forced your hand, but you and your ward are guests. Come."

Eugrator was a day's march over the Ykris Mountains. He had to keep Nippi safe, even after his mistakes and the Fates' schemes. He gazed at the little girl, her wide red eyes filled with wonder. Morvelving grunted. *"Were you following along?"*

Nippi nodded, serious.

At least, she remained vigilant. He prayed to the Moon Goddess that Nippi wouldn't suffer for his own weaknesses. *"Stay close to me."*

Nippi stepped closer.

Morvelving followed Keissus as the other centaurs fell into line around them. He slowly wrapped and sheathed Penalty, handing it and his dagger to a centaur's extended hand. The weight it represented heavier than the sword itself. There was no easier path now. Had he stayed vigilant, looking for escape . . . would it have helped? The Fates had been waiting to set this trap. He had to weather the storm.

12

Cold mountain air blew against his face.

Morvelving squinted at the distant Eugra Valley. Nippi stood next to him, her arm shielding her eyes from the dusty wind. The valley was in the foothills of Mount Eugrathos, whose white crown dominated the horizon. Grass and scarce oaks among the local osage trees decorated the rolling hills that mountain streams had carved into place. Large circular tents and wooden huts dotted the hilltops. Clusters of centaurs moving and working among the structures. He marveled at the sight. Keissus had implied the Roxanar Clan was small. Instead, a sizable host occupied a large valley. They were either making a show of strength or preparing for war. Either way, Morvelving became increasingly concerned about how he was going to get Nippi out of this.

A large flock of geese passed overhead as Keissus stomped next to Morvelving. Six centaurs carried on past Keissus and down the path that led into the valley, their hooves spattered with dirt. Dust wafted up Morvelving's nose. He and Nippi sneezed. They had been left alone on the journey—Keissus had been more of a watchful escort than a prison guard. Still, Morvelving had never found a moment to escape.

"Welcome to the home of the Roxanar," Keissus said, his deep voice hushed by the howl of the wind. "For three star-veiled Rifts, we have lived here."

"A warm welcome," Morvelving stated.

"The stars have shone upon us," Keissus said, obviously ignoring Morvelving's smugness. "Yet, we outgrow our land. For four seasons now, we have praised the old warriors who leave for war in the south. Their exodus allows us to keep growing. Come, I will take you to our Kazar. Then we will eat and march to the Sky-Struck Menhir—where King Agos will talk."

The Roxanar were too populous. Their lands weren't large enough for their posterity. Their old volunteered to leave with the purpose of dying. Morvelving glanced around, his apprehension mounting that he may have slain Roxanar in Makoidake fighting for the Pella people. It was unlikely, as the Roxanar were taller than the centaurs he had fought. Still, he had to consider everything that could be at play. After he was done with his task, what would keep the centaurs from deciding to hold Nippi and hand her over to the Phoithesens? Based on the little he knew, if he helped them with their negotiations, he and Nippi would be free to be on their way.

He noticed Nippi watching Keissus speak, and then she signed up to Morvelving, *"When can I ride on one? My legs are tired."*

He shook his head and signed back, *"That would be very rude, and we are in danger here. Please, be careful."*

Nippi bowed her head, her smile gone. Morvelving felt sick. She had been trying to lighten the mood. It wasn't her fault they were in this mess.

Once they were down the slope, the wind lessened. Several troops overtook their small party. They hailed Keissus, gave Morvelving and Nippiktua quick glances, and hurried on. Their hooves made a low rumble in the earth. The valley was bustling with activity everywhere he looked. Crops—wheat and barley, Morvelving recognized—were being harvested, the centaur workers lying on the ground so their hands could reach the vegetation. Hunting parties rushed past, game slung across their backs. Morvelving wrinkled his nose at the overwhelming smell of sweat and dung. In all his life, he hadn't seen centaurs among their homes and land, so he looked at their practices with curiosity, despite the circumstances. More armed patrols were present than he deemed necessary. Perhaps raids were frequent.

Nippi poked Morvelving and gestured toward the young centaur and centua engaged in a competitive activity. He was fascinated to learn male and female children played together like Mulranei. The dust kicked up and now formed a cloud, concealing the inner workings of the games from Morvelving's sight. They passed a large gathering where centaurs were training, numbering in the hundreds, perhaps even a thousand. The archers rode by, their arrows thumping against the arrayed targets and their hooves pounding. Other centaurs with spears and shields and their strange, curved swords were being drilled in formations.

"Your warriors show remarkable discipline," Morvelving said to Keissus. "Do you expect war with the city of Ugris?"

Keissus met Morvelving's gaze for a moment, then returned to the road. Morvelving tilted his head inquisitively and sniffed. Only the scent of sweat, dirt, and dry grass filled his nose. Still, his question had been either too on the nose or too far-fetched.

"A few times a season, we must defend against raiders," Keissus said in a noncommittal tone. "I'm sure Mulranei know we of the stars are warriors first. Hunters and farmers second. We have not forgotten the wars before our comforts below Eugrathos's Crown."

A vague explanation. There was more Keissus wasn't saying. Morvelving decided against pursuing the topic any further for now. Keissus was doing his Kazar's bidding. Morvelving would wait to hear it from their leader. His own tribe trained for war, after all, even if they avoided large conflicts.

Keissus called the circular towns hompi. They passed many hompi as they traveled along. They looked more like nomad camps to Morvelving. Circular or octagonal tents were arranged neatly, built tall and wide enough to be comfortable. Large wooden workshops, with tall tables, stands, and stalls, marked a smithy or tanning shop. Centaur crafters worked on their trade, the din of hammers filling his ears. Centua worked large spinners for linen or wool. Clearly, in adulthood, centua and centaurs did labor based on their gender. He shook his head. Among Mulranei, it only mattered who was more skilled or by interest. Except him . . . He blinked the thought away.

A white-haired centaur crossed their path to the main hompi. A brass bell hung from his neck and was making a mighty racket. Hundreds of bleating sheep followed behind him.

Nippi looked up at Morvelving, confused. *"How does he make them follow?"*

"It's the bell around his neck," Morvelving signed to her. *"The sheep follow for protection, but primarily for food."*

Nippi watched the shepherd for a moment longer.

Morvelving caught Keissus eyeing their interaction. "Ever had dealings with the Frystlin?" he asked Keissus, prodding.

Keissus shook his head. "No, the endless cold waters lay between. Do they all speak with hand motions?"

"No," Morvelving said. "Nippiktua is deaf and lost her tongue when her tribe was a victim of tribal raids. It is traditional there for captured enemies."

"A harsh tradition for a harsh land," Keissus stated. "The Kazar had traveled far in her youth. Perhaps she will recognize the Frystlin child for what she is. I did not, but now I know what a Frystlin looks like. We have arrived at the Kazar Hompi."

Now they stood at the bottom of two hills. A large hompi surprised Morvelving when they rounded the bend of the path. The Kazar Hompi was like the others, except for the size. The tents were larger, and there were fewer workshops. At the center stood a longhouse with high oak beams and intricately carved woodwork. Centaurs gathered around fires or under their tents, their chatter a hum in the air.

As they drew near, Morvelving looked long upon the tall longhouse. Each oak pillar was carved and painted in rich yellow, purple, and green, depicting moments in Roxanar history. A ramp led to the large wooden doors, each carved with the image of a centaur rearing below a crown of stars. Two guards stood vigil, one on each side of the doors. Here, Morvelving was further struck by the Roxanar's wealth. The guards wore bronze full-plate armor, which was heavy and expensive. He could now understand why they needed to keep trading with the king. They were used to wealth and plenty. Their justification for needing him still needed clarification. Morvelving steeled himself. He would have to be tactful, not allow himself to continue rolling down the hill of his mistakes.

Each guard remained motionless as Morvelving and Nippi followed Keissus and passed through the doors. Their curved swords in each hand crossed over their chests. Nearby braziers cast light on the armor, making shadows dance across them. Nippi stumbled twice, looking up at the guards, her mouth open. Morvelving kept his eyes ahead. Despite the foreboding atmosphere, he admired what the centaurs had built as they now made their way through the great hall.

The interior of the longhouse was open. At the heart, a marvelous hearth blazed. Columns of smoke rising sluggishly to the rafters. Numerous large beams, each carved with natural depictions, maintained the integrity of the structure. Unlike human and Mulranei structures, there were no closed-off rooms or sections. Some half walls served to set aside space for food stores or shelves of pottery, but they were still open. One entire wall was being used to mount weapons and tools for display. The Kazar's longhouse was a place to gather and store.

Despite the high ceiling and open space, the room was stuffy with the scent of too many people. Sweat-soaked hair, unseasoned chopped vegetables in large wooden bowls, and tart wine. Morvelving kept himself from sneezing, hoping no one noticed the moisture around his eyes.

Many centaurs were enjoying wine pressed from nearby vineyards and talking around the hearth. A few youngsters galloped through, weaving playfully around the bemused adults. Keissus called a greeting to several family members or friends. Morvelving couldn't tell them apart as Keissus led them to the end of the vast hall.

Upon a wooden rise, the Kazar sat with her horse's legs tucked to one side, bracing her right arm against an array of gold-laced cushions. Morvelving knew centaurs were an active race; the Kazar lying during a gathering marked her dominance. Others had to seek her out to show their respect or broach clan matters. The Kazar had palish flaxen fur, and her shoulders and face were a light brown. Her long, cream-white hair was intricately braided into a crown upon her head and shoulders. Morvelving was aware her pale eyes had not left him or Nippi since they had entered.

The Kazar sat straight. The firelight glistened on her ceremonial bronze breastplate, and the purple silk tassels danced with the movement of her powerful form. Silence fell as Morvelving and Nippi approached. Morvelving smelled a tension, an unease, like a pine branch about to snap under excessive weight. He understood why. The Mulranei were not innocent of bringing bloodshed upon centaurs. Still, interactions between their peoples had been nonexistent for so long. In his lifetime, he hadn't heard of or seen any Mulranei–centaur conflict arise. Except for his own—the two centaurs he had fought in Makoidake. Without Penalty or even his cuirass, he felt vulnerable and hoped this whole affair would be over swiftly.

The onlookers remained silent so they could witness an exchange unseen for centuries. Even though the exchange had been forced upon him, he wasn't fit to represent his kind. He was here so Nippi wouldn't be alone again and sold off to answer a draekurm's riddle with her life.

"Kazar," Keissus said, bowing. He raised one hoof as his upper body lowered, his chin reaching for his chest. "The stars shone, and we followed. Here stand the Mulranei called Morvelving and his ward, Nippiktua of Frystgalen. The child's ears are deafened."

His bow finished, Keissus waved to Morvelving. "Mulranei, witness and behold our Kazar Roxanar, the Luminous Star Idanphyrus Roxa, descendant of Gargilpythes the Great."

He bowed to Kazar Idanphyrus in respect and wonder at her ancestry. As he did so, Morvelving glanced down at Nippi. The intense gazes of the gathered centaurs were distracting her too. He noticed the youngsters pointing and whispering at her.

"May the moon and stars shine bright tonight, Kazar Roxa," Morvelving said, gritting his teeth. "Nippiktua and I are honored to be your guests. Your proposal was . . . compelling." Nippi hastily followed Morvelving's example. Her bow was quick, and she almost lost her balance. He added, "The Wiseneyes sang the tale of Gargilpythes the Great when I was young. He challenged the fallen god, Nameless, to single combat. Is it true he was able to mar the mortal god, once on the arm and once on the lower jaw?"

Idanphyrus raised the gold goblet perched between two fingers and took a delicate sip. Morvelving was able to catch the smirk she hid. The goblet's embedded emeralds and sapphires caught the firelight. Her pale eyes never left his. "Mulranei Wiseneyes remember well. It is said Gargilpythes missed Nameless's throat by a hair's width. But Nameless slew Gargilpythes and cursed his lineage. At least, that is what Nameless wishes us to believe. A brave tale, and tragic." She leisurely swiveled the goblet.

"You travel with haste from the south," Idanphyrus stated, breaking the silent pause. "The Idosse have harried you on your trail."

Morvelving held back his scowl. Centaurs could divine the past and present by reading the stars, their meanings often vague or misinterpreted. They didn't need the stars though. Sophokis must have sent runners ahead to all the Idosse cities. With no reason to deny, Morvelving spoke the truth. "Yes, a band of Phoithesens believes Nippiktua the answer to the dread draekurm's riddle. I disagree."

Idanphyrus's pale eyes regarded him unblinking. She gave a brief nod. "Understandably, the Roxanar prepared for the worst when the shade of Orrothix's wings passed over the land from the east. The gods and Fates have set their gazes upon us." After a pause, the hall seemed to hold its breath, waiting for their Luminous Star to speak again. Idanphyrus spread her arms and smiled. "I call you welcome. Ours is yours. Sit, eat, and drink."

Several slender centua approached, carrying platters laden with orange cheese and golden bread, mixed with assorted fruits—apples, plums, and tomatoes. Nippi took as much as she could carry, smiling after taking a large bite of fruit. Several youngsters gave approving laughs. Morvelving hastily consumed bread and cheese, too focused on the Kazar and deciphering what game she was playing to enjoy the taste.

After many friendly greetings that contrasted greatly with their forced arrival, Keissus approached Morvelving and Nippi. Nippi was trying to learn a hand game a young centaur was teaching her.

"Different signs counter others. A fist is a stone," the youngster said, "which loses to parchment—palm facing down. Parchment loses to knife, palm facing to the left. And stone beats a knife."

Keissus waited till Nippi finished a round with the youngster. Morvelving envied her ability to ignore the danger they were in.

"The Kazar invites the Morvelving and his ward for a stroll under the stars," Keissus said.

"Of course," Morvelving said, tapping Nippi and signing to her, *"The leader wants us to talk to her."*

Nippi was fiercely intent on the competition. *"Wait, I'm going to win this time."* Her lips set and brows furrowed in determination. The confused youngster refused to miss the opportunity to beat her once more.

Dropping his ears, Morvelving stood so Nippi could see him again. *"Nippi, we must go. We have to stick together."*

Nippi glared up at him. Morvelving spared a glance around, hoping no one was watching. Keissus and several others were. Heat rushed to his face from embarrassment. Armed men feared him, yet he struggled to make this child listen.

Thankfully, the child centua shook her head at Nippi and dropped her hands. Nippi's shoulders slumped.

"Show your gratitude for the game," Morvelving reminded her, ending his signs by miming a handshake. Nippi took the youngster's extended hand and shook it once. She loved games but struggled with losing.

"This way," Keissus said, waving toward the end of the bustling longhouse. Nippi grabbed Morvelving's hand as they left.

Outside, the air was cool and fresh compared to the smoky and stuffy longhouse. The young night revealed a thin blue outline of the mountains as the sun set on the western border. Stars were shining on the black curtain of night. A gust of wind whipped at Morvelving's fur. Nippi shivered and hurried over to Morvelving's left and folded his cloak around herself.

Idanphyrus stood alone on a grassy patch. Her arms were slack at her sides, and her tail swayed back and forth. She turned to face them. "You may retire, Keissus."

Keissus bowed to her command and returned to the longhouse.

Idanphyrus's gaze locked onto Morvelving, her eyes no longer pale. Darkened blue, as if reflecting the night sky.

"Let us walk under the stars," she said, turning. Her hooves made soft thuds on the ground. "You understand why I sent Keissus after you?"

"I understand you gave me no choice, Kazar Roxa." Morvelving glanced back at the longhouse. She had brought them out here to speak frankly, so he would. "You need me to warn you if the young King Agos smells of treachery. A request would have been—"

"And would you have?" Her brows rose. "Accepted a request to aid my people when you seek to leave these lands with all haste? No."

Morvelving clamped his mouth shut. She was right. Nippi yawned, unaware of how loud it was. "The journey was at a hard pace for her."

The Kazar shot a glance toward Nippi. "I understand." She ceased the walk and looked up at the sky.

Morvelving took off his cloak and wrapped it around Nippi. She took it with a contented smile and sat down.

Once Nippi was no longer distracting Morvelving, Idanphyrus said, "Agos has refused to secure our alliance. He believes what his father promised is set in stone." She was silent for a moment, as if recalling a memory. Morvelving noted her eyes narrowing and wondered if it was an unpleasant memory. "You must understand that the Roxanar do not trust the promises of humans. Time and time again, human rulers change agreements made five seasons ago—even one season ago. My people have learned: force the humans to make their treaties, trade agreements, and alliances anew, or tempt dispute and war.

"The Roxanar grew and prospered with the old King Bagos. Hundreds of our warriors have died alongside the humans of Eugrator. Bagos understood—every season, he came willingly to barter our alliance. Agos does not. Instead, he makes demands as if we had a treaty."

Morvelving flicked his ears back momentarily, considering. He saw a solution. The solution was straightforward—they had to converse with the young king. Pride often hindered rulers from avoiding misunderstandings. And the scent of pride, heavy like dust in quarries, clung to the Kazar. He imagined the young king would have the same aura. In his mind, both the Eugratians and Roxanar were stubborn. If young Agos offered the same ritual treaty, and if Idanphyrus could renew it each season, then Agos would gain their alliance. All of this didn't help the fact that he was a hostage. He shook his head.

"You expect me to join your side? Kazar Roxa, I am your prisoner. You threaten to have the child under my protection delivered to be a sacrifice." The stress overcame Morvelving—he bared his fangs. "What's stopping me from holding my claws to your throat and using you to leave these lands?"

Idanphyrus flashed a smile so sharp, Morvelving regretted his words. "What *is* stopping you? Mulranei honor? You are an exile, rejected. You protect this child in the small hope one good deed will

redeem you. No, you couldn't do it. My warriors would follow closely —
one arrow to the dear child's torso, and your world is gone."

Morvelving didn't satisfy her with his response. She was right. He
had spoken out in anger. He considered for a moment. Perhaps he could
garner sympathy with the truth. He took a deep breath. "Kazar, please."

Idanphyrus cocked her head.

"When I took the child under my protection, I sought the guidance
of Telunian." Morvelving rubbed at his right eye. "The Goddess refused
to speak, but the Dae of the Night visited me. They manifested due to the
will of the Fates concentrating on the child. I don't know why, but the
Fates have marked this child to be their instrument. I'm trying to keep
her from this doom. Hide her, stall their plans till she can weather what
cruel destiny the Fates have in store for her, prevent it even.

"Please, the longer she remains here, the more I fear war and untold
calamities will continue to befall this land, your people. Perhaps Orrothix
is aware of the child's destiny and is moving her pawns. I can't be
certain. I am certain of the signs. Along our journeys across the west, I
have seen them: flames consumed great forests with no lightning storms,
disease struck Lesgos after we arrived, and Drudan's Herald approached
the child."

Idanphyrus blinked. "You've seen a Stag?"

"Yes," Morvelving answered in haste, hopeful.

"We have not seen signs of Drudan's servants for more than a
decade," Idanphyrus replied, "when many used to walk the peninsula."

Morvelving took a step toward her. "You see that something is at
work, and all for the child."

A smirk played on her lips. "I see you believe your words, but I
wonder why you think the child is whom the Fates have set their will
upon. Great deeds, good or terrible, draw the Fates' will. *He Who Runs*

Shall Mourn Alone." The Kazar Roxa spoke in Mulranei, her dialect surprisingly fluid. "Have you considered that it is you the Fates have leeched onto? Unlike reading the stars, interpreting the will of the Fates is futile, for they are fickle, bitter, and inexorable. My people will dwindle beyond memory before I understand them."

Morvelving yawned to break his frustration. He turned away from the Kazar Roxa—his plea had failed. "What happens now?"

"My kind are hounded out of our lands by the human infestation. If I cannot keep the alliance with the neighboring city, Ugris, others will seek to attack us. And now the Phoithesens are ruled by Orrothix. I cannot allow them to commune with the draekurm."

"Orrothix is playing games with them, giving them false hope," Morvelving spat. "No draekurm will bore themselves listening to humans."

"The stars dim and the world grows old," Idanphyrus said. "Besides, the Phoithesens have vowed draekurm-war on any who harbor her." She pointed at Nippi, who had dozed off to sleep.

"You can't believe—"

The Kazar Roxa regarded Morvelving from the side. "A bluff, I know. Still, even the rumor of a draekurm seeking to conquer the west will draw legions of elves. Humans are bad enough. Rest now knowing I do not intend to deliver this child to the Phoithesens." She raised her palm to stop Morvelving's outburst. "Yet I cannot let you leave."

Idanphyrus surveyed the night sky, her eyes reflecting the darkness, making it look as if she had empty sockets where her eyes should be. "The wolf has hunted the lamb for many nights. I see it now." She pointed at the night sky. "The stars do not lie. Our interpretations often do. I must be ready for any contingency. My people have prospered, and I will not see that change under my rule. The young king assembles his warriors in greater numbers than required. Even hiring mercenaries. The outcome of our negotiations, and your aid, will dictate my intent for you and the child."

Morvelving's claws dug into his palm. Her words were convincing. However, the scent of her ambition was stronger. Yes, she wanted him to alert her if the young king was going to betray her, but she was also tired of the alliance with the city of Ugris. Mustering her people and taking such lengths to bring him here meant she was making assurances for a different plan. One he wanted no part in.

"That isn't enough," he growled. "I accept the task you have for me. I want no part of your plans. Your path is one of war and death. Give me your word, sworn under the stars, that after the negotiations, my ward and I are free to go."

Idanphyrus stared back at him. Her eyes caught the torchlight, becoming pale again. "When I meet with King Agos, alert Keissus if the king seeks treachery. You will remain complacent for the rest. Keissus!"

In disbelief, Morvelving held back his instinct to pick Nippi up and run.

"Take our guests to their sleeping quarters," Idanphyrus commanded before returning to the great longhouse.

Keissus waved his arm at Morvelving and began to walk around the longhouse. Morvelving gently picked Nippi up, who grumbled before going back to sleep, and followed. He held her tight, glad she could find rest, afraid once again that his mistakes would lead to her suffering. Gritting his teeth, Morvelving began to work out how to get them out of this web the Fates had spun for him and Nippi.

13

It was a cloudless morning.

The sun shone clear, and the sky was a heavy blue. Birds circled and darted back and forth over the small knoll on which Morvelving stood. Nippi was by his side, and they were both part of the Kazar's entourage.

Around them, the cool breeze made the vast fields of wheat shimmer like the sea. They stood behind Keissus, who stood at their leader's left, surrounded by the Kazar's company. The escort warriors' bronze armor gleamed in the sunlight, and banners flapped in the wind from the high spears. Idanphyrus stood at the fore. On her right was her adviser and mate, Gilthan. Morvelving hadn't met the adviser till the morning. They had only exchanged brief greetings.

He was keenly aware of Penalty on Keissus's back next to his and Nippi's travel pack. A clear sign the Kazar Roxa meant to free them both, contrary to what she had said last night. Clearly, she either hoped to deceive him or was blinded by her own certainty. Morvelving ignored his twitching left eyelid—he hadn't slept during the night. Several plans ran circles in his head as he tried to slow his breathing. The Fates had brought Nippi here. Why? He didn't care about the answer—he only wanted to get her out of here.

A menhir stood between them and an army of Eugratians. The stone was as high as a pine tree and split down the middle. The damage to the stone was such that Morvelving couldn't tell its purpose, except as a place for the two rulers to meet.

King Agos was surrounded by his advisers, clerks, and personal companions, and behind them stood the warriors of the city. The line of shields on either side of their king looked like painted fish scales, their spears a forest of bronze torches. Ugris, the Eugratian city, lay beyond the flat wheat fields and behind high stone walls. Their tall gatehouse towers were painted orange to highlight the black lines of images. Morvelving saw the shape of a lion fighting a warrior wielding a club. The city was hidden behind the walls, but the palace and temple stood proudly on a knoll in the center.

King Agos sat atop a raised platform, his chair covered with furs. He was young, perhaps twenty years of age. His hair was light brown and held down by the bejeweled crown on his head. He wore a rich purple and blue tunic under an elaborate bronze cuirass. It, too, depicted a lion fighting a warrior. His sword lay over his lap, and a boy that stood behind him held a high-plumed helm.

Morvelving's nose twitched as he sniffed again. Nippi tapped him, and when he looked down, she signed, *"Is it time to go?"*

"No. Be ready to hold onto me," Morvelving signed. He eyed the backs of Keissus and Idanphyrus. They both gave him as little heed as they had while traveling half the day to the walls of Ugris. He smelled the tension from the humans, who were a shouting distance away. They had yet to exchange any formal greetings. Both sides awaited the other to approach the menhir. Morvelving uttered a muted growl of annoyance at the pride of rulers.

A horn blast interrupted the wind's whistle and the birds' calls. Morvelving gazed northward toward its origin. A rider, bearing only his clothes, laden with dust from heavy travel, approached the king with haste. They fervently conversed. Following behind the messenger, a sizable group of Roxanar arrived from the northwest with a party of fur-clad humans adorned with bones. Morvelving caught their scent. They smelled of mountain cold and pine—and triumph, which made him uneasy.

"Who are they?" Morvelving asked Keissus, stepping up to his side.

"Grece chiefs from the Grecelos Mountains," Keissus stated. "They have come at the Kazar's wish."

Morvelving glared at Idanphyrus, who promptly ignored him. Outnumbered by the Eugratians, she had brought allies of her own.

The Eugratian king quickly stepped down from his throne and mounted his black horse. Accompanied by fifty companions and his advisers, the young king urged his horse forward, a scowl dominating his lips.

Idanphyrus approached as well, gracious enough not to cause further insult. Morvelving motioned for Nippi to follow. His heart skipped—separating from the main centaur host was good for their escape.

"How long are they going to talk?" she asked, watching with intent.

"Not long," Morvelving answered, too focused to explain further. *"Watch closely."*

"I am. I remember what you told me last night."

She understood, and Morvelving was proud of her for remembering to be aware of the dangers. He hid his trepidation.

"You are protected by the Kazar; fear not," Keissus whispered.

Morvelving tilted his head. "Why would I need protection if this is a peaceful negotiation between rulers?"

Keissus had no time to reply, as King Agos halted his horse five strides from Idanphyrus. The two parties faced each other. King Agos and his companions stood before the tall menhir. Idanphyrus and her guard remained adjacent to the split stone.

The king pointed at the approaching Grece chiefs. "What is the meaning of this, Kazar Roxa? I accepted your request to meet and negotiate our alliance, again. Though I grow tired of establishing what has been written and agreed upon already. Why do you bring wildmen into my lands?"

The king's eyes looked at each of them. Lingering on Morvelving for a curious moment. Agos smelled impatient and impetuous—and honest. Idanphyrus remained tight-lipped until the Grece arrived in earshot. The Eugratians looked at them with contempt.

The Kazar spoke. "I invited the Grecians as guests among the Roxanar. They are here to barter for our alliance just as you reluctantly did last season. So the stars tell."

Agos balked. "Reluctant? Kazar Roxa, I saw no need for us to reclaim an alliance that has remained strong and profitable since my father's reign." He looked down at the Grece chiefs. Morvelving followed his gaze. Each one had a bone through an ear lobe or nose—one chief even had a bone through his brow. Their weapons and armor were leather, fur, and bone. Some warriors carried spears with bronze heads. "They have nothing I already offer. My father catered to your yearly requests. I find them completely unnecessary. Is there a grievance you have? Speak it now, so I may know and make an agreement. The treaties and trade between my people and yours have only been profitable."

Morvelving scowled. There were no lies in his words. He glanced at Idanphyrus, Keissus, and the Grece chiefs. They had no intention of establishing an alliance with the Eugratians. Idanphyrus had contrived an intricate ploy for a surprise attack.

"Your father was wise," Idanphyrus said. "He did not shake his fists at 'inconvenience.' He sought our hand in treaty every season. You, King Agos, believe our treaty a right by your crown. This is not so. I invited the Grecians, for they have offered more land. My people have prospered and outgrown our lands."

The chiefs exuded pride as they nodded at her words.

Morvelving kept his ears up from dropping. He took an uneasy step back. They had brought him and Nippi into a war. He needed to find an escape.

"More land?" King Agos said, irony dominating his abrupt laugh. "The Grecians do not own land. What have they offered?"

"The lush Rivers Thren Valley," one Grece chief boasted, his Trade Tongue heavily dialectical. Like the other Grecians, he had a mantle made of small bones resting on his shoulders.

King Agos scoffed. "Kazar Roxa, these wildmen deceive you. The Rivers Thren Valley are lands ruled by Lesgos."

The Grece chief shook his head. "No. The Lesgossan take. We have taken back."

Morvelving's ears couldn't stay up. Agos spoke true. The young man was trying to reasonably resolve the debacle. The Grece chief was lying. Morvelving glanced at Keissus and Idanphyrus. They had only brought Morvelving here to make sure Agos wasn't going to do what they intended for the king and his city.

Deciding to test them and hoping to find his conclusion incorrect, Morvelving whispered to Keissus, "The Grecians lie. Agos speaks true— impertinent and angry, but true. There is no reason to make war upon the Eugratians."

Keissus's eyes darted in his direction. The centaur made no reply. Morvelving looked down at Nippi. She was sitting cross-legged in the grass, pulling the stalks one by one. Filled with worry at the danger they were in, Morvelving quickly glanced across the scene as discreetly as he could, seeking an escape. If he alerted the young king to the danger, he would be killed before he had a chance to defend himself or escape to the king's side. He needed something else.

"What's going on here, Keissus?" Morvelving whispered, hoping a challenge would change what reason could not.

The Kazar, king, and chiefs continued to shout, bartering to best the other. Morvelving sniffed the air and surveyed the surrounding fields while Keissus only stared. To the north, a thin cloud of dust billowed into the sky. Only a few things could create a dust cloud of that size: an abnormally strong wind over a dry field, or—and much more likely— many soldiers equipped for war.

Morvelving moved to face Keissus. Keissus flexed his hand before speaking. "The Kazar wanted you here to warn us if King Agos sought treachery."

Morvelving's lips quivered with a silent growl. "The Roxanar had no intent to make a new alliance with King Agos. That's why Grece warriors approach and your own are not far. I will not be part of this war. Let me take the child to the rear."

Keissus uttered no words.

Morvelving turned to leave. Keissus grabbed him by the arm to stop him, his grip hard. Morvelving showed his teeth. The time wasn't right, and the risk was too great. He would warn the young king, but in a way that would still allow him and Nippi to escape. Morvelving cursed himself for taking piphlid. He should have known the Fates would set a trap. That the Roxanar would forsake peace for war because of their own greed sickened him. Morvelving pulled his arm out of Keissus's grip.

Stepping up so he was inches from Keissus's face, Morvelving was aware of several guards taking a step closer. Finally, Idanphyrus glanced his way, which led King Agos to do the same.

Painfully aware of the danger they were in, Morvelving prepared himself and hoped the Moon Goddess would forgive him for the lives to be lost this day.

Morvelving quickly signed to Nippi, *"Be ready."* He clasped his hands behind his back, hidden under his cloak. He dug his pointer claw into the meat of his left arm, desperation leading him to use what he never wanted to.

King Agos sought Idanphyrus's focus. "What happens now, Kazar? You never told me why a Mulranei was with you."

Morvelving tilted his head to the side to hide the searing pain, waiting for Idanphyrus to respond. He was fully aware of the Kazar's guard—their hands on sword handles, ready to act on their Kazar's command—and Penalty near on Keissus's back.

Before Idanphyrus could speak, King Agos pointed at Morvelving. "Mulranei, what is your business in all this?"

Morvelving met the young king's gaze. Keissus and Idanphyrus were waiting for him to keep their treachery secret. His choices didn't matter. If he gave a warning, the surrounding centaurs would strike. Idanphyrus needed Nippi alive to placate the Phoithesens. A small hope, given that the deaths of hundreds, perhaps thousands, of Eugratians and Roxanar were fated for today. One he wouldn't rely on. His blood began to soak the fur of his left arm.

"I was brought here at the request of the Kazar Roxa." Morvelving stayed near Keissus, ready.

If he lied to Idanphyrus and said the king was planning to betray her, it would accomplish the same result. Morvelving shook his head—all of this because he had relaxed his guard for one moment. He was beginning to believe what Idanphyrus had said—the Fates loved him more than Nippi.

King Agos boldly examined Morvelving and then Nippi. He leaned to one of his advisers, conversing quietly. "Kazar Roxa, are they not the Mulranei and the child the Phoithesens are after?"

Morvelving watched Idanphyrus and worried she could see what he was doing. She turned back to the young king. He hoped the blood soaking his arm was enough.

"Yes, I mean to secure my interests in the southern cities, just as I am in the northern cities."

King Agos leaned forward in his saddle, blinking as if he hadn't heard correctly. "Secure? Our alliance is secure, despite you needing assurances every season."

Morvelving finished tracing the Runic Ring on his arm, blood dripping from his claws. Already, Ergald flowed into him from the earth, accepting his offered exchange: *blood for blood*. The air became dry, making his nose burn. He glanced at the tall menhir. It would have to be enough. *Give and command.* Morvelving bent his will upon the menhir, and squeezed his wound—*balanced or bled, a soul damned*—taking all his control to not show the icy pain spasming through him.

Keissus and one of King Agos's advisers noticed.

"What are you doing?" Keissus faced Morvelving.

"Someone summons Ergald! It's an attack, my king!"

Idanphyrus hissed and pointed at the young king, who drew back the reins of his horse as his face screwed in shock. Two of her guards charged, one's lance pivoting into the king's adviser's chest. The second swung his sword at the king, but Agos had time to defend himself with his drawn sword, bronze ringing.

With a dull crack, one side of the split menhir began to fall over. Morvelving's spell was successful. All eyes shot up to the stone pillar as it descended, seeking to crush all of the Kazar's guard who stood behind Morvelving. The Kazar's guard rushed forward, weapons drawn and spears couched, to meet the Eugratian king's companions, who charged in a fury to defend their king.

Morvelving, dazed from the loss of blood, picked Nippi up and dove to the ground as the menhir crashed onto the earth. A cloud of dust rose, obscuring his vision and hindering the centaurs. He rolled out of the way of pounding hooves and stood, holding Nippi close.

Amid the screams of confused fighting, Keissus still found him.

Keissus raised his sword to strike. Morvelving stepped toward him to catch his wrist. A force hit his shoulder — a human knocked over from the fighting.

Morvelving stumbled. He instinctively rolled again. Cold bronze nicked his ear. Morvelving shouldered Keissus as he stood, hindering the next swing of his sword. Keissus grunted and then screamed in pain.

A spear, thrown randomly or intentionally, protruded through the flesh of his back leg, making Keissus trip and fall to the ground. He frantically tried using his arms and forelegs to stand, but the struck leg was useless and tangled the other beneath him.

A screaming human, one of the king's companions, rushed Keissus, sword aimed for his throat.

Morvelving hurried around the fight, his back to the fallen menhir. He moved Nippi behind him as the melee raged around them. The dust began to settle, allowing him to see the army of Roxanar, hooves shaking the earth, charging into and harrying the Eugratians' shield wall with their bows.

Keissus was pinned.

"Stay down and right here," Morvelving signed, motioning for Nippi to remain.

The brave girl nodded, pressing against the fallen menhir.

The king's companion regarded Morvelving with crazed eyes for a curious moment as Morvelving stole Penalty and Nippi's pack from Keissus's back. Morvelving couldn't risk retrieving his pack, which was on Keissus's flank. It was fortunate Morvelving's belt and his father's dagger were strapped to Penalty's sheath, but their food and his salve were lost.

Unable to hinder Morvelving, Keissus cried out in frustration and pain as he defended himself against the human.

Morvelving jumped back from Keissus, who had fended off the human enough to turn and strike at him in vain. He hurried back to Nippi.

Dae of Acraces, the god of war, darted like red fireflies through the fighting and toward the city of Ugris to feast on the misery and violence.

Nippi flinched when a centaur cut off a man's head. Morvelving quickly got her attention. *"We can't stay here. Hold my hand."*

Her small hand pinched his blood-soaked palm. Morvelving quickly removed Penalty from its harness, tied his belt, and shouldered Nippi's pack. The battle had moved on to the city. Morvelving encouraged Nippi to move, tugging her arm. She was fixated on the war.

"You won't get away," Keissus croaked. Morvelving spared the centaur a glance. He had killed the human, but the man's sword had cleaved into his right shoulder. Death was stealing the life from his eyes.

Furious that his one mistake had led to him being part of all the death that day, Morvelving didn't wait for Keissus to take his last breath, however much he wanted to. He needed to get Nippi out of a land being attacked and plundered.

14

Spending no more thought on the war behind him, Morvelving hurried Nippi eastward, away from the city of Ugris. Morvelving kept the menhir behind and the hill in front to cover their retreat as long as he could. The fields on either side of the road they had traveled were trampled. Wailing like cursed spirits made Morvelving look back. From his vantage, he could see the dark wave of the Grece host approaching the city. Already, smoke rose in the distance, centaur warbands raiding the outlying villages.

He directed Nippi toward a basin that a small river had carved into the land, further deepened by irrigation. Keissus knew he and Nippi had escaped, but he was dead. The real danger was the surrounding raiders who sought to plunder and kill. They needed to leave unnoticed. Morvelving heard the company of centaurs before he saw them and crouched low to hide in the basin with Nippi. The company passed, rushing to a small village in the south. He tapped Nippi's shoulder for her to keep moving.

Morvelving had been in unfortunate, wartorn lands before. The people who worked on the land were the first to be harmed, their homes burned and their folk butchered. Armies often fought to starve each other, and when cities were plundered, all those within either were murdered or taken as slaves. No distinctions were made for those caught in the middle; war only knew prey and predators.

The Eugratians knew this. Morvelving caught glimpses of bands of humans running to cover. They knew their best chance was to wait till the blood ran cold. When the fighting was done, they could hopefully return to their lives under the victor. Morvelving knew the Roxanar would rule. Idanphyrus had planned well, with the Eugratian king likely dead and the city besieged on the same day. No help would arrive soon enough. No other stronger city-state, like Lesgos, could arrive to take advantage of the chaos.

Morvelving let go of Nippi's hand so she could navigate the rocks lining another small stream and tucked Penalty under his arm. He uncovered and licked his wound, then wrapped the leather several times around his arm to stop further bleeding. Sunlight warmed his back, adding further weight to the risks he had taken. He had lost a lot of blood. Morvelving took two unsteady steps forward, his tongue hanging out of his mouth, panting. He caught up to Nippi once he found his stride. The short ravine was steadying out. Surveying the area, he saw no threats ahead. The air was rank with the dank smell of blood, and his ears twitched at each clang of bronze.

Ahead, the fields cut off, blocked by a line of forest. Across the land to the north and west, skirmishes between humans and centaurs raged. Homes were burning, the innocents fleeing or being slain. Ugris's walls were besieged. Already, smoke rose from within the walls. The sack had begun. Morvelving thought he saw a large human shield formation fighting its way out of the city, with centaurs swarming around it like locusts during harvest.

Morvelving sneezed at the horrendous conglomeration of smells, and his ears filled with the terror of it all. Idanphyrus was ambitious and had only brought more war to her people. Perhaps they wanted it. Maybe they desired to conquer before being conquered. He spat, disgusted, and rubbed at the pain in his chest for his part in it.

Nippi was watching him, concerned. If she was the Fates' tool, destined to bring about calamities, how could he stop them? Staring into those small eyes, which only showed compassion and fear, he began to doubt his conclusions. And what Idanphyrus had said continued to muddle his mind.

The way was clear. *"To the forest—go,"* Morvelving signed to her. The brave girl nodded and hurried ahead. She knew what was happening. Morvelving shadowed her, watching for anything. They made it to the forest. Only a few steps in, and he smelled them. He put his hand in front of Nippi.

She looked at him expectantly.

He smelled the fear and heard the gasping breaths, trying to stay quiet.

"We're passing through. Don't hinder us, and I won't harm you," Morvelving said to the humans hiding in the underbrush. The quick gasps and hushing told him they were hoping he would pass.

"Go straight ahead. There are people hiding," he signed to Nippi. *"Leave them be."*

"Can't we lead them away? I'm the best at sneaking."

Morvelving instinctively whimpered at her good heart. He shook his head and signed, *"They will follow if they want. But this is their home. Come on."*

Nippi hurried in front of Morvelving. He was tense, ready to hurry to her defense. From his height, he could see human faces peeking through the cover of bushes and shrubs. They watched him and Nippi enter their patch of the woods without a word. Nippi tripped over several people.

Hooves thundered from behind. Morvelving hissed under his breath and shoved Nippi to the ground, dropping next to her. His wound burning, he stole a glance behind. People around him flattened to the ground.

A troop of centaurs rode up to the shaded forest, their bronze armor and weapons darkened with blood. Morvelving held his breath. Had they seen him and Nippi enter? He could smell their hot breath, lusting for death. They spoke in their own tongue, pointed north.

A baby wailed. The centaurs halted and shouted, pointing their weapons deeper into the forest. A chord of terror rippled through the woods. People ran screaming, the men behind their loved ones. A desperate few charged the centaurs armed with farming tools. Without mercy, the centaurs swiftly cut them down.

"Telunian, no," Morvelving pleaded in vain.

The centaurs rushed forward, let their arrows fly, and began slashing with their swords. More deadly and swift than any human on a horse, they cut down man, woman, and child. Trampled the fallen and alive indiscriminately.

Morvelving grabbed Nippi's arm with his left hand and hefted Penalty in his right. His limbs felt weak, with fear accompanying the pain from his wound. Gods above, why had he taken piphlid?

Centaurs rode through, killing, their eyes bright and faces distorted in mad grins. He couldn't defend these people and live. Nippi's life was dearer to him. But he wouldn't simply flee without doing something. Panic and fear moved him into precise action. Morvelving barked three times, yielding his Eifgald. Sudden and sharp, Morvelving's barks, dipped in his power, made the centaurs and humans pause for a moment.

"Use the trees to evade them! They are weak from above! Run!"

Morvelving shouted and howled his war cry. The howl sent the humans fleeing with greater fervor and made the centaurs waver. It also made them recognize him and Nippi. He picked Nippi up and ran, using the trees to evade any arrows and charging centaurs. There was no doubt in his mind—the centaur warriors were out for blood. Whose blood didn't matter.

Amid the screams and dying, hooves hurried after him. Morvelving put his back to a large oak. A centaur came around, swinging his sword at Morvelving's throat as he pivoted. Morvelving blocked the blade with Penalty and swung a rising cut, Penalty's longer blade cutting off the centaur's arm. Blood gushed forth, darkening the green foliage. Morvelving drove Penalty's point into the centaur's throat. Blood sputtered and evaporated on the blade's glowing runes like water on coals.

Morvelving hurried forward. A woman holding her child ran past, an arrow shaft protruding from the child's skull. Morvelving weaved around a centaur, who was trampling a screaming man while skewering another with his spear. Several people collided with him, making everyone stumble. They cursed and screamed. An arrow shaft whizzed across Morvelving's path. He spared a glance down at Nippi. She was unhurt and clinging to him. Vomit ran down his side near her mouth.

A woman ran into Morvelving. He spun around from the impact to see a centaur aiming his spear at him. Morvelving leaped to the side, tripped over a corpse, and tumbled into the underbrush. Nippi grunted painfully. He lost her.

Panic overwhelmed Morvelving—he sprang to his feet. The forest was a storm of slaughter. Red blood, black stains, brown bark, and green ferns. White. Nippi looked up, eyes wet with fear. Seeing him, she ran toward him. A centaur spotted her too, his glazed eyes wide and teeth bared in mad bloodlust.

Morvelving growled. He had to reach Nippi before the centaur. Had to. Now there were two. Two people ran into him. Morvelving shoved them aside. His jaw ached from his fangs grinding together as every fiber of his body exerted forward. Three centaurs now. They saw him and saw a challenger. Morvelving grabbed Nippi. She cried out as he threw her to the ground against a tree, out of the way. *Telunian, please,* he begged before meeting the centaurs' charge.

Morvelving crouched to dodge the first centaur's swinging sword. Penalty carved through the centaur's front legs. The disoriented and screaming centaur crashed into him. Morvelving's fangs sank into flesh, his claws screeched against bronze.

He stood in time to see the second centaur thrust his spear at him. Morvelving diverted the spearhead with Penalty and countered with his own thrust. Penalty's point, then its blade, divided flesh and bone, and Morvelving slipped in the bloody mud.

When he scrambled to his feet, he found two centaurs dead, and the third was screeching like a hawk as he collided with Morvelving.

Morvelving's breath left his chest when he hit the ground. A force struck his breast, and the centaur's hoof pinned his arm holding Penalty. He grabbed his dagger in time to stop the centaur's blade from cutting his throat. Morvelving growled when the hook at the end of the curved blade cut his snout. He kicked and clawed at the centaur's underbelly. The centaur hissed, moving away and kicking his hind legs at Morvelving.

He tried to evade—one hoof hit his chest. Penalty left his hand just as the air left his lungs from the impact. Morvelving hit the ground again.

Shaking the lights from his eyes, Morvelving clutched his father's dagger and began to stand. The centaur came at him again. Weakened from blood loss and the kick to his chest, Morvelving tripped over a corpse and barely blocked the centaur's sword with his dagger. He couldn't do anything except try to roll out of the way of its kicking hind legs. A blow to his shoulder forced him onto his back.

The centaur was above him, sword swinging for Morvelving's throat. He barely blocked the attack with his dagger, the strike missing him by an inch, and kicked himself away to keep the centaur from stomping him to death. Blood filled his mouth as he bit his own tongue, straining to stay alive. Nippi cried out, but he couldn't see why as the centaur's free forehoof pinned him to the ground. Morvelving saw the triumph in the centaur's sharp grin as he fought to free himself and live.

A tremor reverberated through the ground and into Morvelving. His breath caught. The centaur halted, scowling in confusion. The leaves of the forest shuddered and shook as if a storm were suddenly upon them, yet there was no wind. The air smelled burnt from the magic at work. A deep roar filled his ears like the earth itself was moaning. The sound transitioned into a high-pitched screech.

Both Morvelving and the centaur covered their ears, but the wailing seeped into his very bones, making him writhe and cry out in pain. The earth shook and shuddered—began to move under his back.

Then the centaur was no longer above him. A Stag rammed into the centaur, silver tines stabbing into his torso and gut, sending him to the ground. By the Stag's scars, Morvelving recognized it as *the* Stag that had approached Nippi. The centaur groaned and cried, cursing and sputtering in pain as the Stag raised its head. The centaur's blood shone bright red on the silver rack. The Stag's gold eyes were brimming with blood, and Morvelving noticed its old wounds were bleeding again, the fur matted.

Drudan's Herald roared again, tears of blood dripping from its eyes, nose, and mouth. The earth shook, and the trees swayed. Morvelving covered his ears again and cried out from the painful noise piercing his skull. Through blurry vision, he saw Nippi. She was standing, her back to a tree, one hand braced against it, as she watched the Stag in wonderment, evidently unaffected by the Stag's mighty display of Ergald and Eifgald.

All the remaining centaurs and humans fled in a pained frenzy, hands on their ears, bewildered and terrified. The Stag ended its roar with a heavy snort, shaking its head and body, light shimmering off its black coat.

Morvelving scrambled to Nippi. *"Are you hurt?"* He checked her for wounds. The blood on her wasn't her own, and her vomit would wash off. *"You're not hurt. I'm so sorry, Nippi. We're safe now."*

She absent-mindedly nodded and took his hand. Morvelving sniffed back his tears. She was in shock. This was his fault. The noise of conflict reached his ears, reminding Morvelving that they were not wholly safe.

The Stag approached them, sniffing each in turn. It began to walk eastward up the slope toward the Ykris Mountains. Morvelving realized the Stag wanted them to follow. He scooped Nippi up, then found his father's dagger and Penalty. Morvelving followed the Stag. Drudan's Herald must have been following them. Its purpose was hidden, but one thing he was certain of: the Fates—and now Drudan, even in her slumber—had their footprints in the sands of Nippi's destiny. And they relied on his stupidity.

Once they were out of the Eugra Valley, Morvelving set Nippi down. The Stag began to forage, still staying with them, still leading them. Nippi paid no mind to the pine needles that covered the ground, the blood on her hands, or the dribble of vomit on her chin. Her eyes were wet, and tear streaks lined her dusty face.

Morvelving whimpered. Hating himself would come later. He stared at his fingers to force them to relax around Penalty's hilt, then set the sword on the ground.

Morvelving poured water over her hands, cleaned her face with the fur on the back of his hand. Thankful he had been able to reclaim her pack, which still held her bow and a few useful items, like the waterskin and rations.

"Here, rinse your mouth." Morvelving offered her the waterskin. Nippi took a drink, swooshed it, and spat, all without blinking. He let her cling to the waterskin. Wishing he had an elixir or ale, he rummaged through the small pack for something to soothe her. He wrapped her blanket around her shoulders.

Morvelving surveyed the towering rock structures that rose from the ground like spearheads. The Ykris Mountains were a long ridge of layered rock that jutted out of the earth at an angle, with some cliffs pushing up almost vertically. There was no sign of life.

When he looked back at Nippi, she let the blanket fall from her shoulders as she handed the waterskin back. Her face was skewed, as if she were in deep thought.

"I thought I was back in my igloo when the Qilatuuga attacked, killing and taking. I barfed." She paused before continuing. *"I–I thought the centaur was going to kill you like the Qilatuuga killed my—"* Nippi shuddered and wiped new tears from her eyes.

Morvelving took a deep breath and sat down next to Nippi, putting his arm around her. He didn't know what to say. His stomach twisted at the pain he had caused her, and he vowed to burn any piphlid he stumbled upon.

Morvelving watched Nippi rub her hands and said, *"It's good you made friends with the Stag."*

The child smiled and glanced over at the Stag, who was watching them patiently. *"How can I thank him?"*

"By telling him, I think."

Nippi approached the Stag. She bowed and signed, *"Thank you for saving my Fluff and me."*

Morvelving chuckled, releasing the stress. While Nippi interacted with the Stag, he checked his wounds, licked the deep cut on his arm, and found a cloth in Nippi's pack that worked as a bandage. The natural healing of his people would have to be enough for now. If he was right and the Stag was leading them northeast across the River Ykris and the Ykris Mountain range, he would be able to find ingredients for a salve along the way.

The Stag allowed Nippi to pat its flank, then moved further up the rocky path. Morvelving understood: they needed to distance themselves from any centaur patrols. He gathered their things and hurried Nippi along, painfully aware that she was still in shock from the day's events—and that he was to blame.

15

Morvelving let the Stag lead Nippi and him northward on paths that critters of the wild had created along the western ridge of the Ykris Mountains. Both found a meager amount of calm. Morvelving mended his wounds, foraged the ingredients for his healing salve, and hunted the abundant game in the high mountain valleys. Each simple task in the daylight kept his mind off the events of the past days, but sleep avoided him. That first night, he stared without seeing as his mind lingered on his impulsive decision to take piphlid. That one mistake had led to the plunder of a city and had nearly killed both Nippi and him.

The next morning, the child remained quiet and docile. Morvelving didn't know what to do until he noticed her watching him practice with Penalty to get his mind off his mistakes. At his prompting, she picked up her bow and started practicing. They were one day from the plunder of Ugris, and Nippi was being her usual self. Either human children were more resilient than he could imagine, or she hid her feelings. He wondered, not for the first time, if she didn't trust him anymore.

He caught the Stag's golden eyes on him.

Nippi skipped in front of Morvelving and waved at the Stag. Drudan's Herald slowly blinked and began to scrape its crown against fir trees. Now that the Stag was evidently taking a break from their trek, Morvelving hoped to gain answers.

"Herald, did Drudan send you to us? Has the Goddess of Ervi awakened?" Morvelving scowled as the Stag continued to ignore him. He tried in his native tongue, as his ancestors and the Wiseneyes had communicated with the Stags millennia ago. Still, the Stag didn't even acknowledge him. Morvelving glanced down at Nippi, who was watching him, and shook his head.

"The Stag doesn't want to talk?" Nippi used a fir tree to scratch her back, mimicking the Stag.

"Either he won't or can't." Morvelving ran his claws behind his ear. *"In the Lay of Ivalin, Drudan's Herald followed Ivalin for three days as he told Ivalin the mysteries of the world."*

"So Goldeye doesn't speak?" Nippi shrugged. *"Neither can I. Maybe that's why he helped us."*

"Huh." Morvelving couldn't argue with that.

The Stag's crown scraped long strands of bark off the tree, each of its movements more aggressive than the last. Morvelving tried to catch the Stag's scent and discover what it was trying to accomplish. An audible snap made him flinch. One of the silver tines hit the carpet of pine needles at the base of the tree.

"Goldeye broke his antler," Nippi signed up at him.

Morvelving recognized what the Stag was doing now. *"It isn't a natural break. There is more magic at work here. Watch."*

Nippi waited as the Stag nudged and kicked the silver tine until it was before Nippi's feet. She gasped. *"Is it for me?"*

"Yes." Morvelving smiled.

Nippi picked up the tine and held it close to her chest. *"What do I do with it?"*

"You keep it," Morvelving laughed. *"It's a gift. A rare and valuable gift. Stag tines can be used for many things. They are stronger than bronze. The*

shape of this one will be a perfect dagger for you."

Nippi gazed upon her gift in wonderment.

Morvelving knelt to her eye level. *"This is a tool, like your bow. Do you understand? The tine didn't break naturally, Goldeye made it happen. You are meant to have this gift."*

Nippi nodded with confidence and tucked the tine behind her belt. Morvelving chuckled. The Stag was watching them.

"Thank you." Morvelving signed to Goldeye. *"I was loath to give her such a tool, but the last several days have proved that I was too confident in my ability to keep her out of harm's way. She, unfortunately, may need it."*

The Stag snorted. A scent like resolve emanated from the Stag as it began to make its way north down the sloping woods. Departing after imparting a gift was a common ritual for Drudan's Heralds. Morvelving rested his hand on Nippi's shoulder to stop her from following.

"Where is Goldeye going? Shouldn't we follow?"

Morvelving faced Nippi so she could see his hand signs. *"I don't know. In a way, Goldeye is still the servant of Drudan and must go where her will directs him."*

"I thought he would travel with us."

Morvelving grunted. *"We may see him again."*

Humans had a wide range of facial expressions he was still learning. He currently found Nippi's face unreadable. Her gaze shifted between the tine at her waist and the Stag. He noticed her fingers twitch and found her breathing to be steady.

Seeing her deal with a possible hurt so soon after their escape from the Roxanar made his chest ache. He hurt for her. The Fates were monsters to make their designs around one child. He lifted a prayer in his mind to Drudan, thanking the Goddess for having the Stag find Nippi. The Dae of the Night had mentioned that the Fates and gods had set their gaze upon Nippi. It was odd to him that the only god to intervene had been the one dormant and no longer worshipped. He wished the child didn't have to part with her new friend so soon. Now he waited to see how significant the Stag was to her.

Nippi turned back to him. *"Where will he go?"*

Morvelving sighed. *"To remain in the wilds. Humans have forgotten to respect the old heralds of many gods and hunt them for their hides and tines, so he may be hiding. We should continue."*

"It makes me sad. His Goddess is gone. We don't have families; we should stick together."

Morvelving's eyes stung as he sniffed and whined, amazed at her heart. *"I am sad as well, and we should stay together."*

Nippi extended her arms up for him to pick her up and hold her. Morvelving obliged, carrying her along with her knapsack, and continued to walk. Nippi kept her face buried where his neck met his shoulders.

Morvelving hummed a tune his mother had sung when he'd been distraught. Although lacking lyrics, it was titled "The Soul of the Wind." It had worked to calm him; he hoped, through the vibrations of his throat and chest, it would help calm Nippi.

She began to stroke his fur. Annoying as it was, Morvelving endured it. Perhaps she was doing it for her own comfort. Her words hung in the forefront of his mind—*we don't have families*. He felt sudden fear. Was that what he was to her now? He had taken her under his wing. Wynthrim had said that to redeem himself, he would have to face the responsibility.

Morvelving was walking a fine line. The Phoithesens were after Nippi, and she had found herself amid two warring nations that would have killed them both. He scratched the scabbing cut on his snout and rolled his shoulders, uncomfortable. Why was he surprised?

After a while, Morvelving's arm grew tired, and he put Nippi down. She wrinkled her nose and rubbed the sleepiness from her eyes. Nippi looked back several times at the wooded path behind them.

Gray clouds hid the blue sky above the trees' red leaves. The land along the shores of the Fryst Sea and the northern arm of the Ykris Mountains was difficult to navigate. Morvelving found their way east through cold gorges and ravines that baked in the afternoon sun after the eclipse passed. Cold wind from the sea tickled his tongue. On a ridge, they were able to see the Idospont, a small strip of land connecting the Land of the Idosse to the seemingly endless mainland. The Fryst Sea to Morvelving's left glistened sharp and silver, and the Idryiva Sea to the right hugged the lands' crook like a blanket of sapphire. Flocks of seabirds harried the rocky coasts. To the south, the city of Thressea surrounded its harbor, its painted stone and marble barely visible, its farms built into the fells of the Ykris Mountains.

A breathtaking view, but Morvelving had hoped not to see this land again for a century at least.

After they climbed down the ridge into a ravine with forested cliffs on either side, Nippi turned to Morvelving. *"Did you make that big stone fall behind the centaurs?"*

Morvelving stalled his steps for a moment in thought. Her curiosity about Ergald was natural but worrisome. He had told her he wouldn't use it, but then he had. He couldn't hide his contradictions. *"Yes."*

"How? I didn't see you draw the Runic Ring."

"I did." Morvelving showed her his arm. The wound was healed, but where he had traced the Runic Ring on his arm, the fur was burned away.

Nippi was amused. *"You're sneaky!"*

Wanting to make sure she understood and wouldn't try it without guidance, Morvelving waved for her to stop and watch. *"I took a risk to*

make a distraction and start what was going to happen, but by doing so, I
weakened myself. You understand?"

The child nodded.

"Ergald is dangerous, remember? I had to practice it for many years before I
could gauge how much of my own blood was required to summon enough Ergald
for each task. And the Runic Ring isn't the key. It is the focus. Expert casters
don't have to draw the Runic Ring."

"Like the Stag!" Nippi signed, face alight. *"It used Ergald! I knew it. I*
felt it."

Morvelving nodded. *"Yes, the Stag is a being created by Drudan, who is*
the one who nurtures the flow of Ergald within the earth. What the Stag did was
a feat of power not seen for millennia. It took a toll on the Stag though."

Saddened again, Nippi seemed to understand. *"That's why it went*
away—it's more like an animal now?"

"Perhaps." Morvelving lifted her chin. *"Or it had another Nippi to save*
somewhere."

"What? There's only one of me!"

Morvelving chuckled. *"Thank the gods."*

That earned him a slap on the wrist. He ran from her second
attempt, Nippi's throaty laugh chasing him. Persistent, she didn't stop
chasing Morvelving till he let her catch him. Out of breath, Nippi leaned
against a moss-covered boulder.

A distant horn call made his tapered ears swivel. Morvelving quickly
surveyed the ridge to the north and south. He couldn't see anything, but
he could hear the baying of hounds and cries of men. A hunt was
underway.

Birds fluttered from their hiding places along the northern cliff. The
wind blew from the right direction for Morvelving to catch the scent.
Men, dogs, horses, and . . .

Movement drew his eyes along the ridge. Dark shapes in the shade of trees, distinctively a human and a hound. Further ahead, he caught a scent that surprised him—it was the Stag. Morvelving couldn't believe it. The Stag's scent suddenly made sense now—it had known. That was why it had left them. He stole a glance down at Nippi. The child had followed his gaze, and by her hands on her mouth in shocked worry, he knew she had spotted the Stag.

They both watched as the hunters surrounded Goldeye. Not even Morvelving could see all the action, but the Stag stumbled on the edge of the ridge and fell. Morvelving reached for Nippi.

Nippi took off running before he could reach her. Morvelving called after her blindly. He quickly caught up to her. There was no path, so he led her to the fallen Stag through heavy brush and around jagged rocks.

In the depths of the ravine, the light of the day was already dimming as they made their way to the Stag. Morvelving heard the baying of hounds and human commands quieting. Hoping they had given up on their quarry, he helped Nippi over a fallen tree. Nippi's face was stark determination. She felt no need to stop and converse. Morvelving was proud of her. He would have chosen to leave the Stag and move on to avoid entanglement with the hunters. Her childlike focus drove him along with her, and it was the right thing to do.

Morvelving sniffed out the Stag's direction and then diverted into the rocky woods of the gorge, following the growing scent of death, which made him whine, knowing what awaited Nippi. Already, scavenger raptors began circling in the sky. In the distance, he heard the calls of wild dogs. They would leave Nippi and him alone once they picked up Morvelving's scent.

Nippi followed his every step. For the steep slopes, she climbed onto his back. A river ran through the gorge. The mist from its torrents was cool and besprinkled his fur. It interrupted their path toward the scent of the Stag. They were on a rock that hung over the river. The drop to the opposite rocky bank could prove fatal for Nippi.

Morvelving tapped Nippi on the shoulder to get her attention. *"I will jump down, then catch you."*

She nodded, sure and trusting.

Morvelving threw his pack down, tightened the bindings holding Penalty, and jumped. An easy distance for him, he landed firmly. He turned and waved for Nippi to jump down. After a brief hesitation, she did. He caught her without missing a beat.

Deep in the gorge, the air was cool. Heavy moss adorned the trees. Morvelving and Nippi were soaked by the time they found the Stag.

Morvelving whined to accompany the ache in his chest. The smell accosted his nostrils—of death, of hardship unrewarded. Where was Drudan that she would let her faithful heralds dwindle and perish in agony? The Stag lay on its back. Broken arrow shafts protruded from its side and rear haunches. Its legs pointed to the sky, and one of them was broken. The bone, stark white next to the red flesh and black fur, stuck out like a branch from a tree.

A large raven with a small crown of gray feathers was perched above the Stag. It cawed, "A thread for the Crones."

Morvelving watched the raven fly away.

The Fates watched through raven eyes. He shook a cold shiver from his skin. What the Stag had done had clearly upset the Fates' scheme. Morvelving turned his attention to Nippi and regretted his distraction.

Nippi was on her knees crying, a silent sob.

He hurried and knelt next to her, discarding his pack and sword.

As soon as she noticed him, she dove into his embrace. Morvelving resisted the instinct to lick her head as he had done with Windtail when he'd been upset. She couldn't know the omen—to have a goddess's herald save them in their dire need only to see it dead after a horrible hunt. His hate for the Fates grew, that they would torment this child.

Perhaps letting Nippi come here had been a mistake, yet he knew she was too stubborn for him to stop her from coming. He owed it to the Stag for saving his life to honor it in death. His claws dug into his pawed palms at the thought. He hoped. Telunian, let it be so: that the Fates would be satisfied with one life and leave them alone.

Nippi sniffled and moved from Morvelving's embrace. He ignored the wet spot on his tunic.

"Can we stay and bury the Stag?" she asked.

Morvelving swelled with pride. *"That is exactly what we should do. Go—"*

A branch snapped in the woods. Morvelving stood in an instant. The hunters were closer than he'd realized.

Nippi followed suit when she saw him looking around inquisitively.

He sought the precise direction of the noise. Sure enough, several hunters were making their way through the forest and the broken rocks of the gorge.

By scent and sight, they were Thresseans. Their purple and orange tunics marked them as nobles of the city as well. They noticed him now. Morvelving took a deep breath. He should have prepared, knowing the hunters would seek their prey.

He signed to Nippi, *"Stay behind me. The hunters are here. I will talk to them."*

Her eyes conveyed understanding and anger. Morvelving grunted, concerned. He gave her a calming gesture and hurried to his pack and sword in two strides before returning to stand in front of Nippi.

She moved to his side. He showed his displeasure with trembling lips, but she wasn't looking. She was staring at the approaching hunters.

The entourage was now closing in. There were ten men and women, five servants keeping the hounds in check, and a leader in front. Including the leader, five were armed, two with spears—the bronze heads dully reflecting the shadows—and one with a bow. Each of the five had Idosse short swords at their sides with their signature forward-curving blades. Morvelving had seen those blades break through helmets and chop shields apart.

The leader, a broad-shouldered man with a dark beard that lined his jaw and matched his heavy curls, raised his hand to halt his entourage. His tunic was yellow threaded, and he wore gold bracelets with spinel and iolite. Leopard skin hung over his left shoulder and tucked into his belt. He eyed them both suspiciously and with a scent of curiosity and annoyance. He regarded Morvelving with a smugness reserved for men who had lived their whole lives with others serving them.

"Aeputer's gaze upon you," Morvelving greeted them. He kept Penalty wrapped as he held it by the blade above the hand guard, hoping to show he didn't want to fight. The feeling in his gut made his hackles rise.

"And upon you," said the leader, frowning. "I am Leolicides, son of Alkithides, who rules these lands."

Leolicides's four armed followers fanned out in a semicircle behind him. Morvelving guessed them to be his companions. Nobles in the Idosse city-states had a band of close friends or lovers who were elite warriors that protected the royal families. Each one was fair-faced, young, and strong like Leolicides—boys and girls no longer. The two companions with spears carried them with deftness and certainty. Each had her hair tightly braided to her scalp and wore a well-fitted cuirass made of hardened leather and linen. Their muscled arms bore several pink scars that ran the length of each. One met Morvelving's gaze with unease. One man held an intricate recurve bow with an arrow notched. They were all warriors, more than hunters. If it became a fight, Morvelving would be hard-pressed, and he didn't want to take another risk. He moved his left hand from his dagger to hide his growing anxiety.

"I must say, Mulranei"—Prince Leolicides leaned heavily on his left leg—"I'm confused as to why you are here." His face didn't portray his hostility—his scent did. The hounds paced and whined, tugging at their leashes, the servants struggling to restrain them.

Morvelving sighed deeply. The Fates were clearly watching with sick glee. "My ward and I saw our friend, the Stag, fall. We've come to bury Drudan's Herald."

Leolicides glanced at his companions, laughing. "The fall of your 'friend' is the result of my hunt. I had thought we had lost it two days ago when its trail over the Ykris Mountains ran cold. We found it again, praise Aeputer."

"The Stag helped us escape the war between the Eugratians and Roxanar," Morvelving said, hoping the prince was willing to listen, even if he sought profit for himself. Would he change his mind? Unlike the Roxanar, Morvelving might convince the prince to let the Stag rest.

Morvelving eyed each of the companions. They were all tense like a branch snare, ready to snap at the slightest touch. A conflict wouldn't work well for him, especially if he killed or injured the prince or his companions. Morvelving would have another city after him. Once again, he regretted being among the Idosse. Ever since taking Nippi under his care, every one of his actions had played into the Fates' will. He held back the growing sense of helplessness in his chest and replaced it with angry determination.

"Fascinating tale. If I were sitting near my father's hearth with wine in hand, I would laugh and applaud your Dae-tale." Leolicides picked at his fingernail. "Unfortunately, we are not, and I have been in the wilds and am unable to confirm if you speak true. Now, step aside. I mean to claim my kill, as is my right by the laws of my father. Stags are royal game."

Morvelving placed his hand on Nippi's shoulder, sensing her agitation. She jumped slightly at his touch, fixated solely on the prince's words.

Morvelving looked back at the Thresseans and spoke. "The Stag was killed by the fall, not your spear. You and your companions broke the Hunter Pact between Osideyos and Medithera. Besides, the Stag is Drudan's Herald. To hunt such a servant is an offense greater than the Hunter Pact, and the Stag saved my life. It is my duty to give the Stag a proper burial."

"This is absurd," Leolicides scoffed. "Our arrows protrude from its body, and it is known the Goddess Drudan slumbers. Her worshippers scattered to self-sacrifice, and her heralds wander the wild, aimless and mindless." He looked to his companions for assurance, which they gave eagerly. "The rituals of the hunt we adhere to as our forefathers have done. You're intruding on the very laws you proclaim I've broken. I have listened only out of respect for your kind, Mulranei. Yet I ask you to leave now."

Morvelving tilted his head. He gave a quick glance at Nippi; she was staring keenly at the prince, hand on the piece of the Stag's antler.

"I hear your reason and smell your impatience," Morvelving said while giving Nippi a slight squeeze on the shoulder. "I have been through Thressea before. Your father's law states that none shall hunt a Stag. I have not, and neither have you. I adhere to the gods' will, and they have willed that a hunted kill shall not be left. If it is, the hunter has forfeited it and their success as a hunter. I advise you: return to your city and make sacrifices to Medithera and Drudan to placate her displeasure." Leolicides scowled deeply. Morvelving continued. "I will bury my friend."

Shaking his head, Leolicides groaned in frustration and said, "I shall be the one to interpret my father's will, Mulranei. Now, I command you: be on your way."

"Prince Leolicides, I intend to bury my friend."

Leolicides threw up an exasperated hand. "I will bury it after! Your kind does not rule here. Now go, before I force you to."

Wholly aware the prince meant to remove the Stag's precious crown and leave the rest to decay, Morvelving said, "Don't be foolish. Fighting me will not end well." His words were clear and loud enough that some birds flew away from their hiding place.

"Is that a threat, dog?"

Morvelving curled his lips at the insult and spoke calmly and clearly. "A caution, I—" He didn't finish his sentence. Nippi was evidently none too pleased with what Leolicides had to say. She stepped forward, the Stag antler in hand, and growled from her throat.

Neither the prince nor his companions cared for Nippi's threat. One even sniggered. Leolicides wasn't laughing. His eyes were on the antler. He looked up and pointed at Morvelving. "You hypocrite! How much of the tine are you keeping for yourself?"

"Peace," Morvelving said hurriedly while stepping past Nippi and giving her a quick hand sign to be still. He held Penalty by its handle now, the cover loosened by his grip. Half a glowing rune shone, a thin wisp dissipating from the surface. "That piece was broken off on its fa—"

Leolicides spat at Morvelving's pawed feet, drawing his sword. The two companions with spears lowered them, and the one with a bow drew it. "You are a liar and a hypocrite. Stand aside now and hand over the tine."

Morvelving took a deep breath, wishing he had his bronze cuirass. He signed to Nippi with his right hand for her to run back. He removed the hide cover from Penalty and took off his cloak. Each companion assessed the length of the rune-enchanted blade. Relief and anticipation pressed against his nerves; the centaurs had taken away his choice. The Fates continued to make all his choices play into their will. This one felt like his and Nippi's choice—to make sure their friend rested in peace.

Resolved for a fight, he set Penalty in a middle guard position, directing the blade's point at Leolicides, his hands tucked at the right side of his waist, his left leg forward, blade up to quickly displace a spear thrust. He flicked his right ear back to hear Nippi's steps. She was moving away. None of the companions were focusing on her. Good. His advantage was that he was sure they hadn't fought his kind before. The disadvantage was being outnumbered by four warriors and the prince.

The hounds began to chorus their challenges.

Morvelving snarled. The archer flinched, sweat glistening on his brow. He was the most inexperienced. Morvelving may not need to worry about him.

"Set the hounds on him!" Leolicides commanded. The servants were all too eager to release the beasts straining against their collars. The hounds bolted to surround and rip and tear their prey.

Morvelving barked three times, imbuing each exclamation with his Eifgald. The prince and his companions jumped back, and the hounds ran in a shrieking frenzy, tails tucked, followed by the servants.

Leolicides mouthed his disbelief, recovered from the outburst, and pointed his sword at Morvelving. "Kill the dog."

After a battle, Morvelving had overheard men in a tavern speak of how he had fought. Quick and precise for his height, with a speed no human could match, and fearless, fighting a flanking shield wall alone. It was indeed true, but not according to their expectations. He was faster and stronger than humans. The Moon Goddess had created his people to be that way. A small comfort when his life and Nippi's were on the line. He swallowed his fear.

A fighter must respect every opponent, as any could be their last. The companions may have trained to fight since they had been Nippi's age, younger even.

When Leolicides ordered his death, Morvelving moved with a snarl. He lunged at the archer, who yelped in surprise while raising his bow.

Morvelving slashed at the bow—he didn't have time to kill the man. The broken bow was enough for now. He kept moving past the archer, knocking him down. He parried a spear thrust aimed at his face.

The spear-woman had thrust too deep, allowing Morvelving to throw a cut at her. She realized her mistake and fell back, grunting when she hit the stony ground, trusting her sister companion to attack Morvelving.

Her trust was well-placed. Morvelving sidestepped another spear thrust and moved away from the cluster of his opponents. He felt the wind from a missed sword swing behind him. Morvelving turned in time to see the swordsman swing again, seeking to cut Morvelving from shoulder to waist. He brought Penalty up in time, catching the attacking sword where the blade met the handguard and aiming Penalty's point at his attacker. The man skewered himself on Penalty. He cried out, blood spluttering from his mouth, his face contorted in pain and surprise that his attack had failed.

Morvelving withdrew Penalty from the man's chest and defended himself against the two spear-women.

The archer and Leolicides moved to either side to block his escape.

Morvelving kept moving side to side, sword out, trying to deflect the thrusts that would hit him.

The spear-women were skilled. They attacked him separately and then together in tandem, all the while maintaining a distance from Morvelving's measure. They poked him twice: once into the meat of his shoulder, and the second a slice against his side.

He jumped back, barking. The pain was hot, and it sought to claim his focus.

"Finish him!" Leolicides yelled impatiently.

Morvelving ran to their right to get to better ground while watching for an opening.

They stayed together.

He growled, stalling their advance. He needed to separate them. They were approaching with caution.

Morvelving lunged toward Leolicides in a feint. He switched his feet, evading the spear thrusts, drew his dagger with his left hand, and threw it at the archer.

The man cried out in pain, looking down at the dagger protruding from his right breast.

When one spear-woman glanced at the dying archer, Morvelving lunged. He grabbed her spear and cut her down with one swing to her throat. Her head bounced twice on the stone, blood pooling.

The other wailed her battle cry at the loss of her companion. She lunged at him. Morvelving deflected her spear and grabbed it, pulling it away from her grip. He didn't have time to use it, for she drew her own sword and attacked. He yelped and snarled in surprise.

She came at him with a quick flurry of cuts driven by anger and vengeance, keeping close to him. He blocked the first two. Failed to see her feint on the third. He snarled as the blade cut the flesh of his arm.

Overconfident, she feinted once again. Morvelving caught her arm and, in the same motion, stabbed her with Penalty.

Morvelving let the spear-woman fall to the ground. He withdrew Penalty and looked around. The archer was still dying. Leolicides was out of sight. He flicked his ears, hearing a grunt and a growl.

He hurried over to the sound. Leolicides walked into the clearing, holding Nippi, sword to her throat.

16

Morvelving flared his fangs. Nippi held onto Leolicides's sword arm with one hand, her body rigid but her face displaying defiant anger.

"Settle, dog. Or I'll cut her throat," Leolicides commanded, grinning. Morvelving closed his lips, concealing his fangs.

"Drop your sword."

Morvelving let Penalty fall. Making a loud metallic clang as it hit the ground.

"Now," Leolicides said. "You're going to remove the Stag's crown and skin its hide. Do it, or I'll slit her throat right here."

While he was speaking, Nippi was signing with her hand at her side. *"I. Bite. Arm."*

"No," Morvelving signed back. His signs were upside-down, but he was confident she understood.

Nippi threw both arms up, grabbing hold of Leolicides's sword arm with her weight, and bit him.

"Ah! Aeputer's co—"

Morvelving sprang then, panic and instinct taking over, full tilt into Leolicides. His fangs sank into the soft flesh of the prince's throat, scraping off bone, breaking and tearing flesh. Morvelving pinned Leolicides to the rock wall, holding his sword arm down, and shook till there was an audible snap of bone. Leolicides's body became limp.

He released the prince and wiped his lips, licking the taste of blood from his mouth. Morvelving hurried over to Nippi. She was sitting down, holding her throat with one hand. His heart fell to the earth. He knelt and moved her hand. She only had a shallow cut. Morvelving breathed again. Only a thin line of red, so dark against her blue skin.

"Are you hurt?" he asked.

She shook her head and signed back, *"You meant 'no,' didn't you?"*

Morvelving laughed, a deep laugh, up from his chest to release the panic that boiled within him. *"Yes! Yes, I did. Don't worry, Nippi. You were incredibly brave. I am so glad you are safe,"* he signed quickly for her sake and to distract her from what had happened.

"I didn't want that prince to butcher Goldeye."

"Nor did I." His heart still pounded in his chest from how close he had been to losing her. His relief prevented him from being angry. *"It's over now."*

She gave an apologetic smile and dove at him, giving him a hug. He returned it, not caring if she got his blood on her. He would have to patch his wounds afterward.

After a long moment, Morvelving released Nippi and signed, *"We need to move away from here. Can you carry your pack and hold Penalty? I will carry Goldeye."*

Nippi nodded with enthusiasm. Morvelving wiped the blood from Penalty, wrapped the blade, claimed his dagger from the dead archer, and retrieved his cloak. He quickly applied the healing salve to his wounds, hissing at the stinging pain, and prepared himself for the exertion ahead.

The Stag was much heavier than he had imagined, and Morvelving regrettably had to drag it along the forest floor. He led Nippi until he found a patch of compacted earth where they could bury Goldeye.

Breathless from their trek, Morvelving told Nippi, *"Gather any stones you can carry. Make sure you draw your strength from your legs. I will prepare the body."*

Nippi stood straight, her fists clenched with determination as she looked around. She spotted one rock and began her work in earnest. There were many stones among the ferns and broken old trees that had fallen from the cliffs.

Setting his pack down and removing his cloak, Morvelving approached the corpse. He drew his black dagger, its bone handle wrapped in leather, feeling comfortable in his hand. The dagger belonged to his father and his father before him. It was crafted from metal Drudan had brought down from Celemith to help shape the foundations of Ervi. A time when Nameless still had a name. Morvelving found it fitting to use it to properly prepare Drudan's Herald to enter the Song of Life.

The dagger cut flesh easily, and Morvelving removed the arrows methodically. He placed them in a pile to burn later. Morvelving set the Stag's bone back into flesh when Nippi's back was turned. He found a place to dig a hole.

One of its antlers had broken off from its fall and lay before him. These antlers were the main reason the Stags were hunted, which made him more enraged—the Stag hadn't deserved an end like this. The prince's life of ease and luxury had made him devalue what was valuable.

Hand-paws and feet completely muddied, Morvelving finished his digging. He took hold of the Stag's thick fur and tugged. He pulled and pulled until it was within the hole. Morvelving positioned it in a more dignified posture, with its legs to the side and its nose facing up. Morvelving faced Nippi.

She was resting next to her formidable pile of rocks. Morvelving smiled at her. She merely wiped the sweat from her brow and continued. Morvelving put the dirt back in the hole, covering the Stag, and then went to assist Nippi.

Picking up a boulder as large as Nippi, Morvelving moved it to the burial site. Nippi watched as he set the stones around the dig site, and then she mirrored his actions.

They were joined in mind and purpose to right a wrong. It reminded Morvelving of a pack set on their task among the tribe. An instinct, a will to complete what was given. There was no thought to improve oneself but to complete a task. There was no enjoyment, only solemn purpose, which was its own reward. He had missed this sense of family and community.

Nippi made a grunting noise. *"Like an igloo in Frystgalen."*

Morvelving smiled. *"Yes, here. Climb there, I will hand them to you. We're almost done."*

Nippi climbed onto the stacked stones. Morvelving helped her find solid footing and began giving her the smaller rocks. He didn't need her help to finish, but he wanted her to be involved. In this way, they completed the burial mound quickly.

Nippi stood, taking deep breaths, and watched as Morvelving picked out an etching stone and used it to sketch elven hieroglyphs depicting the Stag's life. He hadn't taught Nippi elven hieroglyphs yet, something he would need to do. The knowledge not only empowered the individual but would also be beneficial as they traveled further east—the elves ruled many lands.

Morvelving could feel the eyes of the forest watching them. Whispers in the wind passed the word that a creature had been honored. He put his memory of the Stag into the hieroglyphs—his initial fear for

Nippi, then his calm at seeing it accept Nippi and save them from the centaurs, and the hallowed memory it had gifted to her—to gain a friend only to lose them. Had it sensed her life's story, the sadness and tragedy set by the Fates? Was it his own story it had sought? Had Drudan directed Goldeye to them to intervene against the Fates? No way of knowing now.

Nippi was sitting cross-legged, resting her chin on her hands, elbows propped on her knees. She glanced at him with a small, exhausted smile. In moments like these, he knew he had done right by the Moon Goddess and his people by taking her with him. He had failed Windtail, but he wouldn't fail Nippi. Wynthrim was right.

They sat together for a time in silence and meditation. Morvelving had attuned himself to his inner Eifgald. Nippi attempted to mimic him, at least his posture—legs crossed, back straight, and hands on knees, with eyes closed to focus on her breathing.

What they did was spiritually grounded in what they had just offered to the earth: the buried Stag. It would decompose, and its spirit would return to Drudan, unless the Goddess truly was dormant. Then it would linger till the next Rift.

Morvelving eyed the child when she sniffled. Once again, he was struck by how brazen Nippi was in the face of death. His eyes stung that someone so young and small contained so much loss.

She caught his eye. *"Do we need to go?"*

The forest was silent, and the sun was starting its descent. *"We can stay longer."*

"My people burn the dead," Nippi signed slowly. *"Amua said it lets their spirits free. Will Goldeye be free?"*

"I am certain."

"What do Mulranei do?"

Morvelving licked his lips. *"We begin the Vhinde, the Dance of the Dark Moon. A dance and song that send the spirit of the dead to reside with the Wardens of the Wild till the Rift."* His eyes fixed on the burial, warding off the vision of Windtail.

"Can we do that for Goldeye?" Nippi sat straight, eager.

Morvelving whined. *"No, unfortunately. The Vhinde needs the knowledge of those who knew Goldeye the best. Heart to heart. Among the Mulranei, it is a mother or sibling or . . . "* He couldn't sign it for fear of reminding himself.

"A father?" Nippi finished for him.

Morvelving nodded and quickly wiped the tears from his eyes. Not wanting her to press further and bring what he worked so hard to bury to the surface, Morvelving moved to stand.

Nippi placed her hand on his palm, stopping him. *"Was that why you were exiled from your tribe? For missing your son's Vhinde?"*

Morvelving's heart stopped a beat, vulnerable and in awe of her insight.

The child noticed his shock and quickly confessed. *"The night you ate that shroom, before the centaurs. You said a lot in your sleep. I'm sorry, I couldn't help but read your lips. You mentioned the Vhinde and Windtail."*

All was laid bare; she had even recognized the connection between the piphlid and his deep sleep. She understood the significance of his son and the Vhinde. Morvelving had a strong urge to run away. Instead, he eased back to sit, taking back control of himself.

"Yes." Morvelving took a shuddering breath. *"That was the final mistake. I couldn't bear to be seen with my shame and guilt. It was all my own fault."*

He waited for her to look at him in disgust and want nothing to do with him. It was everything he deserved. Nippi sniffled. A tear ran down her cheek, making a glistening path on her dusty skin.

"*I wish Goldeye never met me.*" The child faltered. "*Why did he have to help? Why didn't he stay with us? You've said the gods and Fates are watching. I thought that was supposed to be good. I don't understand.*"

Morvelving embraced Nippi as she cupped her face in her hands, sobbing. How selfish he had been to not see her questions weren't about him. She felt the weight of what she didn't understand. Morvelving didn't understand either. Why had the Fates chosen her for a path he couldn't see? Was it to punish him or her? The Fates were timeless, and he would turn to dust before deciphering the whims of the Fates and the gods as they played with mortals and immortals upon Ervi.

All he knew was that their intent was upon Nippi.

Nippi pushed away and viciously wiped her eyes and nose. Morvelving whined, not sure what to say.

"*Goldeye wanted to help,*" Morvelving began. "*I think he interceded by his own will. Stags are ancient creatures. He saw the touch of the Fates upon you or me and knew he had to help, and the Fates punished him for it. There are great forces at work upon the world—for forces of good can sometimes cause horrible things to happen, and forces of evil can sometimes bring good. Remember the Song of Life?*"

Nippi nodded. "*Yes, life turns to death that nourishes more life. The life isn't wrong and the death isn't evil—it only is.*"

"*I think he left us not to hurt you but to keep us out of harm's way.*"

"*He should have let us help him back,*" Nippi stated angrily.

"*It was Goldeye's choice,*" Morvelving signed slowly. "*Just as it was ours to defend his body for burial.*"

This seemed to satisfy Nippi. She wiped her nose again and stared at the burial mound. Morvelving's tall ears rose and fell as he watched her, worried for her.

He got her attention. *"Nippi, we can't do the whole Vhinde ceremony, but I will show you the dance. Would you like to learn it?"*

His plan to put her mind on continuing to honor the dead worked. She loved to dance, and he was happy to teach her. The Dance of the Dark Moon was sacred to his people. Morvelving didn't care if Nippi knew it. If the Fates needed to make her life miserable, he would do everything in his power to keep her safe and give her peace.

17

Morvelving gently placed the healing salve on Nippi's neck wound. She held still until he was done, smiling the entire time.

"That tickled," she said.

Morvelving laughed as he put the pouch of salve back in the small bag.

"Like this?" he signed and then tickled her neck. Twice in three days, they had found themselves in mortal danger. They deserved some lightheartedness.

She jumped back, squealing with laughter.

"No." She hurried ahead of him.

Morvelving looked back across the Idospont for any signs of pursuit. The waves of the Fryst and Idryiva Seas battered the coast's jagged rocks, pounding in his ears. From their new vantage point on the eastern cliffs of the Idospont, he could see the western end of the crossing. The air was unusually clear for the Idospont. He took a long breath; it was time to leave the Land of the Idosse behind. Thinking of all that had happened made him feel more tired than he was.

The salve was healing his wounds, forcing his body to work harder. He couldn't bring himself to leave the bodies of the prince and his companions near the Stag. So, he had carried them out of the ravine and given them small burials, marking the site with rune-carved stones to

name those buried there. The servants who ran would have to be fools
not to find it. King Alkithides would learn who had killed his son. Now
Morvelving would also have a bounty on his head, not just Nippi. The
Phoithesens, the Roxanar, and now the Thresseans were against them. At
least he had left the Makoidake Pella and Agrothicans on reasonable
terms.

He wanted to pass through the lands of Monbargar to avoid the
Fyrancean Desert to reach the remote land of Srel. Menici lands were
wide and open—it would take longer than eighteen days to cross them,
longer with their luck.

Morvelving took a heavy breath after cresting a steep hill. Nippi was
arguing with her windswept hair, stepping in his way twice before lying
face down on the ground, performing one of her "I give up" acts.
Morvelving snorted and surveyed the land to the east. Pines with
reddish-brown bark and green needles now dominated the landscape as far
as his eyes could see. The only features that broke the sea of green were the
Great Elven Road to the east and the Althek Mountains to the north, beyond
which lay the frozen land of Frystgalen. He had made this journey thrice
now in a decade. His pawed feet were sore from the thought.

The Great Elven Road was a dark line snaking through the land.
Spanning the known reaches of the continent of Bregalen, it was wide
enough for two wagons to cross simultaneously. The Mithvarn elves had
made it for the first wars against Nameless, allowing them to move their
armies faster across the land.

Nippi ran to the first menhir they had approached on this road and
traced her fingers over the elven hieroglyphs. The menhirs marked
distances along the length of the road. When she caught up to
Morvelving, she pretended she had to jump over the lines between the
paved stones. He marveled at her ability not to linger on the unfortunate

events of the previous days.

Nippi faced him, signing, *"Thank you for keeping the prince from Goldeye."*

Morvelving tilted his head and drew his left ear back. *"Why do you say that?"*

"How you were talking to them—I thought you were going to let them take him," she signed, then quickened her pace to get ahead of him again.

"I wasn't going to, but I wasn't planning to kill them before I had tried to reason with them," Morvelving answered. *"It is better to resolve differences through talking than through fighting. Remember when Sophokis told me to hand you over?"* She nodded. *"I didn't kill him. It should be the last resort."*

Nippi looked up at him. *"The centaurs didn't seem to believe that."*

"No." Morvelving bristled, still ashamed that his lax guard had led to their involvement in the centaurs' war.

"I don't think the prince was going to bury Goldeye after," Nippi said after a long moment. She kept switching her gaze from Morvelving to her feet, as the paved stones were uneven in places.

Morvelving kept his expression neutral. He was proud of her for assessing what had happened. What amused him, though, was how she had already made her conclusion.

He signed back to her, *"We can't know for certain, but it was clear he only wanted the crown. Goldeye deserved to be buried in peace for saving us. I sought to let the prince leave peacefully because of the risk he posed to you and me."*

Nippi stopped walking, her head tilted to the side. Morvelving had seen her do that before when she wanted to think about something. Windtail had done the same.

She ran to catch up to him and said excitedly, *"So you were going to fight if they started it? And you pushed them into it."*

Morvelving answered, *"I was, but you did that for me."* He wondered, not for the first time, whether they could have avoided the fight if Nippi hadn't shown them the tine.

Nippi nodded, as if satisfied. She became distracted by the sights nearby. Tall trees blocked the sun and fenced the road in. A few white clouds drifted leisurely across the blue sky. Morvelving could see the crown of a storm cloud far on the eastern horizon. He had hoped to avoid any more storms.

He noticed the smoke then. It barely registered among the trees, causing him almost to dismiss it. He didn't recall any villages so close to the Elven Road. They were near the border of the Menici kingdom of Adrea. It could be an Adrean patrol camp.

Morvelving looked back. The Idospont was a small strip of land, like a branch between two vast seas bridging the two landmasses. He sucked in his breath. Movement caught his eye. He squinted. A mounted band— had to be Thresseans—still far, but gaining.

He ran ahead of Nippi so she could see his hands. *"The Thresseans are following. Come, follow me."*

Nippi glanced behind briefly. Morvelving could hear her quick footfalls hurrying after him. He moved off the Elven Road. The forest was silent. He weaved around trees and bushes, checking periodically to see if Nippi was following his steps.

A murder of crows flew away from the branches above.

Morvelving swore under his breath. The rapid clatter of hooves was drawing nearer. Their pursuers must have spotted them and spurred their horses faster. Morvelving sought a place to hide. Finding none, he cursed under his breath and waved for Nippi to stop so he could pick her up.

With Nippi clinging to his left side, Morvelving ran through the woods, weaving around trees and bushes. He went deeper into the forest, away from the road, but mountainous rocky cliffs soon blocked their way. There was no immediate path to take or handholds to climb within reach.

Whatever lead he had gained ahead of the riders would be moot if he continued through the forest. He didn't know what manner of people had created the smoke, but he had to take a chance. If they were Menici, they may help Morvelving against the Thresseans. He couldn't hide for fear the Thresseans had seen where they had fled the road.

Decision made, Morvelving focused on sprinting toward the smoke.

To his dismay, the high cliffs sloped. Giant boulders had fallen among the forest, pushed from a storm. He saw no way to climb, the angles too sharp.

"Gods above," he hissed and signed to Nippi. *"Hang tight."*

The shouts of the Thresseans came to his ears.

Morvelving hurried to the Elven Road and glanced back. They were undoubtedly Thresseans. They had stopped, several riders dismounting and checking the forest where Morvelving had led Nippi off the road. Tall spears in hand and leopard skin on the saddles of their horses. Their helms were tall, with painted feathers and horsehair plumes. The king's own companions. He couldn't discern if any looked kingly before one spotted him and shouted.

Growling, Morvelving sprang onto the road and ran toward the smoke as fast as he could while holding Nippi. He could smell humans and roasting lamb.

The thunder of hooves became louder behind him.

Penalty's blade slapped his leg with each sprinting step, and Nippi pulled at his neck. He wasn't far from where the broken cliffs no longer blocked the forest paths. The riders were gaining. He could feel their spears aimed at his back.

The camp came into view. A large party of humans equipped for battle, and by their round bronze shields and spears, they were soldiers of Adrea. No doubt making a patrol along the borders of the kingdom. Already, many were pointing at Morvelving and gathering their weapons.

"Thresseans!" Morvelving shouted. "Thressean raiders!"

There was no way to know if the Adreans would help him. It was either try or die. The Adrean company formed up quickly and ran out toward Morvelving. Their shields reflected the gray shine of the overcast sky. Morvelving readied himself to evade their spears as he ran along their line toward the woods.

One man from behind their shield line waved his arm and shouted, "*Edu ve*, friend Mulranei! Get behind the line!"

Morvelving rushed past the two men who made way and pivoted to see the Thressean riders pulling their horses' reins and stopping ten feet from the Adrean men's spears.

"Halt in the name of King Obyrace of Adrea!" shouted the man who had waved at Morvelving.

"I am Paloticus, Companion of Alkithides, King of Thressea. That Mulranei has murdered the king's son. I demand—"

An Adrean made loud raspberries to the laughter of others. Morvelving took a step back, not wanting to be in another melee. These men laughed, but their scent and posture showed their stress and fear of a fight. There were over fifty Adreans, but few archers. The Thressean king's companions were warriors, if the prince's companions he fought were any comparison.

"*Edu ve*." The Adrean spokesman stepped forward, hands on hips. "You are in Adrean lands now, *ruequs imabo*. We do not heed the demands of your king."

Morvelving's brows rose at the insult. The Thressean, Paloticus, scowled and waved his hand at a younger companion to stop him from taking the bait.

"You understand King Alkithides will not take kindly to Adrea harboring fugitives and thwarting his justice."

"*Moni devu*, King Obyrace doesn't care what Alkithides takes kindly to or not. Now, *edu ve*, go! Or I'll let our arrows loose."

Across the Elven Road, more Adrean soldiers revealed themselves from the cover of the woods, their arrows notched and spears down. They must have been lying in wait before Morvelving arrived. It was now thirty Thresseans against a hundred Adreans.

Paloticus's deep scowl remained even as he spat at the Adrean commander's feet and pulled his horse around, giving Morvelving a sharp glance. The other companions followed.

The Adrean commander shouted in his native tongue. His men dispersed, a large group following the Thresseans. He eyed Morvelving.

"Thank you. I am in your debt," Morvelving said as he set Nippi down. She remained still, her eyes darting to the surrounding men. She held his hand tight. Morvelving understood why she was afraid. Once again, they were close to being in another fight so soon after escaping the last one.

The commander waved his hand dismissively. "*Edu ve*, Mulranei. We have no love for Thresseans here in Menici. Their crimes in the last war still burn hot. I must know, what are your intentions for entering Adrean lands?"

"Only to pass through to eastern lands. My ward and I have overstayed our welcome among the Idosse."

"Gods-damned Idosse."

Morvelving nodded. "I hope to pass through Sene. Is the town still there?"

The commander's eyes brightened. "Aye, *edu ve*, yes! Best for you to remain on the Great Elven Road. Landslides have blocked the roads through the mountains. Do not fear for the Thresseans. My company is going to follow them all the way to the Idospont to make sure those horse *imabo* don't slip by."

"I shall not forget your kindness."

The Adrean commander bowed from his waist. "The gods bless your journey and shit on Thressea, *moni devu*."

Morvelving thanked the commander again. The Adreans seemed to be in a hurry, for they cleaned up their camp and marched west. Not until they were out of sight did Nippi let go of Morvelving's hand. He raised a prayer of thanks to Telunian for their fortuitous escape from the Thresseans.

After midday, heavy clouds covered the sky, and heavy rain descended as Morvelving and Nippi continued east. There was no wind, so their cloaks kept them dry, though Nippi's puddle jumping caused her new trousers to get soaked.

They passed a northern road that led to the Althek Mountains. Morvelving wondered if Nippi recognized it as the way they had taken south from Frystgalen and whether she was thinking of home.

"Nippi," Morvelving signed. *"Do you miss your family?"*

Nippi nodded. *"It's hard to see them. I think about the Qilatuuga."*

"Do you wish vengeance on them?"

"Yes. No?" Nippi hesitated a moment. *"Amua said we must fight them, but I can't remember why. They cut out my tongue. Could I cut out all their tongues? I don't really want to. I don't want to go back to Frystgalen."*

Morvelving whined. *"I don't want to either. I am sorry for making you remember."*

"It is well." Nippi accepted the dried meat and fruit Morvelving handed her from their pack. *"Do you think about your family?"*

"Yes, but it pains me too." Even now, Morvelving felt Windtail falling.

"Who were they? What were they like?"

Morvelving steeled himself. *"My son, Windtail, and his mother, Wildriver. Windtail was much like you but timid. He would have played any game you wanted him to."*

Nippi smiled. *"Windtail is smart. Wildriver sounds intimidating."*

Wiping his brimming tears, Morvelving chuckled. *"Wildriver is a force of nature. A mighty huntress and the best dancer. She wouldn't let you get away with anything, but she also causes as much mischief as you do."*

Nippi marveled. *"I want to be the best dancer! And I am not mischief. I am Stag Blessed."*

Morvelving's smirk left his lips. The creak of wagon wheels and a faint clatter of hooves came to his ears.

"Something comes from the northern pass," he signed to her. *"Follow me off the road."*

Whoever it was, they were not Thresseans, as they came from the north. Morvelving didn't want to take any chances. He led Nippi off the road and under the cover of trees till he found a place for them to hide under the roots of a tree hugging a boulder. With haste, Morvelving checked to see if Nippi had left behind any signs of their passing. Proud to see none, he directed her to crouch and climb into the dank and cool shade of the boulder. Then he lay on his stomach so he could see the road and remain hidden. Nippi tried to crawl forward to see. Morvelving made her lie back down, motioning for her to stay still.

Soon enough, the caravan caught up with them.

By what Morvelving could see between the trees, a company of mounted elves guarded the vanguard and rear. He could tell they were Mithvarn elves by their gold, crimson, and white banner with a centered image of dark Celemith eclipsing the sun.

Each elf wore a green cloak and harnessed themselves in bronze plating. The company's militant appearance made Morvelving glad he had opted to take cover. Only elves wielded the weapons made by their slaves. Penalty would have stood out—the elves would have assumed that Morvelving had stolen it or slain an elf to get it.

One of the lead riders separated from the company and approached the spot where Morvelving had led Nippi off the road.

Morvelving sank even lower to the ground and motioned for Nippi to stay quiet. Elven ears were keen and their eyes sharp.

Like the others riding in order behind him, the elf wore bronze full-body armor and a helmet. The elegant armor fit the elf's form perfectly, showcasing the unmatched skill of their dwarven slaves. The elf's helmet had a dyed sapphire plume that danced with each bounce of the horse. He carried a long spear with a small green banner marked with a golden sigil hieroglyph that read "House Kizniksu." A minor house Morvelving didn't recognize. At his side was a twohanded sword, its blade slightly curved and its hilt decorated with a jade-colored wrapping.

The elf stopped his horse and rested his spear on his shoulder so he could untie his mask. The bronze sculpture with eye and mouth openings resembled a snarling face. With his mask lifted, his squinting green eyes shifted across the forest before him. He removed his helmet and scratched an itch on his head.

With his gray hair tied back in a knot, the pointed tips of his ears were prominent. His face was fair and stark, blemished by a bright pink scar that ran from ear to throat.

Morvelving looked past the lone elf to the oxen-pulled wagons moving by. Through the crude bronze bars, Morvelving could see forlorn faces, frightened, and sad eyes. Beards matted and filthy. Each wrist bearing manacles.

Morvelving's body tensed to maintain his composure. Their scent was unmistakable. He had helped some of these dwarves cross Frystgalen, though not all of them, and he didn't recognize any faces. Each wagon must have contained fifty dwarves crammed inside. His eyes darted from face to face, looking for Wynthrim. What if he found her? What would he do? Follow the army of elves, find a means to break their chains, barter for Wynthrim, or incite revolt? Three hundred chained dwarves against two hundred elven warriors. It would be a massacre, even if they gained weapons. No doubt the elves knew by now that an exiled Mulranei had helped the dwarves. Once they spotted him, they would disarm him and put him under guard.

Nippi placed her hand on his arm. Morvelving didn't take his eyes off the dwarves. She must have noticed that he was disturbed. Nippi was the weight that kept him prone. Even if Wynthrim was among the captives, he wouldn't bring Nippi into such danger.

A long, interconnected chain of dwarves hurried behind the wagon. Morvelving's chest burned to aid them. He saw one dwarf who still held his head high, his eyes a furnace of unbridled hate directed at the nearest elf. Morvelving was powerless to help them. He had seen that look before, and he hoped, perhaps knew, that maybe he didn't need to. The dwarves would endure and free themselves. It didn't stop him from hating it.

When the lone elf returned to the head of the caravan and the noise of their passing faded, Nippi pulled at his hand, urging him to glance her way.

"What was that about? You looked like you would attack them."

Morvelving took a deep breath. *"I wanted to help those dwarves. Some of them I knew in Frystgalen. They were free then."*

"Before you found me?"

Morvelving nodded.

"Why can't we help them?" Nippi asked. *"Is it like with Sophokis? Do*

the elves have a draekurm?"

"What? No. Elves fight draekurm," Morvelving signed with haste. *"I want to help them, but I won't put you in harm's way. Besides . . . "* He watched the last sight of the elven troop turn out of view, remembered the dwarf he'd seen and the feeling in his eyes. *"Besides, I think, for better or worse, this isn't my fight, if it ever was. I only stumbled upon an ancient struggle mired deep in so much hate that when the dwarves do revolt, it will shake the continent."*

Nippi paused in thought. *"If I wasn't here, you'd have fought the shiny elves?"*

"Not directly." For Nippi to be absent, Morvelving would have needed never to have rejected Wynthrim's offer. *"But I would have done everything I could to help them. Before you ran into me, the dwarves had offered for me to stay with them. At the time, I was too scared, too afraid of being accepted to remain with them."*

He watched Nippi. The girl brushed pine needles from her tunic.

"I'm glad you didn't stay with them," she signed. *"I don't like seeing people tied up. The Qilatuuga did that to me. When we find somewhere safe, we should help the dwarves!"*

"Perhaps we will." If they did find somewhere safe—if she grew up and still wished to aid the dwarves—then they would. The fur on his back bristled, guessing how much the Fates would love that, and his heart ached. Nippi grown and choosing to go into battle. Morvelving dismissed the thought and surveyed the woods and road. *"We'll travel off the road for now."*

Nippi brushed her hands together and continued walking forward. They were near Sene now.

18

"Welcome, travelers, to Sene! *Edu ve,* an odd pair you are." Morvelving and Nippi stood still, watching the gateman. An old man, he limped over to them with the help of an ancient flintstone spear that looked like it would snap under his weight. Wrinkles covered his face, the skin stretched from years of smiling. The smile he flashed right now provided a decidedly unpleasant view into his mouth, filled with decaying and missing teeth.

The gate was a small wooden thing held up by two rotten posts. There was no fence or wall.

Morvelving blinked, perplexed by the presence of a gateman at a gate that anyone could just walk around. He went to speak, but the old man continued.

"Oh, er, I forgot myself. Rule of visitors: 'state your business before being welcomed.' Yes, that's the one. No *buts*, now. Oh, and I'll need your names, *moni devu.*"

Nippi giggled. Morvelving admitted it was amusing to watch him fumble with the gate lock, the posts visibly rocking back and forth.

Morvelving introduced himself and Nippi. "We are only passing through. A night or two."

"Oh, say. I've always found Mulranei so fascinating," the old man said. "When I was a lad, *edu ve,* a magnificent huntress passed through

Sene. Well, it was Galbaeth then. Uh, anyway, loved watching her talk. Forgive me, I ramble. The missus says that's why I'm the gateman, so newcomers only have to hear me once at the gate." He was still smiling. "*Edu ve*, my manners. I am Gauntio, and welcome again to Sene."

"Thank you, we—"

Gauntio cut Morvelving off again, oblivious to his words. "You can find the Green Olive just down yonder. We don't have much else here. As you can see, there's a mustering."

That was the truth—the large inn at the center dominated the town. A few shops and a large barn were on either side, with the ringing hammer on an anvil from a blacksmith nearby. Some residents were already looking at them and chatting among themselves. Three homes stood beyond the town, all of them farmsteads. Olive trees dominated the landscape, though one home had a patch of apple trees. And a great many tents were lined up along the outskirts of the town, with men, young and old, tramping about with shields and spears, which was concerning.

"Gaia, the innkeep, is renowned for her hospitable establishment, fine olives, and wine. Ah, those were grand evenings," Gauntio said dreamily, then shook his head ruefully. "Don't rustle the bush, so to speak, or you'll be guarding the gate, eh? Ha ha! Yes, the wine is from the vineyards further—"

"Thank you, Gauntio," Morvelving said quickly. "Have there been runners with news from the west?"

"*Edu ve*, from that rocky centaur-infested Land of the Idosse! No. And good thing—we have our problems to the east. You'll hear it all at the inn."

"We'll go straight to the Green Olive then." Morvelving was relieved news of the Phoithesens' bounty hadn't come this far.

"Yes, yes, of course, *edu ve*. Here, let me unlock the gate—silly me." Gauntio shuffled over to the gate and fiddled with the key.

Morvelving waited. Nippi giggled and ran around the gate.

When Gauntio succeeded with the lock and opened the gate, only to see Nippi already waiting on his side, he sputtered, *"Edu ve*, child, you little—heh, well, what does it matter? Be on your way. Think you are clever, little miss? I know you can walk around my gate. A man needs work, especially at my age, or he'll dream and dream."

Morvelving thanked Gauntio again and caught up to Nippi. She was already casting curious glances at the people of Sene. They were looking at her too. Her red eyes, white hair, and light blue skin were markedly different from their white skin and dark eyes and hair.

He thought it strange—Frystgalen was not so far to the north. He would have thought seeing *him* would have had more effect on the townsfolk. He doubted Mulranei had frequented these lands within several human generations, unless the gateman had been telling the truth about the Mulranei huntress.

Sene was a small town, yet the Green Olive Inn was large. Dominating the town's center, it stood at the edge of a crossroads. One post with three signs marking the roads: "West to Adrea," "East to Aqualea and Threvicio," and "South to Padamo and Altanan."

The building itself had two stories with many windows. Its foundations were stone, the walls were hardened clay painted green, and the roofing was wood with clay tiles. The wooden sign for the inn swung back and forth in the wind with a weak, creaky noise. Through the windows, Morvelving could see shapes of people moving back and forth and the outlines of patrons enjoying their drinks. Clearly more people than the small town was accustomed to.

Nippi ran toward the door, but Morvelving grabbed her in time.

"Behave yourself," he signed.

"I would never."

He gave her a look and said, *"Stay near me until I know it's safe."*

Nippi nodded and then pulled him impatiently toward the door. He opened it and entered. Quiet humming of family members and longtime friends talking and laughing jovially. All of them gave him and Nippi two glances—a quick first, a lingering second—and promptly continued their conversations.

Morvelving had to hunch to keep his head from bumping into the ceiling. A mustering indeed—most of the patrons were men, all with clothing dusty from travel. He stepped out of the way of a chandelier as he approached the counter. A young woman was staring wide-eyed up at Morvelving. Noise from the kitchen spilled out as a portly woman, wiping her hands on her apron, opened the door.

She spoke a few choice words in her own tongue to the young woman. In the Trade Tongue, she said to Morvelving, "Welcome to the Green Olive, Mulranei. I am Gaia. What are you called?"

Morvelving approached the counter and introduced himself, explaining that they were passing through and offering to work for a meal.

When he introduced Nippi, Gaia looked down at the girl in shock. *"Edu ve,* Morvelving, look at the girl! She needs to eat; my stew is almost ready. Go sit down. An inn hand shall take your things to a room—I have just the place. No. No, I insist you eat and sleep! I am honored to host a Mulranei. There's a spare room. Most of these men have their tents, praise the gods. The poor girl! One mistake, she'd fall and snap! She would break in two. No further questions now. Go sit! I insist."

Morvelving had no chance to speak beneath the swift deluge of Gaia's compulsive words. The power of which reminded him of his tribe's Allseer. He felt heat on his scalp at the reprimand and the unlooked-for hospitality. Morvelving and Nippi ate well for travelers. He made sure of it. It dawned on him that this hospitality was probably a cultural trait specific to the Menici. Several local patrons were smiling knowingly at the scene.

Nippi looked beside herself in enjoyment, evidently having read Gaia's lips during the entire exchange.

Morvelving reluctantly gave their travel pack to the young maid. She had a hard time with Penalty, which drew more curious looks from nearby folk. In shock, Morvelving now stared at Nippi.

"I'm so hungry," she signed with a mischievous smile.

Morvelving shrugged in defeat. *"Well, you're about to get your fill. Whether or not you want it."*

"I like Gaia. She knows how to treat children."

"Glad you're acknowledging your own age," Morvelving quipped as a maid brought him a small mug of wine and one filled with milk for Nippi. Sitting in the undersized chair, he couldn't shake the feeling of being out of proportion, and the rickety old table only added to his discomfort.

The chair was too large for Nippi, but her head and shoulders were above the chipped surface.

"Gaia will bring out your meal shortly," the maid said.

Morvelving grunted. Surveying the room for anyone who appeared to be too interested in them. He found nothing alarming and only smelled contentment and goodwill. Like waking to the warmth of the sun and the sound of birds singing.

One patron rose from his table and approached them. A middle-aged man, suntanned, with thick locks of dark curly hair atop his head. He raised his mug in greeting. "Fair travels, Mulranei. Welcome to Sene."

"Fair, indeed. No wind accompanying the rain, and the Elven Road was quiet," Morvelving said. It hadn't been, but this man didn't need to know. "Is there a festival near?"

"Nay, I wish," the man said as took he a gulp of wine. "We locals are outnumbered, though I'll let Gaia give you word. She'll wallop me if I give up any of the gossip. Enjoy your day and the wine. That white was pressed from the harvest two seasons ago."

"I shall wait for Gaia then. My thanks." Morvelving lifted the mug to the man. He took a sip and held back his grimace, careful not to instinctively lap it up with his tongue. Conscious of the eyes on him and not wanting to draw further attention. The wine was too sweet for his liking. Of course, the ermuk in Frystgalen and the hopped ale in Idosse had dominated his tastes for a long time.

Nippi was gulping her milk as if she had never tasted it before. She put down the mug with a satisfied sigh. Morvelving chose not to tell her about the milk on her upper lip.

Gaia arrived, her arms laden with two large bowls of stew and a plate with a loaf of bread. Wisps of steam were rising from all three. She placed Nippi's bowl down beside her and then fretted over the milk on her lips.

"Goodness me, girl. Not so fast or you'll get the hiccups, and that'll shrink your stomach," Gaia said while giving Morvelving a pointed glance as she set his bowl of stew down. "Your room is all set—second to left after the stairs. Oh, girl, that will not do!"

Nippi had picked up the bowl and was about to sip the soup. Gaia stopped her and handed her a wooden spoon. "It is hot! You'll burn your tongue. Here, like this, then blow on it. I must ask, Morvelving, has she eaten civilly at all?"

"We've been on the road for the past four seasons," Morvelving said after trying the stew. It was warm and delicious, and the mushrooms in it made him think of the ones his mother had prepared. "Please, allow me to labor for the costs of the room and food."

"Nonsense!" Gaia said, rubbing her hands in her apron. "You are my guests. I would not have it said, 'Gaia's Green Olive doesn't feed starving children and honor Mulranei.' "

Nippi laughed her throaty and snorty giggle.

Morvelving clamped his gaping mouth shut. He didn't know why he felt the need to defend his care for Nippi and push back against being so pampered. He held it back though. "You are too gracious, Gaia. We journeyed far—"

He stopped, for Nippi was signing. Morvelving surveyed the room quickly—no one took notice. *"Fluff takes good care of me,"* she said, smiling up at Gaia.

The innkeeper put her hand to her mouth and looked at Morvelving. *"Edu ve,* forgive me, what is this?"

Nippi looked at Morvelving, confused.

"Nippi is deaf and mute," Morvelving answered. "She can read lips in the Trade Tongue."

"Oh, you poor child!" Gaia said as she patted Nippi on the head. "Good Morvelving, is there a way to know what she says?"

Nippi nodded enthusiastically at him when he looked. He sighed; this was new to him. How Gaia talked and moved must have made an impression on Nippi.

"She knows Trade Runes," Morvelving offered. "If you have a quill and parchment, she can communicate with you."

"Oh, of course I have a quill. Without knowing her runes, a girl won't get far. I'm impressed, Morvelving," Gaia said, and Morvelving swelled with pride but was flustered. Why did he need her affirmation?

"I shall fetch some parchment. Enjoy your food, and I shall see what work is available, as I recognize you may be shamed by my gifts. But I'll be forward: there isn't much work in Sene, with all the old folk and women staying here while the men from the countryside and cities are passing through." Gaia patted Nippi on the head again but this time took a strand of her hair, inspecting it, and tsked twice.

"Why is there . . . " Morvelving stopped, for Gaia wasn't listening as she continued to tsk at Nippi's hair.

"A bath is in order, dear child. It looks like you've never brushed it too," Gaia was saying as she walked off back to the kitchens.

Nippi curiously played with her hair then smiled up at Morvelving. *"I like her."*

She continued to eat in earnest. Morvelving was content, despite his fur being ruffled. He had been afraid that Sene wouldn't be welcoming, even after the aid the Adreans had given them on the road, as small remote towns were often wary of strangers. He glanced at the other patrons again. Farmers were talking about their crops. There was also a rough group, though only in their worn travel gear, enjoying their food in silence. The packs at their feet held the shapes of equipment of war: helmets and greaves. The locals also greeted them. An older man approached them. Morvelving listened to their conversation while he ate.

"You lads off to Pilla Falen?" inquired the old Sene local.

"Aye," said the closest man. "News travels fast. The call was made in Adrea. We've come so the Graal won't make it to our own lands."

Morvelving's worry piqued. He had not expected Graal to be in Menici lands. Graal were migratory creatures. They lived on the surrounding land, and when the supply went dry, they moved on. He was unaware of any colonies in the far west.

"I thank you for it," the old farmer said. "There are too few of us and many too old to go marching."

Gaia returned then. Nippi was staring at nothing, drowsy from a full stomach. She perked up when Gaia placed a quill and ink with a long piece of parchment on the table before Nippi. The parchment was strapped to a clay tablet so Nippi could carry it with her. She vigorously folded and tore it into numerous small pieces. This was no small gift if parchment was as expensive here as it was in Idosse cities.

"Now use it sparingly, this is all I'm giving you," Gaia said, looking at Nippi.

Nippi nodded and stood up with her knees on the chair so she could reach the quill and parchment.

"I can't thank you enough," Morvelving said. "The food was delicious."

Gaia waved her hand dismissively. "Enjoy it while it lasts. There may be hard times ahead."

"I couldn't help but overhear—a host of Graal has entered these lands?"

Gaia nodded gravely. "Aye. As you can see, men from the countryside, Adrea, and Puntas Valley are marshaling at Pilla Falen under Aqualean standards. The field's half a day's march from here."

That explained why the Adreans on the road were in a hurry. "I don't recall the Graal coming so far west. Was this recent?"

"Perhaps. There were signs they haunted Mount Medthana north of the Elven Road," she said, scoffing. "You'd think the almighty know-it-all elves would have cleaned them up. You said you're looking for work? I remember . . . well, since there's no work here—not that I recommend persons to any battle—but I'm sure the leaders will hire any they can. The runner says a large host of Graal split from the main and is heading west toward Pilla Falen." She rubbed her hands anxiously. "I hope all goes well—as well as can be in a battle."

Morvelving hummed in thought. That meant there may be a battle in two days at Pilla Falen. He had little time. Morvelving looked at Nippi. She was writing runes to Gaia, thanking and complimenting her. He wondered if leaving Nippi here while he left for the battle was prudent. There was a risk that the Thressean king's men might disguise themselves, enter Menici, and arrive while he was gone.

Perhaps even Phoithesens could come, though he doubted one city under a draekurm's rule had the reach. He had made sure their trail ended ten miles from the Elven Road and appeared to head east, not south. A minor risk compared to hiring himself for a pitched battle. But he felt compelled to help, especially after the aid the Adreans had given him on the Elven Road. Unless it was a slaughter and the Graal won. He asked, "How many are gathering at Pilla Falen?"

"*Edu ve*, I'm not sure," Gaia admitted. "I've had hundreds of young men pass through Sene from Adrea and southern farmsteads. The runners say the entire Aqualean army is there. See, the city has no walls. That's how they've always defended themselves: 'with our shields.' " She said the last bit ironically and with a mocking manly voice, then looked down at Nippi's runes and smiled. "Aw, you are all too welcome, child. Master Morvelving, she needs a bath, and her hair is simply undignified. I'll have one of my girls warm a tub in your room."

Morvelving drooped his ears. "Rest and a bath sound wonderful." He stood and almost knocked his head on the ceiling. All eyes were on him. He looked at the young men heading to the battle. It always amazed him how humans sent their young to the horrors of battle, despite human mortality. The differences were always stark. He would never get used to it.

He let Gaia gather their mugs and bowls. Nippi gathered her newly acquired treasures with care. "Up the stairs and the second door on the left," Gaia said before she started bantering with one of her townsfolk.

Their room was spacious, enough room for a large bathing tub in the center, two beds, and wood cabinets for cloth and garments. A candle stood on each table. A stool near one window, which faced north, had a washbasin.

The inn maid started when Morvelving walked in. She quickly looked away, saying, "The water is nice and warm. There are cloth wraps for drying, and the matron provided soap."

Nippi ran to the bed, set her parchment down, and climbed onto the bed, rolling and jumping on it.

"Thank you," Morvelving said, stepping out of the doorway.

"I'm to help the girl bathe," the maid said calmly.

That was undoubtedly wise. He saw their pack with Nippi's bow behind the bed. His sword was leaning against the wall, still wrapped.

He got Nippi's attention. *"The maid is going to help you bathe. Best do it now while the water is warm."*

"I'll see to our things. Let me know if you need me to tell her something," he said to the maid. Her shoulders relaxed. Perhaps it was Nippi who had frightened the maid.

Nippi didn't make it easy, first trying to jump into the tub as if it were a lake. Morvelving had to tell Nippi to do as the maid instructed with the soap.

Nippi protested, wanting to make more bubbles as soon as she knew she could. She relented eventually. Once out of the tub and wrapped in dry cloth, the maid went to work combing Nippi's hair. Morvelving gained a quick glance from the maid when he unwrapped Penalty to check the blade for blemishes.

"You've both been through a lot," the maid stated, pointing at Nippi's neck scar as she worked out the knots in Nippi's hair.

Nippi was sitting on the ground, leaning against the young woman's knees, eyes closed and content.

"Yes, a few unfortunate events among the Idosse," Morvelving said as he reorganized the contents of the pack. He was happy for a distraction from his thoughts.

"What's your name?" he asked after introducing himself.

"Cassea. I've never been to the Idosse lands," Cassea said. "But Nippiktua is Frystlin, yes? I've heard tell their skin is blue. Thought it was hearsay, thought they just painted themselves."

"We came down from Frystgalen almost three winters ago. You live in Sene?"

"I do now. My apa and pepa sent me to Matron Gaia to learn her trade, and I have learned so much," Cassea said enthusiastically. "Soon I will go to Aqualea. Her hair is so uneven. Did you cut it?"

Morvelving swallowed. "Um, yes. A while ago. She didn't make it easy."

Nippi crossed her arms, staring up at him, having caught what he said. He winked.

"Well," Cassea said, "perhaps if I have time tomorrow, I can mend it. Can you tell her that?"

Morvelving did. Nippi nodded enthusiastically, smiling up at Cassea. Morvelving was happy Gaia and Cassea were treating Nippi so well. Others shied away from her.

The Frystlins rarely came south, and those who did were often rogues and brigands, rarely pleasant company. Every scent he gathered from Gaia and now Cassea was genuine care though.

"That is all I can do for now," Cassea said, standing after wrestling the comb through several hard knots. "I'm sure Matron Gaia needs me downstairs. Shall I bring you anything?"

"We are content, thank you," Morvelving said. He handed Nippi her bow. She made a noise, setting it down on her bed.

"You should check the strings and put this wax on," he signed and then handed her the little pouch of beeswax.

Nippi took it, then tried on a clean white tunic Gaia had provided and tied her belt around her waist. She did as Morvelving had told her to, pulling out the bowstring and easing the wax up and down it.

Finished, she set it down. *"Are we going to stay here?"*

"For a little while. Why?" Morvelving asked.

"I like it here. Gaia treats me important," she signed as if she were a noble girl. Morvelving sniffled and whined at her. She caught his expression. *"Why can't we stay?"*

"We may," Morvelving answered. *"But I fear we need to put more distance between us and any Idosse. There may be war coming with the Graal. I'd rather not be here for that."*

"What are Graal? I don't like what people say about them. They were never in Frystgalen," Nippi signed, then put her bow back in her pack, the top sticking out.

When she looked back at him, Morvelving answered, *"The Graal were created by the God of Pestilence, Kragius. They are like lizards but resemble humans more. They stand on two legs and have short tails and scaly skin."* Morvelving ignored Nippi's perturbed face. *"They are isolated creatures, only interacting with other races to take from them. I've heard rumors some do trade; I've never seen it though."*

Nippi kept her face skewed in disgust. *"I don't want to see Graal. They sound gross. Not putting them on my list. I added more to my list today!"*

"That's good," Morvelving signed, hoping to finally know what this secret list was. *"What did you add?"*

Nippi looked at him shrewdly. *"I'm not telling!"* Then, after considering, she added, *"Are you going to help them against the Graal like you helped the Pella people?"*

Morvelving grumbled. *"Maybe, I—"*

A knock came at the door. "Yes, come in," Morvelving said. Gaia opened the door; she had a smile on her face that immediately fell flat when she saw Nippi. She shook her head. "This won't do, Nippi. Master Morvelving, I placed a clean dress—ah, see it's still there. That's a sleeping gown. Here."

Morvelving had no time to translate, nor did Nippi have time to evade Gaia's mothering. She had Nippi in a loose flannel dress with a small yellow tunic before either could protest.

"Hmm, your hair looks healthy now. Does it feel better?" Gaia asked. Nippi nodded.

"Good. Now, it's almost time for supper. You are welcome to come down anytime. There will be mead and music. Will you be leaving tomorrow for Pilla Falen?"

Her tone was so matter-of-fact, Morvelving questioned whether he had already agreed to go.

"I'm not sure," Morvelving said. Gaia placed her hands on her hips. Nippi saw her and mimicked her.

"Well, it won't do to bring her to a battle," Gaia spoke firmly. "Let her stay here. I'll keep her busy and safe, and it'll be good for her. If the battle goes poorly, I will take her with me to Adrea. I know you Mulranei are wise, and I'm sure you know what you want to do."

Morvelving raised his brows and perked both his ears forward.

Nippi was smiling at him mischievously. This was what she wanted. He didn't want to bring Nippi into a battle again. He didn't want to become embroiled in another conflict either. There were several times he had to, but nothing like this. He knew little about the Graal. He knew they traveled in great numbers. It occurred to him then—he hadn't sensed or smelled any ill will this entire time. Sene was a small and safe town, secure in its good-natured people.

He faced Nippi. *"Is this what you want? To be with Gaia and the inn while I'm gone?"*

"Yes!"

"You'll have to do as she says and stay out of trouble. No 'my list' nonsense."

"Yes! Yes! Absolutely no list," she signed with finality. Morvelving very much doubted her answers.

"I will take you up on your offer," Morvelving said to Gaia. "If I decide to accompany the men to Pilla Falen."

Gaia nodded, evidently pleased at Morvelving's good sense. *"Edu ve,* good. Very wise. Now to supper."

Morvelving watched her leave, wondering if she had pressed him to join the men out of fear for her own people.

Downstairs, each table was full of Sene townsfolk, and many were pressed against the walls. Gaia had a table for them in the far corner, away from the door. It was where the ceiling was the highest. Several locals called out to him in greeting.

"Gods with you, Mulranei."

"Welcome to Sene!"

A troubadour played music, the middle-aged man strumming a lyre for a few ballads, then a lute for dancing. Nippi joined in the dancing when many children and adults alike cleared tables out of the way. Morvelving enjoyed watching her move out of sync. She tried to apply the Frystlin dances she knew to the Menicians'. A noble attempt. Menicians enjoyed large, quick steps while her dances were full of small, quick footwork.

Morvelving was on his second mug of mead when the dancing stopped. Nippi didn't return to the table. He saw her near the kitchen counter. She was showing her dances to a boy and girl her age. They were trying to mimic the patterns. Nippi was moving too fast, but they were all enjoying themselves. Morvelving eased back in his chair, content, the soft warmth of mead holding back his worries for now.

"Pardon, Mulranei," a middle-aged man said. He stood in front of Morvelving. A farmer with tanned, taut skin and a kind face. "May I accompany you?"

"Of course," Morvelving said, introducing himself and extending his hand. The man flinched at Morvelving's claws, which poked his hand briefly. "What should I call you?"

"Paunt Dim, at your service."

"You farm the land here?"

"No, I'm from the Puntas Valley along River Beaut," Paunt said. "Me and some lads have joined the call against the Graal. If those vermin get past Aqualea, they'll wreck the Adrean kingdom and terrorize all of Menici."

"That is my concern. I plan to cross the Menici lands to the east. I'd hate to deal with a roaming horde on my own. I am impressed at how the Menici have banded together," Morvelving said, then chuckled. "I've come from Idosse, and they would have either fought the Graal as individual city-states or attacked the kingdom that was currently fighting the Graal."

"Indeed, well, the Idospont protects them from Graal migrations, I'd imagine. Tell me, Morvelving, is a draekurm ruling over Phoithese?" Paunt asked, shivering at the word *draekurm*. "I've only heard rumors. We don't hear much from the Idosse—the Thressean barbarians control the Idospont. Did the Phoithesens make a blood pact with the beast and now serve it and are gearing up to make war in Nameless's name?"

"Hmm," Morvelving grunted, unhappy to learn the rumors had reached so far. Knowing the Menici had no care for the Thresseans was a relief, a sentiment he loved to continue hearing. He was worried the death of Leolicides would be known. "I was not that far south, but I did hear the tale. Orrothix has captured the city, demanding devious payments. The Nameless rumors are unfounded. Orrothix is acting of her own will. It is unfortunate—draekurm will often travel far from Nameless. Do you receive much news of the east in the Puntas Valley?" Morvelving asked, hoping to redirect the conversation.

Paunt shook his head. "I can only imagine staying in a city ruled by a draekurm. Aye, yes, trade comes from the gulf and up the River Beaut. Narsh raiders have been seen. One galley was even pursued to Altanan's port by the pirates—imagine that! The Monbargars are in turmoil. Trade has stopped from that wild land, no telling why. I talked to a trader from Threvicio who had crossed the Burnt Lands from Suknol. He said he left the Midden Lands. 'War on every field,' he had said. 'The Mithvarn elves were retreating to their mountain strongholds, not because of Nameless's advances. Something else is brewing.' Anyway." Paunt shrugged. "Now Graal migrating south from Mount Medthana. If enough men don't join at Pilla Falen, they could sweep over Aqualea, and only the walls of Adrea could halt them."

"You fear there won't be enough men?" Morvelving asked. This was the first he had heard of doubt. He couldn't afford to engage in a losing battle. Who could, truly?

Paunt shrugged and shook his head. "Perhaps. The Aqualean companies are well equipped and organized. The city's Prime Enator, Arastus, is one of the best commanders, I hear. He has served the old King Aquailor his whole life." Paunt was silent for a moment, considering something. "I wonder, Morvelving, where are the Mulranei? Do not the tribes hunt Graal anymore? I remember old Gran's tales when I was a small lad."

Morvelving lapped up more mead. He then glanced at the man. What tales had been told? "Huh, your gran must have mixed up Graal with minotaurs."

"Is it them your people hate so? I'll take your word for it," Paunt said. "Minotaur headhunts haven't reached our lands for some time."

There was a reason for that, a reason soaking in pain and blood. Morvelving didn't like where the conversation was heading. He couldn't keep a growl from escaping his throat.

Paunt looked at him sharply, surprised. "Apologies if I caused offense. It was not my intent."

"It wasn't you, friend. There is a reason the Land of the Menici has been free of minotaur marauders," Morvelving said. "My people still hunt any that go beyond the Goreth Plains. The blood debts are still warm between our peoples."

Paunt seemed satisfied with the answer and aware that Morvelving wanted their talk to end. He excused himself. Morvelving continued to brood. The talk of minotaurs made him think of the one he'd fought, the dwarves and Wynthrim he'd helped, and the dwarves in chains on the road. Where were his kin when strong tides of evil washed across the land? Morvelving took another drink.

The music and dancing had died down, with the troubadour now playing a slow tune on the lyre. Lovers embraced or left for privacy. The troubadour began recounting the tale of two boys, lost in the wilderness, who were guided to safety by a raven. There, upon the roost of ravens, the boys grew to men who founded the city Altanan, which rests still below Raven's Rock.

After the song, others brought songs from their homes. Pleasant songs dominated the rest of the evening, waxing eloquent about the growing plants of the Sene farms.

Nippi found her way back to Morvelving. He had settled and was enjoying the simple songs; he preferred the ones praising life in the world over the tales of wars and great deeds. Nippi slouched into her chair, a tired smile on her face.

"How were the dancing lessons?" Morvelving asked.

She beamed, eyes glowing in the candlelight. *"The best. Timon couldn't do it, but he tried so hard. He lives at the vineyard to the south, down the road near Peraphos Grove. As if I knew what that was. Fyrla was amazing at dancing! She says she dances every night with her pepa."*

"They come to the Green Olive every night?" Morvelving wondered aloud. Nippi put her elbow on the table, her hand pressing on her cheek. She stayed there a moment, either ignoring his question or thinking about all that had happened that evening.

"I don't know," she finally admitted. *"Fyrla says her pepa is going to fight the Graal. She seemed sad at that. Isn't that what you are going to do? If you do, keep her pepa alive, or else she can't dance with him every night."*

Morvelving felt that implication at the bottom of his throat. He looked at the middle-aged man holding Fyrla in his arms, listening to the songs. Suddenly, his hesitation to go and leave Nippi was gone. He was a son of Telunian, Goddess of the Moon. The Graal were vermin of Kragius, whose wicked mischief sought to hurt these simple and wonderful people. His tribe had cast him out to mourn, but he wouldn't let grief stop him from doing what he was called to do. These people had welcomed him and Nippi, given them the fruits of their honest labor. He reminisced about their pleasant songs of gardening, drinking, and sunlight; he would fight for that.

Morvelving nodded to himself. He was practical as well; if there was coin, he would take it. Joining the effort to stop the Graal advance was even more practical—he and Nippi wouldn't be safe on their journey if a horde of Graal were plundering the land. He memorized the man's face, considered going to introduce himself.

"Fair Mulranei!" the troubadour called from the other end of the room, quieting Morvelving's thoughts and the rest of the room. "Please, join in and share a song. Legends speak of the wonderful Mulranei songs. I hear people in the far east have made instruments to mimic their tunes."

Many others took up the call. His heart skipped as he recalled how he used to sing at the rising of the moon or at the wind, in the peaceful woods with Wildriver and Windtail.

He raised his hand to hush the beckoners. "I would be a poor guest if I didn't oblige. Sene and the Green Olive have been a blessing, an unlooked-for rest from many travels and dangers. I will sing. But prepare yourselves; the sounds may remind you of dark nights in the wilds by firelight, fearing the shadows. Know that it is not so."

Morvelving sang then. He sang a song of life and rising silver moonlight. The guide it offered in the dark, its promise of morning, which gives life. He sang about the wind and its whispers, how it moved over water. He sang about the mountain rivers, torrential in spring, lazy in autumn. Finally, he sang of running in open fields—the joy and exaltation as his chest burned from the hard exertion—and of respite under a shaded tree. He knew all the listeners heard were howls in a variety of tones and notes, but he sang still.

The power was in the feeling the song provoked. The listeners were in rapt silence. Many jumped when the Mulranei began his song. A howl of a wolf to them, yet more potent. As if a mirror had been placed before each listener, and instead of offering their reflection, it offered a window into the song. Of the moon in its glory, the beauty of the mountains, rivers, and creatures, small and large, at peace, giving hope, promise, and life. After that night, some said that Telunian had touched the town of Sene and they should erect a temple. Others held the memory, treasured it close, through hard seasons or war or famine—their moon in the dark. Indeed, the Song of the Moon would not be heard in Menici lands again for centuries and centuries. When the next season of crops grew, it was marked in Sene's small chronicle: the fairest crop on record. The growing infants who listened from their mothers' wombs that night grew to be beautiful, wise, and strong. Their stories would go on to be written in runes—stories of their deeds for the betterment of themselves and others.

When Morvelving finished, the silence was deafening. He heard distant replies to his song from wolves far off in the night, mournful yet grateful.

Morvelving took a deep breath, looking at Nippi. She was sleeping in her chair, a large grin on her lips. He stood and picked her up. She humphed but did not wake.

As he was walking up the steps to their room, he heard Gaia break the silence. "The hour is late. Out, the lot of you. Settle with me or earn my ire."

19

Nippiktua was floating.

No, she lay in the inn's bed. The softness of the pillow and mattress made it feel like there was nothing underneath her. She stretched, kicking the blankets off. She was too warm, something that hadn't happened in the morning for years. Dim light crept in through the cracks in the curtain. Fluff wasn't sleeping. He was sitting on the bed facing her, one of his eyes reflecting the light. He must have been up for some time, she guessed, given he already had his belt on and their pack next to him.

"How long will you be gone?" she asked.

The thought of him leaving and not coming back put a pit in her stomach. But Fluff would not leave for good. He would always come back. Not like the others.

"Two days, three if nothing goes according to plan," Fluff said. His hand signs were so good now. She was an excellent teacher.

"Before I go," he added, *"I want you to listen very carefully. Can you do that right now?"*

Oh, Fluff was serious. She nodded, curious about what he had to say. She moved the pillow to the bedside and used it to prop up her head.

Fluff straightened his back. *"While I'm away, you must listen to Gaia. Do as she says. She is gracious to watch over you. Keep your things here—no one needs to see the Stag tine. If any new people show up here, avoid them. We are still close to Idosse lands, and however unlikely it may be, those who are after us might come this way. What did I say?"*

Nippiktua sat up, her face hot. Fluff didn't need to ask her to repeat anymore. She wasn't little. *"Listen to Gaia. Keep my stuff here. Stay away from strangers and newcomers."*

Fluff nodded. *"If someone recognizes you, run south and then east. Do you know which way that is?"*

"It's where Timon lives," she signed and pointed in the direction.

"Good. I will show you east. It is the direction I will be going." Fluff took a deep breath. She thought he was refraining from saying more. *"Try to hide though. I won't be gone for long. Oh, and please avoid doing anything on your . . . list."*

Nippiktua moved to the edge of the bed and smirked. *"Fine. Why do you have to go?"*

Fluff regarded her for a moment. *"Gaia and these people have been good to us. I wish to help them, and doing so will help us too. If the Graal aren't confronted, they will terrorize the land—the lands we are intending to cross. I'd much rather face the Graal with an army than by myself. Do you understand?"*

Nippiktua nodded. *"I think so. Graal sound scary."*

"They are often a blight." Fluff stood, looking resigned. *"Are you hungry?"*

Nippiktua bolted out of her bed and put on the weird clothes Gaia had given her. They were amazing, though they made running difficult. She tried to imitate how Cassea had combed her hair with the wooden comb. Frustrated, she handed it to Fluff. He did it almost as good as Cassea! She was going to make sure he did it more often. It reminded her of her parents by the fire after a day's work. Despite not liking the idea of Fluff leaving, Nippiktua was excited for the day. However, there was so much to do. She was going to ask Gaia or Cassea how she could braid her hair like theirs.

She raced down the steps and had to halt on the last step.

Gaia stood before her, waving her hand with her pointer finger out. Nippiktua held her breath at the universal sign for *"no, no."* She couldn't catch everything Gaia said, but she knew she wasn't supposed to run down the steps. Gaia became distracted by Morvelving. Nippiktua went to the table the matron had pointed to.

Other people were dining. The food smelled so wonderful, it was making her stomach angry. She followed their lips after she got into her seat. Fluff was instructing Gaia on how to take care of her. Nippiktua crossed her arms. She wasn't a baby. Gaia was looking at her. She missed what she said—oh, she had forgotten her parchment!

She made the signs to Fluff.

"Go on and fetch it then," he signed.

She hurried off but didn't run up the stairs. Cassea was walking down, a folded bundle of cloth wraps in hand. Nippi waved at her excitedly. Cassea smiled and said, "Good morning." Nippiktua pointed at her hair, made combing motions, and then pointed at Cassea's braids.

Cassea said something too quick for Nippiktua to catch and then lifted her bundle, indicating she needed to continue. Nippiktua smiled at her and continued on her way. The people here were so nice. Fluff should have brought her here sooner. When they stayed in—what was it? Lesgos. The people in Lesgos had been angry, even after Fluff helped them. Fluff hadn't told her, but she knew they'd called her a Dae-beast.

When Nippiktua returned to the table with her parchment and quill, she found her breakfast waiting for her: a plate of steaming eggs mixed with potatoes, some fruit or vegetable she didn't recognize, and a mug filled with milk. Nippiktua didn't care that the food was unrecognizable; she was starving. She got in her chair and ate. Neither Fluff nor Gaia could interrupt this holy rite, and she was using the fork. She finished by gulping down the milk. The room lit up when someone opened the door to leave. She enjoyed looking at the carvings on the inn's big wooden beams. There were grapevines and olive trees engraved in the wood.

Fluff stood then and walked over to where Gaia was wiping the tabletops. He looked funny, hunched over to keep his head from bumping into the candle holders that hung from the ceiling and the crossbeams. Nippiktua watched Cassea carry out some wooden trays. She wished her hair had the same braids.

Fluff stood in front of her. *"It's time I was off. Walk with me till the town's end."*

Nippiktua followed him out. Fluff turned to the eastern road. The morning sunlight blinded her for a moment. No one gave them a second glance. The center of the town had a well. She would have to drop a rock down at some point. She counted three houses and the smithy barn surrounding the center. The Green Olive was the tallest. The barn was the largest. She could smell the horses there, and several men were working outside the barn on some projects. Ahead of them, she could see a group of men walking east as well. They all had spears—going to the battle like her Fluff.

Fluff stopped and knelt so he was almost at eye level with Nippiktua. He had to place his sword on the ground. Nippiktua appreciated it when he did that. She was abruptly filled with a longing, as if he were already gone. She buried her face in his neck fur. He gave her a tight squeeze. She tried to squeeze as tight as she could, but his neck was too thick. She scratched behind his ear where he liked it but would never admit it. He put her down.

"Be safe, be attentive. I won't be here to speak for you, and I know you don't need me to," Fluff signed. He looked sad and worried, his ears back and eyes glossy. She resisted the urge to pat him on the head, knowing he

didn't like that. *"I won't be gone for long — two days. Fewer if the battle doesn't happen or if there's an ill result."*

"I will," Nippiktua signed assuredly. Older people always needed reassurance. As if she would disappear or run away from her Fluff. Ridiculous. *"I'm going to learn a lot from Cassea and Gaia."*

"Remember to care for your things. Don't — " Fluff playfully poked her. She giggled. He always went for where she was most ticklish. It wasn't fair. *"Don't practice with your bow. I doubt Gaia would appreciate that."*

Nippiktua nodded and gave him another hug. He returned the hug, then stood and waved farewell. She watched him walk away. As the sun caught the bronze pommel of his sword, flashing, she was suddenly filled with a thrill. Nippiktua was on her own. Fear filled her, and she shivered. No, she could do this. She was Nippiktua, Stag Blessed and Daughter of the Moon, a great huntress. She wasn't a child anymore. Fluff trusted her.

Hurrying back to the Green Olive, Nippiktua entered and immediately gathered her quill and ink and parchment on the clay tablet. There was no one eating anymore. One old woman with skin that looked like melted wax was sipping from a steaming mug of tea. Nippiktua hurried over to the counter, climbed onto a stool, and placed the tablet and parchment down. She wrote what she wanted to say, then walked to the kitchen.

She was almost knocked over by one cook. They must have exclaimed because Gaia found her and spoke to her. Nippiktua only caught a few words: "Careful here . . . What . . . Come on, girl."

Nippiktua raised the parchment so Gaia could read what she'd written: *I can help Cassea so she can braid my hair like hers.*

Gaia laughed, head tilted back, her mouth calling for Cassea. Cassea entered the kitchen, confused until she saw the runes on the parchment.

Her smile was contagious. She and Gaia talked, then Cassea waved for Nippiktua to follow her. Nippiktua skipped in triumph, almost dropping her ink.

Cassea took her out back behind the building, where a big tub stood filled with soapy water. She watched as Cassea took dirty laundry, soaked it, and then rubbed it on a wood plank with ripples carved into it. Nippiktua set her parchment down away from the wet mess, then picked up a dirty rag, rolled up her sleeves, and did as Cassea did.

When that was done, they went to meet an old farmer. Nippiktua helped carry the goods Cassea had purchased for the inn. On their way back, Nippiktua saw Timon in the big barn. He saw her too and waved. She smiled at him and shrugged. Her hands were full, and there was no time to drop the basket of eggs and write a greeting.

Back in the Green Olive, Nippiktua was surprised at how many crows were on the inn's roof. She remembered what Fluff had said about crows and the Fates but still thought it was silly crows would snitch on her.

She let Cassea take the basket of eggs, and then Cassea gave her a broom and pointed at the floor. Nippiktua couldn't help but give Cassea her best stink eye. Cassea laughed and made brooming motions. Of course she knew how to sweep. She showed Cassea. The young woman nodded and walked to the kitchen. Nippiktua swept the entire room. She didn't hold back. She swept between the tables—moving the chairs and tools—and around patrons as they ate and drank.

Nippiktua handed Cassea the broom and pointed at her hair. Cassea smiled and pointed at the far corner table. She hurried over after grabbing her parchment. Scribbling with fury, she held it up: *THANK YOU. FINALLY.*

Cassea shook her head, her smile still showing her perfect white teeth. She motioned for the pen and wrote: *Thanks for the help. Now sit down and face away from me. First, we will try to trim and cut your hair even.*

Nippiktua looked wide-eyed at the bundle on the table next to Cassea. There was a comb, a small thread of ties, and a weird knife with two holes for a handle. She scribbled, *What is that?*

After giving her a quizzical look, Cassea replied, "Those are scissors. We use them to cut hair. A trader from Threvicio had them. They said they purchased them from the elves."

Nippiktua marveled at that—elves, who had dwarves as slaves, made incredible tools. Cassea put a cloth around her neck, combed her hair, then went to work with the scissors. Nippiktua became drowsy as Cassea tugged and combed her hair and began braiding it. She focused primarily on the movement of Cassea's fingers. She liked how it felt, the tug and brush. Cassea's hands were so gentle. She was done too soon.

Nippiktua hurried to her room, the only place she knew had a mirror. Her white hair was taut against her scalp, woven into intricate braids that rolled down to the back of her head. Her cheeks burned from smiling. Without her hair going in every direction, she looked like one of the boys in her village back home—when it had been her home.

She realized she'd forgotten her parchment! *"Thank you,"* she signed to Cassea and gave her a hug.

Cassea accepted her hug and tapped her shoulder. The young woman was holding a lock of her own hair and pointed at Nippiktua. It took her a moment to realize that Cassea was asking her to try braiding it herself. She jumped up and down.

That was when Gaia found them. She talked hurriedly with Cassea—Nippiktua couldn't catch enough of her words to understand. What she said made Cassea jump into action and hurry out the door. Gaia handed Nippiktua her parchment on the tablet. She nodded her thanks.

The parchment read: Timon is waiting at the door for you. He is done with his chores, and I have too much work to watch you. Go with him. The children have some Sene games to show you.

Nippiktua nodded, swallowing a sudden lump in her throat. Other kids. Timon was nice and was good at dancing, just not at Frystlin dances. Were the other children nice like Timon? She couldn't remain in her room to wonder, for Gaia ushered her out and down the stairs. She had no choice.

Timon waved to her from the front door when he saw her. She waved back with her free hand, the other holding her parchment. Timon had darker skin than Cassea—he was out in the sun more, Nippiktua guessed. His curly brown hair almost covered his green eyes. A tight belt held up his breeches at his waist, and dust and dirt had darkened his tunic, which had been light blue that morning.

He waved for her to follow him, saying, "Come on, Nippiktua. We have a game I think you'll like."

She followed him across the yard. Seeing the well again, she stopped and hastily picked up a pebble and tossed it down like her older sister used to when they'd been on the southern fells, where the snow melted enough for deep pools to form below the cavernous ice. She kept her free hand on the stones, waiting for the vibrations of impact. There was a second before she felt it. She laughed and tossed another one. It made a longer vibration. She tried to look down but almost lost control of her parchment.

Nippiktua was happy she could scratch that off her list. Which reminded her of Fluff's caution that she shouldn't do her list. As it was the only one on her list she *could* do, she had done it. Nippiktua promised herself she wouldn't add any more.

Timon led her around the barn. She hesitated for a moment,

wondering if he was like Chub and Thin. If he was, she would run faster. She crept cautiously. The smell of horses, pigs, and goats filled her nose. There was one enormous pig in a fenced pen. Then two tall horses were chewing on some dried grass. Nippiktua had to crane her neck to look up at the nearest one. Timon ran ahead of her to a colossal oak tree, its branches spread wide, giving plenty of shade from the warm afternoon sun. Three other children waited for them.

They smiled at Nippiktua and waved in greeting, putting her at ease.

The two girls were tall and looked just like Fyrla, except one had golden hair and the other's was black. They both said their names, but Nippiktua couldn't read their lips. The boy was short and stubby. He smiled sheepishly at her. He looked like the youngest.

Nippiktua held up her parchment, hurriedly writing. She showed them: I'm Nippiktua. I'm staying for a night or two. Can you write your names?

She remembered Chub and Thin not being pleased with her nicknames for them. She wanted to make sure she knew their names. The two girls excitedly wrote theirs. Timon said something to the shy boy, whose head drooped, and Timon wrote his name for him. Nippiktua read the names: Jenlin, Ylinan, and Neotum. Timon took the parchment and scribbled.

While he was doing it, Jenlin and Ylinan pointed at Nippiktua's braids. She was able to read Jenlin's lips. "Who did your braids?"

Nippiktua drew Cassea's name in the dirt with a nearby stick. The girls seemed eager to read the news. Hopefully, Gaia would give her less work next time in exchange for the more important braiding. Timon showed Nippiktua what he'd written: *The game is called "Skip Adrea." See the boxes drawn in the dirt? We see how fast we can skip over them. I think you'll do great because of how you danced last night.*

She looked up in time for Timon to demonstrate. There was a line of connecting squares drawn in the dirt. The line broke into separate squares, sometimes one square, sometimes two side by side. Timon saw Nippiktua watching and started. He leaped onto each square, then put one foot in a separate square as he made his way down. Nippiktua couldn't hold back her excitement. She could do this!

By the time the sun began its descent, she had become an expert. She, Jenlin, and Timon were tied for the fastest. Neotum made the most improvement; he was the youngest, so it was harder for him to coordinate his movements. Ylinan was tired and watched. If Nippiktua was honest with herself, she was tired too. Her clothes were damp from her sweat, and dust clung to her face, making her sleeve brown when she wiped her brow. She felt an incredible need to be the fastest and wanted to beat Timon and Jenlin. She tried it again, moving as fast as she could. Her legs burned, but she had to do it.

When she finished, Timon showed her the time with his fingers. It was the same as her last. Nippiktua grumbled in frustration. She had to be faster. Fluff had to carry her whenever they needed to get away from danger. Nippiktua paced. If she was alone, she had to be able to take care of herself.

When she glanced at Timon, he only shrugged. Jenlin was smiling but tired as well. They talked among themselves; she didn't care to follow their words.

Her heart felt like it would beat out of her chest. She tried to control her breathing. Her frustration at not being fast enough sought to overwhelm her. No, she could do it faster. She—

Cassea found them.

The young woman's smile made Nippiktua take a deep breath. She wasn't alone, and she'd had a lot of fun. She wrote to Jenlin, Neotum,

Ylinan, and Timon, thanking them. They clapped their hands together.

Cassea said something that made the others hurry away. Nippiktua waved Cassea over to watch her do the skipping game. Cassea shook her head and pointed back to the Green Olive with a reassuring smile. Nippiktua slouched but gathered her things.

When Gaia saw Nippiktua, she placed her hand over her mouth, shaking her head.

"Goodness, girl. Did you roll in the dirt? Go upstairs and wash up and come back down for supper."

Nippiktua laughed and weaved through the crowd as the townsfolk filled the inn. She made a note of the crowd. It was mostly women and children and old men. Several women looked at her, surprised, pointing and calling someone behind her as she climbed up the stairs. Gaia would talk to her for now. Nippiktua realized how ravenous she was and wanted to wash up so she could eat.

The rest of the evening passed in a blur. Nippiktua had supper, and then there was music and dancing again. She stared up at the ceiling. The night's cool light shone in through a crack in the curtain as she thought about spinning and spinning with the other kids. She had to watch the rhythms of the dancers to find her own. She couldn't hear the music, only feel the vibrations or see them on the strings of the instruments. Nippiktua was suddenly sad and wished Fluff was in the other bed instead of Cassea. Her chest was rising and falling steadily in her sleep. Nippiktua stared back up at the ceiling, still wondering how people and things sounded. She fell asleep with those thoughts and dreamed.

20

Morvelving crested the rocky outcropping, which sat high on the hills south of Pilla Falen. He honed his anxiety. This felt right—unlike the centaurs' demands and the horrible disagreement with the Prince of Thressea. Still, he worried about Nippi. The wide plain filled with wheat stalks stretched between two wide rock ridges on either side. Further east stood tall pines. Under their shadow lay the Great Elven Road, and beyond that were the Althek Mountains, their faraway white-capped peaks visible above the tree line.

A small dirt track in the valley led to the many tents clustered within the narrow gap between the two ridges. Columns of men from across the land marched on makeshift pathways and formal roads toward the camp. Morvelving was struck again with human differences based on their given place and cultural identity. Both men and women fought in conflicts among the Idosse. Here in Menici, it seemed only the men fought.

Morvelving scrambled down the hillside, joining the column of men from Sene as they continued to Pilla Falen. He had accompanied them since Sene. Experienced at marching order, they had stopped once for some food. Seeing the city of Aqualea from a distance was the only eventful thing that had happened along the way.

The stench of human sweat and defecation and the acrid aromas of livestock entered his nose from the easterly wind. There had to be a couple thousand men at the camp. What struck him further was a stark scent he had never smelled before. It had to be the Graal, hiding further east.

The commander, Arastus, had a sense of strategy. If the Graal were making their way west from River Ath, they had to pass through Pilla Falen or march to the Elven Road further north. The rock ridges were passable, but scaling them came with high risk. Morvelving eyed them with scrutiny. There were several outposts where men stood watch, though the dense trees to the east provided ample cover. Seeing the land—and how the Graal could approach unseen till Pilla Falen—made him hasten to the camp. Hopefully, the commander had scouts. If not, Morvelving would offer his services. He needed to know if the battle was winnable, and humans were terrible at scouting.

"What did you see, Morvelving?" Paunt called out. Fyrla's father, Farlan, stopped with Paunt to watch Morvelving approach. Their tunics soaked through with sweat from marching. Farlan's shield was painted green, the picture long faded from use. Both had their equipment tied to the shafts of their spears, which rested on their shoulders. They had told him the weapons and armor were their fathers' and their fathers' before. Brief lives, and the stitched linen and leather cuirasses showed their age with patches and old cuts.

"Pilla Falen is a good place for a battle. Arastus knows his command," Morvelving said. "I'm afraid the Graal can approach unseen. I must get to the commander with haste."

"We'll come with you."

"I'll find you after," Morvelving said, putting up his hand to ease their readiness.

Men moved aside for him as he walked the main path through the city of tents toward the commander's tent. Rows and rows of them—men sat or stood, seeing to their equipment. The ringing of sharpening swords and the clatter of smithwork filled his ears. A tall pole held the Aqualean banner high, where it danced lazily in the cool wind. Its golden-crowned white eagle, wings spread against a dark blue sky, was much like the local raptors Morvelving had seen earlier, flying high in the sky.

Outside the tent, several guards stood on either side of a wooden table. A man sat there in armor much like the guards: polished bronze greaves, vambraces, cuirass, and helm—all painted purple with red trim. His helm, unlike the guards', had two red-painted feathers jutting out on either side of the brow and was topped with a tall crest decorated with red- and white-painted horsehair, a sign of command. He held a feather quill and was writing on parchment. The guards saw Morvelving, but the man at the table had his head bowed, his thick black curly hair trying to escape the braid that kept most of it out of his face.

"Prime Enator," a guard said.

The Prime Enator looked up to see Morvelving. "*Edu ve*, by the gods," he said, standing and giving a slight bow. "There was a rumor a Mulranei sellsword was spotted on the road. I am Arastus, General of the Pilla Falen defense. I am honored you have come to assist us against the Graal."

"Greetings," Morvelving said, introducing himself. "I was in Sene when I heard. You have a strong position here. What are your contract rates?"

Two guards eyed each other. Arastus scratched at his dark beard, trimmed on the sides but long at his chin. Morvelving could hear the hushed whispers of men watching him.

"Uh, yes, rates are ten aulos per battle with two aulos per injury.

Make your mark here." Arastus moved over a long parchment, a long list of runes and marks filling the page. "Give the name of who will receive your payment if you perish."

Morvelving nodded. It was the same rate among the Idosse. He dipped his pointer claw in the ink and drew his mark and wrote: *Gaia, owner of the Green Olive in Sene.*

"I see you have weapons," Arastus added as Morvelving wrote. "If you need armor, see our smiths, though I doubt they can find something to fit you in time. We fight in the shield wall with spears. Adrean and western arrivals will be assigned the flank, if that's where you wish to be?"

"A shield wall would be most needed, and that will do well." Morvelving stood straight again. "You have scouts? The Graal can approach from under the great pines without being seen. Even by your watchers on the ridge."

"I have sent several scouts. They haven't returned yet," Arastus answered thoughtfully. "I will not lie to you, Mulranei. You can probably smell a lie?"

Morvelving crooked a brow, left ear flicking to the side.

"The host has not been seen since it split from the main host at River Ath."

"They are near," Morvelving stated. "I can smell them. How close, I can't discern yet. With respect, I ask that you assign me to scout out ahead and find them. I will return. When I do, it may be with a host of Graal on my tail."

Arastus grunted, nodding several times. Bronze scale pauldrons protected his shoulders, and stitched linen lay under the bronze of his cuirass. Up close, Morvelving could see how the stitched linen's blue dye mixed with purple at the abdomen. Morvelving imagined he would be easy to find on a battlefield, and surely that was the point.

He spoke to one of his guards. "Send word to Boragatis: Mulranei sellsword will guard his flank with the Adrean volunteers." Arastus looked back at Morvelving. "I'm assigning you to Eagle Claw Company on the west flank under Commander Boragatis. Report your findings to me, then him. When do you depart?"

"Now," Morvelving answered, picking up his pack and tightening it around his torso. He had taken his minotaur-hide cloak off earlier and was glad he had, as it would have made him too warm for a run. "Look for my return by nightfall."

Arastus began to speak; Morvelving chose to ignore him. Urgency filled him. Men called out to him in surprise as he jogged out of the Aqualean camp.

The Field of Pilla Falen was a flat grassy land with a tall ancient menhir at the center. Morvelving stopped his sprint there and sniffed. If the Graal had scouts, one of their young could have sneaked under the cover of the grass to observe here. The old menhir, cracked and crumbling, stood alone on the hilltop. There were no markings on it, and no scent of Graal.

Morvelving sniffed in the wind again. It was still there, coming from the east. He raced to the cover of the trees, holding Penalty in hand now. It was too cumbersome on his back and would catch on the forest's underbrush.

Under the expansive boughs of the red-bark pines, Morvelving moved swiftly and without a sound. He caught the scent of Arastus's scouts and followed their trail. The smell of Graal weakened the further north he went. He turned east, even though one of the human scouts had continued north. He knew he was close when the woods became as silent as a tomb.

Morvelving crept, ears forward, listening. He sat still in front of a long stretch of heavy brush. The trees grew too close to each other, some hanging dead from others, having been choked of space and light. The land began to descend into an old riverbed formed by flooding. They were there, but he could not see them. How was a host so quiet? Morvelving looked up into the branches, found his purchase, and climbed.

That was when he came face-to-face with his first Graal. The creature's slight, bright-green eyes regarded him with surprise. It lay on a large branch, human-like arms and torso wrapping around the bough, its stubby tail lax. Its skin was a tapestry of greenish-brown scales. It wore worn hide clothing and studded armor on its shoulders and legs. The Graal pulled out a flint axe from its belt. A hiss and growl emitted from its stubbed snout, parting to reveal small, sharp teeth. It bent its back, trying to look larger than it was. It was only four feet long—young.

More hissing made Morvelving look up. Hundreds of green and yellow eyes looked down on him. They'd hidden themselves by camping in the trees. He kept his breath steady; they were assessing his threat and would attack. He had a moment. Morvelving looked down at the slope of the land. Below, more and more Graal moved, looking up at him. He almost fled when a large Graal, ten or twelve feet tall, stood up from its hiding place, having been camouflaged in the underbrush where it had lain. It held a tree trunk for a club.

He had overstayed his welcome. Something in one of the Graal's mouths caught his eye: a human arm, one of Arastus's scouts. Morvelving leaped down, jumping and hanging from the branches he'd just climbed. He landed on the ground and immediately sprinted back southwest. Hisses and roars came from behind him, and the sound of hundreds of clawed feet scraping and thudding. The large one must have made a command, for many of his pursuers fell back, and a few heavy footbeats kept up the chase. An arrow landed in a tree trunk Morvelving had passed a moment ago. They were on his heels, much faster than he'd expected. One leaped at him; he dodged it. Its claws passed through the fur on the back of his neck.

The sun was setting in the west, and the light under the trees was darkening in the twilight. Their arrows were now even further off the mark. Finally, he heard a frustrated hiss and an unusual bark. He stopped and hid behind a tree, listening and sniffing. They had given up.

Morvelving hurried on. His father would have scolded him harshly for allowing himself to sneak right into a hostile camp. But there was nothing new there. He was ever a disappointment to his father, the mighty Thundereye. He had no one to blame for his destiny but himself. The thrill of escape kept him light on his feet despite the weight of memories flooding his mind. Windtail falling. His returning grief sought to take his breath. There was solace in the fact that he was on the right path.

He broke into a sprint as he left the forest and passed into Pilla Falen. Arastus needed to know. Battle would likely come early in the morning, though if the Graal were cunning, they would attack tonight. Already, the shadows of night were growing as he approached the sentries outside the camp. He hailed them, giving each a start.

"The Prime Enator warned us of your return, Mulranei," the guard said after Morvelving explained his errand, letting him pass.

He didn't run through the camp. Despite it being night, the camp bustled with activity. Companies had placed their tents around their fires, keeping their spears and shields stacked nearby. Men sharpened swords or axes and checked their armor. Laughter and games distracted from thoughts of battle.

He found Arastus where he'd left him, except now there were men with an air of command and importance surrounding him. They were looking at a lean young man who was dirty and tired, sitting on the ground. A man with a bald head and an eyepatch over his right eye noticed Morvelving first. He gave a start and instinctively placed his hand on his sword's hilt.

"Arastus, he's returned," the one-eyed man announced. All of them looked up at him. Morvelving only drooped his ears in response.

"Morvelving, you've returned after nightfall, just as you said," Arastus stated. "These are the commanders of the companies from all three kingdoms of the Menici. We will dispense with introductions. One of my scouts has returned with news: the Graal are heading northwest to the Elven Road."

"We must break camp and head north immediately," said the one-eyed man.

"Peace, Boragatis," Arastus said. "Morvelving, what did you find?"

Morvelving told Arastus what he'd discovered. "I was only able to see a few hundred, but by the strength of their scent, their full number is likely in the thousands. Otherwise, they would be heading northeast for easier prey. Unfortunately, I almost fell into the same trap one of your men did, so they know I saw them. They may attack tonight or at first light."

Some commanders shook their heads at that. It was difficult to keep an army fresh and ready if all the men didn't rest.

"They could still be heading northeast," one man said.

"I trust Morvelving's account, Shulgatist," Arastus stated. "Who here can claim to be a better tracker than a Mulranei, who hunted the lands before Man had even crossed into Bregalen?"

Shulgatist fidgeted like a child, which was amusing to see, given his old age and wide girth that strained to escape the strappings of his cuirass.

Morvelving eyed Arastus with scrutiny. His words smelled honest. Yet he was a man of power, and they often twisted their words for their own ends. Idanphyrus came to mind. Was Arastus hoping to blame him if the battle never happened or went ill?

Arastus commanded, "I want half of each company awake and ready for battle. Move the other half to the back of camp to rest."

The commanders were nodding and talking among themselves now, deciding which company was to be positioned where.

Morvelving turned to go. He had done what he could for them to be ready. He had to admit this was the strangest battle he had been a part of in over fifty years. Perhaps the largest as well. Morvelving wasn't looking forward to it. The Graal were full of ill intent. He'd gathered no sense of fear from them. Rather, they feared him because he had sneaked right into their camp, but they weren't acting out of fear. They were simply doing what they thought they had to. Why Kragius had made them was beyond Morvelving. Who could explain the whims of the God of Pestilence? He couldn't, yet there was reason to the Song of Life. Pestilence often led to new growth. It didn't feel right with the lives of people at stake.

He knew well that Nameless used and bred the Graal for his armies. Was this host of Graal trying to avoid that fate here in the west? There was a possibility he was overthinking the whole thing.

Morvelving made his way through the camp to the northwest flank where the Eagle Claw Company was stationed. The younger men looked up at him with wide-eyed awe. Older men shook them, warning or informing them.

Morvelving held his right ear back to catch what they said. "Careful, lad. The Mulranei are ancient creatures. Stare too long, you'll get moon drunk."

An absurd statement. There was no such thing. He refrained from barking at the man to call out his nonsense. The only spell his people would cast on humans was common sense.

He found the Eagle Claw standard. The yellow claw seeming to flex as the banner rippled in the breeze, stark against the crimson field.

Tents were arranged in rows on the flat ground as the land gradually climbed toward the rock ridge. Groups of men watched him from their seats by fires. Others were busy at their work, sharpening weapons or maintaining their armor near a long line of oval and round shields with crescent dips on either side. They were designed for the wielder to jab their spear through a shield wall.

Elves had devised the formation, and men called it a phalanx. It was how they fought, relying on long spears, interlocked shields, and heavy infantry. A sound strategy for pitched battles, better than the mad skirmishes he had fought in, where it was difficult to discern who was friend and foe.

The men he saw were hardly heavy infantry; few had more than a cuirass and helm. Short Graal would be able to cut shins and ankles. He wondered if men with greaves would be on the front line.

"Morvelving, over here!" Paunt called, breaking Morvelving's thoughts. Sene and Adrean men looked his way as he approached, their faces half lit by the campfires. "They said you went ahead to scout. What did you find?"

He found an unoccupied space and sat, setting down Penalty and taking the offered wooden cup of water.

Morvelving told them.

They spoke among themselves, hushed and aloud.

"Sooner than we thought," Paunt stated.

"It's why we came, isn't it?" one man said.

Their talk filled his ears. Morvelving didn't listen as he took the wrapping off Penalty. It shone bright in the firelight, the dwarf runes glowing a hazy blue, a lazy mist rising from one mark. Despite the water, his mouth was dry.

He ignored the stares from the men present. His thumb found several notches on the edge of the blade. He began working on them.

"That is no sword made by humans," Paunt stated as he sat down next to Morvelving. "Elven make? I've never seen runes like that."

"It's dwarven made," Morvelving said, eyeing the man. "You are well learned; you weren't always a farmer?"

Paunt shook his head. "No, when I was a boy, I took the pilgrimage to Don Warthia and studied under the Crafters of Ivalin. Their methods are . . . rigorous. I didn't last long."

"To manipulate Ergald requires sacrifices. It can change a man." Morvelving's arm burned where he had clawed it to bring the menhir down.

Paunt nodded in agreement, his eyes glazed as though seeing memories in the flames that danced above the blackened wood. "It certainly can. I saw it . . . *Edu ve*, I will not recount that tale. I wanted to ask, why change your path for us? You didn't have to risk your life for us. It can't just be for the aulos."

Morvelving was silent for a moment before he spoke. "Most often, coin is all it is, I'm afraid. Kingdoms are not my concern. I need the aulos, but your people touched my heart at Sene. In my travels, I've found it rare for people to offer simple hospitality and kindness to a stranger. If fighting alongside you is how I can repay it right now, it gives me purpose. I've intent to travel through Menici, and if the Graal horde goes unchecked, it will be difficult for me to deal with them alone."

"Reasonable and honorable. We are thankful," Paunt said. "Tell you true, I'm scared. Fear I'd shit myself at any moment. I've been in a couple of battles—skirmishes, really—between two villages or against raiders from Monbargar or Elg Narsh. This is far, far worse."

"I'm scared too," Morvelving said without hesitation, though an urge for piphlid spiked. "The Fates and Acraces's Dae love battles; many threads will be cut short. It isn't any easier to bear that possibility of death if you face it. There's a saying among my people: 'better to chase than be chased.' It's the courage to accept your fears and face them rather than run. Tonight, or tomorrow, that is what we must do."

Whether his words helped Paunt, Morvelving didn't know. He couldn't understand how it was to be human, to have such a brief life, and yet go willingly to death's door. Morvelving had tried and failed. He had lived for over five human lives. His mistakes haunted him. He kept his hand from reaching for the piphlid that wasn't in his belt pouch. If he died before he could right his mistakes . . . Nippi was depending on him. He needed to get back to her, and he evidently needed her near to avoid the itch for piphlid.

Morvelving trusted his skills in battle, and he would do what he could to keep Paunt and Farlan and the rest alive. His arrogance may have doomed them all. The Fates loved their tragic irony. He prayed to Telunian, asking for her protection upon them.

21

———

The Graal didn't attack at night or in the morning, defying logic. Instead, they gathered at the foot of the large menhir in the center of Pilla Falen around midmorning, watching and waiting.

Morvelving stood among the rows and columns of the men of Adrea and Sene. A head taller than most men, he could see down the ranks and across the field. Banners of all colors and shapes fluttered in the soft cool wind. Spears shifted or stood still as the men stood ready. The scent in the air was of anticipation—like a tensed branch about to snap—stifling fear and sweat.

The fear had already made Morvelving sneeze once. It hung above the army, tickling his nose like the morning mists that still clung to springs below the ridge. He wasn't beyond his own fear—fear of not returning to Nippi, of never seeing her again.

He squinted a glance at the sky. The sun was bright behind a thin cloud, and Celemith was dark below it. A reminder the gods watched. He wondered if Telunian was watching him now or if Kragius was looking on with amusement at what violence his spawn may cause. The Moon Goddess taught to help those who sought to keep their simple lives, to continue in the Cycle. He was here for the kind folk in Sene. He would do what he could within his means.

Commander Boragatis was making his way through the ranks to the front. Morvelving noticed movement among the Graal as they milled about in the center of the field. Part of him hoped they would turn back. The Graal did not. They began making noise, jumping up and down, raising their weapons in challenge.

The men around him stirred, spears held straight and shields raised. Boragatis turned to glance at Morvelving. He took a half step, then planted his feet, motioning for Morvelving to come to him.

Morvelving didn't care for the man's posturing. The scent of pride hung about him in a dense cloud, shrouding him in his need to never ask for help. Yet Boragatis needed it. Morvelving had gathered that when Arastus had assigned him to the flank under Boragatis.

The Eagle Claw Company was under-equipped and comprised primarily of younger men. Arastus must be afraid they would break and knew that Boragatis wouldn't ask for any troops to bolster his position.

"What is it?" Morvelving asked Boragatis after he had weaved his way through the ranks of men to the commander.

Boragatis eyed Penalty. Morvelving held it with one hand, its blade resting on his right shoulder, while his left hand held a shield he'd acquired.

"Sure that thing won't break?" Boragatis scoffed.

The Graal were still making noise across the field. Morvelving looked down at the man. "It hasn't yet."

"Hmph," Boragatis grunted. "Well, some fix we are in. Keep the big ones off the men, can you do that?" When Morvelving only stared at him, he looked away. "Do what you need to do, as will I."

Morvelving took the dismissal and walked down the line. Ignoring the sense of being used by the man so he could feel important. "Humans," he grumbled loudly.

The first two lines were veteran warriors, men middle-aged or older, with scars from previous battles and in full armor, helms high-crested with painted feathers or horsehair. Their shields had painted or gilded faces of mythical creatures: phoenixes, gorgons, trolls, and chimera. Some weren't mythical: a Stag, wolf, raven, minotaur, or centaur. The men looked up at him as he passed, then focused on the Graal.

The host of Graal was moving. A host it was, not an army. They moved in clusters, then would stop, howling and hissing. A few Graal loosed arrows from their thin bows, the arrows falling short, getting lost in the grass.

Men laughed. Morvelving understood the Graal were testing the range. The smaller ones, by their age, were inexperienced. He focused on the clusters of older Graal, all five feet or taller, the tallest being a seven-foot brute.

They seemed to be talking among themselves. Down the line toward the center, Morvelving spotted the huge one. It towered over the scrambling younger Graal, even as it kneeled on one knee, its fist under its chin. When it stood, it would be almost as tall as the menhir at the center of the field. It seemed to study the army of men who stood before its younger cousins.

What was it thinking? Was it hungry, sizing up its food? Was it resting? Or was it creating a plan to defeat them? He prayed to the Moon Goddess that it wouldn't join the fight.

Calls rang out, followed by the blowing of horns. The men marched forward. Morvelving arrived at the flank of his line. The lightly clad young men with javelins and slings made way for him. He recognized a few from Sene and nodded to them.

Archers with hunting bows loosed arrows overhead at the Graal. Arastus was tired of giving the Graal time to plan their attack or retreat. His impatience risked exposing the army's flanks.

The army moved forward a step at a time, the front two lines keeping their shields locked. Morvelving followed, marking his targets.

The taller Graal spread among the clusters of the runts. They were armed with clubs, spears, and axes with heads of sharpened stone or flint. Some Graal were armored with stolen bronze, faded to sickly jade. They clearly didn't know how to maintain the metal.

Another volley of arrows whistled overhead, this time falling into the ranks of Graal. Screeches of pain filled the air as many found a target. The Graal still waited as the human army moved toward it. Morvelving walked over several Graal arrows.

The enemy released a second volley; the arrows fell among the men. Morvelving spotted one coming for his torso and blocked it with his shield. Feeling exposed, he wished he'd had time to be fitted with a helmet and new cuirass.

The human slingers began loosing deadly small stones overhead.

The hardest part of the battle began: a slow crawl to reach the enemy as each side peppered the other with missiles, hoping to weaken the other.

Morvelving rolled his shoulders to release the growing tension. He could hear the heavy breaths of the surrounding men, catch their whispers of prayer, and smell the sweat soaking their tunics.

A young man screamed, an arrow protruding from his shoulder. It had missed the hardened leather of his cuirass. He clutched at it, falling to his knees in pain. The surrounding men ignored him, shuffling around him and keeping their shields up.

Arrows ricocheted off Morvelving's shield, bouncing harmlessly at his feet. The Graal and the line of men bristling with spears were close. Men were calling, "Hold the line! Hold!"

Graal were screeching and roaring guttural calls that made his skin crawl, riling up their courage. The large one at the center stood—visible to all—raised its tree-trunk club, and yelled. The signal was given.

Readying himself, Morvelving crouched. To his surprise, and to that of all the men, the larger Graal began throwing the smaller ones over the front ranks. Some of them landed on top of men or at their feet while many were skewered on spears, forcing the spear bearers to drop their weapons. A mad frenzy—ludicrous, if it weren't so morbid.

The short Graal had small daggers and slashed at ankles or stabbed at throats. Then the host sprinted the short distance into the ranks of men holding on by a thread of courage. A dull thunderous clap split the air when thousands of bodies smashed into the shield wall. As hundreds of Graal were skewered on spears, cries of battle and pain followed.

Morvelving rushed in, barking and flaring his teeth, chasing small Graal away from the flank so Paunt and Farlan and the others had a moment to prepare for the impact.

A large Graal threw a small one, three feet tall at most, at Morvelving. He cut it in midair with Penalty. Blood spraying him as its two parts landed on either side of him. He noticed the older Graal holding back as the younger and smaller ones wreaked havoc on the men.

They waited for a break in the line. Morvelving stole a glance east across the battle. Already, several breaks were imminent. Thankfully, the giant leader was still holding back, watching.

Younger Graal tried to flank the line—Morvelving engaged them. He cut one down, torso to rib; still, its jaws snapped at him as he removed the head of another Graal. Seeing two dispatched so quickly made the other young Graal falter and flee.

The slingers continued to pelt the Graal, dropping them by the tens. Morvelving noticed the larger Graal pointing at him. They made some calls in their hissing speech, and the Graal moved away from pressing the front line.

"Ready yourselves," Morvelving called out to the young men with slings and javelins. "Paunt! Take them together!"

They didn't understand at first, not until they saw the wave of Graal moving toward them. He heard them draw their swords before meeting the rush. He had to keep an eye on his feet or the small Graal would slash at his ankles. Morvelving danced in his battle stance, swinging Penalty in precise sweeping arcs and keeping the shield close to his torso, cutting Graal like a butcher with slabs of meat. Penalty's runes boiled the blood on the blade.

Men joined the fight, which dissolved into a gnashing, slicing, and grunting brawl.

The Graal and men fought with weapons. When the weapons were lost or broken, they fought with teeth and limbs.

The cries of pain deafened his ears as Morvelving kept himself away from the small Graal and targeted the Graal as tall as a man or higher, who were moving for the flank of the phalanx. Morvelving leaped over a small Graal and cut down a large one from behind, turning to finish the first.

A Graal challenged him and furiously swung its two heavy clubs, each crowned with a sharpened flint stub. The flint splintered on Morvelving's shield, a small piece flying off and cutting his left ear as he blocked the first two attacks.

The Graal tried to block Morvelving's stroke with its club. Penalty cut through the wood and lodged in the creature's throat. Morvelving pulled the blade free in time to stab another, block another attack, and finish that Graal by opening its throat.

Once the large Graal were dead, the younger ones scattered—they'd succeeded in beating the Graal's attack back.

Men cheered and moved to retrieve the wailing wounded.

Morvelving took the moment of respite to survey the battle. Their line down the field had fluctuated in several locations, and a few points were broken, but most held firm.

The giant Graal still stood back and watched. It seemed hesitant to engage yet also showed signs of thought and care for the battle. But why hold back? Morvelving imagined it didn't want to engage, for as soon as it did, all the human archers, slingers, and spearmen would direct their attacks at it. Hundreds of Graal, perhaps over a thousand, lay dead on the field, their blood muddying the soft earth and accosting Morvelving's senses.

The giant raised its tree-trunk club to its shoulder. Morvelving held his breath. The Graal were faltering, stumbling away from the advancing line of men and killing any who were close. If it entered the battle now, it could change the tide, and what would he do? Morvelving wouldn't be able to watch. He would have to face it, and he was unsure of the outcome.

The giant raised its arm and bellowed something in its own tongue. Almost instantly, the host began to trickle away from the human ranks, leaking into a full retreat.

Every man was as stunned as Morvelving.

The Graal swarmed around the menhir, milling about as if trying to organize themselves. Meanwhile, the large Graal walked down to the center of the Menician army. It stopped a bowshot away, set down its tree trunk for a club, and sat down, cross-legged. Its stubby tail curving to one side. The Graal waited, saw no one approaching, and waved its arm, beckoning for someone to approach.

Around him, men began to talk among themselves, the noise like footfalls on dry leaves. Morvelving ignored them. He was intent on the Graal. Its body language told him it was agitated. He sniffed the air, hoping to gain more hints about its motives. The wind blew any scent away from him.

A runner was making his way down the ranks to the flank. The boy faltered, saw Morvelving, and hurried to him.

"Mulranei . . . " he called, halting to catch his breath. "The Enator . . . " Another breath. "Wants you under his banner. At the center."

Morvelving's ears flexed down and up. So, he was going to approach the Graal. He nodded and hurried down the line.

The front rank still held their shields forward and interlocked. Behind them, men gathered the wounded and checked their weapons.

Morvelving maintained a jog, the shield and Penalty cumbersome but not as hindering as the bodies he tried to avoid.

The large Graal followed his movement all the way and lingered on him as Morvelving approached the Prime Enator.

Arastus stood under his banner, his arms covered in the Graal's dark green blood. A boy held his sword and shield. His companions stood around him, all just as bloodied.

"Morvelving, good," Arastus said, looking up at him as he approached. "What do you make of this?"

Licking his dry mouth, Morvelving gave a quick shrug. A human gesture he'd found to universally signal uncertainty. "I admit, I have little experience with Graal, except for the obvious."

"What is the obvious?" Arastus asked. "You think it actually wants to talk?"

"There's a chance," Morvelving admitted. "It attacked and now wants to parley. Perhaps it doesn't want more of its followers slain."

"Perhaps it wants single combat," a companion stated. Obviously disturbed by that honored possibility. Single combat was sacred to the gods in its simple solution: a few lives for many.

"Only one way to find out," Arastus said, resigned. "I don't like it. Admittedly, I don't like any of these events. If it means to talk and make a deal, I'd hear it before more blood is spilled. Morvelving, can I convince you to represent my banner and converse with the giant? If it means ill, you have a better chance of escaping than I."

Morvelving flexed his ears forward and back, showing his unease, and grunted with a snort. He could evade the giant if it came to a fight. The Graal's smell gave him reason and hope—a curious hope—that the Graal did want to talk. Find a better solution than the total slaughter of the other. Looking now at the Graal and the host behind it, he had the unpleasant thought that they were holding back.

"I'll go," Morvelving said, looking ahead at the large Graal sitting on the ground, staring back at him. "I have a feeling it wants to talk to me. What are your terms?"

Arastus thought for a moment. "They must depart these lands. If they are willing to bargain to leave without more bloodshed, I will hear it."

Morvelving looked at Arastus with more admiration. The man was a leader—and a levelheaded one at that. He understood they'd won the engagement yet was reasonable enough to use more than just the sword to make sure the Graal left. Morvelving nodded and made his way to the Graal.

He'd come here to prevent as many men as possible from dying. If this offered a means to that end, he would risk it. He looked to the sky. Moon Goddess willing, this would have a better outcome than his confrontations with the Roxanar and Thresseans.

The wind tugged at his ears as he strode toward the sitting giant. Tall grass was trampled and churned from the Graal's charge. A few lay dead with arrows in their corpses. Morvelving didn't slow his stride to the

Graal. Everything he knew about Graal came from tales spoken by the Wiseneyes, and those tales involved large battles long ago. He was curious to see if this Graal sought a different resolution beyond what its kind was known and feared for.

The Graal watched him, its slit green eyes never blinking. It rested its snout on one arm. As he drew closer, he could see the array of bandoliers strung across its torso and waist, holding many accoutrements. Mainly bones of all sizes, though he also noticed several strips of armor. Torn from past enemies. All of them looked like trinkets. Morvelving stopped ten feet from the Graal. He still carried his shield and held Penalty by the blade near the hilt. He hoped it would make him less threatening.

Morvelving remained still as the Graal lashed its tongue out like the small blue lizards he had seen along riverbeds.

It pointed a large, stubbed finger at the army behind Morvelving. When it spoke, its voice was rasping and grating, the sound struggling to escape the sporadic array of rotted teeth and long tongue. "Theys going to stand there or go?"

Morvelving closed his mouth, almost biting his own tongue in surprise at how well it spoke the Trade Tongue. He was sure if Arastus were standing with him, the man's mouth would be open in shock, an expression he had seen Nippi perform many times. The Graal could speak. Morvelving suddenly felt silly for thinking they couldn't. It went against all that was taught of the Graal.

"They are staying there as long as you are here," Morvelving said slowly.

"Huh," the Graal grunted. "Why are you here? Instead of softskins. Yous snuck into camp on yestersun."

"I speak for their leader," Morvelving answered. There was no reason to deny his scouting venture. "Stumbled more like. Your camp was well hidden." He doubted Arastus would have the patience or understanding to listen to this Graal. He was confident he could escape if words turned to action. Yet they could surely find a more reasonable solution—if the Graal was willing. "I scouted for the . . . softskins. They wanted to know where you and your friends were."

"This 'ems," the Graal said, pointing at the host behind him with his large thumb. "No friends, trouble grunts. Tunnels too crowded, hunger. Find food or lose 'em. Less hunger."

Morvelving stalled at that. " 'Lose' them? You mean 'kill'?"

The Graal nodded. "Toos many. You scared thems, walked right ups. Thoughts I's had lost them. We's go to finds you and. . . Lo! All theses softskins."

Morvelving considered the situation. The Graal was more difficult to follow than he'd realized. Was he more concerned about Morvelving or the army of men? He felt a tickle of fear that he would blunder the parley and more men would die. He wondered if the Graal was rambling to buy time or to make Morvelving voice the first offer. Perhaps this Graal was content with the amount of his kin slain—however odd and horrible the possibility may be—and now wanted to end the confrontation. Morvelving had tried to reason with Prince Leolicides, and it had ended in disaster. His mother would say, *If it came out wrong the first time, adjust the ingredients.* She had been talking about making stew, but the idea was still applicable. Thinking of her made him wonder what she would think of him now. She had passed her Vhinde two Rifts ago.

"The softskins do not want you to pass further," Morvelving said, resolved. "If you do, more of your grunts will die. The softskins are willing to let you leave without pursuing you." Morvelving pointed south past the Menici host and Pilla Falen. "Those lands they claim and will defend them. You must find food elsewhere."

The giant Graal waved his hand dismissively and scratched an itch under his armpit. He looked Morvelving up and down, and then at the spears and banners of the Menicians behind.

Morvelving sniffed, taking in the Graal's scent. He ignored all the smells of its flesh and found the aroma of its emotions. They were faint, as if the creature wasn't feeling much at all. Or was hiding its emotions. It was mainly bored and a tinge uncertain. Morvelving had to let that sit. Moments before, it had sat and watched its kin fight and die for being "toos many." Now he wondered if the creature was bored from being unsure what it should do.

There was nothing he could have done with the Roxanar, and he didn't regret defending Goldeye against the Thresseans. But he considered whether he could lead this creature from its current path. He'd been alone among different peoples and had seen how they took advantage of and manipulated others—the most recent example had been the Roxanar and Grecian's move against the Eugratians. Could he redirect the Graal from their current path to another? To Frystgalen? East across the Burnt Lands? Or perhaps west to the Idosse and directly to Phoithese? It was just a thought. One he dismissed. There were too many innocents that would die. He'd had no control over the innocent lives lost in the sack of Ugris. Here, he doubted he could live with it, knowing. No, there had to be another way.

The large Graal was uncertain, meaning it felt responsible. Whatever the cause, their hunger was reason enough for the Graal to attack. Not to win—only to decrease the number of mouths to feed. It pointed its finger at the Menician host again. "There's food."

"Yes." Morvelving hung his head, taking a breath of patience. This was worse than explaining something to Nippi. "That food will fight back. Unless you want *all* yours"—Morvelving motioned to the host of

Graal with his shield arm—"slain."

The large creature looked back and shrugged, its eyebrows skewed in thought. "Less good," the Graal said.

Morvelving licked his lips, wondering if Arastus would agree with any other offer. He *had* said he was hoping to avoid more bloodshed. Morvelving wanted to return to Nippi as quickly as possible. But what he had in mind held the potential of crippling the Aqualeans while strengthening the Graal. He wasn't confident. The Graal had to have lost hundreds, if not thousands, in the battle. Considering how nonchalant this creature was about the deaths of its younger people, Morvelving knew what he could demand: the Graal could slay each other. He felt queasy even thinking about it.

"The softskins can give food," Morvelving said, no other way in sight. "If you and yours leave these lands."

The Graal looked puzzled, scratching behind its ear. It spoke, its tongue lashing out, "Theys gives food."

"Then you leave," Morvelving said quickly. "All of you." He motioned again at the host of Graal. Many of them were milling about, restless.

The large Graal lashed out with his tongue, nodding. "Good. Thens we come back morrows."

It spread its massive arms wide like it would take Morvelving in an embrace. Morvelving took an instinctive step back. Hastening to correct the Graal, he shook his head.

"No, you will never come back," Morvelving said. "You lost as many grunts as you wanted. Come back, and you'll lose all of them."

"Wheres go, then?" the Graal said, adjusting his position in agitation. "Back where's no food? No."

The world was a strange place. If someone had told Morvelving he would be standing here advising a Graal where to go, he would have said they were under the influence of piphlid. He blinked away the thought of the shroom.

Any direction he suggested could lead to the suffering of innocents, and he was taking too long. Even now, a cluster of young Graal split off from the main host only for the older ones to shepherd them back. He wanted this whole debacle to be over with.

Northeast was the best direction, he decided. If they kept to the path, the lake people of Oro Ath could flee to their boats, and then they'd become lost in the Gregalen Heights. And if they made it out of that natural maze, they'd arrive in the Plains of Goreth, where the minotaur clans roam. Morvelving took a deep breath. "Don't go back, go northeast till you reach the sea. Wild lands of plenty. No softskins to stand in your way."

The Graal only stared unblinking at Morvelving. He licked his lips and added, "There are the fire sands to the east or the frozen wastes to the northwest. What is your decision?"

Morvelving watched the Graal's eyes dart back and forth as it considered. The Graal was more ponderous than he had first guessed. Odd creatures, quick to violence when they aspired to be. Perhaps it was the age of the large Graal that made it consider first, whereas the younger ones would act first.

The Graal broke the silence between them. "Wes will go. Softskins bring food and no burn ours dead. No nasties dry breads neithers. Live things."

"Leave your dead?" Morvelving asked.

The giant looked at him quizzically. "Yes, theys good eatins."

Morvelving stared, mortified. Livestock it was then. He distracted himself by wondering whether Arastus and his commanders would agree. If they meant to agree in the first place. He thought of Idanphyrus, how she had created a facade to hide her true intent. The Prime Enator could be doing the same.

The Graal stood, gave Morvelving one long look, and spoke again. "Brings food here, leaves dead. Wes go back to woods."

He didn't wait for a reply from Morvelving. He turned and strode back to the camped host.

Morvelving turned his back to the Graal. If the Menicians were planning treachery, he would have no part of it, even against the Graal. They chose a violent path by instinct; it was why they were created. If the gods' accounts were trustworthy. Perhaps it was all they knew, and until someone taught them a different path, they would linger in their ways. Who would teach them? Not him, no.

Putting his thoughts of the Graal and the swirling currents of human politics away, Morvelving strode back, hoping the Prime Enator wouldn't take offense at his agreement with the Graal.

The Prime Enator and his entourage of commanders waited for Morvelving to approach. Calls of victory and the murmur of thousands filled his ears. Wonder and rejoicing. The Graal were leaving. They had beaten the foe. Defended their lands. He had made it possible for more men of Sene to return home. It felt far better than being known for the skill of killing.

"Hail, Mulranei," Arastus greeted when he was among them. "Well done! I see our foes are retreating. Tell me, what was the agreement?"

Morvelving eyed the other commanders. Boragatis and Shulgatist both looked at him with incredulity. Officers were calling for order in the ranks, keeping the men in line. Some clusters were trying to march back to camp.

"The Graal have agreed to leave these lands," Morvelving answered.

Several of the Prime Enator's companions grinned, slapping hands on shoulders, congratulating each other.

Morvelving pressed on. "I discovered the Graal were intent on conflict, but not for the reasons we'd expect. Their . . . colony, I suppose, was overpopulated. The giant I spoke to was mainly looking to kill off the small young ones so there would be fewer mouths to feed."

Shulgatist spat, "Barbarians." His spittle didn't clear the girth of his gut. Instead, it added to the stains on the stretched cuirass.

"It agreed to leave on two conditions: you must provide them with livestock and leave their dead. You can gather the herds and their dead, then leave them up the hill at the tall menhir," Morvelving said hastily, looking Arastus in the eye. He ignored the outrage from the short man, Boragatis. Arastus stood, hand on his chin in thought.

"We do this, what's going to stop them from returning and demanding more?" Boragatis said, spittle flying from his mouth with each word. Morvelving wondered if he ever swallowed.

"You've crippled our own supplies with the cold season near," Shulgatist said, his fist clenched at his side.

"They demand we pick up their dead as well? What for?" Boragatis asked.

Annoyed, Morvelving didn't hold back. "They eat their dead."

"Barbarians," Shulgatist whispered.

"You can choose to march after them," Morvelving said simply. They were right, and he hoped they would come up with a better solution. "I wouldn't advise it though. Fighting the Graal in the heavy woods would be far worse than losing livestock. We never agreed on the details, so the decision is still up to you. The herds that accompany the army will do. Aqualea isn't far, and the Land of Three Kings is rich. Your men won't go hungry."

Arastus had to shout to silence Boragatis. "I've decided. Morvelving, you have placed my people in a difficult position. To succor the invaders makes us look weak, and Boragatis is right. What will keep them from returning?" Morvelving eyed the stillness of the guards. "Nevertheless, we will meet the agreement. I told Morvelving to avoid more conflict, and that is what he has done. The livestock we brought to feed this army would be forfeit either way."

"This is an outrage!" Boragatis cried. "We can't—"

"You are welcome to engage the Graal with your company," Arastus dared the shorter man. "Though any Aqualeans placed in your command are free men and may choose to walk away without repercussions."

Morvelving's brows rose. He was impressed with Arastus.

"This will ruin you, Prime Enator," Shulgatist said quietly.

"If my career is ruined so more men may live another day, then so be it." Arastus eyed the two commanders, then spoke more quietly so only the commanders could hear. "Let the Graal think we are succoring them. As Morvelving said, we are not beholden to them. If they do not leave, we will attack while they feast. Come! Back to camp. We will see to our wounded and the Graal's parting gift."

Grunting, Morvelving hefted Penalty to rest on his shoulder and made his way to the camp, ignoring the frowns from the other commanders. He wore his own frown at Arastus, wondering if the care he showed for his men was political. Morvelving shook his head. He had had enough. The battle was over. He needed to return to Sene for Nippi.

"Morvelving, Morvelving, do you see that! They are gone!" Paunt was yelling as he pointed up the hill where the Graal had been. Blood—Graal's and his own—covered his face, and he had scratches all over his right arm. Farlan next to him was holding up a man grimacing with an arrow in his thigh.

"I see," Morvelving said. Pleased to see more than just Farlan and Paunt rejoicing, and that the battle was done.

After the cheering ceased and they heard their orders, they returned to the camp. Morvelving helped to carry several wounded. After cleaning and gathering his belongings, he then returned to Arastus's pavilion. Commanders surrounded the Prime Enator, congratulating and offering gifts to Arastus. He waited till Arastus acknowledged him.

"Mulranei, come forward. Hear all! I sent Morvelving to speak to the giant in my stead. His silver tongue convinced the beasts to leave our lands. I also hear you defended the flank single-handed." Arastus sounded elated, thriving on all the praise and gifts.

"A combined effort with the men," Morvelving answered humbly. "I wish to settle my contract. I'm needed back west." Several men commented on his poor timing.

"You mistake our gathering," Boragatis said. "We offer gifts in honor of the Prime Enator's successful victory, Mulranei. Wait till we're done before demanding your pay."

"That's enough, Boragatis." Arastus spoke over the man. "Morvelving isn't bound to our customs, and it isn't in his contract. Here." He motioned to one of his servants; they retreated into the pavilion and returned promptly with a small sack. Arastus walked over and handed it up to Morvelving. "Your payment plus extra for being my voice to the barbarians."

Morvelving flicked his ears back. The weight of the aulos was hefty. "I am glad to have helped more men leave with their lives today."

"Fare you well, Morvelving," Arastus said. "The gods' blessings upon you." He leaned forward, whispering. "If you return to Aqualean lands, be warned: I can't guarantee you will not be blamed for our losses."

Morvelving acknowledged Arastus's farewell and threat with a passive glare. Phoithese, Thressea, Eugrator, and now Aqualea. Four cities he needed to avoid due to becoming involved. Maybe Nippi had the right idea to keep a list. Leaving the commanders, Morvelving kept his senses tuned for treachery.

The Menici custom of gift-giving after a victory was unique. Despite his urgency to depart from the camp, he stopped by the tents filled with the dying and wounded. The air smelled of iron and rot and excrement. Men in pain were moaning or crying while the Apothurgeons, in their blood-covered white tunics, walked among them, administering aid to those they could.

Morvelving approached one Apothurgeon, who was mixing up herbs for administration.

She examined him up and down. "You are not injured?"

"No, I was just with the Prime Enator," Morvelving said. "He was receiving gifts for the victory. It is custom to give after a victory?"

"Yes, commanders and enators tend to receive such after they do something great," she answered. "I speak above my station. Please, I have many men who need these herbs."

"Here, take this." He set down his pack and pulled out the small pouch of salve. "This is my people's gift from the Moon Goddess. We call it ambrosia, the Moon's Nectar. It is a healing salve. Use it among your wounded. A fingertip's worth will heal most wounds."

It was all Morvelving had. He would have to make more. Mulranei saliva had healing properties, and his people had made it into a salve for centuries.

The Apothurgeon looked at the pouch in his extended hand with shock and wonder. She took it gently as if it was a rare fragile treasure, saying, "The tales of Mulranei healing powers are still told at the

Apothecary. Our ancestors would have been destroyed by the Harrow Plague if not for the Mulranei Tribes that roamed the lands then. Thank you, noble Mulranei. This will help ease the suffering of many."

"Good, use it well," Morvelving said, turning to leave. He had thought of giving it to Arastus, but he had a feeling the salve wouldn't have made it to those who needed it.

"Wait, Mulranei."

Morvelving turned back to the Apothurgeon.

She walked close to him, considering her words. "What are the ingredients? There are so many sicknesses and deaths we could prevent if we were able to replicate the ambrosia." She looked up at him, hopeful.

Morvelving growled, not showing fangs. She took a step back. He then gave a brief whine. If humans or even elves knew the chief ingredient was their saliva, then Mulranei would be hunted down and massacred. One of many reasons the tribes now roamed in the wilds and seldom interacted with other civilizations.

"It was a gift. Accept it as is," Morvelving said, his voice low and angry. He wasn't angry at her but at the pain it would cause his people if this secret were known. Perhaps it was a mistake to give the salve away. Should he snatch it from her? No, his time with humans had made him change his mind all too often.

The Apothurgeon nodded, looking away from him, ashamed. "I will accept it as is. Please understand, I only wish to help those hurting."

"As do I. It was why I gave it to you rather than the commanders or generals," Morvelving said in finality.

She gave a quick nod and held the pouch close to her chest.

He turned his back to Pilla Falen and began his short journey back to the one human he wanted to be around.

22

———

Nippiktua woke up and didn't want to leave the bed's warmth and comfort. A dull hum filled her ears as it always did. She smelled it. No, that was her breath.

Gaia walked in, and Nippiktua couldn't hide that she was awake fast enough. She glared at Gaia as the woman shook her pointer finger, spoke quickly, and whipped the covers off.

Nippiktua snarled up at Gaia and pulled the blankets back over her head.

Gaia still had her up, and by the time she was dressed, her drowsiness was gone.

Gaia wrote on her parchment: *You slept late. Follow me to the kitchen. There is work to be done, girl.*

Downstairs, Nippiktua consumed a portion of bread and creamy brie before one of the cooks instructed her to clean pots and pans.

With five pots clean and shiny, Nippiktua dried her hands. She ran over to her quill and parchment. She held it up to Gaia as the woman walked through: *Where is Cassea? I want her to show me how to dance.*

Gaia took a deep, exasperated breath; she seemed to do too much. Adults tended to do that. Nippiktua handed over her parchment. Gaia wrote: *She is out on errands and will be back by noon. Now follow me.*

Nippiktua did. The Green Olive never stopped moving. She

wondered if the evening was the only time when everyone enjoyed themselves. She missed being in the woods with Morvelving, going wherever he wanted. Seeing the birds and squirrels among the branches. She wanted to go climb the oak that stood where she'd played Skip Adrea. She looked for an escape, but when she tried to slip away, another one of Gaia's workers spotted her and shooed her on to follow Gaia.

When Gaia noticed, she said, "None of that, girl. There is work to be done. You'll have time enough to play." Nippiktua caught every word because Gaia stooped, putting her face very close.

Nippiktua nodded and did her best out back washing clothes: she helped a nice old woman fold the blanket, brought water from the well (yes, she threw more pebbles down), and swept the floors.

That's when Cassea returned. As noon drew near, Celemith's passing caused the sunlight to dim. Fluff had claimed that was where the gods resided, which Nippiktua didn't fully believe. Why would the gods live in a dark circle? She waved at Cassea. Cassea gave her a quick smile but hurried over to Gaia, looking concerned. Nippiktua couldn't read what they were saying, for the door to the Green Olive opened, and a tall woman stepped in.

Nippiktua had never seen a woman so tall. The woman had to duck her head to enter through the door. Her hair was dark red yet bright, like hearth embers. It was short and painstakingly braided tight to her scalp, patches of scalp revealing scars and skin-carvings. Her face was stern and sharp, dominated by a pink scar that ran from her right eyebrow over her nose. Her neck and shoulders were broad, arms ropey and hard. Over her blue tunic, she wore a cuirass of waxed linen threads and leather with a circular bronze plate at the center, like men wore to battle. She glanced down at Nippiktua.

Nippiktua took an involuntary step back. The woman winked at her, then walked past. She held a scabbarded sword in her hand and had a heavy pack over her shoulder. The pack had a helm with a crest dangling from it. She was a mercenary, like the ones Fluff had worked with, Nippiktua realized. Just as she remembered she wasn't supposed to be around strangers at the inn. She stalled. Should she run or walk backward? Nippiktua couldn't decide, so she remained.

The strong-armed woman approached Gaia as men of all shapes and colors entered the inn. There was even a Frystlin man, his long white hair a thin and greasy veil covering his red eyes. He regarded her with surprise and spoke to her in Frystlin.

"I wouldn't have guessed to see another Frystlin this far south, let alone a Frystlin child. What's your name, girl? Your tribe? Hey, you know our tongue. I see your eyes understanding. Too shy, eh?"

The men next to him started speaking. Nippiktua couldn't read their lips, for Cassea approached and told her something, pointing to the kitchen.

Nippiktua nodded and hurried off, feeling terrible, as she had done what Morvelving had told her not to. She felt a pinch of guilt that she hadn't acted faster. Fluff would worry for her. She wished he were here. Nippiktua counted the time. He had been gone a day and a half. He should be back soon.

———————

Ezrilkath watched the Frystlin girl hurry into the kitchen. Odd little thing. She set her heavy pack down with an audible sigh. Her men were filing into the big open room. The strong smell of warm, savory food filled her nose; it would be good to eat properly for once.

The stocky woman who approached her eyed her with trepidation. Ezrilkath understood. She knew what she and her men looked like: after their long and unpleasant journey, vagabonds at best.

Ezrilkath spoke. "Greetings. I am Ezrilkath of Monbargar, the captain of this sorry lot."

"Worse for wear," Ezrilkath heard Odrys mumble. She continued, "We are mercenaries, here for some rest and food. We have coin—drakma and aulos—and we will make no trouble." She directed that last bit to her men. This time, Odrys, her second in command, grunted behind her.

"I am Gaia, matron of the Green Olive, and be welcome," Gaia said.

Ezrilkath didn't feel welcome. Every eye was on them as if they would burn the place down. Well, she would if there were profit to be gained, but there wasn't. Besides, she was feeling good about today.

"Find a seat," Gaia offered. "You've arrived in time; a meal is almost ready. Keep the war equipment outside, thank you."

"As you wish, Gaia," Ezrilkath said, turning to see who the perpetrators were. "Gruss and Dressus, you know better. You get your food last now. See to the horses."

They grumbled when she handed Gruss her sword and Dressus her pack. They left the inn to meet their tasks.

"Shall you need stalls for your beasts?"

"No, they'll eat in here. Oh, the horses," Ezrilkath said, smiling and sitting down with a grunt. "We're only staying for the meal."

"Ha. Ha." Odrys sat next to her, rolling his eyes, unamused. Gaia wiped her hands on her apron as all twenty of Ezrilkath's men entered. They were dirty and worn from the road. She wished they'd had time to clean up a bit. Her attempts to get them to clean themselves in the rivers were some of the hardest battles. Ezrilkath didn't know how she held them together. *With your unbending will,* Odrys had said once. Which Ezrilkath knew was a dung-cake lie. Truth was, she kept them alive in battle so they could live to spend their coin as they wished. That's why they stayed with her. They were all her Monbargar kinsmen, besides the Frystlin, Pulasuq, who was scratching his white chin hair as he looked toward the kitchen. And Odrys, who was an Idosse.

"You are on your way to Pilla Falen then?" Gaia asked when she returned with a plate of bread and cheese along with a pretty serving woman carrying a few mugs of ale.

Ezrilkath pleasantly watched the sway of her hips as she weaved around the tables and men in chairs. The men ignored her, seeing Ezrilkath's eyes.

The young woman caught her stare; Ezrilkath gave her a small smirk. The serving woman ignored her. Ezrilkath wished she hadn't said they weren't staying long. Couldn't go back on that now. Besides, it was clear to Ezrilkath that the serving woman didn't like her staring. Ezrilkath sighed in resignation. She missed her homeland, where the women weren't so high-strung.

Ezrilkath finally answered Gaia, ignoring her silent accusation at her ogling. "Yes, I heard about the Graal five days ago in Agrothica. We've been on boat and road since."

"You may be late," Gaia said, not hiding her irritation. "The men left a day and a half ago."

"Have you heard if there was a battle?"

"No, but—"

"Well, then you don't know," Ezrilkath said, interrupting. She found Gaia's frustration amusing; obviously, few interrupted her. And Ezrilkath enjoyed how adorable she looked when flustered. Perhaps tumbling with her would be more pleasant. She placed a pouch of drakma on the table. "For food and drink. Thank you."

She devoured her food. The loaf was warm, and steam wafted gently from it as she tore another piece. The cheese was buttery, flavored with berries and herbs.

Gaia took the pouch of coin, counted the drakma and aulos. She didn't react when she counted more than was necessary. Odrys eyed Ezrilkath with a vexed look. Yes, she had done it again. She'd forgotten to count the coin. Truth was, they would have more than enough after the battles with the Graal.

"Stew will be ready in a moment," Gaia said, then left to the kitchen.

"That wasn't *all* our coin, I hope?" Odrys asked. His muffled voice was a whisper with the food in his mouth.

Ezrilkath shook her head before taking another deep drink of the brown ale. The men were hushed. This pleased her.

When she had first formed her band, they couldn't get work for all the brawls they'd started in towns and cities. She had needed to tighten the belt. Now they moved in and out without incidents . . . most of the time.

Leaning over to her, Odrys added, "If we miss the fighting, we'll be scraping again."

"We won't. Gaia had no news. Their men haven't returned," Ezrilkath answered while she watched Pulasuq. His Dae-eyes hadn't left the kitchen. She threw a chunk of bread at him. "Stop staring, Pulasuq. How many times do I have to tell you how unsettling your Frystlin eyes are? Gods above."

Pulasuq nodded and hurried over to her. He was a lean man, and short. She swore his stature was a god's joke to make people underestimate him. He was lethal with his twin bronze daggers. He looked like he had just discovered the meaning of life.

"Captain," Pulasuq whispered. "That Frystlin girl is the one the Idosse were looking for."

Odrys glanced over at the kitchens.

Ezrilkath did too and glimpsed the Frystlin girl's white hair bobbing behind the counters.

"So? That's all the way back west in Phoithese. I've had my share of Idosse and all the centaurs galloping around. Odrys is the only Idosse I have patience for," Ezrilkath said and was disappointed Odrys ignored her.

"They were offering more coins than any commander of a battle will," Pulasuq said hurriedly.

Ezrilkath waved him back to his seat. "You're so quick to sell your own, huh? Aethra's tits, go eat more. You're greedy when you're hungry."

Pulasuq obeyed, thankfully. Ezrilkath enjoyed another bite before being attacked by Odrys's scowl.

She ignored it, for Gaia and the pretty serving woman returned with the stew. She caught the Frystlin girl peeking from the kitchen door before watching the sway of the young woman's hips again. Ezrilkath enjoyed looking at the details of her soft cheeks and her rich brown eyes when she set down her bowl of stew.

"Thank you," Ezrilkath said. "You look like someone with big dreams. How long have you been apprenticing? By now, you must be able to run a place like the Green Olive."

The serving woman cast a wary glance at her but gave a small, embarrassed smile.

Ezrilkath had guessed right. She praised the gods in her mind. It was a wonderful smile.

"It's definitely a possibility," the serving woman said. "Enjoy your meal."

She walked away before Ezrilkath could ask for her name. Ezrilkath pinched herself. That was what she got for staring too intently. Why had she said they weren't staying long? She was going to go blind among all these ugly men. After dealing with the Graal, she would take them to Aqualea, spend a few coins for warm and beautiful company.

Draining her mug, Ezrilkath gasped in contentment. Her belly was full, and a minor buzz was settling in from the heavy ale. It was time to move on. Some men had started a game of Rock Down, a dice game she'd never liked. "The day is passing us by. Time to go, boys. Let's—"

The door burst open. Ezrilkath pivoted, ready for anything, along with half her men.

"Gaia!" a young lad called as he came through the entranceway. He stopped to gape at Ezrilkath but hurried past. "Gaia, Gaia!"

"In Aeputer's ear, what is all this noise?" Gaia barked as she walked out of the kitchen.

"Gaia, the Graal were defeated at Pilla Falen and turned back and heading away northeast!"

Gaia gave a quick sharp glance to Ezrilkath. "That is wonderful news."

Well, perhaps she had more reason to linger now. She couldn't see the serving woman. She would have to at least get her name.

"Captain," Odrys whispered next to her, his back to Gaia. "No battle, no coin. If that Frystlin girl is the one the Phoithesens are after, it would be an easy profit. Enough coin to return to your lands, hire more warriors, and take it back from the Ketlans."

Ezrilkath tilted her head down to look at him. Gods, she despised the Ketlans. "I do hate it when you're right," she said, resigned.

"I don't like it either," Odrys admitted. "But we've been stretched thin, and the men won't like another dry spell."

He was referring to their months among the Idosse. Where they'd become entangled in Lesgossan and Makoidakian skirmishes. And then barely escaped the Roxanar warriors at the sack of Ugris, going unpaid and losing over fifty men. Their employers continued to die before paying them. Kragius, the god of mischief, loved her.

Ezrilkath caught Pulasuq's eye and gave him the signal to be ready.

"Time for us to go, ready the horses," Odrys said as he pulled two of the men aside.

She was going to walk into the kitchen when the Frystlin girl hurried out, holding a parchment with freshly scribbled runes. It read: *What's happening, Gaia?*

The girl held it up to Gaia, who instantly took it and chided her. Why did the girl need to write her question? Why hadn't she overheard the message boy yelling? Like an unsuspected slap to the face, Ezrilkath realized this was the girl the Phoithesens thought would free them from their draekurm overlord. She spat. More dirty work. She hated it, but she hated the Ketlans more.

Gaia was already looking at Ezrilkath, at the realization on her face as it changed to shock and anger. The pretty serving woman's eyes widened in terror, which hurt the most.

"We'll be taking the Frystlin girl off your hands," Ezrilkath said.

"Aeputer's cock, you will," Gaia said, standing in front of the girl.

Pulasuq was already in position and too quick. He hurried right past Gaia and grabbed the girl, who let out a gasp and a silent scream.

Ezrilkath took two long strides to catch Gaia and the serving woman with each hand. Gaia almost knocked her over. The woman knew how to use her weight. The serving woman scratched at Ezrilkath's arms, drawing blood.

"Odrys, get the men to restrain them," Ezrilkath called between her clenched teeth, nodding at the other locals moving in to help Gaia.

"Aeputer curse you, you Monbargar brute," Gaia spat as she pushed and shoved.

Ezrilkath pulled her into a neck hold. Another kitchen aide ran out with a pan and bashed Ezrilkath on the shoulder. She growled to shake off the dull pain, and one of her men grabbed the woman and pushed her away.

Pulasuq cried out in pain. Ezrilkath looked to see the Frystlin girl had poked one of his eyes and was running up the stairs.

"Kragius's flaccid cock—Pulasuq, you useless idiot, after her!" Ezrilkath barked. The Frystlin girl ran up the stairs, swift and silent as a fox.

"Run, Nippiktua!" Gaia yelled, still struggling against Ezrilkath's neck hold. "Cassea, go after her!"

Cassea tried to bolt up the stairs. Ezrilkath grabbed her wrist in time. "Ah! You monster! May you never burn and your spirit wander forever," Cassea cursed and screamed.

"Now, that's not fair," Ezrilkath said between gritted teeth. "Only— ugh, hold still. Only trying to live. In . . . " She was going to lose her grip. "This. Gods. Forsaken. Place."

Cassea was about to bite her hand when one of her men jumped in and grabbed Cassea and Gaia, pinning them to the wall.

Ezrilkath took a relieved breath. "Hey, don't hurt them! Just hold them back."

"That won't redeem you!" Gaia spat. "You're a fool and a monster."

Cassea had her teeth bared as she stared at Ezrilkath, tears streaming down her face from her exertion and helplessness. Gods, Ezrilkath was tired of this.

"I'm not a fool for taking an easy job. The girl is worth more than this whole town," Ezrilkath said as Pulasuq came down the stairs with the still-struggling Frystlin girl. She held a bow and quiver of arrows, expertly made, against her chest as she wiggled to get free.

"Nippiktua, be brave!" Cassea called out. "Nippi!"

Some men laughed. "She can't hear you," they teased.

Cassea screamed and struggled again.

Ezrilkath knew that scream would haunt her dreams. "About time, Pulasuq. We're going. Get rid of that twig." Then she turned to Gaia and pointedly said, "Don't follow us, or we won't be so nice."

The matron of the Green Olive spat at Ezrilkath's feet. "You're a fool. You have doomed yourself and your men. That girl is under the protection of a Mulranei. He will track you to the ends of Bregalen, and I hope he rips out your throat."

Ezrilkath scrutinized Gaia. The innkeep was telling the truth. She looked at Odrys. He became more urgent, skin as pale as his hair.

"A Mulranei? In these lands? Nice Dae-tale," she said, walking out, ignoring the cries of frustration and anger.

Pulasuq had the girl on his horse. The little thing was still struggling. Odrys held the reins of Ezrilkath's horse while the men mounted.

"This little animal has bitten me thrice now," Pulasuq complained.

"Deal with it, but don't hurt her, or I'll smash your stones," Ezrilkath said. "We don't know how the Phoithesens want her." She looked pointedly at Odrys; he flinched, recognizing her anger. "A Mulranei? By itself and caring for a human child. How true can that be?"

Odrys handed her the reins. "There is only one Mulranei I have heard of in the west: the mercenary called the Sword of Mourning."

"Fuck," Ezrilkath spat, knowing full well who that was, and leaped up onto her horse. "We ride with all haste to the Port of Adrea. Odrys, you better hope he doesn't catch us before then."

The Sword of Mourning. She couldn't believe her ill luck. Gods above and below, she had hoped to meet the mercenary. He was a legend among sellswords: a Mulranei wielding a dwarf-made, two-handed sword who was undefeated in battle. The mercenary camps always had a cluster of men talking about where the Sword of Mourning had been seen last.

Four mercenaries from Old Aphoeria and Danare had joined her band before the sack of Ugris. Every night, they had told stories of their chance meeting with the Sword of Mourning, to the envy of others. She had spotted him with the Roxanar outside Ugris and was thankful he'd been absent from the fighting. They had heard he killed the Prince of Thressea and his companions. Now he would be after her.

She checked her weapons needlessly as they rode out of Sene and instinctively checked if they were being followed. No one. Good. The day had started so well—if only it had finished differently.

Nippiktua kept screaming, but she might as well have been gagged for all the help it did. She was so angry, sad, and terrified—she felt like she would burst. Her throat was raw, and her wrists hurt where they were tied. She had been so close to getting her Stag dagger and Fluff's whistle before being grabbed again. The thought made her resume her screams and struggles to fall off the galloping horse. And her *sanitja*— gone. What she'd been planning to do with the bow, she didn't know. Try to stick an arrow in the tall, strong-armed woman?

The Frystlin man had put her Stag dagger in his pack. Nippi had to get it back. Why had she run out to Gaia, asking what was happening? Fluff would be so mad at her. This was all her fault.

She thought of Fluff then, how sad he would be when he came back and found her gone. Would he come after her or be so mad he'd give her up? No, Morvelving would come after her. He had said he would never abandon her. Why couldn't she be better? Nippiktua wondered if it had to do with what Morvelving had said about the Fates, that they were watching her. That possibility only made her more mad. What did they want from her? She was important, but to the Fates and gods? She hit the horse's neck in frustration. It ignored her. The Frystlin man didn't. He tightened his arm around her. Her teeth marks made dark blood pool on his blue skin. She'd given them to him when he'd carried her down the stairs.

That made her think of Gaia and Cassea. The way they'd fought for her surprised her and made her even angrier. She'd hurt them too. It wasn't fair! Thankfully, the brute woman with fire hair hadn't hurt them. She was riding ahead of Nippiktua. The horses were moving fast over the road, heading toward the sunset, too fast for her to jump off safely. She didn't know where they were taking her. She would have to be smart, like Fluff, to escape.

Her anger and determination dried like her tears as they rode into the night, her captors lighting torches to guide their way. Nippiktua fell asleep, hungry and exhausted, only to be welcomed by a nightmare where Morvelving was always out of reach.

23

———

The morning sun was warm on Morvelving's back.

He had slept poorly during the night. His dreams kept showing him returning to Sene to find Nippi hurt. Her wanting to stay with Gaia, no longer choosing to be around him. The last possibility had hurt him the most. In them lay the doom of his choice to look after Nippi. One day, she would grow old and no longer need him, and her spirit would pass. While he would remain, till he was killed or too tired of the world to continue.

He wiped the tears from his eyes. Sene was visible in the distance—the tall oak's branches like a crown over the small town—and the Green Olive's chimney puffed out a steady column of thin smoke. Morvelving sniffed the air and stopped mid-step. In the eddying breeze, the stench of fear replaced the soft morning's scents, corrupting his breath like pollen in spring. There was anger and sadness as well, all coming from Sene.

Morvelving sprinted the rest of the way. Was it Nippi? Was something happening right now? His ears were up to catch any hint. The scent wasn't fresh; it was thin, lingering. Telunian curse him if something had happened to her. Several folk called out to him, their words muffled as he sped past toward the Green Olive. He dropped his small pack, keeping Penalty in hand.

When he burst through the door, the patrons jumped in their seats and stood, eyes wide.

"Nippi! Nippi, are you here?" Morvelving half called, half barked. Nippi wouldn't hear him anyway. There was startled alarm in the kitchen. A woman's voice called for Gaia. The room smelled of struggle and food. One table's leg was broken.

Cassea ran down the stairs.

"Where's Nippiktua?" Morvelving demanded, approaching the young woman. She choked on her own words and began sobbing, dropping to her knees, hands up.

Morvelving checked himself, hiding his fangs and changing his growls into short whines. "Cassea, what happened?" he said as quietly as he could as a tempest of pain swelled within.

"Mercenaries," Cassea choked out. "I'm so sorry, Morvelving. We did everything we could. They grabbed her before we figured out what they were up to. They knew, or guessed, who she was. I–I—" She couldn't finish.

Morvelving noticed the bruise around her neck. She was in pain. Gaia burst into the room.

"Aeputer's might, Morvelving," Gaia said, going to Cassea and comforting her in an embrace.

"I'm fine," Cassea said. "Morvelving, you must go after her. They left yesterday afternoon."

"I will. The mercenaries. How many? Who commanded them?" Morvelving said, impatient. They had a good head start. He recognized Nippi's broken bow up against the wall in the corner. He'd have to leave it.

Quickly taking a step back from his loud questions, Gaia answered, "Twenty or twenty-five, mostly Monbargars, led by a red-headed Monbargar monster. They headed west on horseback for the Port of Adrea."

Morvelving swore under his breath. He turned to leave; he would have to travel only with necessities. He stopped at the door, taking a last glance at Gaia and Cassea, feeling sudden guilt. He should have known it wouldn't have gone well for them to watch Nippi. He should have never departed from her.

"Gods-damned Fates," he cursed under his breath, further risking their ire.

Retrieving his pack, he set it on a table, grabbed the pouch full of ingredients he had collected on the way for a healing salve. He dropped his coin pouch on the table.

"I don't blame you, Gaia and Cassea," Morvelving said as he displayed the contents of his pack, sheathed his dagger, bundled his cloak around the two pouches, and tied it around his torso. Penalty he would hold in hand. "I have no need for any of this now. Keep it and do with it as you will. I will not forget your kindness and care for Nippi."

"We—"

"You did too much," Morvelving barked, interrupting Cassea. "You are lucky you weren't killed, and I thank the Moon Goddess for that. May your kindness be rewarded."

"Go! Go!" Gaia said, eyes brimming with frustration, her voice angry. "Get your daughter back."

Morvelving hesitated at her wording but needed no further encouragement. He sprinted out the door. Several villagers called out in surprise, their voices lost to the wind in Morvelving's ears. He caught the scent of horses and the unwashed odor of humans. They only distracted him from his worry for a moment. It followed him like a shadow—the fear that Nippi would be harmed—or worse, killed. He had failed Windtail. He couldn't do the same for Nippi. He would not. Morvelving ran faster; he could not let that happen to Nippi.

The land fell before him as he crossed the plain filled with vineyards and cornstalks. He would run at a full sprint till nightfall to gain the distance lost, then jog to save his strength. If the Monbargar leader was clever, they would not rest till they reached the port, and they would try to divert their trail to lose him. He also kept his senses tuned to the scent of narroot. The root grew in damp earth and away from the sun. Mulranei warriors used the plant in battles to take away their fear and give themselves bursts of unfaltering strength. He would need it to sustain himself. He thought of piphlid. Would narroot ensnare him like piphlid had? It was a risk he couldn't consider. Finding narroot meant catching up and rescuing Nippi.

He knew the mercenaries were hoping to cross the Idryiva Sea to one of the Idosse ports, then travel by land to Phoithese. Morvelving had to reach them before they reached a port. Otherwise, they would gain two days on him if there was no ship to carry him. There was a worrying possibility that they were already aboard a ship. Morvelving couldn't consider that. The trail was fresh. He let his instinct carry him onward. Nothing mattered, neither town nor village. A patrol of Adrean soldiers hailed him and pursued him for a time. Nothing stopped him. He kept running till the sun set and the night hid his movements.

Between heavy breaths, his tongue lapped on the side of his jaw, tasting the cool wind. Morvelving beseeched Telunian to protect Nippi. That he would reach her in time. He would do anything for her to live, simply live a life where she was loved and cared for till she no longer needed it. Why did the Fates want to torment her? What glee did they gain from the sorrow and doom that surrounded her? Was it simply the life-strings they collected and coveted? The Dae of the Night had said the Fates held his thread. Or was it Telunian? If the Moon Goddess was punishing him for his mistakes, let Her take his spirit now and do with it as She will. Only leave Nippi at peace . . . That couldn't be it.

The sky was dark and gray where clouds floated; the stars were dim when visible. There was no moon. It wasn't the right time for a dark moon. He felt the omen of Telunian shunning her favor.

The mercenary trail split: one west, one north. Morvelving stopped in his tracks. His chest heaving, he sniffed the air. Their leader was clever. There was no immediate difference between the two trails. Morvelving brought his nose to cover every inch, tracing the curve of the horses' hooves in the soft ground, the scent like many rivers leaving their mark on the land. There. Nippi. No mistaking her scent. A thick cloud of anger accompanied it, lingering like rotten cherries at the foot of the tree. Was she angry at him for leaving her? He could only hope that wasn't the reason for her anger. Find her, then he would know.

They were still heading west. Morvelving continued. His heart raced and his legs burned. When he caught up with them, he would have to focus. The Monbargar were clever. Undoubtedly, they could use Nippi as a shield if they were desperate. Yet it would be a bluff, for they needed her alive to gain the Phoithesens' reward. Even so, would they risk her life?

The land passed under the constant rhythm of his feet, and a steady rain soaked his fur as his thoughts battered him with unchecked fears and terrible possibilities. Even now, they constricted his breathing. He felt a great pressure closing around his chest like a vise. Morvelving braced himself against a birch tree, gasping for breath and coughing. The birch roots hung over a small stream that continued on its way, unaware of his flight. He lapped up some water, cool and invigorating. He cupped water in his palm and splashed his face. His chest was no longer constricting, and he quelled his fears.

His eyes widened at the scent of narroot. He dug furiously near the tree's roots and found the dark blue stem with orange veins. Morvelving cut the root with haste and held a piece of it before his mouth. Should he do this? The piphlid's pull was no longer strong. He had resisted, and his mind was partially free of it. Would he have the same reaction to narroot? He would need the fervor it provided. Mulranei warriors used it in battle to fight far beyond their limits. He put the piece in his mouth, chewing. The root was ice cold and already burned down his throat, his legs cooling with renewed energy. The feeling was a cousin to piphlid's, and he swallowed his panic with the bitten stem. This was a necessary risk to help him save Nippi. Morvelving quickly gathered the remainder of the root.

He lifted a prayer to Telunian that the root would not hold sway over him as piphlid had, then continued his pursuit.

Nippi's scent was clear—he was getting closer. The Monbargar had tried to confuse him several times now, but he had gained on them during the night. He leaped over the stream and ran up the small hill. The land was wild and rough, its mountains defending against the might of the Idryiva Sea. Morvelving avoided the roads, hoping to catch up to the mercenaries who followed its winding trail. The thought of Nippi being transported across the sea and given to Orrothix crossed his mind. He steeled himself against it. *Focus on the path, assay the prey, and determine how to approach them when you catch up to them.* How his father had instructed him. He had run harder and longer than this in his early years, but not with a loved one's life at stake.

24

———

Ezrilkath didn't hire a ship at the Port of Adrea.

She saw another chance to muddy their trail and make it harder for the Sword of Mourning to catch them. She was under no illusion that a Mulranei would be fooled for long. Besides, it was difficult to commandeer a ship in a city. She swore to herself as her horse made its way down the rough track to the port. A small town, only ten buildings. Dim candlelight shone through the windows in the coastal haze. There were many fishing boats and one large trader. The sea and its wind were like a constant drum in her ears. Clouds, dark gray, hung low over the swells.

"Gods above," she sighed in relief. Ezrilkath adjusted herself in her saddle. She was sore, cold, and exhausted. The Frystlin girl—Nippiktua, the pretty serving woman had called her—was finally asleep. Ezrilkath had kept her from falling. In her attempt to escape, the girl had given Pulasuq an elbow to the groin. Ezrilkath was impressed with the girl. She cried, yes, but her screams were full of rage, and she never stopped trying to escape. The girl grunted in pain when the horse jolted on a misplaced step. Ezrilkath wanted to race to the docks just to get off the horse and be away.

The men weren't happy either. Ezrilkath had taken a risk by making no camp, only necessary stops. On top of that, she kept them all battle ready, including herself. Which was another reason she knew they would have had trouble at Adrea. The city guard wouldn't have taken kindly to mercenaries dressed for battle entering their city. A necessary addition to their discomfort, but they could rest when they made it on the ship.

"A large enough vessel down there," Odrys called from behind. "Not for the horses though."

"I can see that," Ezrilkath snapped back.

Almost to level ground. From here to the Idospont, the Menician coast was a wall of hills and cliffs with sharp, broken rocks. As if the land had put up a wall to defend itself from the sea. The small port town had built a dike to break most of the fiercest waves, but still she could see the docks getting washed over every third wave. Why anyone would live here was beyond her. She respected it though; life was hard and cruel, and people who lived through it deserved more than what they were given.

"We'll sell our horses. The coin will pay for the ship," Ezrilkath called back. "Take them to that barn there. I can see a few horses there already."

"Would have been better to sell at Adrea," Odrys retorted.

"Yea, then we'd have the Mulranei on our ass and the city against us once he arrived," Ezrilkath said, then called out when she finished her descent to level ground. Her horse didn't like the broken rock but still managed to correct itself. "Dismount and to the docks. We ain't grabbing anything but a ship!"

She groaned; her legs felt like they were covered in burning poison. The Ketlans in Monbargar put poison on their spears. She shook her head. A reminder of why she didn't like this whole situation. Nippiktua was Ezrilkath's age when the Ketlans had attacked her town, killing and capturing. The Ketlans had raided her town, cut down her father and mother, and taken her captive. Those god-cursed animals had made her watch them cook her parents' corpses and eat their flesh.

Now she was taking the child away from her loved one. Ezrilkath slung Nippiktua over her shoulder. The girl moved then, kicking and making her weird gurgling noises, which didn't make Ezrilkath feel any better.

"Gods above, stop squirming, you Dae-ling." She swore at her luck. She needed the drakma. Enough to return to Monbargar, buy land, hire warriors, and make war on the Ketlans. Cut their limbs, tear out their tongues, and drink from their skulls like the Monbargar heroes of old.

Nippiktua's ankle hit Ezrilkath in the face.

"That's it." She dropped Nippiktua on her feet, squeezing both her arms. "Listen, girl. Yea, read my lips. I see you with your knowing Dae-eyes. We're getting on that boat so you can go to help the Phoithesens. Any more fussing or escape attempts will lead to your death at sea." The girl only stared back at her with what Ezrilkath thought was her angry face. "Fine. Pulasuq! Get me rope."

She tied up the kid and picked her up like a small sack of potatoes. Odrys and two men took the horses to the large barn. Many locals were already watching them with worry or contempt. Ezrilkath ignored them; she would have done the same, been wary of twenty men in bronze plate with horsehair crested helms, tall spears, and round shields entering a small damp town. She took long steps on the muddy road, her legs protesting each movement as she headed straight for the moored ship.

"Keep the crew on the ship and be on the lookout for others returning," Ezrilkath told Kasgalathan. "We'll round them up if we have to."

"Yes, Captain," Kasgalathan said, motioning for some men to follow him. They spread out and fell behind Ezrilkath.

The dock was slippery. Ezrilkath had to steady her feet as sea spray washed up and soaked her legs, leaving the ends of her tunic and cuirass heavier. Aethra's contempt, it was cold.

Sailors saw them approaching and called an older man to the deck rail. His beard and hair were salt-crusted, and his skin was dark and leathery from sun exposure. The tunic he wore used to be green—now it was gray. At first, he had an alarmed expression, but he quickly regained control.

"Does the ship sail today?" Ezrilkath asked, looking at the older man.

He looked down at Nippiktua and then at her armed men. "Aye, Monbargar, across the Idryiva. We cast off when heaven passes the sun."

Ezrilkath couldn't wait till noon. She lithely hopped onto the deck of the ship. The old man cursed, surprised at how quickly she'd gotten on board. Her men followed her.

"You'll cast off with due haste," Ezrilkath demanded. "I have precious cargo and only so many days to deliver. My man will return with aulos for your trouble." She cut off his protests. "There will be more regrettable trouble if you decide to fight this."

The captain of the ship looked up at her defiantly. He surveyed her men and his own. In that moment, he calculated and nodded, saying, "Gods-damned Monbargars. Fine! The Idryiva is rough enough, I don't need more trouble. When will your men return?"

Ezrilkath looked back down the main street of the town. Odrys and company were heading to the docks. Kasgalathan was guarding the dock with five men. Their helmet plumes limp, soaked by sea spray and rain. Villagers were moving about their homes again, some still watching from open windows or covered decks. "They're on their way now."

The ship's captain nodded and shook his head as he turned from her, calling obscenities and giving commands to his crew.

Ezrilkath let Nippiktua stand and signaled her to stay. The girl only fidgeted in her binds. Ezrilkath was about to check whether she had tied the girl well enough when a sound split through the roar of sea and wind. It bore into her like a Ketlan's burning needle under her fingernail. The dreadful howl that filled her ears seemed to freeze the waves as it did her heart. Cries of terror echoed from the village.

"Kukran! Kukran!"

Fools. Ezrilkath had been in a Kukran attack. This was far worse. Kukran were mindless, cursed beasts that only sought to feed on blood.

This was a Mulranei: clever, calculating, and determined. And he was coming for her. Ezrilkath, her limbs shaking, looked up at the rocky cliffs above the village. She thought she saw a gray shape descend. Shutters and doors slammed in the village. Odrys and the two men ran down the last steps to the dock.

"What in the Darken Depths have you brought against me?" the ship's captain squealed at her.

Ezrilkath ignored him, her heart pounding. She couldn't die now. She couldn't die now. "Cast off now! Odrys and Kasgalathan, get aboard. Men, repel the Mulranei."

"Mulranei! Gods-thrice-damned-shit-for-brains Monbargars!" The ship's captain continued to curse.

Ezrilkath ignored him. "Cast off! Men, get the ropes! Bring in the anchor!" She didn't like how stunned the sailors were. This wasn't her men's first journey on a ship, and Monbargars knew ship craft.

Nippiktua hopped to the deck rail.

"Aeputer's cock," Ezrilkath cursed as she lunged for the girl. She had wiggled out of her leg ties.

Odrys landed on the deck, and Kasgalathan and three men were pushing the ship off when she grabbed Nippiktua.

"Pulasuq!" She tossed the girl to him; they both fell to the deck floor. Sailors were working on the oars now. Ezrilkath was pulling one of Kasgalathan's men on board when she heard a crash and a scream. She looked toward the noise—no movement.

The village seemed deserted. Her peripheral caught movement. She glanced up at the roof of the fish barn that stood near the dock. Ropes and pulleys slack. On the roof, two silver orbs for eyes blazed through the haze, and at their side, a long blade with burnished blue runes steamed like hot coals. The Mulranei had positioned himself perfectly.

"Look out!" Ezrilkath called, pointing, as the Mulranei leaped from the roof. A humanly impossible leap, passing over the surging waves, down onto the dock behind Kasgalathan and three other men.

They turned in time, but it didn't matter. The Mulranei landed sure-footed, eyes still burnished silver, fangs flared. A growl drummed from his throat, deeper than the sea's tempest. The Sword of Mourning was tall, seven feet, sinewy muscle visible under wet fur, accompanied by the rune-glowing great sword. His fur was spotted black, gray, and silver. He lunged with a rising cut behind a man's shield, so precise and swift it cut his arm clean off. Before the armless man had fallen, crying in pain, the other two were felled: one with a thrust and the other bitten in the throat and tossed into the bay.

Kasgalathan attacked like the brave and foolish Monbargar he was. He was one of Ezrilkath's best swordsmen. The Mulranei blocked his attack and returned it with a cut that would have taken his head. Kasgalathan blocked the attack with his shield. It didn't matter. The Mulranei kicked and swept Kasgalathan's legs out from under him and cut his throat while he was in free fall.

"Aeputer's cock," Ezrilkath spat as she rushed back from the deck rail and the Mulranei leaped onto the ship, barking and snarling, killing another man. He swung at her. She blocked the blow with her drawn sword, distancing herself from his long reach. The blow numbed her entire arm. "Spears! Repel him! Get him off!"

Five men rushed him with spears, making him back up to the rail. The ship was drifting too slowly from the dock, the oarsmen struggling. Her men had given them a breath before the Sword of Mourning cut one spear, using the opportunity to get behind the other spear points and subsequently knock them down, killing or tossing overboard each of the five men.

Ezrilkath caught the dryness in the wet air, odd within the sea haze. She looked over at Udrothan. He had cut his hand and was drawing the Runic Ring for casting Ergald.

"Udrothan, you fool!" Ezrilkath spat. "Mulranei are immune to direct Ergald."

They couldn't fight him. The hard truth was a heavy blow. Nippiktua was struggling with Pulasuq. Ezrilkath saw the Sword of Mourning's eyes on her. She had to act; the ship was making its way out onto the sea. Three men had crashed into the Mulranei, one holding down his sword arm. They were being clawed and bitten. Ezrilkath looked around in haste.

Odrys called to her. He had returned from below deck and tossed her a small barrel. "Oil!"

Ezrilkath caught the barrel and the idea. She broke the lid and cast the oil at the Mulranei's feet just as he tossed another man overboard.

"Man overboard!" a sailor called. Some of them tossed a line. The Mulranei picked up his sword and caught her eye. He took a step toward her as the oil hit the deck at his feet. He slipped. Ezrilkath took three strides and jumped feet first. Her feet caught him in the chest, and her weight carried him overboard.

The rail slammed into her ribs, and the Mulranei's claws cut into her right calf. She wrapped her arm around the rail in time to catch herself, cold seawater enveloping her legs. The rail creaked under her weight; she heard the splash.

Odrys and his two men helped her up. She looked back.

The Mulranei resurfaced from the water. He barked twice and then emitted pitiful, gut-churning howls. She looked over at Nippiktua. She was crying, half hanging over the portside rail, held by Pulasuq, and slamming her fists against the wood. The Mulranei wasn't swimming toward them. He knew he couldn't keep up in the sea swells, not with the wind in the sail and the oarsmen beating the water. She looked at the slain and wounded men.

"Gods above and below, Odrys," she said finally, adding in relief, "Aethra's tits and Eorhath's ass. Get the girl below deck and tie her to a post so she doesn't jump off. Aeputer's brow, Odrys." She threw her anger at him.

"I didn't know the girl was watched by the Sword of Mourning, Ezril," Odrys said as he checked the wounds on the men.

Ezrilkath growled and stalked off with a string of curses. She hoped the gods would hear and strike her down. She helped the sailors finish pulling Udrothan out of the water. She had lost eight men, and four were wounded.

The ship's captain was staring daggers at her. She rolled her shoulders, deciding to be angry at someone else instead of old Odrys.

Morvelving coughed and breathed out the bone-numbing seawater. Furiously pushing with his arms and kicking, he desperately swam for the ship. His body ached and his wounds stung in the salt water. His heart burned. Nippi was right there, so close. Yet he couldn't get to her. Penalty was heavy in his hand. His chest heaved and forced a wail out of him. A sensation he'd buried deep returned: the memory of Windtail's limp body. He howled again in misery. Morvelving cursed the sea, which took him under and expelled him roughly onto the shore. A water-Dae wanting rid of him.

He stood up and shook himself, the heavy water leaving his fur. Townsfolk rushed back to their homes. Morvelving couldn't repair the fear he'd caused them. He'd acted more like a Kukran than a Mulranei. No, he had to rescue Nippi. He should have stayed with her. Now he rued that poor judgment. He rubbed his chest. The mercenary captain had played a mortal dance and won, but he would out-endure her. It took two days to reach Idosse lands, and two more to Phoithese. He had to reach the city by land or sea before then.

Morvelving quenched his thirst at a water trough. He checked his wounds. They would mend. He would have to finish his salve on the way. Taking a deep grunted breath, Morvelving began running out of the town, away from the fear he'd caused. He would take the coastal road, looking for a ship that would cross to Nos Isle and land near Theba. He shook his head. No, there was a possibility he would find a ship to Nos, then none to Agrothica. His best option was to make the six-day journey on land in four days.

If nothing hindered him, and if Nippi's captors faced unfavorable sailing conditions, he could be on the Agrothican coasts as they made port. Then he could lay a trap. He had been desperate seeing them loading onto the ship, ready to cast off. Now he would have to be patient and hope Telunian would let no harm come to Nippi from the sea. The Moon held a thin sway over the water. Though Ulyss, Lord of Waters, held bitterness toward Telunian for dictating the tides, and his grudges were deep. He may take small vengeance. Morvelving brushed the thought aside to quell his own panic.

To stop would be to abandon Nippi to a terrible fate. Nippi would not know loss again.

"Hear me, Goddess," he said between hoarse breaths. "Keep her safe." The unquenchable feeling of powerlessness and a need to prove otherwise flowed through him like it did when he saw Windtail's broken body. He couldn't handle it. His hand went to his belt pouch for piphlid and found narroot. He placed another root stem in his mouth, recognizing the danger, but he didn't care right now.

They would make it across, and Morvelving would wait for them. No thought for the ache in his limbs and chest. He ran north. Morvelving didn't stop, passing farmsteads, villages, and herds of livestock. He paused only for water and the scent of narroot as he ran. His journey would pass through Thressea, and he was confident the king would have a watch set for him. Nothing could hinder him—nothing. At night, he howled to the starlit sky, hoping Telunian would hear his plea.

25

The ship's deck was slippery with oil and blood when Nippiktua dove
for the tall railing with bated breath. She couldn't believe it when she saw
the strong woman jump and kick Morvelving off the ship. He was always
steadfast, unmovable. Ignoring the salty spray stinging her eyes, she
lifted herself over to see. She saw Fluff's head rise from the dark water,
saw his mouth move—he was barking. The rest she couldn't see due to
the tears blurring her vision. She banged her tied hands on the wood as if
it were the cause of all her problems.

Strong hands took hold of her. She didn't fight, straining for one last
glance at her father. He had tried so hard. Her wrists were still tied.
Stuck. She couldn't do anything, and it made her grind the ropes in her
teeth till her lips bled and her jaw cramped. It was too late.

Her traitor kin carried her below deck. He tied her to a post and
tossed her a blanket. She didn't care. Fluff was gone, and she . . . she
should have been better, older, stronger, so Fluff didn't have to take care
of her. Nippiktua pulled the blanket that smelled like fish over her head,
deepening the dark. Then she let the pounding of the sea against the
wood fill her mind as she cried herself to sleep.

When Nippiktua woke, the sea's pounding still reverberated
through the wood against her skin. She smelled salt, fish, and blood, and
her head throbbed. Was she bleeding? Something poked her on the

shoulder. She flung the blanket over her head. Dim now, the only light shone from the hatch where the steps led to the main deck. Shadows moved back and forth. Once her eyes adjusted, she saw what had poked her. It was a *who*. Nippiktua pushed back from the mercenary captain.

The captain said something to her. She didn't catch it; Nippiktua was too angry to look at the woman. She placed a bowl of porridge next to Nippiktua. Her stomach protested her own defiance. The captain only looked down at her, searching her face. Nippiktua wanted to tear her eyes out.

A shadow dimmed the light of the deck steps. Someone must have called the captain, for she turned her back to Nippiktua to speak to them. Nippiktua remained defiant, ignoring the food. The strong-armed woman peered down at her. Noticing Nippiktua wasn't taking the food, she picked up the bowl and shook her head.

Nippiktua's stomach grumbled again. She watched Strong Arms pull out pieces of cooking charcoal. The fire-haired woman scribbled on the wood. Strong Arms showed her the runes. They read: *I'm Ezrilkath. You need to eat.*

Nippiktua bared her teeth like Morvelving did when he was angry. This was what he'd meant—this was the right time to show her teeth. The strong woman shook her head and walked up the steps to the daylight. Thankfully, she'd left the food behind. Nippiktua looked down at the bowl. It looked like porridge. Her stomach grumbled at her. Morvelving would tell her to eat too. The thought of him—his head bobbing in the water, fur all wet and not fluffy—made her sad again.

Once she'd wiped the tears away and blown her nose in the blanket, she ate. It was gross, no flavor, but she was too hungry to care. Nippiktua slept after, content with a full belly. Morvelving was in her dreams. He was running with her in the woods. She was fast and strong, weaving through brush and around tall trees. They were running for the joy of it — the freedom of it. The wind cooled the sweat that soaked her braided hair. It still held together how Cassea had pinned it. Nippiktua breathed in the warm summer air, then the fall's and winter's. They ran unceasing through the seasons. She was a goddess, unyielding to time and weariness.

The forest of tall white trees ended on a precipice. Morvelving stopped in time and moved to catch Nippiktua. She evaded him. Nippiktua didn't need to stop. She leaped from the cliff and was weightless. The wind tore at her face as she laughed, hearing her voice. The land below rushed toward her like a long-lost friend with open arms of greeting. Nippiktua wasn't afraid. She was free and unyielding. She simply moved on. Weightless as a leaf, she soared on the wind, higher and higher toward the sun. It blazed like the will of her heart to keep flying.

There was Celemith, a place of bliss where the gods live. It was black against the sun. As she drew near, its shadows dissipated to reveal a world with massive trees and mounds of snow, like the ones her father had made for her and her siblings to slide down.

Nippiktua laughed, unable to contain her excitement, flying closer until she could see her mother and father. They still wore their bear-fur coats. Three hunched shapes stood behind her parents, hidden in their own shadows, bright sapphire fishing line threaded between them — village elders Nippiktua didn't recognize. But she felt their gaze, cold and dark, yet beautiful and welcoming.

Movement diverted Nippiktua's gaze. Her two sisters moved first to the elders and then to her parents, bundled in furs and pointing at Nippiktua. She called to them.

"Stay with us," she heard her mother say.

"No," her father said with pride. "She is free."

Suddenly, a shadow hid them from her sight. Nippiktua turned to look up. A great draekurm with fierce, blazing red eyes descended.

She woke up, crying out. Nippiktua looked around. A sailor with an apron looked over at her from the small stove. He was cooking, as indicated by the potent scent of fish and the blaze of the fire. Ezrilkath sat cross-legged near her. Nippiktua sharply turned away.

Ezrilkath lifted a wooden board with parchment. Nippiktua had to look. It had a list of items Nippiktua didn't understand. She understood the runes Ezrilkath had written. She was going to untie Nippiktua. She immediately thought she should run, but where? She was stuck on this ship. Nippiktua made no response as the mercenary undid her bonds. Nippiktua was surprised by the gesture. She didn't know what game Ezrilkath was playing, but she would not take part in it the way the woman wanted her to.

Once free, Nippiktua felt a hot fire within her and swung her fist into the woman's chin. Nippiktua gasped—her hand burned with pain while Ezrilkath didn't even blink, which made Nippiktua mad. Ezrilkath didn't strike back but wrote runes on the parchment again. She was using a large white feather as a quill now. Nippiktua glared, shaking her hand, trying to relieve the pain.

Several sailors walked by, hurrying to their tasks. One mercenary, the older one with white hair, peeked down from the top deck.

Nippiktua looked at the runes Ezrilkath showed her: *Don't cause trouble or I'll tie you up again. It's two days to Agrothica. You can't escape. I am sorry.*

Nippiktua looked into the woman's eyes, scowling and not trusting her. They were dark blue with a grayish tint, pretty—which confused Nippiktua. Why would such a mean person have pretty eyes? Even more confusing was her apology. How could she be sorry? If she were sorry, she wouldn't have taken Nippiktua. Despite her own anger, her loneliness and fear, Nippiktua motioned for the parchment.

Ezrilkath handed her the quill and ink as Nippiktua took the parchment. Looking at it closer, she saw that it was some sort of log for the ship. The mercenary must have taken it from the ship's captain.

Nippiktua wrote, asking, *Why are you sorry? It's your fault.*

Ezrilkath took a long time to write back. Nippiktua rubbed her wrists, waiting. Her lips were also cracked and scabbed. There was a water jug next to her that Ezrilkath must have brought down. Nippiktua crawled on her hands and knees to grab it. She drank deeply. Ezrilkath noticed her and seemed to remember something, for she dropped the quill and twisted around, holding a bowl of porridge and offering it to Nippiktua.

There was a strange feeling spinning in Nippiktua. She hated this woman for taking her from Fluff. Yet she needed the woman to survive the next few days. She didn't understand why Ezrilkath was trying to be friendly if she was just going to hand Nippiktua off. Ezrilkath was taking her to the draekurm. This was not how Nippiktua wanted it to happen. She'd hoped to stumble on a draekurm together with Fluff. Now she was going alone. She had to be brave.

Taking a bite of the flavorless porridge, Nippiktua read what Ezrilkath had written: *You're not wrong. You travel with the Sword of Mourning. He's a mercenary. You know he works for coin so you can eat. I'm doing the same. We must eat and survive. The world is cruel, and the gods above have abandoned us to the Fates. The battle was over, so I needed an alternative . . . I was hoping your friend wouldn't catch up to us.*

Father, Nippiktua corrected quickly. Ezrilkath nodded. Nippiktua added, *You're still mean, and I don't like you.*

Ezrilkath's lips twisted into a small smirk. She stood up. Nippiktua had to strain her neck to watch the woman go back up the steps. Fluff would be proud of her for sending Ezrilkath away. The mercenary was right though: she couldn't escape into the sea. Fluff couldn't have given up on her. The thought lingered in her mind, dark and consuming. No, she couldn't give up. She looked down at the parchment Ezrilkath had left. Her words confused Nippiktua. They had to eat and survive, and they had taken her so they could make coin from the people who wanted her to talk to the draekurm. Grownups were so weird and mean. Then she considered, wondering if she had the right measure of them, and decided that, even so, they weren't evil. They didn't mean to harm her. They simply didn't consider—or want to consider—how their actions hurt her.

Nippiktua had felt that way when that pigheaded prince wanted the Stag. She hadn't thought about what the prince had wanted, only her own anger and sadness, and she'd wanted to blame it on the prince. She didn't know how she could think about how others felt, especially when they felt like enemies, but she decided she would try. The heavy thoughts made her lean back on the wooden beam. If Ezrilkath was only thinking about the coin, then she was like Nippiktua had been with Goldeye—not caring about who got hurt. She took another bite of food.

The sailor-cook was working at the stove. He only peered down at her and shrugged. She watched him cook, enjoying the delicious smell. And waiting for a chance to take something to eat without him seeing. She decided then that she would trust that Fluff was coming for her across the sea, and she wouldn't try to escape from Ezrilkath. Not for now, at least. She finished her porridge.

26

There were many reasons for Nippiktua to be annoyed with grown-ups. She stood on the ship's deck out of the way of the sailors, who'd pushed and bonked her twice already for being in the way.

There were ones like Cassea and Gaia, who were nice. Then there were ones like Ezrilkath, who did mean things but weren't evil and did nice things too. It was perplexing. Why couldn't they just be one or the other? Ezrilkath had taken her from Fluff, Cassea, and Gaia. Nippiktua hated her for that.

Now, Ezrilkath let Nippiktua walk freely, gave her the best food, and even let her play the pebble game the sailors played. And Nippiktua liked her for that. Ezrilkath was only mean when she had to be.

Nippiktua wondered if most evil things were genuinely that way. Ezrilkath had said she needed the drakma, so maybe evil was wanting too much. What would Fluff call that? Greed.

The ship was a wide-bellied thing, but it glided when the wind blew. The wind was weak now. Nippiktua watched the eight sailors on each side of the boat pulling the oars. She had to behave because otherwise Ezrilkath would make Nippiktua pull the oars. By the look of it, pulling oars was something Nippiktua *never* wanted to do.

A sailor was climbing a rope and wood ladder, moving up to the nest on top of the mast, where the sail hung limp. Nippiktua wanted to go up there too, but the fear of falling kept her from asking.

The old mercenary Ezrilkath called Odrys stood in front of her. She'd thought he would let her pass, but he just stood there like a caribou with a bloated belly. Nippiktua scowled up at him, hands on hips.

Odrys clasped his hands together. Nippiktua watched as he tore his thumb off! What? She couldn't believe what she was seeing. The old man moved his hand again. His thumb was back! Nippiktua jumped and grabbed his hand, looking for any sign of a cut. Odrys didn't let her look for long, forcing his hand from her grip and walking away, chuckling.

Nippiktua shook her head in disbelief. Clearly, he'd used magic. She would have to ask Fluff how to do that.

Being on the main deck felt fantastic. She had stayed below deck yesterday after Ezrilkath had talked with her. She had watched the cook, become tired, and cried herself to sleep. This morning, she decided she wouldn't let people decide her fate without her. Nippiktua was going to be involved. If she paid attention, perhaps she could find an easier path to escape. She was confident Morvelving was waiting for her across the sea, and she didn't want him to kill Ezrilkath. The ship's captain was doing something with a piece of quartz stone. She ran over to watch.

Ezrilkath watched Nippiktua hurry across the deck to the ship's captain, Contivo.

He was using the old quartz trick that was prominent among boatsmen to navigate the seas. Ezrilkath couldn't escape the guilt she felt for taking the girl and for the many men she'd lost to the Mulranei. Her leadership was at risk. She held a weight too heavy to carry, and instead of feeling determined to see the job done, she wanted to give it up. She watched Odrys approach.

"What was that all about?" she asked.

"Just showing the child my trick."

Ezrilkath rolled her eyes. "The missing thumb trick?"

Odrys, recognizing her glare, didn't chuckle with self-amusement, which was equally infuriating.

"For the reward, it was a good choice," Odrys said quietly. With the slap of waves against the ship's hull and the splash of oars, she barely heard him. "The men know this. Even with some of the good men lost."

"More coin for the lot of us," Ezrilkath stated, trying to act like his words weren't hitting her on the nose.

"Though I know the amount of the drakma from the girl will set us up nicely," Odrys said, ignoring Ezrilkath's hard play, "some are concerned you won't go through with it."

Ezrilkath gave him a warning side-glance.

Odrys locked eyes with her, unwavering. "You've spent a lot of time with the girl."

He was referring to Ezrilkath writing with Nippiktua during mealtimes. She had found it pleasant and discovered Nippiktua had been with Morvelving for almost three years. Nippiktua had wanted to know why Ezrilkath had taken her. Though she couldn't find a good answer, Ezrilkath had given the child an honest one. It was all for the coin. She needed to survive and return to Monbargar. The girl seemed to understand—she had to. It was how she had lived her life with the Mulranei.

She'd also learned Nippiktua knew the Phoithesens were after her.

They think I can talk to the draekurm. Make it stop being mean, Nippiktua had written. Ezrilkath thought it was absurd and wasn't looking forward to dealing with any Phoithesens. She had heard of the draekurm in Phoithese and kept her company far from those fanatic southwestern lands. Now she was heading there. Telunian's toes. Who was mad now?

"She reminds me of me at her age," Ezrilkath confessed. Odrys only nodded, leaving a moment of silence. He knew her past, just as she knew his. Soldiers often confessed their stories the night before a battle. She and Odrys had lived through many.

"You are not what the Ketlans are," Odrys said, moving away from Ezrilkath, spitting on the deck at the mention of the Ketlans. "But I do want to know: what do you intend to do?"

Ezrilkath had been considering this for some time. She knew she couldn't just let the girl go after losing men to the Mulranei. Her men had to see a profit. They had sold slaves before for a lesser price. They didn't like it, but that was how it was. She watched Nippiktua hurry over to a sailor bundling rope. The sailor saw her watching and handed her the rope. She tried unsuccessfully to wrap it the way he did.

Ezrilkath had already informed Contivo that interfering with her on Nippiktua's behalf would have dire consequences. Thankfully, the ship's captain wasn't the noble type. Or if he was, he was also smart, not challenging a Monbargar on the open sea.

"I'm not going through with this," Ezrilkath said after a long moment. Odrys only nodded. "The gods may judge me for taking the girl. I've caused pain to many people and received my share as well. This is too close. She's just a girl, and the Phoithesens think sacrificing her will change a draekurm's mind? It's madness."

"What do we do with her then? And how will we pay for our journey back to Monbargar and have coin remaining?" Odrys asked.

"Gods above, Odrys." Ezrilkath rubbed her temple. "The only road we have—double cross. We take the Phoithesens' drakma, shadow the girl, and get her back as they take her to the draekurm. We're too small a band to worry about reputation."

"What if they leave her in the city?"

"I'll work out the details. I—"

Odrys continued interrupting her. "And what if the Mulranei catches us before then? You know he is on his way. I have no doubt."

"Aethra's tits." Ezrilkath ran her hand through her short, braided hair, damp with sweat. The sun was warm, even hidden by clouds. The Mulranei was a rather large knife at her side. She should never have taken the girl. There was a chance the Sword of Mourning *and* her men wouldn't listen if a confrontation arose.

"I doubt we have the numbers to fight him off," Ezrilkath said. "The drakma means nothing if we're dead. No, if he catches us before Phoithese, I'll give him the girl. You really think he could make it in time?"

Odrys shrugged. "I have seen many things in my time and heard about more. Mulranei are an ancient race. The life of their goddess still runs pure in them, I think. My mind says it's impossible for him to make it to Agrothica in two days across land, but I still fear he is there waiting."

"Don't get superstitious on me," Ezrilkath chided. "It would be physically impossible, even if he ran full sprint night and day. Go. Tell the men to rest up. It's going to be hard once we make port."

Odrys did her bidding. Ezrilkath took a deep breath. Admitting she'd made a mistake in taking Nippiktua eased her conscience, but the fear that the Mulranei would intercept them and not listen to her plea made her knuckles white. Perhaps the plea didn't need to be *hers*.

Nippiktua was sitting with several sailors who were out of their rotation. Each had a mug of ale and a pipe for smoking. Ezrilkath didn't know why the girl was so fascinated. She looked to the west.

The sea swells rose and fell, and several large white birds followed the ship. They would make port in Agrothica by the morrow. Ezrilkath had been to the small city-state before. The Agrothicans were a cunning lot; other Idosse cities hired their leaders as tacticians or builders. Surprisingly, Agrothica was a rather unimposing city. They enjoyed simple functionality over extravagance.

Nippiktua took the offered mug from one sailor and tried it.

Ezrilkath moved to their side of the ship. She may have taken the girl from her loved one, but she had standards. The last thing she needed was a drunk child. Ezrilkath took the mug from Nippiktua, but she didn't get there in time to stop her from taking a drink.

The girl grimaced at the bitter ale.

"Fucking Idosse, what have you? Brains of a fish?" Ezrilkath said, chiding the sailor and thrusting the mug into his hand. It spilled heavily.

The sailor looked up at her with contempt. "What're yous, her captor or mother?"

Ezrilkath didn't give the sailor any more of her attention. Some people were hardly worth the words. She ushered Nippiktua along. The girl needed no encouragement. She hadn't taken a liking to the ale, with good reason. Ezrilkath had tried the brew, and it was sour, having been fermented too long. Undoubtedly how the sailors liked it.

Nippiktua kept a space between her and Ezrilkath. Good, the girl was smart enough to not be as quick to trust as other children. How Ezrilkath was at her age.

She led Nippiktua below deck. It was close enough to mealtime, and Ezrilkath needed to see what the girl had to say about her plan. It involved her cooperation, and Ezrilkath would need her guarantee. Perhaps the girl could be persuaded to save Ezrilkath and her men's necks if the Mulranei caught them before Phoithese, however unlikely that confrontation was.

The light swayed as the ship rocked back and forth. Several sailors were taking their meals, and two of them were her men. Juthan and Kintanther acknowledged Ezrilkath then went back to their tasks. Kintanther was oiling the bronze scales on his cuirass, and Juthan was sharpening his sword.

Nippiktua ignored them and ran to the kitchen. She must have made nice with the cook, for she found a wooden bowl and spoon in one cabinet.

The girl rummaged through all the goods. How she knew where everything was, Ezrilkath could only guess. She looked back up the steps to the main deck—all clear. Ezrilkath doubted Nippiktua could learn where everything was. The cook probably thought it harmless for her to watch, and she memorized where he put everything.

Nippiktua finished rummaging through the cabinets, barrels, and crates, and sauntered over to the other side, effortlessly climbing on top of a barrel to eat. Her bowl had a few *bachka*—hard-baked pieces of bread square-cut for ease of storage—with butter and a chunk of crumbling white cheese. Nippiktua ate with a satisfied smile on her face.

"Hmm," Ezrilkath grunted, amused. Yes, her plan could work. The girl was resourceful. She grabbed the wooden plank with the captain's list of goods. He was unaware he'd let Ezrilkath borrow it. The feather and ink were still there, though the ink was nearly empty.

Nippiktua watched Ezrilkath write as she ate.

Ezrilkath handed the girl the plank, her runes written over the old list of cargo. She told Nippiktua that she had a job for her. She would act like a mercenary when they made landfall tomorrow.

Nippiktua looked up at her, scrutinizing.

Ezrilkath showed nothing. She would not plead for the girl to behave how she wanted. She wanted Nippiktua to act like the band so no merchants in Agrothica would think she was a slave for sale. They needed to be out of the city as quickly as possible, and Ezrilkath didn't want to be haggled. The Agrothicans loved to barter for any wares they set their eyes on.

Nippiktua wrote and showed Ezrilkath the runes, her face stern but for the hint of a smirk at the corner of her mouth.

Ezrilkath read the words: *Will I get a sword?* Ezrilkath's eyebrows rose. Now, what would she want with that? To stab Ezrilkath in the throat as she slept? Or Pulasuq? The girl seemed to hate him the most. Ezrilkath couldn't blame her. She wrote her answer: *A wooden sword.*

The girl looked at the answer and frowned.

Ezrilkath crossed her arms, staring back at those stubborn red eyes. Frystlins were always unsettling to her. No wonder people left them alone. Seeing one of them in the frozen wilderness would be terrifying.

Nippiktua nodded and held out her hand.

Ezrilkath scrutinized her. It didn't take long for her to realize what the girl wanted.

"What, now?" Ezrilkath asked with a snort. "Gods above, I don't have one with me."

Nippiktua flung out her palm, persistent.

"Little Dae," Ezrilkath grumbled as she stood and pointed at her lips. "You'll get your sword. Not yet. Stay out of mischief." She left the girl in the shadows of the ship's hull and climbed back into the sunlight.

Odrys was waiting for her with several of the men: Pulasuc, Kintanther, Juthan, and Diometes. They would tell the others. Pulasuq still worked on sharpening his dagger. He wore a dirty tunic and breeches, sweat glistening on his brow, the only one in the company who was always warm. Kintanther watched her closely. He had always looked up to her, and their losses hit him the hardest.

"We'll be in Agrothica at sunrise tomorrow, boys," Ezrilkath said, looking at each of them. "The girl's going to act like one of us. We slip through the city quick and easy. I want no hiccups or misplaced sandals." She gave Pulasuq a pointed look. "Anyone asks, she's a recruit. This task was supposed to be quick and easy. It's no longer that, but we make do with what we have. The road to Phoithese will be hard. We'll rest after it's done."

"Aeputer's cock, you think the wolfman's after us still?" Juthan asked, unbelieving, his arms crossed, his sinewy muscles seeming to stretch his pink scars. He braided his red hair to his scalp in the traditional Monbargar fashion. "No way he'll make it across land, and by sea would be longer."

"I have no doubt the Mulranei is doing everything he can to catch up to us, make no mistake," Ezrilkath said. "We won't be done at Phoithese. I want to be clear of the Idosse after the deal. I've been gone too long from my scores in Monbargar."

Kintanther looked up at that, nodding. So, he had been waiting to hear that. Good. They had their own scores to settle in their homeland.

"When we get paid for delivering the girl, we sail for Monbargar," Ezrilkath continued. "Quick and smooth, and far richer for it—enough to gather fighters there and strike at the Ketlans. Go tell the others."

The four men nodded and left, talking among themselves. Ezrilkath trusted them to convince the others, so she needn't repeat herself. She felt Odrys's eyes on her. "Aethra's tits, what?"

"You didn't mention your intention to double-cross the Phoithesens," Odrys stated, one eyebrow crooked in curiosity.

Ezrilkath shrugged. "They'll improvise just fine."

"You know you'll be taking the girl from one cruel fate to another," Odrys said thoughtfully. "In Monbargar, the risks will be great for a young mercenary."

"Trying to live is a risk. I can't change that, nor can I change what the Fates devise. With us, she has a chance. I doubt she'll have that chance with the draekurm."

Ezrilkath was getting frustrated now. Not at Odrys but at herself. Why did she decide now to see the harm she had caused and use the girl as a path to redemption? Eorhath's beard, she never should have taken the child from Sene. She could hear the campfire talk: *How did the mercenary captain Ezrilkath die? Oh, she took a child a Mulranei had sworn to protect. And the gods laughed, and the Fates moaned in pleasure.*

Odrys must have been thinking the same thing, for he stated, "We should give up the girl if the Mulranei, beyond possibility, catches up to us."

"We talked about that," Ezrilkath replied. "I will not make the same mistake twice. Even if fifty men join us at Agrothica, I wouldn't keep her from the Mulranei."

The ship's captain was barking orders, and the sailors were returning to their tasks.

Ezrilkath was suddenly tired—tired of being away from her homeland, tired of risking her neck in some idiot's war for a few coins so she could eat. Four years had gone by, and she was as poor as she'd been when she'd started out—and now she was heading in the opposite direction.

"The Phoithesens better be true to their offer," she grumbled to herself. What could she do otherwise?

Ezrilkath watched the ship ride over the waves of the dark sea as she considered her path ahead. She had to be practical. Take the Phoithesens' drakma, keep Nippiktua with her. Return to Monbargar, hire Thrarls, and reclaim her family's land from the Ketlans.

———

Agrothica was exactly how Ezrilkath remembered it: a sprawling city with no walls or towers except the lighthouse standing proud on rough stone, jagged from the battering of the sea. It stood tall, almost as tall as a small mountain, its smooth stone standing against the massive breakers. The great fire at the top blazed. The fine masonry was a stark contrast to the shabby and crumbling buildings of the city. It was true the keeper of the lighthouse worked as a regent to the city called the Plutriach. Merchants and bankers ran the rest of the city, hiring thugs and mercenaries to protect their wares and deliver governance at their whim. None of the other Idosse city-states sought to conquer Agrothica, for drakma flowed through it to the benefit of all the greedy kings.

If the city's sight was an eyesore, despite the lighthouse's attempt at refinement, its smell was a gaping wound. Tar, fish, and human waste wafted up to Ezrilkath's nose, making her cough. Nippiktua was making a show of pinching her nose closed. The baying of seagulls and the cries of goats drowned out the calls of sailors and dockmen. On the rocks along the bay and within the city were goats. The Agrothicans bred the finest goats, sold at high prices for sacrifices to the gods. The land surrounding the city was poor for crops, so the breeding and shepherding of cattle and goats was Agrothica's primary source of goods. Now they simply let the creatures roam.

Contivo brought the ship to dock. Already, merchants called out that their wares were of the highest quality. The ship's captain ignored them. In fact, even the sailors did—they were all looking at Ezrilkath and her twelve men. The merchants gathered, saw the rough-looking mercenaries and the sailors' unease, and made themselves scarce. There were no sales to be made here.

Ezrilkath turned to face Contivo. She could see him working through his options. He could call out to the city watch, which patrolled in pairs along the dock. She recognized them by their polished bronze cuirasses and green cloaks, telling all who they belonged to—bankers or otherwise.

Contivo looked down, seeing her watching him. Ezrilkath wasn't dishonorable. She had taken control of his ship and hadn't paid him for his loss of wares. She dug her silver and copper armband out of her pack and handed it to him.

"For your trouble," Ezrilkath said, handing it to him. "It is better than nothing, and it's all I'm offering."

He did not know that it was the armband she'd won in her first battle. Her people measured a man or woman by how many armbands they wore, won only in battle and given by a lord who had won many. She'd won it when she was sixteen, barely conscious and decorated in gore and her own vomit, her thumbs still in the warm eye sockets of her dying enemy. It no longer fit her arm, and she'd never felt like breaking or reforming it.

Contivo took the armband as payment, grunting and cursing under his breath. He didn't say a word as Ezrilkath led her men off the ship. Merchants immediately accosted them.

"Finest wool this side of the Idospont!"

"Spices from the mysterious east!"

"You'll not find better-forged swords."

Ezrilkath ignored them all. Her men did too. She avoided the patrols of any city watch. Mercenaries weren't uncommon. In fact, she spotted a few outside an outdoor inn called Accopia.

Nippiktua was the only one who seemed to enjoy herself, ironically. She held the short wooden sword Ezrilkath had given her and periodically swung it madly around, her face contorted in rage. When she wasn't swinging at a fly, she was gawking at the people in the city.

Children gawked back at her, pointing and calling out, "Hiya, Blue!

Where can I get eyes like that?"

Nippiktua was blissfully unaware.

A boy tried to get closer to her and taunt her. Ezrilkath chased him away with a glance.

Carts and passersby hurried out of their way as they left the city on the main road east. She would scurry away too if she were a tired farmer and a band of heavily equipped mercenaries approached with spears above their heads and shields on their backs. Their packs weighed them down, and helms clattered against their legs as they marched. Ezrilkath kept hers on her head, signifying herself as the leader, and set the pace.

It was a grueling pace. She felt time was against them, an angry Mulranei breathing down her neck. The men chose not to complain.

When night descended, she sat near the fire, its flames dancing, casting shadows on each of them. The kid was sleeping, bundled in a blanket. In the morning, she had refused to be carried. She hadn't lasted long though—she couldn't keep up, so Ezrilkath had let the girl ride on her shoulders. Ezrilkath's legs were still sore from the extra weight. They had made good time. The constant breeze in the Makoidake Plain sought to take all the warmth from her cloak.

"You shouldn't become attached," Odrys said quietly to her. His blanket covered his head, as if asleep.

The men glanced up and down. Even the two sentries turned their heads. Gods-damned Odrys.

Odrys continued. "Even if everything goes smoothly, there's a chance she will perish along the road. Our paths are dangerous."

"Tell me the sky is blue," Ezrilkath snapped, then sighed and grunted. "Fuck, Odrys. Yeah, I feel guilty. This whole thing is a mess. We get to Phoithese, get the drakma, then grab the girl before she ascends the mountain. I'd rather risk the chance than leave a person—a child—to face a draekurm. Anyone want to comment or question?"

No one spoke. Odrys only sighed.

Ezrilkath continued. "Good. After, we'll grab a ship in Old Aphoeria and sail to Monbargar."

"What of the draekurm?" asked Kintanther.

Ezrilkath shrugged. "What of it? We won't get close enough for it to even smell us. Now get some rest. We leave before sunrise." She leaned over to Odrys. "I understand your concern—and Aeputer's cock, you called me out—but I need you to withhold your badgering and focus."

Odrys nodded and put up his hands in surrender before lying back down on the earth to sleep. Ezrilkath wanted to do the same. The itch on the back of her neck was keeping her on edge. Something was close, and she didn't like it one bit. By midday tomorrow, they'd cross the River Serpres and be at Phoithese before sunset.

She stood and relieved Juthan of his sentry duty. If she could not sleep, she could at least keep watch.

27

Morvelving stumbled into the tall tree, bruising his shoulder, bracing his left hand against the trunk. His claws dug into the bark, tearing it open as he fought to stand. His chest heaved. He was off the road and had crossed the Idospont.

Drums and horns still rang from the city of Thressea. The shouts of humans, the baying of hounds, and the thunder of hooves battered his ears. King Alkithides had set a watch for him, seeking vengeance for the death of his son. Morvelving regretted letting Leolicides's servants flee, however innocent they were.

This was the only way to get to Nippi.

As the beating hooves had approached, shaking the earth behind him, Morvelving had pivoted, leaping down the slope and continuing into the dense woods. King Alkithides and his companions pursued him but had not spied his change in course. They may have passed him by for now, but their hounds would find his scent. Still, his diversion had saved him from being skewered by a long lance.

He pressed on, ripping his claws from the tree, stumbling till he found his stride. Penalty weighed heavily in his right hand. He wasn't running away from what he needed; he was running toward it.

Squirrels and birds shouted at him for running like a drunkard through their peace. His body burned. He wanted to lie down and sleep for two decades. He had only stopped to finish making a healing salve and collect more narroot.

Morvelving brought another stem to his mouth, greedily taking a bite. Strength burned through him, and he shuddered, reveling as the pain became null. It was essential. He couldn't have come so far without it.

Despite the narroot's advantages, he would not make it out of the Thressean lands alive. From the shade of the woods, Morvelving peered at the stretch of road. It wound like a snake through the rocky and wooded land. Beyond his sight were the fields surrounding the River Ykris valley, the natural landmark for the border of Lesgossa and Thressea.

Morvelving had to cross the river. Alkithides wouldn't risk crossing the border into the more powerful city-state. Between him and the river, out of sight, were the king and his companions. Already, he heard the baying of their hounds drawing closer.

Even with the narroot, he stood no chance of outrunning horses. They would catch up to him and slay him. Desperation drove him: there was only one thing to do, but it risked draining him further. He raised his snout to the heavens and sang a song of concealment, feeling his Eifgald ebb and flow, and the land respond to Telunian's verses that had gone unheard for centuries. Stanzas that invoked an unnatural fog to rise from each sea, brook, and river to cover the land.

His legs shook violently, and his chest felt as if it would burst. He had exerted himself too far. He crushed the salve in his palm and spread it on his legs and chest, licking the rest from his fingers. Instead of burning hot, his limbs and chest burned cold, and despite the warm air, his breath was visible as smoke.

Shouts and the gallop of horses drew near.

The land around Morvelving became hidden in a gray haze. A hindrance only, and he was too exhausted to take advantage of it.

There was one other thing he could do. Either it would work, or he would be dead. Taking a long breath, he sang to the wolves of the land. They were out there in the woods, glens, and fields. Hunting or resting, they were out there, and he called to them, telling them of his plight. His howl carried across the land, through the trees and hidden dens. There was no response. Morvelving whimpered, his chest heaving, and ran onto the open road.

It took him several moments to gain a rhythm to maintain his run. He couldn't see, but he could hear and smell.

Cries in Thressean came from behind and to his right. The gray shapes of riders with high horsehair-crested helms and taller spears rode past. The mist swirling in a maelstrom of confusion. Hounds found him, yipping in surprise when he barked at them.

A rider blocked his way. Morvelving almost ran into them. The man shouted, struggling to turn his startled horse so he could lunge with his spear. Morvelving darted around, trusting the fog to hide his movements.

The hounds kept on his heels but didn't risk coming nearer. He hoped the king and his companions, confused by the thick mist, would struggle to follow.

His hope faded just as the fog dissipated. His Eifgald couldn't sustain the Goddess's verses. Their echo dimmed, and the fog fell away. Using Ergald crossed his mind, but it would tax him too much. He spared a glance behind.

The hounds kept pace with him, and a horseman appeared around the bend of the road, pointing and shouting.

Morvelving sprinted into the woods. The road led downward out of the highlands and onto rolling hills, wooded and spotted with fields. His pursuers would have to circle around. Time was fleeting. If they guessed his destination, they could ride ahead to River Ykris to cut him off. His direction was too obvious.

The hounds, sensing his fear, chose now to corner him. One snapped at his leg, testing. Morvelving pivoted and slashed with his lefthand claws and caught the flesh. The hounds fell back, howling and whimpering, their wounded friend baying mournfully.

They didn't try to approach Morvelving again.

He covered his face as he burst through a heavy bush, the thorns of its branches catching his fur and tearing his skin. A field of tall grass lay before him, and beyond it ran the River Ykris, its waters sparkling in the sunlight. The land sloped down toward it; a lone oak shaded a patch where an array of wildflowers grew. The wind made the grass and grain stalks dance like waves of the sea. Morvelving took another bite of narroot, for King Alkithides and his companions were approaching from the west.

Sweat glistened on their mounts. The bronze spearheads and helms flashed. There were thirty. Thirty men on horses, with lances the length of two spears. Thirty men who had trained their whole lives to defend and fight for their king. And now they all charged toward Morvelving to avenge their king's son. They would lance and trample him before he reached the river.

The hounds tried to shepherd Morvelving toward the charging horses. He ignored them, as they were unwilling to test him again. Morvelving growled and forced his legs to move faster. He had to make it. An image of Nippi burned by draekurm fire filled his mind. Windtail falling. He had to. The land flew under him. But it was not enough.

Morvelving swiftly dodged under the first lance. He caught a fleeting sight of the rider's snarling face, matching the roaring bear on his helm. He looked like a harder and older Leolicides. Riders circled ahead of him. He was trapped, and all he could do was try to avoid the horse and lance. He was so tired.

Morvelving collided with a horse. His snout slammed into the shaft of the spear. His back hit the soft earth hard. Hooves pinned his shoulder and stabbed him in the gut. Nippi flashed in his vision. He rolled and stood, growling and ready with Penalty. The magic of the narroot made him ignore the pain and exhaustion, ignore the lack of breath in his lungs, ready to show these humans how Mulranei fought to the last.

Wolves—great gray bounding ones and large dark ones with gold eyes. They came from all sides, more packs than Morvelving could count in his beleaguered state.

The wolves attacked hound, horse, and man. They had heard his plea and answered. Morvelving's eyes burned with tears of relief.

"Flee, He Who Mourns!" they barked. "Run to her who is alone!"

Morvelving obeyed the Wardens of the Wild. He half stumbled, half ran from the high-pitched screeching of hounds, the braying of crazed horses, and the shouting of men. The chilly waters of River Ykris numbed his legs.

His ears flicked back.

"I'll get my revenge, dog! You killed my son! I curse you and your kin, wolfman!"

Morvelving closed his eyes, knowing his actions and the king's curse would haunt them both. He washed the ripples of doom away by diving into the river's current. Swim to the bank, race across the Makoidake Plain, and get to Nippi. That was all.

28

Nippiktua gazed upon the wide valley from where the road crested a high knoll.

The walled city looked so small compared to the white-crowned mountain dominating the western horizon. Her boots were still wet from the wide river they had crossed. The boat had been flat, and the wind had tossed the water onto it. She hadn't liked it one bit. Just like she didn't like Strong-Arms Ezrilkath's plan. She wanted to be done with Sophokis. Letting them take her to the draekurm, then Ezrilkath coming to take her back—it was a dumb plan. Grown-ups always made dumb plans.

If Nippiktua had her way, she would snatch the drakma from Sophokis and flee. Easy—no problem with the draekurm. She considered her list. She *had* wanted to talk to one. But that had been when Fluff had been by her side.

Nippiktua blinked away the stinging in her eyes. She was on her own, no Fluff. She had to think and take care of herself.

Strong Arms was helping, but she couldn't be trusted. Nippiktua smelled burnt wood in the air. A wispy dark cloud hung below the white cap of the enormous mountain. Strong Arms had said that was where the draekurm was. She had been hoping that Strong Arms would see she was a good enough mercenary to take somewhere else. Nippiktua was *good* with the wooden sword now.

Shapes of men were walking toward them from the gate of the big city. Strong Arms had sent one of her men to the city to tell them how brave they were for capturing Nippiktua. One of them shuffled with a stick. Nippiktua remembered the anger in Sophokis's eyes when Fluff had refused him. She was afraid he would be mean to her. She looked up at Strong Arms.

The tall woman looked down at her. She must have seen Nippiktua's worry, for she knelt and pointed at her lips, saying, "We'll come and get you up at the mountain." She pointed to the big scary mountain behind the city. "Do as they say, and they won't hurt you."

Nippiktua nodded. She still couldn't decide if she should continue to listen to Strong Arms or run away from her. That moment had passed. Maybe when Nippiktua was grown and strong enough, she would make Strong Arms pay. Until then, she had to be small and observant. It was the only way to survive without her father. Yes, Morvelving should be her father. It was right.

Strong Arms's mouth moved again. "Do you understand?"

Nippiktua nodded. Strong Arms extended her hand. Nippiktua didn't know why until she pointed at the wooden sword. She huffed and placed it in Strong Arms's hand. Nippiktua had been planning to hit Sophokis with it. She panicked, eyeing the Stag tine at Pulasuq's side. She shook her head. She shouldn't have it. Sophokis would take it away.

Strong Arms nodded. "I'll give it back. They'll take it if you have it."

That made sense. It just wasn't fair. Nippiktua felt empty. Everything she thought was hers continued to be taken from her. Her family first, then Goldeye, Morvelving, and now Strong Arms, however uncertain Nippiktua was of her. What did she have left that could be taken away? She felt the earth tremble beneath her sandals. She looked around. No one else seemed to notice, so she ignored it. The group of men was approaching.

It was easy to tell Strong Arms's man apart from the others. He was a head taller and wider, whereas the men from the city were lean ghosts in their tunics. They had weapons—spears and swords—yet their weapons made them look like children with toys compared to Strong Arms's men. Sophokis's eyes were sunken in his skull. His shining eyes stared at her. Nippiktua felt like something was crawling on her arm.

Strong Arms stepped forward. She was in her war gear, a tall crested helm under her armpit. Her waxed linen and bronze cuirass, greaves, and bracers gleamed, even in the clouded light. With her hand motions, Nippiktua could tell she was speaking to Sophokis. Nippiktua crossed her arms over her chest when they both looked in her direction.

"How'd you free her from the wolfman?" Sophokis asked.

"With great difficulty and loss of men. You have the drakma?" Strong Arms extended her arm toward the man.

"Yes, of course. It's not our plight that urged you to help but the coin."

"What else is there, Idosse?"

Sophokis sneered and held out his hand. One of the taller men behind him put down the large sack slung over his shoulder. He pulled out three large bags bulging with coins. Nippiktua had never seen so much drakma.

Strong Arms waved her arm for one of her men to grab the gold.

Sophokis asked, "Will you be entering the city?"

Nippiktua looked up at Strong Arms, who answered, "Gods above, no. We're going far away."

As they continued to talk, Nippiktua lost interest. There was another tremor in the earth. She looked up at Mount Kydos. She couldn't make out any details. The land and city would have been beautiful if she weren't held captive in it.

Strong Arms's men began picking up their gear. Nippiktua looked around. Some were already leaving. She looked up at Strong Arms—the woman only glanced at her. Nippiktua looked down. Right, she had to pretend this was the last time she would see Strong Arms. A part of Nippiktua suddenly realized that Strong Arms may not come to get her. The thought made her freeze, even as the blindfold was placed over her head and her hands were bound. Smell and touch were her only senses now.

She was afraid. As she was led and carried into the city, she couldn't deny that every touch and shove made her flinch and shudder. Her quick breaths in the bag over her head warmed her face. The smell of the men's sweat filled her nose, followed by the smells of the city. Animal and human smells, food smells—sweet and spicy. She was walking on a stone-paved road now, and it trembled underfoot. Someone poked and pinched her, making Nippiktua jump.

She could imagine all the people looking at her blue skin with wonder. Were they angry that their savior was a foreigner, or were they glad they didn't have to sacrifice their own? Nippiktua didn't want to be a sacrifice. She had no choice but to be carried, jostled, and pushed on through the city.

They carried her up steps, made her stand for what seemed like the whole day, and then carried her down steps. It was really frustrating. If they had removed the sack from her head, she could have walked the whole way. Why did they need to hide her face? Perhaps it made them feel better?

After a long sleepless dark night, they removed the sack from her face, and the cool air dried the moisture from her breath off her face. She squinted in the morning light as the sight struck her: a small footpath twisting like a snake up to Mount Kydos.

The path followed the crest of the mountain's arms, with steep rocky slopes on either side. Several men walked ahead. They held shields and spears yet still wore their poor tunics.

Someone pushed her on, making her stumble. Her ankle scraped against a boulder. Nippiktua looked back. It was Sophokis.

Nippiktua scowled at him and tried unsuccessfully to stop the tears from brimming in her eyes. She was worried. Strong Arms hadn't rescued her yet. She couldn't rely on anyone but herself. Sophokis had to let her go up the mountain herself soon. When he did, she would slip away.

The draekurm must be at the end of the path. Nippiktua couldn't see anything ahead beyond the mist, and it made her want to run in the opposite direction. She wondered if the draekurm would let her go after a couple of words. Given everything she had heard about draekurm, she knew that wouldn't happen. She reluctantly followed the three men in front of her, marching up the rocky path one behind the other. She didn't know if she should flee or play dead, making them carry her to her death.

Nippiktua looked to the sky, half expecting to find a draekurm swooping down to eat her whole. A canopy of clouds hung heavy around the mountain as if the wind held no sway over them. The wind was cool, and the air smelled of burnt wood and smoke.

The small winding path began to straighten and steepen onto a great slope with withered old trees. Sophokis's hand struck her shoulder, making her move faster. She considered running from him now. They would catch her.

She tried regardless, and one man grabbed her arm painfully before she could gain speed, stopping her attempt as quickly as it started. Rubbing the bruise on her arm, Nippiktua decided she would have to trust Strong Arms.

When Nippiktua had had enough of climbing, they entered a flattened area. Large rocks that had been gouged out of the mountain lay around the perimeter. At the end was a shadowed path marked by a tall stack of stones. It stood alone, like a doorframe at Gaia's inn, but without any walls or roof. Nippiktua took a step back when she noticed the skeletons lying out in the open. The bones lay on the blackened stones, resembling their color. Nippiktua saw what looked like weapons scattered in disarray upon the rocky ground, their melted metal now hard again.

The men had stopped before the stone doorway, not wanting to move further. Sophokis faced her. His sharp jaw and sunken eyes cast shadows on his face. She tried to be defiant and stare back—she couldn't. She looked at the ground.

Sophokis waved his hand. She looked up at him as he spoke so she could read his lips. It was difficult. They were thin and tight.

He pointed at the path ahead. "Beyond there, Orrothix awaits. There are no other paths. We'll know if you follow us back or wait and return at nightfall. Though I doubt Orrothix would let you. Orrothix already knows we are here. Go, tell the draekurm its impossible demand has been met. Free us of its oppression."

Nippiktua barely had time to finish reading his lips before he untied her hands and pushed her on. There were six men, but she was the bravest. They acted as if the tall stone archway would crush them if they walked under it. Nippiktua walked past them without getting flattened. She looked back. The path remained hidden. A shroud of smoke, steam, or fog—she didn't know which—completely hindered her from looking back. There was only one thing to do. She walked on and hoped that Strong Arms would be brave enough to pass under the standing stones.

<h1 style="text-align:center">29</h1>

Morvelving shook the wetness out of his fur, sending droplets in every direction. He briefly glanced back at the wide River Serpres. He did not remember crossing it—did not remember crossing the entire Makoidake Plain. Shaking his head, he realized he was half walking, half stumbling through the low brush and loose rocky slope. He remembered barely escaping the vengeful wrath of King Alkithides after crossing the Idospont and running through Thressea.

Morvelving had exerted himself too much in summoning the fog and wolves to aid in his escape. All creatures had limits, his mind told him, yet he had ignored his own for too long. Having consumed narroot continually, Morvelving's body almost moved without being told. A force pulled him, as if a Dae or god were tugging a rope taut, urging him to consume more. Just as piphlid had. It was the same now.

Growling suddenly and trying to steady his feet, Morvelving shook his head again. The motion made his vision blur, and he found himself sitting on the ground, as broken as the dead branches nearby. Only his chest moved with his ragged, rasping breaths. Small fireflies hung around his head. Or was he imagining them? He tasted blood on his tongue and smelled it running from his nostrils. Shapes moved between the trees, their paths like cloudy wisps.

Telunian Silverlight, lend me strength, he prayed. Morvelving forced himself to focus. There were no fireflies, no spirit shapes. He was on a knoll. He had moved. Rough ridges and soft hills were all around, crowned with gnarled trees and straight pines.

He didn't know when he had stood up. When he realized he had, he was under trees and near a road. He drew in the scents by instinct—men and horses. A deer and her fawn, an eagle high above, and smoke. Sulfur, then a reek that made the hairs on his back stand up. Power from Eifgald and Ergald lingered, straining the air, making it dry. A drizzle fell from the heavy clouds, the droplets on his snout multiplying. He was close to Mount Kydos, where Orrothix lay. Which meant Phoithese wasn't far.

Morvelving rubbed at his eyes, slapped his own face. He was here. He had to find Nippi. Fear urged him on. What if he was too late?

A vision of Nippi's body, burnt and broken on the earth, brought his mind into clear focus. He was in a heavy forest. Brush grew green and lush. A squirrel ran across a branch above, knocking dew onto his head. Birds were singing, oblivious to his plight. His senses strengthened. He half stumbled and half ran up a steady slope. After twenty slow paces, the forest gave way to a field. The ground bore scorch marks, and a few stalks stood alone and leaned against the wind. He could see stone walls above the leaves of the trees. He was closer to the city than he had thought. Hurrying back into the cover of the forest, he made his way north.

When he found a road, he also found Nippi's scent. Relief washed over him; she was in the city. So, they hadn't taken her to the mountain yet. Morvelving took some time to consider his path. He breathed heavily, and his limbs shook as if he were chilled. He needed food. With effort, he made his way east around the city and found trodden ground leading up to Mount Kydos. There he would hunt and rest. He would wait till they brought Nippi up the mountain. Once they left her, it would be easy to intercept her and keep her from going up to Orrothix. At best, the Phoithesens would think she had perished.

And Orrothix—he could feel the power of the draekurm over the land like a heavy rain. Her magic was at work, for what purpose he couldn't guess—some forgotten devices of Nameless. Morvelving couldn't bother himself with what evil the draekurm was conjuring. Even her motives were purely selfish and self-preserving. What mattered was taking Nippi far from this place.

Morvelving downed a mountain goat with a thrown stone—there was no strength in him for a chase. He feasted after a quick hunting rite, his fangs ripping and tearing flesh before the rite was finished.

He found a cliff overlooking the winding path up the mountain, lay down under the canopy of heavy brush, and closed his eyes. Nose and ears keen to any scent or sound. No one would pass without him knowing. If Orrothix knew of Morvelving's presence, she made no move to scorch him. It would be a fitting end to all his failures, being burned away, his spirit unable to join the endless hunt.

He had just closed his eyes, yet he woke to find morning light flooding the mountainside. The draekurm haze billowing around the peak. Morvelving slowly unfolded himself. His limbs felt like stone, and noises creaked within him like rusty door hinges. He groaned. His nose was quickest to wake—humans, blood, sweat, and Nippi.

Morvelving forgot the pain of his movements and looked down at the path. The scents still lingered—and the footprints. His head swam in pain, and his vision blurred. Narroot came to mind. He licked his lips. Without thinking, he bit into another stem. Sharp focus stung him, cold like a dagger in the flesh. He unwrapped Penalty and hurried back down to the path, unsteady at first but regaining his balance and fortitude.

Nippi had passed not long before, with Sophokis. Six or seven men, but then there were more footprints. Morvelving recognized the scent—the mercenaries. What were they doing? He hurried up the winding path. Sure enough, as he came around the bend, the scent of blood and death told him what had happened before he saw it.

Sophokis and his companions lay along the path. One was far down the slope, body broken on the stones. It had been quick work, no time for words.

Morvelving blinked several times. The mercenary captain meant to take Nippi back? Now, after all she had done? He growled and hurried on; he wouldn't let them.

Orrothix's scent and magic were strong. He had to get to Nippi before the draekurm woke. The mercenaries were risking their lives and a horrible death for Nippi. What were they up to? Wisdom and patience were the hallmarks of his people, but he was itching to use Penalty, especially if the mercenaries were here to take Nippi again.

A tremor within the mountain made Morvelving run up the path. The haze was thickening ahead. "I'm here, Nippi. I'm here," he said to himself.

Movement caught his eye.

The path led upward, and he could see seven or eight figures, maybe more, moving beyond a bend and out of sight. They were dark shadows, save for the glint of their bronze weapons. If he kept to the path, he would be too late.

Morvelving sprang upon the ridge and free-climbed up the jagged cliff. His claws scraped against stone and dirt as his hands searched for holds.

30

Nippiktua was humming to distract herself from her heart trying to beat out of her chest.

The draekurm's mountain wasn't as scary as it looked, she told herself. Of course it *was*, and the smell was hurting her nose and stinging her eyes.

After she had passed the stone doorframe, the haze had cleared somewhat, and there was a path with large trees and stones covered in faded paintings and figure carvings. She stopped to examine some. On most, hunters with spears chased herds of beasts. She liked a painting of two big people and several little ones. A family. She wondered if the draekurm was even here. The place was still, stagnate. Dusty, but she didn't mind.

She could only see several paces ahead due to the wispy haze and the gray leafless trees which marked the way. The morning light was growing, and with it, the haze seemed to thicken once more, making her realize it wasn't natural. The gray stones at her feet became more broken the further she went, and the path disappeared under dust and dead leaves. Nippiktua looked around with haste. As long as she kept going forward, she wouldn't become lost. She jerked her hand to her nose, grimacing. It smelled like something had farted.

A cool gust of wind blew past her and cleared the haze, revealing the mountain's slope and three giant caves that billowed steam. There was no longer a path. She stood in an open area next to the slope with many piles of broken stone. No draekurm.

A large raven with a small crown of pale feathers was perched on a tall boulder, black eyes watching her. Nippiktua stared back and watched it fly away. She remembered seeing it before when they'd found Goldeye dead. Her brows furrowed, angry.

A glint in one of the piles of stone caught her attention. She walked over, happy for a distraction. It was a spearhead. The shaft of the spearhead was broken. The other half lay a few steps away.

That was when she noticed the hand. Nippiktua was confused. It held the shaft tight, skin like dry leather. There was the arm too. She looked upon the man that lay there holding his spear. She took an involuntary step back with a gasp. His eyes were closed behind his dusty helm. In fact, heavy dust covered all of him as if he had been lying there for years. His skin was taut against his bones. The only movement from him was the dust and ash billowing away from his nostrils. He was alive, yet not living.

Nippiktua's stomach dropped. Eyes wide and heart racing, she noticed the piles of stone were, in fact, people lying in odd positions, just like the young warrior. There was an old man with a shepherd's stick, a woman with a basket, and many young men with weapons of war. She couldn't understand it. Why were they all sleeping? How could they sleep for so long? Despite her fear, she inched closer and nudged the young warrior on the shoulder with the tip of her toe. The warrior didn't budge.

A hand grabbed her shoulder and turned her around. Nippiktua expelled all the air from her chest. She would have stumbled back if not for the firm hand and her heart trying to jump out of her chest. She flailed her arms at her attacker.

Strong Arms held Nippiktua steady. Her eyes behind her helmet were wide and concerned, darting around. Her left arm held her shield and sword. The sword had dark wet streaks on it.

"Gods, girl, you needn't have gone so far," Strong Arms said.

Nippiktua stopped swinging and focused on recovering from the shock, so it was easy to watch the woman as she handed Nippiktua her wooden sword and tine dagger. Nippiktua dropped the wooden sword and clutched the dagger close. Strong Arms's twelve remaining mercenaries fanned out behind her, looking around with unease.

"Come, we must leave, no need—"

Movement behind the mercenaries made Nippiktua look away from Strong Arms. Something climbed down from the rock wall. It held a long blade with glowing runes, and its eyes were shining silver. The rest of it was still in shadow, but the movement of the tall ears gave him away.

Nippiktua couldn't believe it. She pushed past Strong Arms, evaded her hand, and ran to Morvelving. He was alive, and he had come for her. She wasn't alone or forgotten. The sting of tears filled her eyes, yet she was smiling. There was no way for her to know what she was feeling. It was a storm swirling and breaking against her. She ignored the fierceness of his wild fur and her burning eyes as he came to her, hand outstretched. He was watching the mercenaries with an intensity that almost made her stop. Almost.

She burrowed into his chest just as he knelt. His fur was wet and smelled awful. She didn't care; she squeezed as hard as she could. His heart was beating incredibly fast as his left arm wrapped around her and held her tight. She wanted to stay there forever. Everything was better now. Fluff was here.

———————

Morvelving watched the mercenaries as he held Nippi close. Her sobs and trembling body rendered him unable to move, only to hold her.

The leader, who they called Ezrilkath, had gathered her mercenaries into a defensive position, shields facing him. Morvelving had heard what she had said to Nippi, confirming the double cross.

He searched the sky. The steam blocked his vision, emanating from the mountain's three holes. He didn't need to see Orrothix to know she was near. The air was dry, despite the silent trickle of water dripping steadily down rocks from many spells. Orrothix must have laden the mountain with runes of power. They needed to leave.

Keeping Nippi close, Morvelving growled at Ezrilkath. One mercenary took an involuntary step back. Nippi was sniffling and wiping her eyes.

"Why did you do it?" Morvelving snarled at the mercenary captain. The narroot made him crave action. He swallowed the desire to leap at the mercenaries and cut them down, give pain to those who had caused him pain. He flexed his fingers on Penalty's handle, hoping for an excuse. Morvelving inhaled slowly. He only wanted to lead Nippiktua away. Dealing more death was unnecessary, he told himself, even as his right leg involuntarily took a step.

Ezrilkath's eyes watched his sword hand and flinched at his movement. "I was wrong to take her," she said, her voice resolute, truthful in her admission. He recognized her: she was the one that had kicked him off the ship when he'd been so close to Nippi. "It was all for drakma. But I couldn't leave her to the draekurm."

"That hardly absolves you. You were foolish." Morvelving spoke quickly to keep from barking. "And your men paid for it."

Ezrilkath, tall and tense, seemed to droop, and her head bowed as if tired.

That surprised Morvelving. He sought her scent. She was sincere and regretful. He grunted. "You profited and paid in blood. Tell me why I shouldn't—"

Nippi tugged at him. He looked down.

"*Don't hurt Strong Arms,*" Nippi signed up at him, the white of her eyes red from her tears. Her hair was all braided up—like Cassea's, he realized. "*She was nice after . . . She just wants to go home. Claim her land. Make things right.*"

Morvelving licked his lips, releasing his snarl. Her soft words made him check himself. He gave Ezrilkath a stern look and tucked Penalty under his arm. The mercenaries breathed again.

Morvelving signed to Nippi. "*I'm not going to. You're with me—that's all that matters.*"

"*I thought you were gone, that you gave up on me.*"

"*I'm here.*" Morvelving knelt again and leaned down so his nose was almost next to hers. "*I'll never give you up. I promise.*"

Nippi burrowed herself into him for another hug. Morvelving felt a weight lift from his shoulders. Nothing else mattered—his past, his mistakes. Her embrace was like the golden, searing light of the sun breaking through the clouds.

Ezrilkath motioned for her mercenaries to follow her back down the mountain.

He watched them. They needed to go too. They had lingered too long. He noticed the bodies behind the mercenaries, camouflaged by the ash and dust, and was suddenly afraid. The reason for the scent and sense of spells was clear. They had to leave now.

He stood, saying, "The draekurm has enthralled those people. We must go now!"

"Enthralled what?" one mercenary asked.

Bellowing laughter filled the air, answering the man. It cracked the air like thunder, and the ground shook. The quake of her wings echoed as if a giant were beating a drum. The air seemed to ripple like water after a thrown stone hit its calm surface. Steam and haze danced overhead. An ancient creature. Far more intelligent than giants and far more terrible. Morvelving snarled, suppressing the memories of kin burning and shrieking in a battle long ago. Orrothix was here—a draekurm, a lord of sky and fire, a spawn of the traitor god—Nameless.

The long, winged shape of Orrothix passed overhead, dominating the whole sky. Ezrilkath and her mercenaries crouched down, cursing. Morvelving kept Nippi close.

Orrothix must be teasing them, like a cat with a mouse, or they would have been dead already.

"Hmm, an odd pairing. Amusing," came a voice from the sky, booming against Morvelving's ears like wind gusts on window shutters. "Son of Telunian, you trespass."

"What—gods above!" a mercenary called out, stumbling and struggling away from a body. It stood then, joints snapping from being still for so long, flesh pale. Eyes blazing like two red suns.

"Go! Go!"

"Gods save us," another mercenary called out. The enthralled were standing up all around them, blocking any escape.

Morvelving cursed himself for not seeing the trap sooner.

"Thralls," Morvelving growled, gripping Penalty. "They are under the draekurm's spell and will fight fearless of injury or death. Defend yourselves!"

Already one thrall with a spear was lunging at a mercenary. The man stumbled back, barely escaping.

Ezrilkath swung her sword at the one holding a shepherd's staff, her blade cutting from shoulder to ribs. Blood spilled down, exposing bone and flesh. The thrall stumbled back, then continued swinging its staff at the tall warrior. The blow struck hard against her shield.

"Shit on this," Ezrilkath spat. "How do we kill them?"

"Their minds are already dead," Morvelving called out. "Break the bodies to stop their advance. Orrothix has had time to build her defenses. Group together—fight them off or die!"

Morvelving's limbs shook violently. He was so tired, but the narroot kept him moving while keeping Nippi by his shin. She was clutching tightly and moving with him. The brave girl had her Stag tine out.

He swung Penalty upward at a thrall reaching for him. It was a woman, seeking to grab his throat. The blade cut through flesh and bone. Her arm seemed to float before it fell to the rocky ground. Morvelving kicked the thrall away, the motion making him half stumble.

Orrothix flew overhead. A wind followed that knocked over one mercenary. Orrothix's laughter continued to batter Morvelving's ears.

The thralls were closing in—one mercenary was caught among them, cried out in terror and pain, his calls overcome by the sounds of his butchering.

The mercenaries yelled to each other. "Cut it down!"

"Watch out!"

"Hold, Juthan!"

Morvelving kept his back to Ezrilkath's group, training his focus on the thralls still coming at them. He cut one clean in half. Another blocked his blow—he kicked it back. He grabbed a spear, its thrust aimed at Nippi, and cut the head off the thrall. Its body lingered, standing for a moment till it fell.

He saw why the mercenaries followed Ezrilkath; she cut down the thralls precisely and efficiently, keeping them from her exposed men.

Now that they were together, the mercenaries formed a shield wall in a semicircle, holding against the brute relentlessness of the thralls.

Morvelving had cut down two more thralls when he felt the wind shift—he looked up. The draekurm was swooping down.

"Break! Break and run," Morvelving called out as he picked Nippi up and ran toward two thralls blocking his way. He pushed one down and blocked the other's sword with Penalty. A great roar of flame exploded behind him, and the heat burned against his back. He dove to the ground, tucking Nippi into his arms and rolling.

The world lit up as if a sudden sunrise had split across a flat plain. Then the ground shook, making Morvelving lose his balance. An immediate heat dried his fur.

Orrothix landed amid a cloud of flames, making the jade-colored scales all over her hide shine, outlined in shadow. Orrothix's underbelly was covered in pale green scales, while the spines and scales along her back were dark jade. Her eyes were two blue suns cut down the center with darkness. Her neck was long and serpentine, flowing into a lean torso with sapphire flesh webbed between the spikes along the length of her spine. Sinew under scales stretched into wings larger than ship sails, pale jade and thin yet tough as the crown of horns spilling from Orrothix's skull. The draekurm's short, strong legs held her above the ground, her long tail swishing in the air. Three claws at the joint of each folded wing served as her forelimbs. Sharp fangs lined her long snout, some bent out and in, and others broken in half. Flame dripped from inside her mouth like saliva from a thirsty animal.

Ezrilkath hurried out of the clearing with one of the older mercenaries. They fought off thralls as they hid behind a great boulder. The others scattered in panic—one rolled on the ground, trying to put out the flame on his arm. Orrothix took one look at the mercenary and lunged her long neck, fangs ending the man in an instant.

Orrothix spoke. "I slept for a moment—bored and tireless—only to be awakened by warriors sent from those Phoithesen cockroaches. Have you come to take my throne? To plead for freedom?" Her voice was tremendous as sea waves yet smooth and coaxing as a slight morning breeze. "A pitiful attempt—my thralls alone would have finished you. No, you are here for different reasons. Ah, dire reasons." Orrothix set her eyes upon Morvelving. "I rule here, Moon Pup. There is no righteousness here for you to claim unless you have come to ask for my assistance. Do you tire of Telunian's collar? Shall I free your mind?" Her eyes flicked to Nippi for a moment. "Curious. You harbor a human child."

To Morvelving's surprise, Nippi stood in front of him and signed at the draekurm. *"Let us go. We did nothing to you."*

"Fascinating! So, the Phoithesens found an answer to my riddle. The fools." Orrothix lifted her head high with her long neck and croaked a laugh. "Oh, Moon Pup. I do not understand how you can linger among them. The mortals. The humans. You give them a small hope, and they look for that hope tirelessly. Ignore the disillusioned few who come to chase me away on their own when they could have challenged me the first day I arrived. How did Aeputer phrase it? Ah, yes: 'The courage of humans' No, it is 'the hope of humans'! They believe it as blindly as they believe in the gods' love. As the gods, I answer to no law or word given."

Morvelving kept his teeth bared, tense and ready, his hair bristling. His instincts urged him to show his strength. He barked, "We've come for nothing of yours, lord of the sky, queen upon the mountain. The girl did not wish to ascend but was forced. I am here only to take her away." He hoped to keep Orrothix talking and distract her with praise—his and Nippi's lives depended on it. He had to tread carefully. He could distract

Orrothix long enough to gain a window for escape. Orrothix was only twenty strides from him.

The mercenaries either struggled against the thralls around her or hid. She didn't care for them; she knew he was the greater threat. He had to get Nippi away. Ezrilkath and the mercenaries were making their way back down the path, fending off the thralls that pursued.

"Fair words will not save you, Moon Pup. Many lords now rest and reform in the deep places of the world because of your kin's fervor," Orrothix said, looking to the side at the mercenaries. "I am not finished with you, little roaches. None may go without my leave." She crawled and slithered toward them. The mercenaries fell back in disarray. A foolish man, brave, ran at Orrothix, sword raised.

"No! Flee! Don't look into her eyes!" Morvelving warned and moved to intercede. He didn't wish a draekurm's spell on any being. Orrothix turned to him and belched a pillar of flame. Morvelving sidestepped and dove back, getting Nippi out of the way. When he turned around, the brave man was standing in front of the draekurm, arms limp and eyes already glowing like the other thralls.

One mercenary drew the Runic Ring, conjuring Ergald from the wound on his leg. Morvelving sensed the dryness in the air, and the earth groaned. He couldn't guess what the man was trying to do, but it was too much. A resounding clap added to the cries of battle, and the Ergald-crafter stood there, eyes dumb, bile dripping from his mouth. A thrall cut his arm and throat—still, he stood, motionless and uncaring. In his desperation, his exchange of blood had not been equal to the spell he'd cast.

Morvelving was only himself—one Mulranei, tired and worn, and with precious care for Nippi. Even if the legendary warriors Stormfang and Swiftpaw were here to aid, he doubted they could triumph, only prolong an inevitable defeat. Fleeing was their best chance of survival. Ezrilkath was on her own, despite what she could mean to Nippi. Nippi made a noise. He turned down to her. A legless thrall had grabbed her leg and was trying to pull her close for a bite. Morvelving quickly cut the arm and kicked the thrall away. Then he picked Nippi up and ran. This was their chance. Something hit his back with tremendous force, and he felt weightless, and the world spun. Pain filled his body, and his vision turned white. He shook his head, feeling for Nippi.

She wasn't there.

31

Morvelving stood, his vision returning.

He was on a ledge near the clearing. Ezrilkath and the older mercenary were fighting their own men, who were now enthralled by Orrothix. Where was Nippi? He frantically searched the ground for her. Penalty lay next to a dead thrall. Something caught his eye—movement on the ledge near one of the mountainside's dark openings. Nippi. She was jumping up and down, waving her arms. What was she doing? In horror and wonderment, he saw Orrothix suddenly swoop down from within the thick haze and land just in front of her.

"Nippiktua! No. No. No." Morvelving leaped down in two strides, panicking. Legs and joints burned. Picked up his sword, breath didn't come, still moved on.

Orrothix was staring at Nippi.

The small girl held her Stag tine in defiance toward the draekurm.

Orrothix met Morvelving's gaze, then lifted herself into the air, snatching Nippi with one of her clawed feet. Nippi's legs dangled as she clutched onto the draekurm.

Nippiktua knew she had to be brave. Her father was here for her; he had come after her, and she had Strong Arms too. Everything had happened so fast, yet she felt sure of it. Like the day with the Stag, everything was right—not special, not significant, just so. That was why she waved the draekurm to her. She had had enough. Orrothix would not hurt her friends. She was going to talk to it.

She had to remember to breathe when the draekurm landed in front of her. She kept her tine in front of her to stab Orrothix if the draekurm tried to eat her, and she still held it raised when Orrothix picked her up. Nippiktua held on to the draekurm for her life as the world fell away, like in her dreams, and the wind sought to rip her away to a quick death. She didn't understand why Orrothix had to take her away. She didn't much care. Orrothix listened to her. She, Orrothix, was a she-draekurm, and she talked to Nippiktua in her mind.

You really can hear me? Nippiktua thought, hoping to focus less on the fact that she was high in the sky.

Suddenly, Orrothix swooped down to the mountain. Nippiktua's stomach was in her throat. A large gaping shadow marked the entrance into the mountain.

Yes, little roach.

You are amazing. No one has done that for me. I always have to work hard to read how their lips move —

Be silen —

It's exhausting. People talk too fast. And then they never learn to sign to me! It's not fair. Except Morvelving. He learns quickly.

SILENCE.

Nippiktua felt Orrothix's talon close tighter around her, seeking to crush her. She held on as Orrothix dove. Her landing jolted Nippiktua, and all the air escaped from her chest. She coughed. Orrothix released her, turning to face her again.

The draekurm's bright blue eyes held Nippiktua's reflection in them.

She didn't care how terrified she looked. She was—but she had to do this. Father said everyone was afraid. It shouldn't keep her from doing what she needed to do. Which was to talk to Orrothix.

No, Nippiktua thought as she stared back at her reflection in Orrothix's eyes. *You listen. You brought me up here for something you need. Well, I need something from you.*

Orrothix's lips curled, revealing her rows of fangs, some as long as Nippiktua's arm.

Fascinating, Orrothix's voice boomed in Nippiktua's mind. *So small, yet bold beyond the measure of gods. Naivety. What does a little roach want from me that I would bequeath to her? I do not need you. Only what you carry.*

Nippiktua looked down at the Stag tine in her hand. She had utterly forgotten it.

This? she asked.

It is the only thing you carry.

What do you need it for? It's very important to me, but if giving it to you means you'll listen to me, then . . . then I'll give it to you.

Orrothix cackled. *How amusing. As if I need you to give it to me. I confess this is one of the most intriguing events that has happened in centuries. The oddity, the absurdity! The Fates tugging and pulling upon my endless thread. Centuries have passed with nothing new, nothing changing, and now a sudden novelty. This moment is a treasure more precious than all the gems of the earth. I'm feeling benevolent. What is it you want, little roach?*

Nippiktua swallowed. For a moment there, she'd thought the draekurm would eat her whole. *For starters, you can stop eating the city people down there. I think you've terrorized them enough. You bothered them so much they came after me and Morvelving, and that's not fair. They wouldn't bother you, I think, if you just stayed in your mountain. For second, you can let me and Morvelving go. Oh, and Strong—uh, Ezrilkath and her men go. We didn't mean to trespass.*

Orrothix seemed to only half listen as she moved toward the opening in the mountain. *Is that all?*

Yes, that's everything. Not very difficult for a magnificent draekurm. Now, what do you need the tine for? Nippiktua thought it was a very reasonable offer.

Follow, little roach.

She didn't at first. But something unseen tugged at Nippiktua's feet, slightly stinging her ankles. She looked down as she followed the draekurm. There was nothing there; it was as if Orrothix's will had forced her to follow.

Nippiktua was afraid she wouldn't be able to see inside the cave, but the light from outside billowed in, showing the roughly cut stone gouged with claw marks. Orrothix slithered and crawled on her belly through the tunnel, her wings tucked against her body. There was plenty of room for Nippiktua. A burning vapor was the prominent scent, along with Orrothix's smoky breath. A large part of her told Nippiktua not to follow the draekurm into the mountain. That would be the smart, grown-up thing to do, but she wanted to see what the draekurm was doing. Besides, she wasn't sure she could act against the power that made her follow.

I am fortifying my brother's resting crypt, Orrothix said, as if in answer to Nippiktua's questions. *He was slain in the east. His spirit fled here, lingering within the mountain, to rest and grow. The humans discovered it, thinking it was a treasure. I am strengthening his resting place with protection. The Stag tine will be sufficient, as it is a piece of Drudan. The goddess is still in her forced slumber. Her power within the tine will strengthen my brother's rest.*

Despite her fears, Nippiktua hurried in front of Orrothix and looked ahead. Before them, a large orb floated above the center of a stone basin, suspended by pillars decorated with glowing lines. More lines were etched on the floor. Nippiktua guessed the magical rings and runes were keeping the orb safe. She couldn't understand why a draekurm needed so much protection. Then she saw the small fragile shape suspended in the orb. It was a tiny draekurm. She looked at it in utter fascination; it was the most incredible thing she had ever seen. That such large and terrifying creatures could be so vulnerable.

Why not seal him away from the humans? I doubt they could find him then, Nippiktua suggested. When she looked up at Orrothix, the draekurm was looking at her in a way she didn't like at all. She tried to take a step back but couldn't.

How astute. In fact—Orrothix slithered around the earthen rune-marked orb till she was facing Nippiktua, her bright eyes like two sharp knives delving into Nippiktua's mind—*you and the Stag tine are the last pieces I need. The Fates' will. Destiny. Small items, small hands to reach where I cannot and tie the bind. There was a rumor that Drudan's Harolds were still upon the land. The Stags hold much power, though not enough to go searching. But now a piece is here, and you will do well sealed within, finishing my work while I seal the entrance. Place it there.*

Orrothix pointed her nose at the glowing lines and runes etched into the stone floor in front of Nippiktua. Despite herself, she placed the tine on the stone and stepped back.

Now, Orrothix said, *look into my eyes. This will bring you ease and be far less . . . messy.*

Nippiktua didn't like the sound of that. *Oh, I don't like staying underground. Too stuffy.*

She took a step back, terrified. But she couldn't stop looking at those eyes. They dominated her vision. She felt a tugging, as if she were being pulled down into those eyes to swim in them for eternity. A release, a peace. No more pain, no more hurt. It was wonderful—so warm, like being wrapped in a thick blanket next to a fire. Nippiktua wanted to stay here.

A howl, mournful and harrowing, reverberated within her mind and shook her body—cold and clear. The blanket of warm power was flung off her as if a mighty wind had rushed into the cavern. Nippiktua shook her head and blinked. She had *heard* Morvelving.

Orrothix's snout was right in front of her, blazing eyes behird.

Nippiktua ran.

Morvelving saw the entrance. Eifgald was at work. Orrothix was enthralling Nippi. He howled a song of declaration, of interruption. In his desperation, he would do what he had to till he fainted. He swallowed the last bit of narroot, its effects making his muscles spasm and his eyes twitch. There was a roar, and a light flickered from within the shadows of the entrance. He hurried over.

Nippi came running out. Morvelving sprinted to her, relieved beyond words to see her alive. Behind her, the darkness erupted into flame. He swept Nippi up and dove to the side as the flame flurg out of the mountain.

The air was sultry, and the ground shook. Orrothix made for the entrance. Morvelving turned around, keeping Nippi behind him, just as the draekurm's head appeared out of the mountain.

Penalty met Orrothix in the middle of her snout. Its blue runes flared, and sparks flew. Morvelving had swung with all his remaining might, yet he had not cut through her scales. Instead, he had made her head crash into the rocky ground. She was vulnerable at the entrance, wings tucked against her body. Morvelving had to keep her there. Beat her back, make her retreat, so he and Nippi could escape.

Orrothix recovered and snapped her jaws at him.

Morvelving swung Penalty to meet the lunge. Orrothix belched flame from the hit, and Morvelving lost the feeling in his arms as he stumbled back. He glanced back at Nippi. The clever girl had climbed up and into a cleft, hidden.

He snarled. "Back into your mountain, worm. Leave us be."

He continually battered Orrothix's head with his sword. He swung with no precision or proper form, only brute aggression. The draekurm recoiled in a rage, spilling a wave of flame from her mouth. Morvelving had to leap back. The gifts of Telunian protected him against direct Ergald, but a draekurm's fire was their Eifgald, a powerful force that even their Goddess could not protect Mulranei from. He leaped over the pools of flame. He had to beat her back into the mountain. If she took flight, she would strafe the entire mountain from the safety of the sky. Morvelving lunged for her underbelly, evading her jaws. Penalty's sharp point slid along her scales, sending out a trail of sparks. Morvelving grabbed one of her horns and tried to climb on top.

Orrothix's winged arms were out of the cave entrance.

"Ah," Orrothix roared in frustration. "Curse your Moon Goddess, rodent."

The draekurm shook and twisted violently, flinging Morvelving off. His bones vibrated as he hit the ground and rolled, quickly standing and diving out of the way of flames. Orrothix trailed his movement as he ran for her wing. She was moving out of the mountain.

"No!" Orrothix growled, lunging at Morvelving. He had to stop to evade her snout in front of him. He pulled out his dagger just as she whipped her head against him. The dagger blade stabbed her near her eye. "Argh, vermin. Pest. Burn! Burn!"

Morvelving couldn't stop. He lunged, swinging Penalty at her eyes, moving to her left and then to her right. Orrothix roared and snapped her jaws at him in frustration. A minor victory. It was only a matter of time before his body gave up and he slipped. There was no victory in a fight like this. Orrothix lunged with her mighty legs and twisted, pushing herself out of the entrance. Morvelving had to jump out of the way to avoid being crushed.

Her powerful wings spread, almost knocking Morvelving to the ground. He stood and faced her, Penalty at his side, dagger in the other hand. His chest heaved, and the pain sought to numb his mind. He noticed Orrothix's nostrils flare and her tail droop. She was tired too.

Fangs showing, Morvelving snarled. "You know this will end ill for both of us! Do you wish that? Are you so tired of eternity that you wish to spend the next century reforming?"

Orrothix snorted. "And you? Do you wish to risk oblivion for one child who will die before you see the end of your days? 'He Who Runs.' " Orrothix shook her head mockingly. "Take your cowardly mantle and run along, pup. Your destiny is pain, rodent. Loss and pain. Mourning, forever alone. You think you are noble, but you are a fool. She will grow and forget you; all your sacrifices will mean nothing. She will love others and grow old while you linger till she turns to dust. Is that what you'll fight for?"

"Yes," Morvelving answered, absolute and resolute. He had found what Wynthrim wished him to, and he wasn't going to run. He ignored her words, though they pierced like daggers. "You can't understand it. Nameless made you too powerful to understand and then used your brothers and sisters in his schemes. I seek to live and cherish every moment till it's gone. What are you doing that you need to crush those you deem so insignificant? What have we done to you? You have the power to end this folly. Let me and the child walk away."

The wind drummed in the silence that followed. Morvelving kept himself ready, facing the draekurm. Orrothix stared into his eyes. He felt the tug of her Eifgald trying to take over his mind, to enthrall him. A desperate attempt by Orrothix. Morvelving took a deep breath and chased her mind from his, hoping it meant the draekurm would cease her demands for Nippi.

Orrothix sighed deeply, steam billowing from her nostrils. She cocked her head, her eyes gleaming. "I understand mysteries powerful enough to break your faith, Moon Pup. I see when the Fates find a thread to torment. They cherish yours—eternal and tarnished. If you care for the mortal child as you confess, leave her to me. Her life will be a blink of an eye either way. One being far less . . . painful."

Morvelving faltered.

"Ah," Orrothix purred. "You thought it was the child whom the Fates loved? Or has someone told you the same? Poor little pup. I see it, the noble quest to shield the child from her terrible destiny. Honorable, worthy of redemption. You are a fool. The Fates intend to build a legacy so wrought in pain and loss it will carry through the ages until the world is broken and the gods perish."

Morvelving rolled his shoulders to make himself appear threatening. The draekurm was lying. She had to be. His limbs shook, and he felt he may collapse at any moment. Orrothix's words held power in the fact that Idanphyrus had said the same. What could he do if the Fates weaved his thread only to torment him, hurting Nippi only because she was close to him? His obsession with piphlid, his son's death, and his exile. Nippi was next in the Fates' cruel pattern. Telunian's grace, Nippi's death was guaranteed. He had to . . . Morvelving shook his head, dispensing with the thoughts, and stared into Orrothix's brazen eyes. He was He Who

Runs Shall Mourn Alone, but not while Nippi drew breath.

"I thought draekurm were wise," Morvelving countered. "To assume the will of the Fates is to invoke their timeless eyes upon you. You may have cut your thread short, Orrothix."

The draekurm's eye twitched. Morvelving's heart skipped a beat, ready for her last attack. Clouds passed overhead; an echoing creak came down from the massive snowdrifts on the mountain's peak. Morvelving prepared himself.

"Nippi, I am sorry. Telunian, protect her," he whispered, waiting.

Morvelving's fur cooled in the breeze. His hand was a vise on his sword. He heard Nippi's breaths in the stillness as he kept his eyes on Orrothix. The draekurm had not moved except for the flare of her nostrils, expanding and shrinking.

Orrothix bellowed at Morvelving, loud and sudden. Her mouth opened wide, fangs clear, tongue black, her voice like drums of war. This was it. The end. Morvelving snarled and barked back at her. The ground shook, and in the far distance, great swaths of snow fell from the eaves of the mountain in answer to their challenges.

Orrothix turned from Morvelving and moved to the entrance. "Go, your lofty ideals stink. Being near you draws the Crones' eye. The Fates may have you, but not me."

Morvelving's heart skipped when Nippi ran from her hiding spot to him. How did she know? Unsure if Orrothix was driven to trickery, Morvelving met Nippi halfway.

Orrothix did nothing. She ignored them and proceeded to etch a Runic Ring into the stone with one of her wing claws. When it was complete, she bent her long neck over so her claw could reach her mouth. She cut her tongue. Dark blood spilled onto the ring. The air bent, and an audible snap filled his ears. The spell triggered. The walls around the entrance collapsed, sealing whatever was inside. Orrothix took flight then, her great form diminishing in the sky.

Morvelving slumped to a knee. He couldn't believe Orrothix had given up the fight. He let Penalty clatter upon a stone. Nippi pushed herself against him, keeping him from falling over. He looked at her, whined, and smiled, signing, *"I'm so glad you're unhurt."*

Nippi smiled back up at him, nodding. She signed, *"I regret putting draekurm on my list. Let's not do that again."*

32

Morvelving watched the waves of the Adrica Sea stretching endlessly across the horizon. He held on to the ship's rail. Nippi was next to him, having just finished telling him about her time without him. She was looking for anything under the water's surface. She was proud of herself, as she should be. He couldn't be more proud. Nippi had lived through a remarkable ordeal. Morvelving hoped nothing like it would happen again. He doubted this was how human parents raised children, and he felt he had aged two hundred years in the last ten days.

Nippi eyed him briefly. She had increasingly become more conscious of him. For the last several days, the urge to consume narroot had almost incapacitated him. He was ashamed of it. The urges were regrettably similar to piphlid.

She signed, hands moving smooth and quick, *"You should give her a chance. She knew where to hire the boat."*

Morvelving's tapered ears drew back as he glanced over at Ezrilkath and Odrys. They were sitting together, enjoying their evening meal. The older man nursed his injured arm. When he and Nippi had descended Mount Kydos, they'd found Ezrilkath and Odrys alive among the dead thralls and mercenaries. Nippi had convinced him to let the pair accompany them, a decision that had proved helpful when he'd blacked out moments later. Ezrilkath and Odrys had found a ship to leave the

Land of the Idosse while he was unconscious. With King Alkithides seeking revenge, it was too dangerous to travel by land.

He didn't like it. Nippi was happy with Ezrilkath. It was peculiar. He had to trust her instinct—it may indicate her need for another human to interact with.

"She is on the ship, Nippi," he signed back to her. *"That is chance enough. I will not get in the way unless she means to take you from me again."*

"Ezrilkath doesn't. She made a big mistake," Nippi said. *"You've made mistakes too."*

Morvelving grunted. He couldn't argue with the truth.

"I'm glad you arrived when you did," Nippi signed. *"How did you? I want to know."*

"I ran, retracing our journey through Thressea and Makoidake." Morvelving was hesitant to recount the story, for he had been in such a dark place. It was time, though, to stop hiding who he was from her. *"The Thressean king, Alkithides, pursued me. He would have caught me if the wolves hadn't answered my call for aid."*

Nippi's mouth dropped. *"You can do that?"*

"I had to do anything I could to get to you. The Wardens of the Wild answered this time. It's not something I could or should do often. I think their aid and the narroot allowed me to arrive when I did."

"That's the plant you kept chewing that made you faint when you stopped?"

"Yes," Morvelving admitted. *"Those things hold a powerful sway over me. Like when I overslept and the centaurs found us. I've done the same before, and that was how my—"* Morvelving stalled, took a deep breath. *"How my son died, and why I was exiled."*

Nippi gave him a hug. Since he was standing, she could only hug his left leg, but he appreciated her awareness and heart. After a moment, she let go and signed, *"But the narroot helped you help me and Ezrilkath and*

Odrys. That doesn't seem so bad."

Morvelving gave a weak chuckle, grateful his confession hadn't seemed to faze Nippi at all. *"True, but I shouldn't rely on it. Thankfully, there is none left."*

Nippi looked out upon the waves, contemplating. She was growing up fast. Orrothix's words about her mortality were true. Morvelving felt the loss already. Before long, she would be a woman. Would she still need Morvelving? He didn't know, but he would be there. He would always be there to protect her and teach her everything he knew to survive in the wide world.

The ship rode the waves, light and swift, oarsmen grunting to the beat of the soft drum. Their heading was southeast for two days, then east. It was a desperate heading, one he would not have chosen. He had no love for the open sea. The Sea Lords of Elg Narsh prowled these waters. The ship was a small smuggler out of Old Aphoeria. The captain swore the route was safe from pirates and the Idosse patrols, so they could approach Menici from the south.

Morvelving looked down at Penalty, which lay next to his pack. No longer a penalty for running, as Wynthrim had said, but a reminder of the wise dwarf, of dwarven enslavement.

One thing was certain: he wouldn't continue to roam. That had been a mistake, and separating from Nippi was a risk he couldn't handle again. They would find a wild land to live on till Nippi grew. However much he wanted to return to Sene for Nippi's sake, he knew they would have to go further east or south. Each path would have its dangers. There was no way to hide themselves from the Fates. He still worried Orrothix had been right: was it him the Fates sought? What destiny was he dragging Nippi into? Morvelving took a deep sigh, deciding to think on it later. Now he would enjoy the calm and safety.

———————

Nippiktua stole a glance up at Morvelving. He was watching the waves, not her. It was silly. She didn't need to check. He couldn't hear her thoughts. She stared without seeing, considering what Orrothix had told her as she had flown away: *The Fates will hold your sapphire thread, little roach. When his mantle falls to you, draw my name upon the stone with your own blood.*

The wet wood of the rail grated against her fingernails. Nippiktua relaxed her hands. She didn't know what Orrothix had meant about the Fates, the mantle, and drawing her name in blood. What mantle? Nippiktua shrugged.

She felt at home. More so because Morvelving had admitted who he was to her. He knew everything about her. Now it was mutual. Nippiktua wiggled her nose to stop the tickle, but her eyes still brimmed with tears.

Morvelving tapped her shoulder and motioned for her to follow.

———————

Ezrilkath eyed Morvelving as he looked out upon the waves. When the Mulranei had blacked out from exhaustion, her guilt had made her help him and the child. She had made too many mistakes; the Fates were enjoying her life-weave. She had to give back somehow. Odrys was eating his meal beside her. A fine mess she was in, and one of her own making.

"Remind me not to make decisions for a good while," she grumbled.

Odrys only grunted. She was thankful for it. Her band was gone, dead. She had more drakma to her name than she had earned in the last two years of campaigning, and for what? She had to start fresh, and there

was the chance they'd be gutted before reaching Monbargar. Morvelving could decide to rip her throat out . . . No, he could have killed her. It was Nippiktua. The girl had a way of making everything seem right. Ezrilkath took another bite of the warm gruel.

She almost choked on the food. Morvelving was standing before her. Ezrilkath cleared her throat. Odrys froze mid-chew.

"What are your intentions?" Morvelving asked. "I can smell a lie."

"I intend to finish my meal." Her answer made the Mulranei growl, a deep rumble in his throat, clearly unamused. "We depart for Monbargar after we land in Menici."

"To take your land back?"

"That was the plan. You know well enough my plans haven't been the best."

Morvelving gave a small snort. "No, they haven't. But neither have mine."

He stood there, looking down at her. She felt his eyes reading her, deciding and deciphering. Ezrilkath was losing patience.

"Aethra's tits," she spat. "If you're going to damn me or toss me overboard, get it over with. Life is too short for all this anticipation."

Morvelving blinked—shocked or annoyed, she couldn't tell. He huffed and gave a brief whine from his throat, Mulranei expressions she didn't understand.

"Thank you for your help," the Mulranei said. "For carrying me and hiring the ship when I was out. Nippiktua and I are going east from Menici. You and Odrys are welcome to accompany us till Monbargar."

Ezrilkath looked at Odrys. His mouth was still full, but his eyes were wide in surprise.

"I'm giving you a chance," Morvelving continued. "There's enough ill fate in the world. Even my mantle is a chance, a chance to do and be better. I avoided it for far too many winters. So, I'm giving you this chance and advising you to take it."

Nippiktua stepped out from behind Morvelving with a toothy grin, holding up a piece of driftwood she had scratched runes on. It read, *I convinced father not to eat you.*

Ezrilkath choked on her own spit. Quickly, she said, "I accept your offer, gods above, and thank you." She looked at Nippiktua. The brave girl was watching her lips. "I will do what I can to mend what I have done till we part ways."

Morvelving nodded. "It appears we both have ills to mend."

He made hand signs at Nippiktua, who rushed over to Odrys. She dragged him to his feet to follow her. Odrys made a reluctant noise.

Ezrilkath watched as Nippiktua began showing Odrys some kind of game. The old mercenary put all his effort into learning it. She rolled her eyes. He had often spoken about the grandchildren he had lost.

"I wanted to speak to you alone," Morvelving said, sitting cross-legged in front of her. Ezrilkath had to adjust her position, suddenly uncomfortable with the tall wolfkin within her space.

"I have no choice but to listen," she grumbled.

The Mulranei's brown eyes stared at her, unblinking. She wondered why they were silver when he was angry.

"Nippiktua sees something in you that I don't wholly understand," Morvelving said hesitantly. "I assume it is because you share kinship as humans. I am not human, and there are many things I don't understand about being a human or a woman."

Absolutely baffled, Ezrilkath kept her mouth shut.

"While we are in company . . . " The Mulranei's shoulders rose and fell. "If you and Odrys can help Nippiktua with these matters and teach me, I would be most grateful. Do you accept?"

Ezrilkath shook her head. "Gods above and below, you would be better off with centaur than me. I am not worthy."

His right ear pointed to the side, giving her the sense that he wasn't impressed.

"I was once told something similar by a wise dwarf," Morvelving said. "She believed in me. I am giving you the same chance."

Ezrilkath didn't know what that meant. She grimaced. "Yes, I will try."

This satisfied the Mulranei. He nodded and stood. "Good. And thank you."

Ezrilkath massaged her brow. Odrys returned, breathless and smiling.

"I just learned an exhausting game and a few signals the girl communicates with," he said. "What did the Sword of Mourning want?"

"He wants us to help Nippiktua be human."

Odrys chuckled. Ezrilkath wanted to join his laughter but was still too perplexed.

"He made it easy for you," Odrys said. "Mulranei are too gracious."

"And praise the gods above for it." Ezrilkath grunted and finished her meal. Yes, she would mend her wrongs. There was time, and the Ketlans weren't going anywhere.

"You know I don't eat humans," Morvelving signed at Nippi, shaking his head. Flustered and shocked that she would say such a thing. Perhaps that was why Ezrilkath seemed so compliant with his request.

Nippi laughed. He didn't know where she had gotten the bit of driftwood. Must have been on the deck. Nippi signed back at him, *"I wanted Strong Arms to appreciate your decision. She doesn't know you don't eat humans. Oh! Guess what?"*

Morvelving sighed deeply. *"Do I want to know?"*

"Yes! I added something to my list."

"Telunian, give me strength." Morvelving gazed to the heavens and signed, *"And what is it now?"*

Nippiktua looked out upon the waves, then back at him. *"Sirens."*

Acknowledgments

There's always a hero in a story. In the making of *Morvelving*, the hero is my wife Hannah, my love and friend and comfort. She is my Samwise Gamgee in this endeavor. Thank you for your patience, encouragement, and enthusiasm.

Without fuel, the fire will die. I owe my childhood friends for countless hours of adventure that fueled my imagination.

One person writes a novel, but it takes the talents of many to complete. Ivan Cakić, the talented artist whose work graces the cover. The editor, Amelia at Amelia Winters Editing, who made the manuscript ready for you. The proofreader, Alissa A., whose added scrutiny is paramount to success.

I am grateful to all the beta readers: Cade Smith, Rohit, Catie, Gil Jackson, Natalie Rowland, Erika Baker, and Obie. *Edu ve*, I owe you all a drink, and I declare you all Mulranei-friend. Special thanks to fellow authors Edward Bagby and A. J. Peterson, who gave their time to critique every word and decipher what I was trying to write.

I admit Erviad started with a dream—like many things, a messy, incoherent dream filled with every fantasy story that sparked my imagination. But it was mine. I couldn't let it go, and here I am. Because of this, I am compelled to name and thank the visionaries who gave me life, purpose, and belonging in their offered escape throughout the years: J. R. R. Tolkien, Robert Jordan, George R. R. Martin, Brandon Sanderson, Joe Abercrombie, Nicola Griffith, Colleen McCullough, Janny Wurts,

Patricia A. McKillip, and Christopher Buehlman.

To my fencing instructor, Brent Lambell, and the crew at Indes WMA: thank you for the endless sword bouts and shenanigans.

Thank you, reader, for giving me a chance. If the story sparked feeling, be it joy or contempt, please rate and review my work. This is a journey, and I plan to learn.

About the Author

C. J. Switzer loves reading fantasy so much that he has worked for more than a decade to breathe life into his own stories, starting with his first publication: *Morvelving*. A graduate of Warner Pacific College with a BA in Social Studies, he enjoys studying history, engaging in a voracious fencing bout, and the challenge of bouldering. He lives in Portland, Oregon, with his wife, Hannah, and his two dogs, Feanor and Turin, who are experts in tragedy and cuddles.

Secret Author Note:

Thank you for reading Morvelving. If you loved the story, let other people know! As a Indie Author, reviews are paramount for my stories to be noticed. Click link to review on Goodreads or Amazon: